T...

...Diego Castillo.

He was also the naked stranger who'd rescued her from
the river, the man whose warm eyes and warm skin had
awakened her to passion. The one whose voice made her
insides quiver with sensual feeling. The one she'd heard
in the confessional chamber.

And the one who'd also heard her. All about her.

* * *

Tempted By Innocence
Harlequin® Historical #854—June 2007

Author Note

Of all the stories I've written, this one you're holding in your hands is my very favorite. Its theme of sacrificial love resonates very deeply in my soul, though I didn't know when I began the story that it would become so important. As Diego taught it to Celeste, he was also teaching it to me.

In addition, it was incredibly challenging to write a hero who was a priest sworn to celibacy, and to have him face true-to-life temptation without being corrupted. There was a very fine line there, but Diego turned out to be a wonderful and noble man whose story involved me so completely that I actually cried as I wrote a couple of the scenes in the latter part of the book. I'm not prone to such tears, so I knew this story was tapping into a rich and deep emotional vein, and I suspected that what moved me would be enjoyable to readers, as well.

Please do let me know if this story touches you as profoundly as it touched me.

Reut
MAH

TEMPTED BY INNOCENCE

Lyn Randal

TORONTO • NEW YORK • LONDON
AMSTERDAM • PARIS • SYDNEY • HAMBURG
STOCKHOLM • ATHENS • TOKYO • MILAN • MADRID
PRAGUE • WARSAW • BUDAPEST • AUCKLAND

ISBN-13: 978-0-373-29454-1
ISBN-10:   0-373-29454-9

TEMPTED BY INNOCENCE

Available from Harlequin® Historical and
LYN RANDAL

Warrior or Wife #837
Tempted By Innocence #854

Praise for
Warrior or Wife

"A highly sensuous tale of courage and enduring love
set in the splendor of ancient Rome. Lyn Randal's
Warrior or Wife is an absolute must-read for those
who love gladiators!"
—Award-winning author Lyn Stone

"A stunning debut... From the blood lust of the
gladiatorial arena to the silken sheets of a Roman
senator's couch, Lyn Randal's story weaves a powerful
and ancient magic."
—RITA® Award winner and bestselling author
Gayle Wilson

DON'T MISS THESE OTHER
NOVELS AVAILABLE NOW:

#851 THE PREACHER'S DAUGHTER
Cheryl St.John

#852 McCAVETT'S BRIDE
Carol Finch

#853 ROGUE'S WIDOW, GENTLEMAN'S WIFE
Helen Dickson

Prologue

Seville, Spain
May 17, 1517

Alejandro Castillo knew this thing he did was shameful, that it was a travesty and an outrage. Worse, he realized the others knew it, too, from the looks cast towards him as he sat in his special box in the Castillo family chapel.

Some of those looks were pitying glances, forgiving him even as they whispered his guilt. But others were hot with censure, and he deserved it. He was Judas Iscariot, leading an innocent to the slaughter.

He didn't look anywhere but forward, not even when his wife squeezed his hand. If he looked around, Anne's green eyes would be his undoing.

She, of all the others, knew the struggle he'd endured, how hard he'd tried to quiet the voices of his royal ancestors. She understood that he wanted to do the right thing for his sweet *palomita*, too—for Celeste, the little English dove who'd be betrothed to his son Damian this day—and how he despaired that he couldn't avoid sacrificing her.

He stared straight ahead. The lawyers droned on, clarifying the points of the betrothal, detailing the financial aspects of Celeste's dowry and the gifts of both the English and Spanish kings. Occasionally they asked him questions. Alejandro answered in a voice so flat he was amazed it was his own.

It was almost unmanly, the way he felt. He wished he were able to stride to the front and rip the gaudy clothes from his son's back, snatch that horrible ring from the girl's hand, proclaim everything a mistake.

But his kinsman the Spanish King, and Celeste's kinsman the English King, had decided upon alliance. And kings made no mistakes.

Alejandro thought of past sins and the judgement of God. Maybe his withered legs and acts of penance had not been enough. Maybe he must now suffer this guilt to expiate the blood that stained his soul.

Alejandro stared straight ahead and tried to find comfort in the familiar smell of ancient stone and burning wax. He would make it up to her. He damn well would do that. Celeste would bear his family's noble name.

Small comfort, that, but maybe soon there'd be a child with her dark eyes and copper curls, with her fiery spirit and affectionate heart. And he, Alejandro Castillo, would make sure that whatever his son Damian might do, the young wife and child would never need a single thing.

Only when he thought of that could he endure the scene before him—the rigidity of Celeste's delicate shoulders, the shaking of her fingertips when she reached for the quill, the way her eyes looked—too wide, too dark, too solemn.

Padre Francisco had scarcely pronounced the official words of betrothal when the chapel doors were flung open with a loud crack, startling Alejandro from his uneasy thoughts.

Midday sun flooded the dim sanctuary, harsh and hurtful. Men rushed in—large men, burly men, a cadre of men whose faces were partially covered and who brandished weapons towards the startled people sitting motionless in carved pews.

"Don't move, any of you!" shouted one who strode to the front. "We're here to prevent this damnable alliance with that filth-ridden vermin who calls himself King of England! There *are* still men in Spain—*men,* I tell you—who'd rather slit their own throats than ally with ill-begotten English refuse!"

Alejandro heard Anne's gasp, and knew her eyes flashed fire to hear her English countrymen so defamed. He looked around and gave her a warning frown, knowing it would help but little.

He wheeled his chair forward, ignoring the swords which immediately swung in his direction. "What is your purpose here?" he demanded.

The leader laughed, a grating and unpleasant sound, and moved towards Damian. Another minute and the tip of the brigand's sword pressed into the richly brocaded vest his son wore. Damian winced at the pain, his eyes narrowing.

Alejandro knew fear then.

"What would you do?" he asked again.

The man gestured. Damian was surrounded by men with weapons. Their leader lowered his sword. His lips twisted; one brow lifted above eyes that mocked. "I'm doing what I must."

He turned to Celeste and bowed. "I almost regret, little English *señorita,* that I deprive you of both your lover and your wedding."

As if in a dream, Alejandro saw the sword being raised behind his son's back.

He pushed his chair forward before he thought, his hands jerking at the wheels, his callused palms hissing against smooth wood. Men rushed towards him like a wave, their features a blurred turning of hard lines and bared teeth, their words lost in the explosion and flash of pain behind his eyes, and he was falling, tumbling into darkness…

Chapter One

❦

Don Alejandro Castillo had wicked eyes. Pirate eyes. They were blue, like the Mediterranean, and intense, like the Spanish sun. They could skewer a soul on the keen edge of a cutlass.

In real life, those eyes always softened when they looked at Celeste Rochester, but in her dreams the night before they had not.

"Don't fail me, *palomita*. Find my son," he'd said, his eyes dark with intensity. "Find Diego and bring him home to me."

"I will," she promised, knowing how great was the need. She sincerely meant and sincerely believed every word.

Such was the power of the dream.

It was harder to have such faith in herself now, released from the night's magic and staring across a smooth expanse of blue sea towards the isle of San Juan Bautista in the Spanish Indies.

This was her destination. Somewhere on that island was the man she sought. Diego Castillo, her betrothed's identical twin.

A shadow fell across her and she looked up. "Barto," she breathed, her hand involuntarily moving to her chest in surprise.

Her companion bowed slightly. "I frightened you. I'm sorry, I didn't mean to."

Celeste smiled at him. He *was* a bit frightening—or at least he *had* been when she'd first met him. She supposed his fearsome aspect was the point, however, since this old friend of Alejandro Castillo had been charged with her protection.

Celeste never doubted Barto's ability, not after having seen him. He was African, a Moor converted to Morisco, a man black of skin and firm of muscle and probably the largest person Celeste had ever seen in her nineteen years. His voice thundered; his arms and thighs fairly strained the seams of his clothing. He handled a variety of weapons with the ease of long practice. Yet, for all his great size, Barto's face usually held a pleasant, almost amused expression whenever he looked at her.

He turned that expression towards her now as his hands rested lightly on the ship's wooden rail. "Are you all right, *señorita?* There is a scowl between your brows that gives me pause. I almost feared to break into your reverie."

She smiled at his gentle humour. "As if you'd have aught to fear from me, Señor Gigante."

She nodded towards the isle they could see in the distance. "I confess to feeling anxious. Tomorrow we will go ashore and, God willing, we shall find Diego Castillo. I worry that he won't be easily convinced of our need. I worry that I won't be successful."

Barto turned to face her, taking both her hands into his and raising them, one at a time, to his lips. "Ah, *señorita,*" he said softly as he lowered them again. "If I were you, I'd be far more worried that I *would* be."

Celeste hardly slept that night, so nervous was she over the task she faced the following day. Instead, she slipped quietly on to the deck and listened to the crew from the shadows as they laughed over their games. She would write down snippets of their conversations in the journal she kept for her six-year-old brother, Jacob. She felt guilty about her months away from him, and writing had become her way to share all she'd seen since leaving England for Spain four months before.

She'd already sent him one book filled with the daily stuff

of her life. It contained her early days with Alejandro and Anne Castillo, pleasant days for her, as they'd awaited the return of her betrothed from sailing aboard one of the vessels with which his family's fortune was made.

Now she walked the decks of *La Angelina* and wrote of far more adventurous things, wanting Jacob to experience with her the taste of lemons and salt seaspray, each glorious sunrise with its chant of morning prayers, and the mournful song of the *guitarra* beneath a dark sky full of stars.

She didn't write of her fears when the fresh morning dawned. Instead, Celeste tried to ignore her emotions as they rowed in towards the first Spanish settlement on the isle.

Caparra. Even the settlement's name sounded exotic, the *R*s rolling deliciously against her teeth like waves rolled against its beaches of white sand.

Captain Jones had smiled when she'd said as much. "Nay, *señorita,*" he'd said with a shake of his head. "You must harbour no romantic illusions about this place, even if the name is a hopeful one, for it means *blossoming.* This isle is fair, to be sure, but the living conditions are primitive. The settlers are men of adventure, busy mining the wealth of this land. They are second sons, my lady."

He'd noted Celeste's puzzled expression. "Second sons. The younger sons of the hidalgo. Unable to inherit the fortunes of their fathers, they strike out to achieve their dreams by whatever means necessary. And some of those means have been brutal. Nay, *señorita.* This land holds promise, but for now little comfort."

Celeste had seen that for herself once they entered the settlement. The buildings were wooden, with roofs of thatch, even the miserable building that advertised itself as the inn and tavern, where they now headed to make enquiries.

As they waited outside for the Captain to conduct their business, Celeste looked about with growing discouragement. Everything was dirty and in poor repair. Roads were few and of thick, dark mud, rutted from the hooves of horses and wheels of carts. The sparse shops had the same tired aspect as the rest of the settlement. Celeste could only imagine how poor their selection of merchandise must be.

Only one building was constructed of stone and stood out from the rest. "The home of the Governor," Barto said, leaning close. "Governor Ponce de León had it built well, for he anticipated problems with Diego Colón, son of the Admiral. They both laid claim to the title of governor."

"Has there been trouble?" Celeste asked.

"Aye, a bit, though the Crown kept violence from erupting by choosing Ponce de León over Colón. But the ill will lingers between the two men yet, or so I hear." Barto made a sweeping gesture and faced her with a sardonic grin. "And all for this nondescript mudhole where the mosquitoes will either kill you or make you wish for death."

Padre Francisco joined in, his lean, ascetic face animated. "Ah, but the mud glitters here, Barto, don't forget that. The promise of gold has made many an old friend into an enemy." He shrugged. "Though that promise, too, has proved a disappointment. Little gold has been found, despite the blood spilled for it."

Celeste nodded, wondering about Diego Castillo and his reasons for coming to this land. It couldn't have been the desire for gold, not with all his parents' great wealth. But he'd come. *Why?*

She had far too many questions about Diego Castillo. It had seemed odd that she'd lived among the Castillo family for months and had never heard of this twin brother until Damian's abduction. Even then, his parents had seemed strangely reluctant to talk about this mysterious twin.

Ten years. He'd been gone for ten years. What kind of man would not return to his family once in ten long years? She feared the answer to that question.

The Captain soon returned with good news. "The Saviour has seen fit to bless us today, my friends," he said. "One within knew our man. Diego Castillo lives on an *encomienda* nearby.

You can find your way there before nightfall." A look of
pleasant surprise passed between Barto and Francisco.

Celeste nodded, tension strumming through her gut. *He
was here. She'd found him.* Even before sunset of this very day
she might have met Diego Castillo and explained her need. She
prayed he'd be willing to help, already half afraid that he
would not. And yet she had to convince him. There was so
much at stake. She'd try anything, promise anything. Almost
anything.

The narrow streets of Caparra were primitive, but Celeste
soon realized things *could* be worse. The rutted courses of mud
which passed into the countryside made even the puddled
streets of the town seem decent by comparison.

Now the cart had stuck again. This was the third time they'd
halted to push the cumbersome vehicle out of sucking mud.
Celeste climbed out with a groan of frustration, lifting her
skirts nearly to her knees without care for propriety. Padre
Francisco took up the reins while Barto eased his way through
the muck to put his strong shoulder to the back of the convey-
ance.

"Hettie," Celeste said, turning to her maid. "While the men
push the cart out, I need to relieve myself. There in the forest.
Nay, don't climb down. You'll soil your skirts. I won't go far."

Hettie nodded. "Be careful, love. And hurry. It shouldn't
take long to get the wheels on solid ground again."

Celeste entered the gloom of the trees with trepidation. This
island was so lush that she expected to find herself in a tangle of
underbrush. Surprisingly, the trees grew tall and the forest floor
was passable. She sought out a sheltered place to answer nature's
call, then looked around at the beauty, so different from the
forests of England, even more vastly different from the dry plains
that surrounded Seville. Curious, she eased farther into the wood,
smiling at the coolness, enjoying the heady fragrance of vividly
coloured tropical flowers. She breathed in deeply, comforted by
the scent of vegetation, of rich, moist earth and...*water?*

She moved forward and soon heard the roar. Moments later she stood on an outcropping of rock, looking down at a froth of rapids below. She sighed with disappointment. She'd wanted to cool her skin, wash her face. But the water was too far down and much too rapid.

She held her place for a moment, mesmerized. As she turned away an exquisite blossom nearby caught her eye, vibrant pink with streaks of peachy orange. She thought of Jacob. He loved flowers. He'd often picked bouquets of daffodils for their mother.

Jacob needed beauty. The physicians had said so. He could have it if she pressed this unusual bloom for him. Maybe she could reach it. It grew on a vine only slightly above her head. She swiped at it without success.

She tucked her lower lip between her teeth and tried again. Her fingertips grazed the delicate blossom, but it remained stubbornly out of reach. She jumped, then jumped again, realizing just as she snared her prize that the earth beneath her feet had shifted, carrying her towards the edge of the cliff on a rolling wave of pebbles. The blossom was crushed, then lost in a nightmare of blurred motion. She sought anything to grasp—vines, roots...*nothing!* There was no solid earth beneath her feet, only the tumbling of slippery rock and the edge, the very thinnest edge, of the cliff overlooking the water.

She fell in slow motion, her arms winding like fragile windmills, her body tipping forward even as her mind screamed. *No! Oh, dear God, no!*

She saw water beneath her before she plunged into the soundless depths of it. For a moment she hung within it, then rose again into sound and air. Down, up again, constantly shoved between the deep green-blue of the river, the green forest, the blue sky.

The current caught in the heaviness of her skirts. She was hurled forward into white froth, then dragged below into dark silence.

She bobbed up, gasping. Stones slammed against her ankles

and her elbows, and scraped roughly against the tender pads of her fingertips. She screamed as she was flung towards a huge boulder. Somehow she managed to avoid it. She was sucked backwards into the eerie silence of water, then just as quickly rushed forward towards turbulence again, helpless to stop herself from hurtling downriver.

I will die and no one will know. Oh, God, don't let me die.

Then, as if God had truly heard the petition, someone was there, someone of flesh and blood with strong arms. Someone made of warm muscle and sinew. Those arms lifted her, pulling her through the noiseless depths and through the froth, pulling her up into air and light and sound. Masculine arms closed tightly about her.

They reached the bank, dripping. Celeste could only cling to him, burying her face into the throbbing pulse of his neck— shaken, trembling, aware now of a thousand chaotic sensations. The tendrils of her hair clinging to his skin. The prickling of scraped places. The heavy breathing that meant she lived. And the breath of her rescuer, hot and harsh against her neck.

He spoke to her in Spanish, in between gulps of air. *"Está bien?"* he asked.

She could not answer, not yet.

He shifted her slightly in his arms so he could see her face. *"Está bien?"* he repeated, the tone more worried, more forceful.

"I'm sorry," she said, gasping. "I don't speak much Spanish."

"Are you all right?" he asked, in her English tongue, the enunciation clear but accented in a heavy, sensual way that made something burn within her. Or maybe it was the voice. So deep. So rich with concern.

"Aye, I'm fine," she managed to say between gulps of air. She pushed her hair out of her eyes.

Celeste wasn't sure what she noticed first, whether it was the rigid planes of his jaw or the clear blue-green of his eyes— eyes that could have been made of river and sky and trees. Eyes filled with a kindness that made her ache, that seemed somehow familiar, though she couldn't recall when she'd ever seen eyes so warm before.

Or perhaps it was his hair, tawny gold and so long it touched his shoulders, or his warm breath against her wet lips. Maybe it was the strength of the arms that cradled her, the thudding of his heart, the firmness of his muscle against her body... She wasn't sure which impression struck her first and most vividly—or if all of them were there simultaneously...as if, in the aftermath of surviving, she could only sense and feel and exult.

It made no sense, the emotion that flooded her. She wanted to reach up and twine her fingers into his long hair, to pull his lips to hers and taste him, to hear him moan inside her mouth and to feel his lean body press itself against hers. It made no sense, what she felt for this man who seemed familiar but wasn't. No sense at all, but yet...it was there.

She made no move, said nothing.

She only let herself breathe and feel his breathing, too, until finally the strong rhythm of lifeblood ebbed and she could speak without gulping at air. "I'm sorry," she said. "I can't swim well."

"Certainly not in all these clothes."

He'd not meant the words to be provocative, but, cradled as she was in his arms, his chest bare and warm against her cheek, she felt such strange stirrings. She couldn't contain the heat which speared her, beginning a burn in the pit of her stomach and igniting a fire that flamed in her cheeks.

As soon as he'd said the words, lust bolted through Diego. He hadn't meant to conjure the image of her as a forest nymph, sliding naked against his skin in sensuous water, but that image had somehow been there, full-blown. *Dear God, what had he done?*

He looked down at her—a girl, he'd thought her at first, for she was quite petite. But, no, she was a woman. An ethereal woodland fairy with rounded curves outlined by wet, clinging garments. A fantasy, with delicate features and long, long tendrils of coppery hair. With eyes large and dark and warm as earth. She was glorious, and he couldn't halt the desire that savaged him. He hadn't expected it, hadn't needed it or wanted it, but it had come.

And—God help him—she must soon know of it, for he could not hold her cradled in his arms for ever. When he put her down, her dainty feet to the forest floor, she would see then that he wore nothing. And all his explanations about his interrupted bath, all his apologies that his linen towel waited on the rock behind them…none of that would explain the swollen heat of his loins, the arousal she could not avoid seeing. *Lord, have mercy.*

The woman looked up at him and their gazes locked.

For the moment, she couldn't seem to find her voice. She could only lick at lips moist and inviting. She seemed to concentrate on words—such poor, poor substitutes for the nebulous something other they both truly wanted.

Words. Think. Words. He could see her struggle to find them.

Words finally came, forming themselves slowly into coherence. "Thank you," she whispered. "You saved my life."

He had as much trouble speaking as she. His eyes traced her features, then fastened upon her lips again. "My pleasure. 'Twould have been tragic to lose you."

The words were simple, and such as any courteous man would have said. But spoken as they were in that richly accented voice, Celeste felt her heart trip. She didn't want to leave the comfort of his arms. She wanted to pull him closer, wanted his warmth to enfold her. The thought was so powerful it frightened her.

"Are you not weary of holding me?" she asked. "Perhaps you should put me down now. I'm sure I could stand. The fright has passed, I think."

A strange expression crossed his face, almost as if he

winced. His eyes became the deep, deep blue of stormy seas, filled with something akin to regret. He dutifully eased her to her feet.

It took a moment for all the details to register. Her eyes were reluctant to leave the rugged beauty of his face.

Soon enough the realization came.

He stood before her in naked splendour, his body tall and finely sculpted. His shoulders were broad, his chest firm, his waist and hips trim, his legs straight.

He was beautiful, so beautiful, with the austere and spartan beauty of a man, with angles sleek and chiselled, with every muscle defined. To look at him made her ache at the careless majesty of his form. He watched her eyes, standing motionless beneath the scrutiny. His own dark azure eyes held concern.

Her first impulse was to step forward, to place her palm against his chest, to feel his heart thudding against her fingertips, to touch him. And then, because the impulse was so natural, so strong and so exquisite, she turned and she ran.

"Wait!" she heard him call. "I can explain! Wait!"

She looked back only once; he'd found a towel and was trying to wrap it around himself to follow her. But she knew what her wicked heart had desired of him, and that such a desire could never be. And, because she knew that, she bent and lifted her sodden skirts over one forearm and ran as if her virtue depended upon it.

Chapter Two

Even with Celeste's best efforts, it was some while before she found her way back through the forest to where the others waited with shifting feet and worried expressions. She hurried towards them. Hettie turned and cried out in dismay. "Lord, child! What have you done? Your beautiful clothes—they're all wet!"

"I fell into the river." Celeste brushed aside the concern, but Hettie fretted over her like a mother hen, plucking at her sleeve and pulling back the heavy curtain of her hair.

The maid clucked her tongue at the ruined gown. "And just now, when we're about to make it to that gentleman's *encom...encom...*"

"*Encomienda,*" supplied Padre Francisco. "Or, if you cannot remember the word, you might call it an estate, like in England."

"Aye, that," Hettie said. "It distresses me that my lamb will meet the owner looking such a pathetic sight. Though perhaps seeing a lady in distress will make him more disposed to offer lodging."

"He'd *better* offer lodging," muttered the priest. "We've a letter in the name of the King of Spain from Cardinal Cisneros himself. One look at that and if the man has any wit in his brain he'll offer up even his own fine bed."

"Nay," Celeste said. "We're not here to inconvenience him, only to find Diego Castillo."

"Let's move along, then," Barto said. He raised the reins and the mules started into motion again, the cart lurching forward over the uneven ruts of the narrow road.

The *encomienda* of Don Ricardo Alvarez was not a grand one, but it had many things to commend it. The location was excellent, with the home of the master well-built and over-looking a valley that was lush, its well-tended fields a testament to the owner's diligent oversight and the hard work of his slaves.

The man himself was another reason to give thanks. Although their appearance was unexpected, he welcomed them graciously, offering them lodging and food even before they'd explained their purpose and shown him the letter with the royal seal. Only once, upon their first enquiry concerning Diego Castillo, had Celeste seen a flicker of discomfort, but as it had been so subtle and so brief she imagined later that she'd let her overactive fancy get the better of her.

Now, as Celeste stripped off her sodden clothing in the comfort of the hacienda's guest room, she sighed and stretched out upon the bed. Blue-green eyes came again to her mind, and she shivered with the wickedness of the fantasy she could not forfeit. Who was he, that tall stranger who'd plucked her from death, only to plunge her squarely into forbidden desire? What evil lay within her heart that she could have such lustful imag-inings even while Damian Castillo's betrothal ring encircled her finger? God help her, she was a sinful wench!

She bounced up upon the edge of the bed, calling to Hettie.

Soon she was gowned, her sleeves tied on, her hair secured in an elegant coil and veiled, hiding the fact that it still had not dried completely. "There," the maid said with satisfaction. "Nobody would guess what a poor sight you were. You look an elegant lady now. What do you mean to do now?"

"I'm going to confession. There's a small chapel on the

premises, built of stone. If I can find a priest there, and if that priest can speak my tongue, I'd like very much to say shrift."

Hettie looked dubious. "You'll not likely find an English-speaking soul anywhere on this island."

An unbidden thought came to Celeste, that of a stranger with warm skin who spoke rich English into her ear. She shivered with delicious feeling, then shoved aside the memory. "Priests spend many years at their education, Hettie. Padre Francisco speaks our tongue—and French and Latin besides. At least I'll attempt it. I've not been shrived since I left for Spain."

"Why the need for confessing, all of a sudden?" Hettie studied Celeste, frowning slightly.

"Oh, I know not. Perhaps in this wild land I feel more strongly the want of it."

"Would it not suffice to say shrift to Padre Francisco?"

Padre Francisco? Saints preserve her! She'd rather die with those sins unrepented than tell the Castillo family priest about her faithless heart!

"Nay, I think not," Celeste said. "I'll seek out the priest who serves this *encomienda,* and if he speaks no English…well, so much the better."

Hettie smiled at Celeste's weak jest and busied herself with straightening the room. Celeste pushed open the heavy door, blinking as she crossed into the brightness of the flower-filled courtyard. The church stood nearby, and she hurried towards the peace she hoped to find there.

Padre Diego Castillo heard the soft tinkle of the bell and groaned inwardly. He'd placed the tiny bell on the door of the confessional chamber so he could work in his private room without missing any penitent who came. Yet he'd begun to dread the sound.

Of all his priestly duties, this one came hardest. It was never easy to hear the sins of other human hearts. He could never feel peaceful about leading others to absolution when he had so much of the world left in his own soul.

He knew the importance of his work, knew as well that all sinned and none stood perfect before God, but yet…how it disturbed him to be made aware of his own black heart, over and over, each time he closed the door of the confessional.

Even so, he was never hard on those who poured out their transgressions, often amid agonizing tears. Their guilt was his own. Empathy kept him seated, still and contrite, while they sobbed out their shame. Empathy made him return to the tight little box again and again, listening through the small latched door, crying his own guilt silently while they cried theirs aloud.

He closed the door and sat down, drawing his robe into a comfortable position around his long legs. "I am here for you, my child."

A woman's voice answered. "Padre, do you speak English?"

Diego's chest tightened. It couldn't be. *Not her.*

"Aye," he answered, letting his accent come out thick and gruff, knowing the fear that as he'd recognized her voice, so she'd know him by his.

Or should he let himself be known? Should he open the latched door that separated them and let her view his face? Would that not be the honourable thing to do—now, before she said another word, before she bared her soul?

What would her reaction be? Diego tried to imagine it. *She would die.*

She'd been held in the arms of a naked priest, a priest whose eyes must have shown the lust that had flamed within him. And even if his eyes hadn't, the rest of him surely had. Oh, dear heavens. He was as trapped as he'd ever been. He couldn't reveal himself. Listening to her confession was the only way to avoid savaging her dignity and destroying whatever semblance of decency remained to him.

"Father, I have examined my heart and am come to make my confession of sins to thee."

He concentrated on the words, on their form, comforted by the movement into familiar ceremony. His response was sure. "You have prayed, then, and sought God's leading?"

"Aye, Padre, prayed to know the true state of my soul."

"And our Lord has led you to knowledge of your sins?"

"Indeed, and I fear what I've seen. There is lust in my heart, Padre. Lust, and unfaithfulness to one who believes me to be true."

Diego could scarcely speak. "You've been unfaithful to a husband?"

"Nay, Padre. I have no husband."

"In what way, then, unfaithful?"

"I'm betrothed to a nobleman in Spain. I hardly know him, but I've spoken vows of betrothal and am to wed him as soon as 'tis possible to do so."

Diego had no words. She paused, expecting his response.

"Padre, are you there?" she asked finally.

"Aye."

"Did you hear me well?"

"Yes. There is more?" Diego knew there would be more, and he did not wish to hear it.

Her voice took on a frantic edge. "Oh, Padre, I'm so ashamed of my wayward heart! I can't control my feelings, though I wish to be upright, to be the fine wife Damian Castillo wishes of me."

Shock impaled Diego's heart.

His next words were stammered, tumbling out before he could hold back. "Damian Castillo? *Damian Castillo?*"

"Aye." She paused. Diego envisaged the way she looked, the sharp way she tilted her head, her furrowed brow. "Padre? You don't *know* him, do you?"

"I…the name is irrelevant, my child. Only your repentance is important now. Tell me more. In what way have you been unfaithful to your betrothed?"

"I felt lust for another man. He was a stranger to me. I don't even know his name. But he rescued me from drowning. And I…I was overcome by a feeling I've never known before."

"Perhaps what you felt was not lust, but some other fierce emotion. Gratitude at being saved, perhaps?"

"Nay, Padre. I'm familiar with gratitude. What I felt was an uncommon lust. I think I would have lain with him, I wanted him so badly."

Diego closed his eyes and leaned back in his seat, his throat tight.

"I don't know why I was affected by him. Something in his eyes held my heart. I couldn't look away. Now I can't forget the magnificence of his body. He held me and our eyes met and something passed between us, something intense and beautiful. In that moment I wished to know him as a man. To be known by him as a woman. I wanted him to kiss me. I wanted to lie with him there in the forest, with green around us and blue above us. Perhaps he wanted it, too, for he—"

Diego cleared his throat. "That's enough. It's not best to dwell further on those images. Memory should serve judiciously. If aught reminds you of lustful feeling, it would be best to put such behind you."

"I know, Padre. There's the coil. I don't wish to forget him."

"Why wouldn't you? The man's a stranger. He means nothing to you. You're already bound by sacred oath to another. You must forget this nameless man and find happiness with him who would be your husband."

Diego heard her sigh. "Your suggestion *is* the proper thing," she said, "and yet I doubt I can feel for my husband what I felt today. Nor am I sure I *want* to."

Diego wanted to groan. "In time you'll come to feel the same passion for your husband."

She didn't answer.

"Listen, my child. What you felt today was a natural thing, given as a gift by a loving God for his divine purpose, to lead mankind to couple and beget children. It's a natural and beautiful thing, but meant to be enjoyed between man and wife. Not corrupted by—"

She cut him off with a low growl of frustration. "Corrupt? No, it was not. Were I to have lain with that blue-eyed man, there would have been something loving between us, something of warmth and care, something transcending all vows. Our *souls* seemed to entwine."

She was quiet for a moment. "Padre, I'm not an immoral woman. Nineteen years old am I, and yet do I remain a virgin. Never have I wanted to make love with a man, not any man ever. But what happened today was wondrous. In my heart, I know our coupling would have been a thing of beauty. It felt good and right between us."

Diego drew in a shaky breath. That much he could not deny. It *had* been wondrous. It *had* felt good and, yes, even right.

He bit back his first impulse, that of agreement. Instead, he did his duty. "There's never a time when sin can be right. Had you lain with him, you'd be guilty of fornication. You might have conceived a bastard child. I know you don't wish for such disgrace."

Diego looked up at the ceiling of the small chamber, realizing how exquisite his own tension had become. "You must close your mind to further fantasies. To continue with them is to lead yourself into a world of folly."

"Aye, Padre." She was near tears.

"Pray God to keep your soul pure and your body untainted until you wed. You must pray this."

"I will."

She cried now. Tightness made his own chest ache. "Put aside your guilt, and with sincere heart seek the will of God. In this way, you are forgiven."

The bell tinkled as she slipped away.

When he was sure she had gone, Padre Diego Castillo bowed his head and prayed for her soul...and his own.

Ricardo Alvarez looked down at his drink and then up at Diego, who paced the floor of terracotta tile in agitation. "I didn't give your presence away to them, you know. But neither can I pretend I know you not. They've a letter with the King's seal, Diego. I dare not lie and tell them you aren't here."

"What do they want with me?" Diego asked, stopping to riffle his hair with lean fingers.

"This I do not know. Could it be your father has…departed? That you're the recipient of an inheritance or something?"

Diego halted for a moment, considering that, then shook his head and resumed his pacing. "That doesn't explain the presence of the girl. Who is she? What does she want with Diego Castillo?"

"I'd hoped you might answer that question."

"My father's not been ill," Diego reasoned, as if to himself. "Doña Elena Ponce de León sends me news of Seville. Her last letter came but two weeks ago and she said only that my brother was…that he is…"

Ricardo looked up sharply and frowned. "To *wed,* Diego."

"He is to *wed.* There, I've said it." Diego stopped and shook his head. "And at the time all I could think was, 'God bless them both,' but that was before…"

Ricardo cocked his head, but Diego only frowned at him. Ricardo frowned back, nonplussed. Diego had been his friend for years, and nothing, not even the priest's ill humour, could dissuade him from their deep friendship.

Ricardo let Diego pace awhile, then cleared his throat. "You must meet them, Diego, and find out why they're asking for you. They're to dine with me this evening; you might as well attend."

Diego stroked his chin. "You could discuss the business with them and tell me of it later. That way—"

Ricardo stood abruptly. "You're the damnedest, you know that? The damnedest! Truly, I've never known you for a coward, but—"

Diego's lips twitched. "And you're probably the only Spaniard I know who gets away with cursing his own priest." He shrugged. "I'm no coward, Ricardo, but there's more to this tale than you understand. I have reason to be loath to meet them. The English *señorita* in particular."

"Well, enlighten me. What's a reason so good that you can't

at least discover their business, especially if accompanied by a fine meal and good wine?"

Diego raised his eyebrow in such a rakish way that it almost offset the pious formality of the priestly robe he wore. "This morning I went to my bath at the river, heard a feminine scream, and before I knew what was happening, had pulled a woman from the water."

"That makes you a gentleman, Diego. What of it?"

"Well, something passed between me and the girl as I held her in my arms."

"Something like physical attraction, Diego? Well, it happens. Even priests are men."

"I'm not supposed to let it happen to me."

Ricardo snorted. "Carnal temptation. As long as nothing comes of it, you've not sinned. There's no ill done."

"Except that I stood naked with the girl in my arms, Ricardo. And then became *aroused*…by her…beauty."

"Tsk. Tsk. Where is a towel when you need one?"

Diego frowned. "This is no laughing matter. I couldn't hold her in my arms all day, and when I put her down… Well, she saw…everything…'ere she fled from me."

Ricardo threw back his head and laughed. Diego scowled at him.

"And let me guess," Ricardo said, still grinning. "Our lovely redheaded guest is the lady of whom we speak?"

"Aye, she is the one."

"So there's the rub." Ricardo shook his head. "You still must face her. Oh, you'll be a bit embarrassed. She'll be quite a lot embarrassed. But it happened, and now it's in the past. She's got to understand that even priests can be men occasionally, and curse it all, *she* interrupted *your* bath. It isn't as if you tried to seduce the girl. You didn't try to, did you?"

"Of course not. Whatever my past sins, I've been faithful to my vows since I spoke them."

Ricardo gestured with the glass of Madeira. "So let the girl see that robe, Padre. She'll get over the shock. She'll cry herself to sleep because her blue-eyed piece of masculine flesh has a higher call than marriage, but she'll get over it."

"Well, there's more."

"Damn. There always is."

"She came to shrift this afternoon and…well, I couldn't let her know that the priest to whom she was confessing her lustful feelings had…uh…."

"Been guilty of the same lustful feelings?"

"Aye, some such thing as that."

"So now she'll know you deceived her."

"And there's more."

Ricardo shook his head. "More? Sweet blessings, Diego! For a priest, you get into the most confounded messes."

"It seems our unexpected encounter moved her deeply, so deeply that now she doubts she can feel the same for her betrothed."

"Her betrothed?" Ricardo glanced up into Diego's face and found it far too grim. "Oh, dear heavens," he said. "Don't tell me. Not…your brother?"

"My brother."

Ricardo sat down abruptly. "Hell. Hell and damnation."

"Ricardo, those curses—"

"It's like the last time all over again, isn't it? You and Damian and Leonora."

"Nay, Ricardo. It is not like the last time. I'll not let it be. I'm under my vows now."

Ricardo shook his head. "Sins of the flesh, sins of the mind. *Cuidado, amigo.* They are not too far apart."

The muscle tensed in Diego's jaw. He said nothing.

Ricardo breathed in deeply. "You can't run, Diego. You must face our guests, including the *señorita.* Come, dine with us this evening."

"She'll be angry when she discovers who I am. What I've done."

"Let her be angry. Let her vent her spleen and hate you. It will be the simplest way."

Diego nodded.

Ricardo walked across the room. He looked back from the doorway. "And, by the way, her name is Celeste."

Celeste, Diego thought when he sat alone in the quiet. Well, it would have to be. Everything about her, even her name, was heavenly.

And that made him feel like hell.

Chapter Three

Celeste dressed for dinner early and, having time to spare, decided to explore the lush gardens of the courtyard and beyond. They were lovely past anything she'd seen before, even though the sisters in the convent where she'd studied had kept beautifully tended gardens of herbs, with captivating masses of English roses thrown in for sheer beauty. Sister Maria Theresa had smiled once when Celeste expressed delight over a particular bloom. "The Lord gives us all things to enjoy," the nun had said. "He means that we find communion with him through the wonders of his creation."

Now Celeste pondered that. She could see how the beauties of blossoms and butterflies and birds, of mountains and rivers and trees, could lead her heart towards a sweet communion with the Almighty.

But the most magnificent beauty she'd seen of late had been the etched muscle of a man, a man with long hair of tawny-gold and eyes of turquoise-blue. And that beauty, she had little doubt, would only lead her further from God's virtuous path.

She thought again of the priest's words. She must put the man from her mind. To think on him would lead to folly.

Yet she didn't want to put thoughts of him aside. She'd

never known desire, not until today. Oh, she'd let a suitor or two kiss her lips, and then had wondered what was so wonderful about it that lovers would brave discovery, the displeasure of their families, and even death itself, to experience the wonders of love. Kissing had been distasteful, to say the least.

After trying it, she'd had little interest in more intimate matters. Such things had seemed vulgar and common. So she'd come to the age of nineteen with her virtue intact and little knowledge or concern for what occurred between a man and a woman in their coupling.

Even when she thought of being married, she never considered the actual act of consummation. Marriage meant running a husband's home, directing his servants towards profitable enterprises and seeing that his children were well trained. That was the role of a woman. Celeste hadn't imagined actually lying with Damian Castillo.

She fingered the bright fuchsia blossom of a vine which covered the wall, and then sank miserably down onto the bench beside it.

She tried to remember Damian's face from the one time she'd met him, just prior to their betrothal ceremony. She wanted to think him handsome, but the leer in his eyes and the sneer of arrogance that turned his lips had made him less than attractive. She couldn't imagine he'd be tender or gentle with her inexperience.

And yet the priest had told her she'd feel desire for him, that she must concentrate on him until that desire came.

The only thing she could imagine coming was a deepening disgust.

Now Celeste admitted her truest feelings. She was not uninterested in love or carnal matters, nor had she ever been. She knew—had somehow always known—that there would some day come one whose touch would stir her passion.

That man had come along this very morn, a man with eyes so warm she'd wanted to fall into their depths, with a form so tall and lean she'd wanted to memorize every hard angle of it.

She envisaged herself kissing him and quivered with the imagined taste of him on her tongue.

When she thought of that man, she knew she couldn't do what the priest asked. The priest was wrong. She wanted to know that man, not forget him.

She arose, a new plan forming. She would ask in the village for a tall, golden-haired Spaniard with eyes sometimes blue and sometimes green, a Spaniard with a knowledge of English and a voice rich and deep. She'd find him.

A soft clearing of a throat behind her made her shift around on the bench. "Barto," she breathed. "It's you."

He moved forward until he looked down upon her, his expression soft.

She extended a hand. "Sit down here with me. I wish to talk with you."

Celeste paused, thinking back over their voyage. At first she'd been wary of the big man, of his size, of his fierce demeanour. But he'd shown her his true self when she'd become seasick, along with Hettie and Padre Francisco and nearly half the crew. Barto had shown incredible gentleness with her then, holding her as tenderly as a child while he forced ale down, one swallow at a time.

When she'd recovered, he'd sensed her boredom and brought out books. Her eyes must have widened with anticipation, for he'd laughed. "Not all of these are in English, *señorita*. There are some in Spanish, too, so you might learn the tongue of your betrothed's homeland." Barto had seemed to enjoy her squeal and excited hug.

A few days later, when the books in English had all been read and the struggle to learn Spanish had begun to weary her, he'd brought out another gift, a simple tunic top and a pair of *zaragüelles,* the wide trousers worn by the sailors, sewn small enough to fit Celeste's petite frame.

Celeste remembered Barto's grin when she'd emerged from her quarters a short while later dressed like a seaman, her hair in a single braid down her back. "No mariner ever looked as good in those breeches as you do now, m'lady. The boatswain will have a hard time keeping the men's minds on their duties today."

But he'd introduced her to José Lorca just the same, and the boatswain had soon begun letting her perform duties with the rest of the men, although she'd suspected they saved only the easier tasks for her. She had grown proficient at knowing the workings of the ship, the names of its complicated machinery, and the tasks of the sailors. While Hettie had complained that no proper lady should become as golden brown as Celeste was becoming, Celeste had enjoyed the sun and the salt and the smell of the sea.

Barto seemed to know her heart, her very heart, and she gravitated towards his company. Barto was patient, and let her tag along behind him. He taught her how to knot ropes. He taught her how to play poque. He taught her sea ditties, even though a few were so ribald that she couldn't sing them for laughing. Padre Francisco had censured him for that, but Barto had merely grinned at Celeste. She'd smiled back. A friendship had been made.

So now, as Barto took his place beside Celeste on the bench, she knew she could ask him the questions that burned in her heart. "I want to talk, Barto," she said. "There are things I need to know, and I trust you to tell me."

Barto raised an eyebrow. "What things?"

"I want to know more about the Castillo family. I sense...I don't know. Something amiss, perhaps."

Barto didn't reply.

"I grow uneasy, although I can't say why. On the surface, naught seems out of place. And yet..."

"Don Alejandro was right in what he said about you, that you possess a keen intelligence to go with a lovely face and exquisite form. He cares for you. You remind him of his own dear Englishwoman, his beloved Anne. Like her, you are warm, emotional, the kind of woman he's always wanted for his son."

"He said that?"

"*Sí, señorita,* he did. And, coming from Alejandro, that's a compliment indeed. In all the years I've known him, he's never been one to carelessly give affection. Anne won his love and she's worthy of it. But you…you've won his heart in a different way altogether."

Celeste smiled. "I like Don Alejandro. When I came to Spain I was anxious about what I would find, whether I'd be welcomed by the Castillo family, and whether I'd find my future husband an old man, plagued by gouty legs and a pox-kissed face. But Don Alejandro and Doña Anne were kind, and Damian…well, he's not old and not gouty, and if his face has been kissed, then 'twas not the pox which did it."

Barto laughed. "You're pleased to marry him, then?"

"I suppose." Celeste shrugged a delicate shoulder. "Our two kings favour the match."

"Aye, but you still have the final decision. No man, not even a king, can force a maiden to wed. With your wealth, you could remain unmarried if you so chose."

Celeste toyed with a blossom. "I need this marriage, Barto."

Barto met her gaze. "The Castillo family needs you, too. Alejandro and Anne long for a grandchild. An heir."

Celeste sighed. "So this marriage will be done and the alliance made, if we're successful in this venture."

Barto frowned. "I don't think we will be. I doubt Diego will be aboard our vessel when we return."

Celeste's breath caught. "Is he such a churl, then?"

"Nay, no churl. Not he. He's the most upright of the Castillo family. I doubt he'll be party to the deception, whatever the cause of it, whatever the worth of it."

"Upright? More upright than even Don Alejandro?"

Barto laughed, the sound booming across the courtyard and down the covered porticos. "Especially Don Alejandro! You don't yet know Alejandro Castillo well enough."

"No?"

Barto grinned, crossing his massive arms in front of his

chest. "Let me clarify. Alejandro's a good man. He always has been. But he's also been…unorthodox at times."

"He doesn't seem so to me. Quite the opposite."

"He's changed. Most men do over the years. Today he's upright in his dealings, gives faithfully his alms to the poor and his tithes to the church, serves God and country with zeal, turns away from sin. Such was not always the case."

"That's often the way of a man in his youth. My own father was a rake until he met my mother."

Barto smiled. "Ah, but there are rogues, and then there are *rogues*. And Alejandro was definitely one of the latter. Aye, and worse than a rogue."

He faced her squarely, one eyebrow lifted as if he challenged her. "He was a pirate. A corsair of the Barbary coast, preying on foreign vessels and making his wealth from the misfortunes of his victims."

Celeste's eyes met Barto's and saw the truth in them. He studied her carefully, waiting for indignation or outrage. She gave him neither.

She knew. Somehow she'd always known. There was something about Don Alejandro that spoke of fierceness, of boldness, of a wildness never tamed.

She looked away, plucking at the petals of the bloom in her hand. "A pirate. Did he kill people?"

"Only such as needed killing."

Celeste frowned, trying to resolve her conflicting images of Don Alejandro. "Then the accident which left him crippled… It was not an accident, was it?"

"Nay, *señorita*. He was injured in a fight for an Italian *nao* loaded with rich cargo. We won the vessel, but our good captain lost his legs, injured by the blade of a scimitar against his spine."

"*We*, Barto? You were there?"

Barto bowed slightly. "Aye, Pirate Barto at your service, m'lady. I was steward aboard Alejandro's vessel, chosen as much for my size and the fierce aspect of my countenance as for my ability to read and cipher. Who among Alejandro's seamen would question the quality of the rations if I'd purchased them? What man dared question his share of the captured loot if I meted it out?"

Barto thumped his chest. "I was—and am—loyal to Alejandro. He lives today because I fought my way to his side before a hideous, pockmarked Italian could finish the job of killing him. Yet I do try to be an honest man, *señorita,* and will not portray your future father-in-law as anything but what he is, a sinner struck down as a man in his prime, humbled by fate or Allah or God, or perhaps by whatever wickedness led him to such a vocation in the first place."

Celeste pondered that. "Doña Anne told me not to feel sorry for him."

"I agree. Alejandro was humbled, but he wasn't debased, for he's a man of intelligence and energetic will. He's not one to bemoan his tragedy. Indeed, I doubt he gives much thought to it today."

Celeste studied the huge Negro's face. "You admire him, don't you?"

"I do. There's much about him which is admirable. Even as a pirate he was never without honour."

There was companionable silence for long moments, each staring at the soothing fall of water in the fountain, or the riot of blooms or the shifting patterns of shade beneath the trees.

Celeste finally broke into the quiet. "Tell me about the sons. Give me the truth, plainly spoken. I'm convinced there's much I've not been told."

"What were you told?"

"That they were twins of like appearance."

"They are similar in looks. Or at least, they *were.* What Diego's appearance is today, I cannot know."

"Are they similar in their personalities as well? Damian seems…" She struggled to express her fleeting impression. "He seems well-mannered."

That much she could say in truth. He *had* been outwardly

courteous, attending flawlessly to minding her chair, even though she suspected he'd used it as an opportunity to view her bosom from above.

Barto laughed, but the short sound was almost bitter. "Well-mannered," he said dryly. "Aye, he's well-mannered. Anne would have seen to that."

"You don't like him very much, do you?"

"I despise him. And now that I'm fond of you, I would that you weren't pledged to him." Barto quirked an eyebrow. "That's the truth, plainly spoken."

"Why do you dislike him?"

"Dislike? I didn't say dislike, *señorita*. I said I *despise* him. I'd almost say I hate him, and not merely for what he did to Diego—"

Celeste held up a hand. "Hold there. What did he do?"

"It's past, and not my story to share. For now, I'll say merely that your *novio, señorita,* is a self-centred fool who's cared for naught but wealth from his youth. The injustice is that he was firstborn and thus the heir, for he'll never become half the man that Diego was without even trying."

Celeste looked down. The jewels of her betrothal ring glittered in the filtered sunlight, mocking her. Tears sprang to her eyes. All her reasons for marriage suddenly seemed weak and illogical. "This man is to be my husband?"

Barto frowned. He took her hand into his larger one. "Don't despair. He'll not do you harm. There are those of us who love you. We'll insist he treat you kindly, even if he'll never love anyone but his own miserable self."

"I don't wish to marry such a man. Help me, Barto. Help me know what to do. I've learned to trust you in spite of what Padre Francisco tells me of your heathenish ways." Her mouth quirked up. "Or perhaps because of them."

Barto smiled and rubbed her knuckle with his thumb. "I'm honoured to have earned your trust. And now trust me in this. Alejandro and Anne already love you. They're growing older and deserve an heir to carry on the Castillo lineage. Theirs is a very noble, very honourable name, and your children will do well to receive it. For their sakes, and for the peaceful union of our two countries, you will marry Don Damian and you will get an heir by him. But once that is done you can forget the bastard even exists."

"Is he so awful, then?"

Barto looked away. He didn't answer for such a long time that Celeste wondered if he'd heard the question.

He turned finally, with an expression both tender and sad. "A heathen I may be, my lady, but even heathens know when the time comes to pray. And I will pray for you that God might intervene and grant you happiness. If anyone deserves it, you do." He dropped a kiss upon her forehead and left her alone to ponder in silence, staring past the gentle fall of water into the shadows beneath the trees.

Don Ricardo Alvarez was a generous host. Celeste could hardly believe the great quantity of food and drink he'd placed before them. She smiled at the thought that even Barto's great hulk must claim satisfaction after such a meal, and Padre Francisco would probably need to ask forgiveness for succumbing to gluttony.

Not only was the fare ample and delicious, but Don Ricardo was an excellent host. He had appeared early to escort Celeste to the table, his doublet and hose of silver contrasting nicely with his tanned skin, blue eyes and black hair. He spoke to her in English, though very poorly, and, since Celeste had learned but a little Spanish, they managed to converse in awful broken phrases heavily punctuated with much laughter.

They strolled through the garden on the way to the large, well-furnished dining hall, and Celeste told him with mispronounced adjectives how lovely the flowers were. Don Ricardo obliged her by picking some of the more exotic blooms and giving her the bouquet, even taking one and tucking it behind her ear. Celeste might have thought the attention flirtatious, except that with Don Ricardo it didn't seem so. Instead, he seemed friendly and kind.

The others had not yet arrived, so he took her into the kitchen and introduced her to Maria and Pablo, a Taino Indian couple in their mid-thirties. He explained in slow, careful English that Maria was his hostess and Pablo his overseer.

"Their names—no Maria, no Pablo—no true. I call this, for names true are words of Indians, words hard, hard to say," he explained.

Maria smiled shyly and pointed to the blossom in Celeste's hair with a chuckle. Ricardo then spoke in Spanish. He'd learned that Celeste understood it much better than she spoke it, and he was obviously tiring of his losing struggle with English.

"Maria smiles because I've placed a blossom in your hair," he said. "I hope I did it right."

"Did it right?"

"Aye. There's a very old custom of flower courtship here on this island. If the flower is placed on the right, it means one thing. On the left, it means another thing. In the centre, something else entirely."

Celeste reached up to feel the bloom. "It's on the right. What does that mean?"

"Ah, now, there's the problem. Being a man, and not the romantic sort, I can never remember the details. It either means you're available to become someone's lover or it means you've found a lover and look no further. I hope I put it on the correct side."

Celeste laughed. She couldn't resist the mischief in his expression. "Which do you think would be the correct side, Don Ricardo? Do I need a lover? Or have I already found one?"

He studied her with amusement. "You're far too attractive not to be pursued by lovers already, *doncella*. However, if you should some day find yourself without someone to call your own, then I stand ready to take up the task."

"Don Ricardo," Celeste said with a smile, admitting that, as he was probably only around thirty years of age and handsome, he had undoubtedly practised his courteous phrases on many a willing maiden. "I see you're a rascal, and a flirtatious one at that."

He laughed and raised one eyebrow. "Rascal? The word hardly does justice to my misdeeds, *señorita,* but I'll let it pass since you don't yet know me well enough to have learned of them. But come, our other guests are arriving. Shall I escort you to the table?"

Now, as they attended the meal, Celeste listened to the lively banter around the table, most in Spanish too quickly spoken for her to follow. Occasionally, however, Don Ricardo sensed her boredom and, like a worthy host, slowed his speech or changed to her tongue to include her in some particularly comical story.

Celeste noted, however, that beneath his polished mien and jovial manner he seemed uneasy. He kept glancing towards the door as if expecting someone. Indeed, another plate had been placed on the table but had so far remained unused.

They were nearing the end of the roast suckling pig with its glazed fruits when Don Ricardo stood suddenly, looking past the open door into the corridor. "It's about time you got here," he said, not pretending to hide his displeasure.

A shadowy figure moved closer to the entrance. "I'm sorry, Ricardo, but the Indian couple who live down near the river bridge lost their baby this afternoon—an early birth, the child too small to live. I went to comfort them and to offer prayer and last rites. I was necessarily delayed."

Don Ricardo's displeasure softened. "Well, come in and eat," he said, gesturing, and the priest entered the room.

Celeste had been looking down at the food on her plate, but when the man entered she raised her eyes to greet him. Her heart stopped beating. It couldn't be. *Not him.*

Ricardo looked around and raised his hand towards his guests. "Nay, don't get up. I can make the proper introductions without hindering our meal. Permit me to introduce the priest who serves my *encomienda.* He's also my good friend. For you, though, he's the end of your quest—the gentleman you seek, Padre Diego Castillo."

Celeste could not breathe. She looked around at the others,

only to find soft amusement on Barto's face and a startled, almost pained expression on that of Padre Francisco.

Her eyes travelled over him quickly. No wonder he'd seemed somehow familiar. He was her betrothed's twin. They had the same height, the same hair colour, the same blue eyes. But there the resemblance ended. Her betrothed had short hair and a full beard. Diego's hair was long and streaked by sun, his tanned face cleanshaven. He lacked the arrogant stance and ostentatious clothing of his brother, and his eyes were far kinder. And, of course, when she'd first seen Diego he'd been thoroughly wet and completely nude, and her mind had been in such disarray that she hadn't been able to put the facts together.

Even now she could barely register them all—that the priest before her was Diego Castillo, the other son of Don Alejandro and Doña Anne. And that he was also the naked stranger who'd rescued her from the river, the man whose warm eyes and warm skin had awakened her to passion. The one whose voice had made her insides quiver with sensual feeling. The one she'd heard in the confessional chamber.

And the one who'd also heard her. All about her.

She sat very still, letting the facts settle. He remained in place across the table from her, watching her with that same concerned expression he'd had earlier.

"Sit down, Diego," Don Ricardo said in a firm voice.

Diego did not sit. He stared at her, willing her to look up at him. Celeste felt his eyes, felt their odd intensity.

She did look up, but only to focus her attention on Ricardo. "I wonder if I might be excused," she said. "I suddenly feel unwell and need a little air." Then, without hearing a reply or waiting for one, Celeste escaped the room.

Diego caught her just outside the doorway, capturing her slender wrist with a firm male hand. "Don't run away from me," he said.

Celeste, startled, looked up into his face. It was determined and firmly set, his blue gaze intently fastened upon her face. Her throat went instantly dry.

"We must talk," he said quietly. "Come with me. The chapel is nearby and will give us the privacy we need."

Celeste looked back towards the open door of the dining room and saw that every pair of eyes in the room had fastened with interest on them. Don Ricardo's face held slight humour. Barto and Padre Francisco's a mixture of confusion and curiosity. "I would be unchaperoned," she stammered. "That would not be proper."

Some of the intensity fled Diego's face, replaced by a hint of amusement. "Perhaps not proper if I were a handsome gallant bent on your seduction. But I think a maiden might visit a priest at any time without fear of ravishment." The corner of his lips gave in to the temptation to smile. "Wouldn't you agree, my lady?"

It was difficult to answer him coherently. Her mind had snagged on the word *ravishment*. That word, mixed with his nearness and the intense blue of his eyes, had set her nerves to quivering. There was too much between them, even here, with every gaze turned in their direction. Too much heat. Too much fascination. Too much *desire*.

There was desire. Oh, yes. Celeste knew she wasn't supposed to feel it, or even be comfortable with it, but at this moment she didn't care. She'd always been far too headstrong and impulsive, had always had to labour to contain her natural urge towards spontaneity.

But now, standing in the corridor with Diego's warm fingers capturing her wrist, the wildness in her soul reasserted itself, and she plunged headlong into feeling.

"Come with me," he repeated. "Tell me why you've come from Spain to seek me out."

Celeste nodded absently, trying to remember again exactly why it was she had come. She'd practised a speech to deliver to him, one that enumerated all the reasons he should return with her. She'd known it by heart only an hour ago, but now could not remember one single word.

She vaguely heard Diego make their excuses, and just as

vaguely heard Ricardo's reply, before Diego led her away through the heavy carved doors and into the courtyard.

Her senses were suddenly alive. The short trip across the paved courtyard became a dream of sensation. The night air was cool and a bit damp, heavily scented with the fragrance of flowers…and man. Diego's warm, soapy essence was new to her, and more pleasant than she'd anticipated. His hand left her wrist and moved to the small of her back as he guided her towards their destination. He touched her lightly, courteously, but her entire body vibrated to the warmth of those elegant fingertips. She'd never been so aware of anything as at this moment, with primitive energy humming through her.

And he was a *priest*. She reined in her madness and focused on that, on the coarseness of his dark robe, on the glinting of his silver crucifix in the moonlight. Diego Castillo was a *priest*.

But, goodness, he was an attractive priest. The maleness of him called out to her, made her flush with desire, made her wish… No, she would not consider any such thing. She was already bound by oath to another, and this…this was utter madness. Her mind coiled around her fascination and captured it. She was here for one purpose and one purpose only: to convince her betrothed's twin to return to Spain. Only then could she procure the marriage she needed. She *needed* this marriage.

That thought sobered her. By the time they entered the heavy doors to the chapel her limbs had ceased their trembling. Her mind had calmed. Maybe now she could concentrate on the business at hand.

The chapel was lit by one single candle near the altar which threw golden glints of light up towards the wall where a silver Jesus hung on his silver cross. The edges of the room were cloaked in comforting shadows. Celeste glanced up at the ceiling's thick hewn beams, and breathed in the familiar smell of wax and incense.

Their footsteps seemed too loud in the quiet, as if she and Diego somehow intruded upon the serene and sacred.

Diego seemed not to notice. Instead, he led her down the aisle to a carved pew bathed in the golden circle of light.

Good, this is good, Celeste thought, glancing around. Surely being in a holy place would help contain the giddiness of her emotions. Surely the nearby death throes of the Saviour and the close presence of the Virgin Mother would remind her of all she'd ever been taught of honour and purity.

But she swallowed hard when Diego swung with lithe grace into the pew beside her and seated himself so near that their thighs almost touched.

She knew the most intense urge to cross herself.

Mercy. God, have mercy.

Odd how she'd never thought of blue eyes as being warm before. But now she felt bathed in concern, baptized in compassion, heated from the inside out by this man's green-blue gaze.

"I owe you an apology," he said. "I should have made myself known to you in the confessional this afternoon. I'm sorry I did not."

Heat flooded her face. Her gaze fled from his direct appraisal.

He took her hand in a gentle gesture of reassurance. The contact burned her skin, so that she almost gasped at the touch. "I considered it, you know, not wanting to hear your secrets, but…well…" Celeste felt rather than heard his sigh. "You had seen me as few others have."

At the hint of amusement she thought she heard, her eyes darted back to his face. The corners of his lips twitched, and she knew he laughed inwardly at himself.

She suddenly wanted to taste those lips, those handsome lips. He would taste so good. Almost she could taste him now. His manly fragrance was all around her. She inhaled it with every breath. He would taste like that smell, that warm and erotic smell, like soap and sandalwood and male, clean and elusive.

Celeste breathed in deeply and forced her gaze away from

that slight smile. The lace on her sleeve became suddenly fascinating. It was quite intricately wrought, with such painstaking handiwork...

Diego waited for her to speak. She sensed his rapt attention on her face, felt his amusement slowly change to concern. His thumb began to stroke her knuckle, an unconscious act of comfort on his part, but to Celeste an eroticism almost unbearably intimate. She pulled her hand away from beneath his, and felt his frown deepen into a scowl.

"You are angry with me?" he asked.

She shook her head, not quite trusting her voice.

"You feel betrayed, then?"

She drew in a deep breath, regretting it immediately when his gaze fell to her breasts as if she bade him there. He caught himself and looked away quickly, but not before she'd seen the blue gaze deepen to the darker azure of desire.

"Nay, not betrayed by you," she said. "You did only that which was required to preserve your dignity and my own. If I have been betrayed, then it was by my own wicked thoughts. I did not know you were sworn to God. I would never have... I would not... Oh, sweet merciful Jesus! To know I felt such things...and for a *priest!*"

She buried her face in her hands.

There was silence. It stretched between them, long and rife with tension.

She lowered her hands, but could not meet Diego's gaze. "I have sinned against God and against you. Please forgive me, Padre."

He did not answer immediately, but startled her by rising from the pew abruptly. "Wait here," he said. "I'll be back. Wait."

He was gone only a short while. When he returned, Celeste saw that he was no longer in his robe, but dressed as any ordinary man in the simple fustian tunic of a common labourer, the garment loosely belted over hose and boots of soft leather.

The clothing was coarse, but clean. Simple, but attractive

on him. It made his shoulders appear broad, his hips narrow, his legs long and powerful. His hair was casually rumpled, palest gold where the tropical sun had kissed it, more honeyed where it lay against his collar. His skin was dark, his teeth startlingly white against the bronzed glow of his face. He was cleanshaven and his chin had a cleft.

He was so handsome it hurt.

She almost wished he'd put the robe back on, so she could think of him as a priest and not be so aware of him as a man.

He took his place once again in the pew and smiled at her. "There now. Let's forget for the moment that I'm a priest. Could you and I not talk more freely if I were merely Diego Castillo?"

She nodded.

He turned so that his body faced hers. "Then, as Diego Castillo, I must be completely honest with you. What happened between us at the river…that was an uncommon thing for me. Not your rescue, my lady. I don't mean that. I speak of the emotion which passed between us, and of the carnal feeling that accompanied it."

Celeste's face grew warm, not from the embarrassment which should have met his words, but from the provocative memory of his beautiful body.

Diego saw her face redden and immediately halted. "I'm sorry. I am too bold." He drew in a ragged breath and raked lean fingers through his hair. "Yet I know of no other way to make this right. Will you give me leave to speak forthrightly? My intentions in doing so are honourable."

"I doubt them not."

Diego's gaze found hers, intense and beautiful. "You freely confessed your sins. As Padre Diego, I was denied the opportunity to do the same. But please understand this, Lady Celeste. If you sinned in that moment on the riverbank, you were not alone in it. I reacted purely as a man. My thoughts towards you were wicked and impure. I wanted—"

He broke off and looked away, the muscle in his jaw tightening.

"You wished to lie with me as I would have lain with you?"

Diego closed his eyes. "Yes. Forgive me. I repent such thoughts." He opened his eyes and met her gaze. "I do repent them."

Celeste nodded.

In truth, she repented nothing. Not one moment could she regret; it had been a wondrous thing. But she understood Diego's need to do so.

She also saw that they must put that moment of pure lust behind them if she were to accomplish her other aims. Should Diego think for one minute that passion could flare between them again, he would never board a ship bound for Spain and spend weeks of sailing time in her near presence.

She smiled, meeting his anxious expression with gentleness. "I cannot claim to be a scholar of the Holy Word as you are," she said softly, "yet I know that carnal temptation is not sin until consummated. We were created man and woman, Don Diego, and our bodies whispered this obvious truth to us in a moment of weakness. But naught came of it, so let us not consider it again."

Diego studied her for a moment, his intelligent gaze taking on a new admiration.

He lifted her hand to his lips. Celeste tried not to shiver visibly beneath the onslaught of fresh desire. "You are as wise as you are beautiful, *señorita*, and I am in deep gratitude of your kindness towards this humble priest." He lowered her hand, though Celeste continued to feel the warm brush of his lips across her skin.

There was a brief silence. Celeste studied the ornate carvings behind the altar, acutely aware of Diego's large body beside her, and of his thoughtful expression.

She was startled by low laughter.

"Forgive me," Diego said with an amused lifting of one eyebrow. "But it occurs to me that perhaps I am taking myself far too seriously. I don't believe you came to this isle for the express purpose of falling into a river so that I might rescue you."

She smiled. "No. I did not plan that."

He stroked his chin and feigned a serious look. "No? A pity. Such a *startling* introduction, and, alas, none can take credit for it!"

At her answering laughter, Diego abandoned his sombre expression and grinned. "You did, however, come to this island in search of Diego Castillo. Tell me why."

Celeste's stomach did an urgent roll. She'd come to the moment of decision. Success or failure would be met in a matter of moments.

"I came to ask you to return to Seville with me."

Diego's face registered momentary surprise, quickly contained and changed to a certain wariness that she sensed rather than saw. "Return to Seville? Why?"

She'd prepared for this. She'd practised a speech. But where was it now?

"Because I need you."

It was a pitiful argument, and she should have expected a snort of disdain or disbelief. Instead, his expression softened the slightest bit. "You need me, *señorita?* Ah, and I am such a heartless beast if I can refuse your winsome face. Please explain."

"Your brother and I were to make a marriage of alliance, arranged on behalf of the Kings of Spain and England by Cardinal Cisneros himself."

"And have you met my brother?"

"Yes, but only briefly, just before our betrothal ceremony. He was at sea during most of the three months I lived with his parents—your parents—prior to that time. I cannot claim to be well acquainted with him. He was taken before we had further opportunity to learn of one another."

"Taken by whom?"

"No one knows for certain. There are several factions in Spain who resist the efforts of your king to establish friendly relations with England. They are growing stronger, gaining strength all the time. The fear is that their constant agitation will ultimately lead to war."

Diego frowned. "The situation is a grave one, then."

"It is, indeed. Your father is anxious that these criminals should not appear victorious. They would gain further support from the people. For now, his gold has bought secrecy. Few are aware that Damian has been taken and the proposed alliance delayed, but the secret cannot be held indefinitely."

Celeste met Diego's gaze. "We need you. If you return to Spain and play your brother's part, the intent of Damian's abductors will be foiled. It's even possible the charade may secure Damian's release. If the marriage is accomplished, with you standing proxy, they will no longer have reason to hold him."

"This is why my father sent you?" Diego's scowl did not bode well. Celeste wanted to plead with him, already hurting over the rejection she anticipated.

"Yes," she said. "He feared the dangers, but I begged him to let me come. My desire to wed is great. I trusted the outcome to no other."

Diego's gaze sharpened. "What does this marriage mean to you?"

She drew in her breath. She hadn't expected this question. *Everything.* This marriage meant everything.

But how could she explain? The story had begun so long ago, and had grown so convoluted. Even she didn't understand all the intricacies and intrigues of it.

Her father had been a kinsman of King Henry. In younger days the two men had shared deep affection and similar notions of what was best for the country, but gradually their ideas had diverged, until finally they had been in sharp disagreement.

Those who were kind and thoughtful of Celeste and her younger brother, Jacob, called the carriage accident that had taken their parents' lives a tragic misfortune. Those less respectful bandied about the words *murder* and *traitor*—though in her heart, Celeste would always believe her father had acted on his highest principles, heedless of possible consequences.

That belief had enabled her to endure the subtle ostracism

of society. Believing that had led her to stand over the newly turned earth of her parents' graves and vow that she would somehow restore the honour of her family, for Jacob's sake. For Jacob, and for his earldom, and for the name Rochester, which he would always carry, she hadn't protested when King Henry had made Thomas Rochester's orphaned children his own wards. Later, when an alliance had been proposed, she'd sensed how dear it was to King Henry's heart, and for Jacob's sake she had agreed.

Certainly she didn't want marriage for herself. Her father had left her half of his great wealth, so she would ordinarily have been in a position to choose for herself the ultimate course of her life. She could have remained unmarried, and probably would have done so. But there was Jacob, and the doctors said...

The doctors. So many doctors. And all in general agreement as to the cause and cure of Jacob's malady.

Her brother had not spoken one word since his parents had died.

Time had passed, the grief had dissipated, but his tongue had not been loosened. Jacob, with his sweet angelic face and golden halo of tousled curls, still remained locked in his own world, unable to find his way out.

The doctors were convinced he needed the kind of life he'd known before the accident. He needed beauty, and peace, and the love of a family to free him of his fear and insecurity.

Celeste had hoped marriage to Damian Castillo might be the means to provide those things.

But now Damian was gone and she needed Diego. Without his help there would be no marriage and no family and no secure, happy life for Jacob.

Diego watched her face, awaiting her response.

"This marriage means everything to me," she said simply.

His eyes narrowed. "Is it money?" he asked. "Do you lack wealth and seek marriage for that reason? Because if it is—"

She cut him off with a low growl. "No. That is not my reason." She drew in a deep breath. "Will you help me?"

* * *

Everything in Diego recoiled at the simple question. Everything about this felt *wrong* to him. But Celeste's eyes were so anguished, so dark with secrets she would not share with him. He couldn't explain why, but he was reluctant to hurt her with blunt refusal.

He gently turned aside her question with one of his own. "What is my brother's appearance now?"

Celeste's face grew hopeful, and he could have cursed at himself for his carelessness.

"His hair is short, not long as yours is. Where you're clean-shaven, he wears a full beard and moustache. His clothing is ostentatious, costly and elaborately embroidered, and he favours the codpiece, after the English fashion."

"He would."

Diego was silent for a while, his mind churning and yet feeling strangely numb. "My father knows I hate deception."

His hands clenched and he made a harsh sound. "But he also knows I owe a debt. Dear Lord God, he knew I'd have to do this."

Celeste looked relieved. "You'll return with me?"

Diego turned, studying her face. Did she not understand? Did she not care? What he was being asked to do went against all he knew, all he felt. And he felt too much in this moment, too much pain, too much guilt, too much desire.

Celeste did not meet his gaze; he wondered what was in her thoughts. What did *she* want? What did *she* feel?

As if to connect to the mystery that lay behind her veiled eyes, Diego took her hand. The contact was so potent it burned him, a sweet living hell, her fingertips trembling against his.

"I know not what is best," he whispered. "I don't want Damian to have you. Not you."

Their eyes met. Diego couldn't look away. Her lips were close. He could almost taste her breath. He watched in helpless fascination as her lips parted. Her tongue flicked out to moisten them.

"You don't?"

"Nay," he said softly. "I don't."

She waited for more, but he could say no more. How could he tell her what he knew—that it would be a savagery to put an innocent like her into the lair of the wolf? Damian would take her without mercy, use her up, bend her to his will by deceit or by force, whichever served best. He would show no concern for her.

Even without words, Celeste must have discerned his thoughts. Her eyes filled with tears.

Diego was surprised by the feeling that came over him then, a fierce protectiveness, something primitive and feral.

Her eyes—so warm, dark as night, dark as the secrets of a man's soul. He stared down into them, feeling a decade of anger rip him apart like a wolf's claws.

He gave in to his darkness, drew her into the pain. He pulled her across the pew and into his arms. He kissed her.

Her mouth was as sweet as he had known it would be, as tender and hungry and eager. As innocent as Eden and as wicked as sin, all at the same time, and worth every moment of the guilt he knew he'd feel.

He tasted her long and deep before he finally pulled away, his body throbbing with what he'd done.

He stared at her, consumed by darkness and guilt, willing his breath to come again, and wishing he wore his robe still, so he could hide the effect of his desire.

He ran his fingers through his hair and looked away, towards the silver crucifix which adorned the wall above the altar. "I'm sorry," he said, without looking at her. "I shouldn't have done that."

Then he stood and walked out.

Chapter Four

〰〰〰〰〰

In his dream he was a man, and not a priest. Diego looked down and the robe was gone. He felt for the heavy weight of the crucifix. Gone, too. He saw his bare feet, his wiggling toes against cool leaves, then his knees and thighs, and realized with delight that he was naked.

The water he entered was still and cool, but she was there, her skin warm against his. She slid against him and his breath caught. "Celeste," he said. "Don't. It will only make matters more difficult." He closed his eyes, already aware of the tingling heat of his loins.

She was a water nymph, a spirit as free as time, as warm as earth. She was a fairy with coppery locks that wrapped around him and pulled his body against hers.

Then he kissed her, tasted the carnal innocence of her mouth and groaned. "I want you, Celeste. I want you," he said against her wet lips, and felt his manhood push aside the water, push aside the flesh, push into her tight, hot sheath…

Diego awoke just as his body betrayed him.

He closed his eyes and let the forceful spasms subside, let his breathing return to normal and his tense muscles relax again.

It had been a dream. Just a dream.

He groaned, feeling shame even though he knew it was irrational. Feeling he'd betrayed his priestly vows.

Even though a priest was a man.

That was the problem. He was a man—a virile, healthy specimen, with all a man's innate drive to pursue, to conquer, to mate. A man who'd kissed his brother's betrothed for reasons he couldn't begin to understand, and who had liked it enough to want more. God help him, he did want more.

Diego smoothed his hands down the front of his robe and sighed. It was good to feel like a true servant of the Lord again. The events of the previous day, the disturbing dreams of the preceding night—what were they compared to the coarse, familiar feel of this robe? Especially when, like today, he had work to do—important, satisfying, soul-cleansing work.

The family of Juan Carlos awaited him in their tiny peasant hut on the far ridge overlooking the valley. His prayers were urgently needed; Juan Carlos was desperately ill. Diego also had coin from the poor box to relieve the hunger of the wife and four small children. Beyond prayer and food, he could do no more. Miracles were still the realm of God.

But when he stood before their dwelling he found there *was* more he could do. The small garden Juan Carlos had planted was neglected and sadly overgrown. Not only that, but the family's lone milk goat helped herself to it freely, her eager mouth nipping the tender tops off of whatever poor, struggling plants remained.

This was charity he could do. He set to work clearing the weeds from the small plot. This was charity to benefit their most urgent needs—aye, and his own as well. The hard labour would drive the sinful folly of the previous day from his mind.

Here, sweating in the escalating heat, he could even imagine that the raw desires of yesterday had been but a strange aberration. His life would now return to normal, with his days spent in service to the people of Ricardo's *encomienda* and in the prayers and study that strengthened the soul.

It was peaceful, his life, if somewhat predictable, with time measured from Mass to Mass and from each holy day to the next—and if in his inmost being he sometimes found himself longing for something more, he reminded himself that he'd chosen this course for his life, no one but he. He concentrated on its rewards, like the gratitude he'd seen in the face of Juan Carlos's wife, and the timid smiles of admiration on the faces of their dark-eyed children. Or the satisfaction he'd felt as he'd left them, looking back at the neat rows of plants, cleared now of strangling weeds and surrounded by a fence he'd contrived of sapling poles lashed together with vines.

By the time he left them it was well past midday. He was tired from his labours, and hungry. He'd grown hot and dripped with sweat.

Plunging into the river would go a long way towards refreshment, even without soap or towel, and he headed for it.

It helped his body feel cooler, but also brought to mind the disturbing images he'd worked all morning to set aside. Celeste, warm and womanly in his arms. Celeste the water nymph, her ripe curves sliding provocatively against his own. Celeste the innocent, her lips moist and pliant beneath his kiss.

He left the river with a growl of frustration, shaking wetness from his hair. A large, flat rock nearby usually held his towel, but today he'd have to let his skin dry by sun and wind. Even out of the water, his thoughts had no respite, for as he looked down at himself, sprawled naked upon hard stone, he saw again the admiration in Celeste's face when her eyes had traced his form.

What madness had seized him? It was insanity, most surely, and he'd come too far to let himself be waylaid by it.

It helped to think of this as a moral test. Lust had been his downfall before. Now it was being presented to him again. His faith was being tested, his resolve tried by the carnality of his flesh. When he thought of that, he was strengthened in his determination to subdue his impulses and conquer his own baseness.

It was only when he thought of Celeste that the whole image fell apart. She was not the brazen temptress it demanded. She was, instead, refreshingly innocent, with scarcely any knowledge of what occurred between a man and woman. A virgin just awakening to the beauty of her own sexuality.

Awakened by him.

And, because he had absolutely no idea what to do about that, he climbed down from the rock, donned his still-damp robe and his sandals, and headed for his tranquil cell. Spending his afternoon in prayer might quiet the confusion and provide the way out of this maze.

Padre Francisco came in the late afternoon. Diego heard his sandalled feet shuffling against the stone floor and raised his eyes from his books just as the elder priest slipped into the seat beside him.

"I knew I'd find you here," Francisco said.

Diego studied his face. The man had aged, but his grey eyes were as gentle as always. "Aye, a priest should spend time before the altar of God," he answered. "I learned much from you, Padre."

"You must have, Diego. I was rather surprised to see the priestly garment upon you last night. I didn't know."

"No more surprised than I was at seeing you and Barto. It was rather a shock to have my past so suddenly become my present."

Francisco chuckled. He gestured with a slight wave of his hand. "You look good. Healthy." He motioned towards the book Diego held. "Studying, I see. That's good. Don Ricardo says you've been a fine priest."

Diego shrugged. "Ricardo's a good man and a faithful friend. He makes sure I have all I need. This land is primitive, but there are many opportunities to serve. The native people here knew nothing of the Lord Jesus, and nothing of Spanish ways. Sad to say, they've suffered at the hands of some of our countrymen. The friars and priests here try to mitigate the evil. Perhaps it's helped. I hope so. I long to give something of value back to the world."

Francisco was quiet for a moment. "Is that why you entered the priesthood? Do you serve God to undo the deeds of the past?"

"What do you mean?"

Francisco studied the younger man's face. His expression was compassionate. "Diego, my son. For ten long years you've wandered in the wilderness."

The words—so quiet, so gently spoken. Yet they sliced Diego's heart. He closed his eyes.

"All the service you render, all the masses you say, all the good you do… It won't bring her back."

"I know, Padre," Diego answered, his voice sounding odd. He raised a hand to cover his eyes.

There was a long silence. Francisco leaned near, his voice not much more than a whisper. "Diego, listen to me. All have sinned. All men fall far, far short of God's standard. And we can't any of us make it up by our deeds."

"I know. I preach this to the people. I know these things." Diego drew a deep breath and looked away. "I know them."

"Yet you've not trusted in them."

Diego's head jerked round. "I've not trusted in them? Good Lord—I've given my *life* to them!"

Francisco shook his head. "You preach the grace of God. You teach of his compassion towards repentant sinners. Yet *you…you* walk in the guilt of the past. This is not trusting, Diego."

"You don't know this. You don't know me. For ten years, ten long years, I've been as one dead. You didn't know where I was or how I fared or even if I yet lived."

"I didn't know where you were, that's true. Yet in my heart I knew you lived, that you prospered. I believed in my own answered prayers, perhaps."

"You knew a boy of eighteen years, Padre. You don't know the man he became. You've not seen me, haven't spoken with me. Yet you come here, sit beside me now, and tell me I don't belong in the priesthood?"

"Aye. Though it sounds strange to your ears, Diego, I don't think you do." Francisco rubbed the tension from the back of his neck with a large hand. "You wanted to be an artist. Do you not remember that? You had the talent. No one had the same eye as you, the same hand as you, the same ability to put ink to paper and create a world of feeling that never existed before."

"That was long ago. My life changed. It had to."

"Aye, some things had to change. But, Diego, God never meant you to live with unresolved guilt. I told you this when you came to me, when you confessed your sin."

"Leonora was dead."

"Aye, she was."

"And my child with her."

"I know, Diego."

"And all my tears and a few Pater Nosters wouldn't undo the evil I'd done."

"Diego, their deaths were not your fault."

"Oh, the hell you say!" Diego stood abruptly, his fists clenched. "I didn't kill them, no. Not directly, not with *this*—mine own hand!" He wheeled and faced away, struggling to breathe, struggling to think, struggling not to race down the aisle and slam his palms against the weighty oak door on his way to somewhere else, anywhere else.

After a moment of deep breathing, he managed to sound calmer. "No, I didn't kill them outright. But it was my sin, Padre. My sin!" He turned and crumpled into the seat. "How could I have done it?"

"You were young, Diego. She was young."

"I loved her."

"Aye, and she loved you."

"She was betrothed to Damian."

"But she loved you."

"I took what was not mine to take."

"The sin wasn't yours alone. She gave you the right to take it."

"And she paid for it, Padre. How completely and utterly she paid for it."

"And you *didn't?*" Francisco's brow creased with such compassion that he was nearly in tears. "Diego, what have you been doing for ten long years if not *paying?* Sweet merciful Jesus, what are you doing now if not paying?" He waved his hand towards the robe Diego wore, towards the cross on the wall. "What is all this if you aren't still paying, paying for a sin that's already been forgiven?"

"You don't understand."

"I do, Diego. I do. More than you know." Francisco looked off, as if his thoughts travelled far beyond the walls of the small sanctuary. "Do you remember the night you came to me?"

Diego swallowed hard. He'd tried to forget Leonora's message, the wild ride that had followed, the realization that he'd come too late. He'd tried to forget the blood, the sight of Leonora lying still and lifeless, the silence—and, in it, the rending of his heart.

How he'd got back to the chapel... He could never remember that part, only the strong arms of the priest catching him as he fell, the truth tumbling out over shuddering lips, the violence of sobbing, both his and the Padre's. The rest, a blur. His parents, their faces pale. Their hands trembling as they placed the purse of gold into his and their voices telling him to go, to ride, to wait until they knew Damian would not kill him.

He'd tried, tried to forget that night. And for ten years it had haunted his dreams, had breathed the poison of sadness into every moment of joy. Oh, how he'd tried to forget.

And now, sitting here so quietly with the Padre, all he could say was, "Aye, I remember."

"I told you my story, that I knew your pain. For in my youth

I also sinned. I have a son, Diego. Unlike your child, mine was born, but he was not whole. He was…is…crippled. Helpless, his mind feeble. The child of my lust." He turned a look of patient understanding towards the younger man. "And it's taken me years to realize the truth, that I joined the priesthood to ease my guilt because my son, my poor son, carried in his marred body the penalty of my sin. In some deep part of my soul I needed to do penance, I wanted to suffer." He held out his arms. "This robe, this crucifix of silver about my neck, my vow of chastity—these were my self-imposed punishments, although I didn't see that at the time. Nor has it helped, Diego. It hasn't helped."

He reached out and plucked at Diego's garment. "I see the same struggle now within you, and I must tell you, before you get too far down this road, that this is not the way."

"Leave me alone, Padre."

"Guilt is a brutal gatekeeper, my son. I know."

Diego looked away, his jaw tightening. "Leave me alone, Padre."

"There's a better way, Diego."

Diego's head jerked upward; his eyes narrowed. "What do you know about it—or me? Perhaps I enjoy what I do, perhaps I find peace in it, perhaps—"

"Aye, you've found some comfort in it; I doubt it not. But you're not completely at peace, are you? There are times when that robe chafes, times when that crucifix feels like a prisoner's chains. You can't fool me, Diego, not *me*."

Diego drew in a sharp, exasperated breath. "Blessed Mother of God!"

"You still long for home, for resolution. You miss your parents and you grieve over the broken relationship with your brother."

That cut to the bone. Beneath the swift stroke into tender flesh Diego could not speak, only stare, his eyes burning.

Francisco cleared his throat. "'Tis time you made those things right. Return with me to Spain. Do as your parents have asked."

"That would be deception, Padre. To pretend to be my brother? To wed the girl in his name? A lie. It seems wrong to me."

"Nay, Diego. What is wrong is you *here,* far from your home and family, an exile from all you ever held dear. What is wrong is you *here,* wearing robes of the priesthood for reasons that demean the sacred. What is wrong is bearing the guilt—"

"And there wouldn't be guilt from this action, too? That girl…and Damian? Just to think of it makes me writhe. She's young, her innocence a fragile thing."

Diego raked his fingers through his hair. "Padre, you know Damian. He'll not treat her kindly. He'll not love her. Will this marriage be good for her? Nay, it will not! How could I feel anything but guilt over my part in it? I cannot do this."

Francisco drew in a long, deep breath. "In some things you've changed, Diego, but in this you have not. You yet think with your heart. It's why I love you, why Leonora loved you."

Francisco stroked his chin with a thin finger. "I shouldn't question the ways of God, but sometimes I do wonder why Damian was born the heir and you were not." He shook his head. "It's true that Damian is unworthy of the girl. She is beautiful and full of goodness. She's loving, kind towards others, exuberant and joyful. She has much that would please a normal man—a keen mind, a sharp wit, and a form…ah, a wondrous form for a man to touch. But Damian won't cherish those virtues. I know that. His taste is too vulgar. Whores, harlots, and worse, for now there are boys—"

Diego held up a hand. "Enough. Tell me no more." He turned abruptly to face the other man. "What I need to know is this—how can *your* conscience be at ease with the thought of giving her to him?"

"Because I'm thinking of your parents. They suffered great pain when you left. They've suffered daily ever since."

The muscle in Diego's jaw tightened. "I know. It grieves me yet."

"They know what Damian does, what he is. They've little hope he'll ever change and be worthy of his fine lineage. Their hope now is for the future."

"They want a grandchild."

"Aye, they do. Their hope of redemption." Francisco drew in a long sigh. "Is that not God's way, my son? That even in the darkest evil there's always a remnant of virtue, a seed of hope for the future? The seed of your parents' hope lies with Celeste. They've come to love her, Diego—for her virtue and her pluck, for her loving heart and her kind ways. They hope that a child of her womb might have her qualities, rather than those of his sire."

"I'm not convinced Celeste wants Damian."

"I doubt she does. She's intelligent enough to sense the evil in him. Yet she has little choice. Her kinsman is the King of England and he's committed her to this course."

Francisco crossed his arms before his chest, his gaze solemn. "Diego, she *will* wed Damian, whether you aid us or not. Your help only hastens the enterprise and eases the hearts of your parents. Should you choose against it, the nuptials might be stayed, but they will not be stopped. You do understand this?"

Diego nodded, but said nothing.

"Damian will be found—indeed, might have been ransomed already for all we know. We might return to Spain only to find the entire voyage unnecessary. However, your intention to do this for him, for your parents, will restore you to your rightful place within the family. It will show your brother your sorrow for the past."

Diego snorted. "As if he'll appreciate that. As if he'll forgive. How am I to know he won't make good his threat to kill me?"

"Ten years have passed. His anger has cooled. He has no reason now to feel threatened by you. He has the title, he has the wealth, and he has the girl. He has it all. What have you, Diego, beyond this robe you wear and this vow you've made?

Indeed, he'll view you with disdain…with pity, even. But he'll let you be."

Diego breathed in deeply. "I'll think on all this, Padre. I promise you nothing but that."

Padre Francisco smiled. "That is enough for now, Diego. 'Tis enough."

Celeste knew Barto had probably thought her request odd, but still he complied. By the time he'd received her message and met her at the stables, she had horses saddled and ready.

Barto's expression was a mixture of curiosity and bemusement as she handed him the reins. "Here," she said. "I chose this gelding for you myself. He's large and powerful, but his disposition is one of gentleness. Rather like you, Barto."

Barto grinned, pulling his large frame up into the saddle. "I don't know about that, *señorita*. Few others have found me tame, but when it comes to you, I'm foolishly twisted around the crook of your smallest finger."

Celeste smiled up at him, then mounted her own horse, a smaller black mare. "The crook of my finger? I doubt that. Yet I do thank you for coming to ride with me. I need your advice."

Barto glanced at her sideways. "My advice? You wouldn't rather have that of good Padre Francisco?"

"Nay, Barto. Padre Francisco would likely shake his head and censure me for my honest questions. You, on the other hand…"

"I, on the other hand, have no room for censure, is that it? Most interesting, this, if it's my heathenish advice that's warranted."

"I need to talk, Barto. I have questions, but no father and no mother from whom to solicit advice."

"You have Don Alejandro and Doña Anne."

"Aye, and most especially I could not say these things to them."

Barto raised an eyebrow. "This must be serious indeed."

"Aye. I know not how to ask even you. I shall have to be direct. Surprisingly so, I fear."

"I guessed as much," he said with a sigh. "You've questions such as any maiden would have, considering her tender state of pending matrimony."

Celeste's cheeks flamed, but she nodded. "You are wise, Barto. Or else I am too easily read, like a book whose plot is overly familiar."

"Nay, there's nothing wise about me or overly familiar about you. Yet truly hath it been said that the most necessary things of life are air to breathe, water and food for subsistence, and a lover with whom to sport. Since air is not your problem, and you eat little more than a cat, I figure the worry in your eyes has mostly to do with the lover, or the sporting, or both. Do you grow disturbed about becoming wife to Damian Castillo?"

"Aye. I do not much cherish the man and dread all I must perform."

"You've no wish for him to bed you?"

Celeste nodded.

"Well," Barto said. "'Twill not be the most awful thing you've ever done, certainly. And, like I said, you can forget him and all further intimacies once an heir is born."

"I can't do it, Barto. He'll find me dreadfully inept. I know so little."

Barto smiled. "I promise you, it won't be a problem. A man prefers that his wife be inexperienced. Indeed, most men relish the thought of such tutoring as that would require. Trust me. What happens between a man and woman is not too difficult to figure out. It won't seem uncommon or strange at the time."

"I want you to explain it to me. In detail, if you please."

"Doña Anne will do it when you return, *doncella*. She's a much better choice than I."

"I want to know *now*. I want to know how a child is made. I know that kisses, even passionate kisses, cannot cause a woman to conceive. But how—?"

"Oh, Lord," Barto said. "Lady Celeste, I cannot tell you these things."

Celeste frowned. "You can. You've lain with women. I heard the Padre say you've—"

Barto groaned. "I can't deny that, but neither can I explain it. Not to you."

"Aye, Barto, you can."

"Sweet heavens," Barto said. "Sweet heavens. I can't—"

"If I wished to arouse a man, how would I do it?"

Barto shook his head. "I promise you, *señorita*. With your fair looks, your husband's arousal won't be a problem."

Celeste frowned and chewed at her lip. "What I most want to know is…how far must one go before a child is conceived?"

"One must go…rather far."

"How far? Will I conceive if I am touched by him…there?"

"*Señorita,* please. I think, if you must know these things now, that I will find an older woman who—"

Celeste's scowl was fierce. "I am asking *you,* Barto, and don't pretend you do not know! Just how intimate will I have to be with this man before I conceive his child?"

"Oh, no," Barto groaned. "Oh, no."

"Will he have to touch me in private places?"

"Aye."

"And will he…?" Celeste took a deep breath. "Will he have to do more than that?"

Barto nodded. "Aye, if a child is to be made."

There was a long silence.

Celeste saw it all. She was not sure of all the intricacies, but her imagination provided her with enough understanding for now.

"I cannot marry Damian Castillo," she said quietly.

Barto looked worried. "*Señorita,* I know that here in the harsh light of day the act of which we're speaking sounds unspeakably unpleasant."

Celeste wanted to scream. No, no, it wasn't the act that sounded unpleasant, only the man. In fact, were she to lie in such fashion with the… Oh, sweet merciful heavens, he was a *priest!*

"I know it sounds unseemly and crude," Barto said. "In reality, 'tis not the way. It can be nice. Very nice. You'll see."

They rode in silence for a while. Finally Celeste spoke. "In Spain, I never thought much about being a wife in those ways. I thought marriage was what I wanted. But I've come here and now I shudder at that which I must do."

Barto glanced at her. "Perhaps when we return to Spain all will right itself. Your time here will seem distant then, like a dream."

"Perhaps." Celeste looked down, her eyes misting. "Perhaps my discontent is merely due to this island's loveliness, to the softness of the moonlight here, to the warmth of its nights. It makes me…"

"It makes you long for love."

Celeste sighed. "I suppose. I do long to be loved." To admit that sounded strange, but it was true. She hadn't felt loved since her parents had died. Maybe that was why she understood why Jacob never spoke, why happiness never touched his eyes. Maybe that was why she felt so compelled to make a family for him again. She looked away quickly, and wondered if Barto saw her tears. "I want to be loved," she repeated softly. "Now I wonder if I shall ever know it."

Barto looked down. He said nothing.

Celeste remained silent during the rest of their ride. She could not admit, even to Barto, that she ached for a man with blue-green eyes and tawny hair. A man she could not have.

"I can't imagine why you're going to do this," Ricardo said as he clipped another lock of hair with shears and laid it on the table.

Diego met his gaze. "Do what? Cut my hair?"

Ricardo held up a thick shock of gold. "Maybe I should save these curls, Diego. That way, if you're ever canonized, people will make pilgrimages from all over the world to see the relics of my humble little shrine. Could be a worthy way to make some money."

Diego shook his head. "You're forgetting something. Most of those saints had to be martyred or some such thing before they were so honoured."

Ricardo sighed and clipped at another curl. "True, true. Though I wonder if you aren't hastening towards your cross with desperate speed."

Diego frowned.

"I can hardly believe you've chosen to return to Spain. Did your brother not say he'd kill you if ever your paths crossed again? And did he not attempt it once before?" Ricardo pushed at Diego's jaw to tilt his head, then drew his hand back sharply. "Ouch!" he said with a grimace. "Damn at the whiskers! Two days of not shaving and you're as woolly as a lion!"

Diego shrugged. "Damian has a beard. I have to look the part, don't I?"

Ricardo grunted. "I don't suppose you've considered how dangerous it could be to play his part. A bastard like your brother has probably made his share of enemies. His enemies, your enemies... And yet you're going back into harm's way, all because some little snip of a wench asked it of you?"

"I'm not doing it for Celeste. In fact, I don't think she much favours the match."

"Not if she's a sensible girl, and she does seem to be." Ricardo clipped and combed, stepped back to look, then clipped again. "So why are you doing this?"

"I owe it to my brother."

"Like hell. You don't owe that idiot anything. If he'd treated Leonora like a gentleman should—"

"It wasn't his fault that she...that we..."

"I say it was. She was betrothed to him long before she met you. If he'd been kind and loving, there wouldn't have been room for you."

Diego frowned. "Forget it, Ricardo. The past is done. But perhaps I can make up to him what I did then...make it up to my parents."

"And what of Celeste? She seems much too dear to be so cruelly sacrificed."

Diego was silent.

"That bothers you." Ricardo nodded. "Well, maybe it should."

"It does. I can't deny it."

"Then you need to listen to the voice of God or your conscience or whatever it is that's telling you not to do this."

"I've tried. But there are other things to consider. My father, my brother's life, and Celeste's own wishes. She says she needs this marriage. She *needs* it."

Ricardo nearly dropped the shears, causing Diego to rise in his chair. *"Cuidado, amigo!"* he cried out. "You could unman me with such carelessness!"

Ricardo shook the shears at him. "You're a priest, Diego. You've little use for all your parts, even if you should lose a few."

Diego sat down again, shaking his head. "When I've finished this masquerade, I'll find another position where I'm not so abused."

Ricardo laughed. "I do abuse you sorely, I know it. Yet you'll deserve all of it and more if you help marry the sweet *doncella* to Damian. But you say she *needs* the match? Whatever for? I can hardly see our little Celeste as the sort to desire gold at the expense of her happiness."

"She says wealth is not the object. I would be disappointed in her if it were."

Ricardo worked on in thoughtful silence, finally snipping through the last tawny curl before handing the looking glass to Diego. "Are you disappointed that she's marrying him, or disappointed that she cannot be yours?"

Diego studied his hair, rubbed a hand through it and across the coarse stubble of his new beard. He stopped upon hearing the question, his eyes narrowing, and stared at Ricardo's reflection in the glass. "What sort of question is that?"

"The sort of question only a friend would dare ask."

Diego lowered the looking glass. "I don't want her to marry Damian. But she certainly couldn't marry me, now could she?"

"There are other roads besides marriage, Padre. And sometimes even priests tread them."

Diego scowled. "Ricardo, if you weren't my friend I'd lay you out cold for that, priest or no."

"Then you won't mind if I try to bed the girl?"

Diego stiffened, unable to control the involuntary reaction even though he was mindful that Ricardo watched him with a relentless stare.

"I cannot, as your priest, condone such immoral behaviour. And she is to wed my brother."

"Aye, she is." Ricardo sighed. "That's what's so tragic, Diego. Such a fair little maiden, never to be loved by a man, never to be pleasured until she loses herself in ecstasy. Merely a container for your brother's seed. God, what a waste."

"I agree. Yet she has chosen the path herself."

"One of us should love her. Just once. So she'll know the joy of true passion."

"Ricardo…"

"I know she's virtuous, but I doubt not that if it were put to her right she'd lie with one of us."

"I should geld you for these things you speak."

Ricardo laughed. "Ah, you do well, Padre. You hide your feelings well. They were but the palest glimmer in the dark, dark blue of your eyes."

Diego stood, rubbed the tension from the back of his neck, and studied his friend. "You talk foolishness, Ricardo."

"Nay, I do not. Were you not bound by your vows, you would have already made love to her."

"She is betrothed to my brother."

"And yet you have already come to love her."

Diego snorted. "Love?" he said, brushing hair from the front of his robe. "Love doesn't come in a moment. Nor in three days. And that is all the time I've known the girl."

"Well, *desire,* then. Hard-driving, gut-wrenching sexual desire. You do already feel that for her."

Diego was silent.

Ricardo laughed again, the sound rankling. "You don't have to admit it. I know well enough. I've seen it in the way you tense when she enters the room, in the way your eyes follow her—and in the way jealousy flitted across your face when I suggested bedding her, even though I did it only to see your reaction. Aye, you want that girl, Diego, priest or no." His lips twisted as he held up the shears. "Are you sure you don't want me to complete the job I almost began with these? It's a long, long voyage to Spain, my friend, and the quarters aboard the vessel far too close and conducive to passion."

"There will be others aboard the ship. Celeste will be well chaperoned. Trust me, I'll not let history repeat itself. If she wishes to wed my brother, then wed him she shall. With her maidenhead intact for him to enjoy."

Ricardo looked unconvinced. "Sins of the flesh, sins of the mind. *Cuidado, mi amigo.* They are not too far apart."

Chapter Five

Diego was avoiding her. That was the only way Celeste could explain it. The ship was no large place; their paths should have crossed by now. But they hadn't, not since they'd boarded a fortnight past. Did he think her a wanton who'd seduce him without respect to his vows?

She wandered the deck aimlessly this morning. Here and there a seaman nodded at her, then furrowed his brow when she hardly seemed to notice. Too late, she'd come out of the daze and mumble a greeting, usually to the man's departing back. It wasn't like her to be so distracted, gazing out with distant eyes over the shifting horizon and sighing as if she'd lost something inestimably precious.

In truth, she feared she had. Diego had not said a total of a dozen words to her—and even those only to keep up social amenities. Her friend the boatswain had told her that Diego came out either very early or very late, times Celeste would be in her quarters. The hours she was wont to come on deck he kept to the small cabin he shared with Ricardo, who'd decided to return to Spain with him. Their close quarters on the *tolda* must be stifling in these humid days of mid-July.

Celeste knew full well why Diego avoided her, but it did not assuage the hurt. Her heart ached to see him.

She'd given him the clothing his mother had sent, garments such as Damian would wear. Strangely enough, the finery looked appealing on Diego, where Celeste had thought them prideful and ostentatious on his brother. Diego looked almost identical to his twin now, with his shorter hair and beard and moustache. Celeste doubted that anyone who watched the wedding ceremony would fail to believe that Damian Castillo claimed his bride.

Only she would know. She'd made a supreme effort to avoid thinking of it, but she knew that when Diego put the ring on her finger and spoke those sacred vows in his warm, richly accented voice, she'd ache with secret longing.

She wanted Diego. She wanted to marry *him*, not his brother. She wanted to know Diego, to lie with him, to bear his children. She wanted to love him and to have him love her, to vow to him her eternal love and to hear him pledge the same.

But Diego was vowed to God.

A priest. Had she known, perhaps she never would have fallen in love with him. She would have guarded her heart better. But she hadn't known, and it had come like a thief, the most intense emotion she'd ever experienced. It was physical attraction, she knew that, but it was more, too.

She wanted to be with him, to talk to him, to touch him, even knowing how dangerous those things would be for them both. Truly, she did understand why Diego kept himself apart from her. Yet she couldn't help thinking that if she couldn't have the important things, at least she wanted to see him, even if from a distance, even if surrounded by busy seamen on the deck of a ship.

But seeing him had its dangers, too. Whenever they were together, their mutual awareness was so potent she feared others must know. She'd once turned to find his eyes upon her, and the expression within them had been hungry. Their gazes had met and they'd been joined, unexpectedly and without help, in desire so powerful that Celeste had sucked in her breath and looked away, hoping none had witnessed the guilty exchange.

But they'd not been so lucky. Ricardo had stood nearby. He'd lifted an amused eyebrow, then turned away after a glance at her reddened face. She'd wondered for three days if she should address the matter, somehow explain to Ricardo that what he'd seen wasn't as guilty as it had appeared. But what could she say? What he'd seen was *exactly* as guilty as it had appeared, even if the sins were only in her mind. So, feeling ashamed and helpless, Celeste had passed two weeks in this maze of conflicting desire, wishing to get a glimpse of Diego, but glad, so glad, that he'd shown enough honour to stay away.

She tried to amuse herself with the same enterprises that had kept her engaged on the earlier voyage. She donned her seaman's garb and worked. She read books to the crew and worked on learning their language. She helped the cook with his cooking, helped the steward with his figures and supplies, helped the pilot, even learning how to use the astrolabe. But another week passed and she could not quiet the restlessness.

She wiped perspiration from her brow, brushed back the dampened tendrils of hair that had escaped the long russet braid, and imagined Diego in his shadowy cot. She wondered if he were miserable in the oppressive heat. She wondered if he were as restless as she.

Her questions and the endless longing finally decided the matter. Hettie hardly stirred when Celeste eased from their quarters in the darkness the following morning.

Only the faintest pink light of dawn greeted her as she made her way onto deck, a light delicately tinged with corals and gold, reminding her of the soft, pearly colours of a seashell. She hardly had time to enjoy nature's display of shifting colour before she spied Diego, standing with his back to her, a lone figure at the rail, partially hidden by the shadows of the upper deck.

The sight of him made her heart clutch painfully in her chest. He faced the wind, his blue sea cape billowing out behind him in the early-morning breeze. Wind played through the soft layers of his hair, taunting Celeste by doing openly what she dared not do.

He stood comfortably, his stance that of one accustomed to the sea. Celeste wondered if he, like his brother, had spent time aboard his father's vessels. She could not help admiring the snug fit of his hose against well-muscled legs.

He turned and her breath caught. His linen shirt, worn without the customary doublet, was only partially buttoned. Celeste devoured the sight of his bare chest, lightly furred with hair.

He stepped forward. Celeste knew the exact moment he spotted her. He suddenly froze, his head jerking up and slightly backwards.

He recovered quickly. His voice was smooth when he spoke and betrayed none of his surprise. "Celeste?" he said. "Are you well?"

She moved forward. "Not completely. I suffer from the strangest malady of late."

His eyes moved over her. "What ails you?"

"It's rather odd, this malady. With each day that passes it grows worse."

He looked concerned.

"I cannot sleep, and when I do my dreams are troubled ones. When I arise, I wander through my days feeling more listless than ever before. I'm addressed by others but do not always hear them. I stare at the horizon for hours, not seeing any of the beauty before me. I divert myself with amusements, but of the pain there is no relief."

She turned. Diego stood near her now, so near she longed to reach out to that warm skin, to grasp the soft linen of his shirt and pull his lips to hers. Instead, she raised her gaze to the burning blue-green sea of his. "I am lost without you, Diego."

His eyes swept her face. Fire ignited behind the darkening pupils. "How am I to alleviate your suffering, Lady Celeste?" he asked quietly. "I have naught which might effect a cure."

"You do, Diego. Here in your presence, I am much improved."

He didn't answer, but turned and walked back to the rail, his body gone rigid. She followed and stood beside him, wishing she could wrap her arms about him and kiss away the tension. She breathed in, smelling salt and ship and the essence of this man she loved. Loved. Even though loving him was a mad, forlorn hope.

"You're avoiding me," she said simply.

"Aye," he said. The muscle in his jaw tightened. "It is the only way."

"I understand why you do," she said. "But I'm languishing for the sight of you. Please, don't think me a wanton that I've come so early to steal a private moment with you. I...I only wished my eyes to touch upon you."

His head turned and he studied her, his expression such a fierce scowl that it frightened her. Was he angry? Had her rash decision backfired and somehow raised his ire?

"Diego?" she said hesitantly. "Do you think harshly of me?"

His growl was impatient. "Sweet mercy, woman! How am I to think harshly of the one whose very breath—?" His voice faltered. He looked away towards the swell of the sea, the curving of the horizon. Celeste waited in the void of words, trembling, not sure if she trembled in fear or in anticipation. Diego's words came so quietly that Celeste strained to hear them. "The one whose very breath is as dear to me as my own."

"Then you've missed me, too? Dare I hope, Diego, that you've missed me, too?"

He turned with a swift, agile motion and Celeste was pulled into his arms. A hawk, capturing a dove. Celeste could not breathe, and didn't care to. She was enveloped in Diego, in his warmth, in his smell, in his taste, aware only of the flood of sensation, of his tongue parting her lips and plundering her, of the moan that answered the piracy. The hard wall of his chest pressed against breasts which heaved and firmed beneath his warmth. And lower, his thighs crushed her skirts, the alien hardness there proof of how much, how very much, he'd missed her, too.

"Oh, Celeste," he groaned as he pulled back to search her face. His eyes stormed a glittering tempest, his hands rough upon her shoulders. "I'm trying to do what is best. Yet I want you with every waking breath. I hate myself for it, but I desire you. Oh, dear God!" His lips came to hers again. Celeste could feel his anguish, the need that waged war with honour.

She should retreat. She shouldn't have come. The torment was too great.

But he tasted so good. For so long she'd fasted from his presence. All she could do now was revel in the feast Diego gave her. He was sensuous warmth. He was rugged beauty. His taste was honey and forbidden desire. His muscles, erotic ecstasy beneath her fingertips.

"Oh, Diego," she murmured. "Kiss me again. I don't want it to end." He kissed her, over and over, until her world was unsteady, made up only of her fast, irregular heartbeat and his ragged breath and thrusting tongue. Her legs seemed to lose strength and he, sensing it, drew her more firmly against his hardened form, her body arching backwards as he trailed liquid fire down her neck and across her collarbone.

When his hand captured the fullness of her breast, she gasped and lurched in his arms. He immediately released it. "Nay, Diego. Don't stop." Her voice sounded strange, harsh and urgent.

He groaned and pressed his hips against her, his words a rasping breath across her ear. "Don't do this to me. How can I deny you?"

"Touch me, Diego. I cannot bear it if you don't."

He touched her. His hand cupped her fullness, his thumb strumming across the hardening pebble of her nipple until she quivered with sensation. Beneath the assault she grew bolder, eager to appease the yearning. She let her hand touch his chest, splaying her fingers across the firm expanse, his skin warm and tight beneath her palm.

So engaged was she in the taste of his kisses, in the stroking of his fingers against her breasts, in her own tentative explorations of his muscle, that she didn't understand Diego's tight, irregular movements at the fastenings of her clothing until he bent and his mouth touched her bare nipple. She cried out and grasped his head, her fingers twining into the soft layers of his hair.

The sensation was too much—the way his tongue licked at her, the way his heat spiralled through her. Her eyes slid closed. She was lost. Lost.

"Diego, make love to me," she whispered hoarsely. "Let me give my virginity to the man of my choosing. Love me 'ere I'm imprisoned for ever."

She didn't stop to consider more, only knew that it was the most ardent wish of her heart at that moment. Yet the words had the opposite effect from that she'd intended. Diego stiffened. Long seconds passed. He did not move.

Her eyes opened, her mind cloudy and confused. He had pulled back and now studied her face, his expression a curious mixture of sadness and longing. He drew in a deep, unsteady breath and pulled her silk chemise up to cover her pale breasts, then hooked her stomacher into place over them. A quick kiss on her forehead, and he released her.

She could only stand, stupidly, feeling alone, the blood still pulsing in her ears. "Nay," she whispered. "Don't leave me."

How could he leave her? She knew she wasn't alone in what she felt. He wanted her, had arched her body against his in a promise that now looked to be unfulfilled. She felt betrayed...*cheated.*

"I'm sorry. Forgive me," Diego said quietly.

"Don't leave me. I need you."

"You are betrothed to my brother."

"But I want you, Diego. I love you."

He turned at that, his eyes warm and compassionate. "You're young and innocent," he said, "and your inherent virtue demands that you justify this...this desire we feel."

He ran lean fingers through his hair. "Our bodies crave one another in the way of nature, but that isn't love, Celeste. Love does what is best for the other person." He looked away. "I've done wrong to mislead you. I never should have touched you."

He turned away, his hands gripping the rail so hard that his brown knuckles turned white. "I'm a priest. A shepherd responsible for others' eternal souls. Including yours."

Celeste was silent for long moments, trying to read the inflection of his voice, seeking the meaning behind the words. "You think me evil, then? A wanton temptress to seduce you?"

He didn't look at her. "The seduction was as much my fault as yours. More so, since you are an innocent and I…am not." He looked at her. "I won't deny my wrong. I won't deny I'm torn in half. Part of me wants to be honourable and maintain your virtue as I should. To deliver you, *virgo intacta,* safely into my brother's arms."

"And the other part?"

His eyes bored into hers. "The other part is a man. A man who wants to touch your silky flesh and taste your fruit, forbidden though it be. Please forgive me."

Celeste looked out over the water, trying to think calmly. Trying to bury the hurt of his rejection. "I was wrong, too," she finally said. "I shouldn't have come. I knew it could lead to this. But I wanted to see you. No matter what you think, I do love you. I feel desire, aye, but I feel more than that, too. I want to know you, Diego, and were you not a priest…"

"But I am," he said. "You might forget that, but I cannot. Were I to lie with you, I'd know bitter remorse after the deed were done."

Celeste swallowed hard. "Aye, I doubt it not. I'm so sorry."

"Shall we be friends, then?"

She shook her head. "I cannot be friends with you. It's impossible to be in your presence and not want more from you than that."

He bowed his head. When at last their eyes met, his were dark and solemn. "Then we must continue as before. I'll keep to my quarters. You must not seek me out again. Do you understand now, Celeste?"

"Aye. I do."

She left him, hurrying away before she lost the will to leave him, before she turned to him again and flung herself into his arms.

The early-morning sun had grown strong. She squinted against its brilliance, but the brightness of the day did not reach her heart. There it was utter darkness.

Diego waited at the rail for Celeste's footsteps to fade, knowing the urge to call her back. He could still feel the silken weight of her breast against his palm. He could still hear her sighs.

It had nearly been too much. He'd almost lost his mind and it unnerved him. Never in all his years as a priest had he been so close to the edge, so dangerously near to falling. So eager to fall.

The more he tried to fight desire, the more it occupied his thoughts. Celeste was in his blood now. He only wanted more.

He sighed and turned from the rail, wondering how the next few days would be endured. He would be true to his word and stay far from her. He would give himself no opportunity for outward sins, but nothing could contain his thoughts. Sins of the mind were as easy to commit as sins of the flesh, and just as dangerous for a man's soul.

A shadow fell across the deck. Diego looked up. Barto stood before him, arms crossed over his massive chest, a curious half-smile turning up the corners of his lips. "Diego Castillo," he said. "It's a bit early in the morning for seeking out amusement, is it not?"

Diego canted his head.

"You should remember, Padre, that a ship is no place of privacy. Even in these early hours there are seamen about."

Heat came into Diego's face. He closed his eyes and swallowed hard. "You saw that."

"I wasn't spying, but, as I said, this deck is no vast place. To tryst privately is not easily done."

Diego couldn't answer. He imagined how the scene had looked to Barto. The big man was no saint, but he certainly knew that a priest shouldn't have been passionately kissing an innocent young virgin, nor fondling her breasts. Especially if that young virgin was already pledged to someone else…like his own brother.

"I don't know what to say. I was wrong in what I did. I shouldn't have touched the girl."

Barto chuckled. The sound surprised Diego. He looked up.

"I saw enough," Barto said. "Enough to know you weren't the only one doing wrong." He grinned and shook his head. "That little woman's been like a keg of gunpowder, just waiting for the right man to light her fuse. And then you came along."

"I haven't… I didn't…"

"I know. I saw you put her away, and I have to admire you for it. You did more than I would have done, given similar circumstances." Barto stroked his chin. "But now I do think I'm beginning to understand Alejandro's logic. When I saw you two together, everything started making sense."

"My father? What's he got to do with this?"

"I'm not sure. It's just an idea I have. You know, I've been puzzled by this whole enterprise from the start. Why send the little *doncella* off on this dangerous voyage in the first place? Proxy marriages are done easily enough."

Diego nodded. He'd had the same thought himself.

"I know Alejandro meant to hide the fact that Damian's been abducted. But, even so, you didn't really have to play the bridegroom's part. There are other ways to convince the world Damian lives." He studied Diego thoughtfully. "So why? Why send Celeste to the Indies to find you? Have you given thought to that?"

"Aye, I've wondered at it, but I haven't the answer. My father's plans are usually well conceived. This does seem unlike anything he would have decided."

Barto smiled. "Perhaps his plans are still well conceived, Diego, but I didn't catch on until I saw you with her. Aye, your father is a wise old fox."

Diego frowned. "What are you getting at?"

"I don't think Alejandro intends for Celeste to wed Damian," he said slowly, watching Diego's face. "I think he means for her to wed you."

"Me?" Diego closed his eyes. "God, have mercy."

"Of course, your father didn't know you'd become a priest. That was the one thing he wouldn't have expected."

Diego felt weak and nauseous. He drew in a deep breath and ran a callused hand across his brow. "But the King of England decreed that she wed—"

"—someone of the Spanish royal family. Damian was never specified by name."

"But Damian's the heir," Diego protested. "Surely my father wanted to assure himself of the continuance of the title."

"Aye, he probably did. Until he met our little *doncella*. She has a strange effect on people. Your father, your mother, all the servants…and I confess even I myself… All have become fond of her. She's an extraordinary woman."

"Aye, she is. But what's this got to do with me and her and what passed between us these few moments past?"

"Well, imagine. You are very like your father, Diego, so it shouldn't be hard to follow his thoughts. Imagine you have two sons, one of whom is a vile man with little bent towards kindness or decency, though he is the heir. Then there's the other son, who's the very opposite and tends towards those virtues which his elder brother lacks."

"Yet that son is not the heir."

"Nay, he's not, of a truth. So when the idea of an alliance is proposed, of course you might choose that the older son marry, with the hope that he'd settle down and forfeit his riotous lifestyle."

"Perhaps. Marriage has helped settle many a rebellious bachelor."

"But think on, Diego. The girl sent could have been ungainly and as ugly as an old mule. She could have lacked wit. She could have been fit for little else besides the breeding to be done."

Diego began to understand. "But she wasn't," he said. "She was a fine, lovely young woman with intelligence and virtue."

"Now you see it. For three months Celeste lived with your parents. Your father was won by her effervescence, by her beauty and her charm." Barto shrugged. "Oh, at first he probably told himself she'd be the very thing Damian needed, that of all women who could tame him she could. Yet doubt must have niggled at him—how could he, in good conscience, cast such a pearl before swine?"

"I still don't understand how I have become part of this," Diego said.

"Well, that was probably decided after Damian and Celeste had finally been introduced. Your father would have watched them carefully. Damian ogled the girl like she was naught but a cheap doxy, and Celeste, sensing something amiss, was uncomfortable in his presence. Your father would have quickly realized the match was doomed to unhappiness."

"Still, Damian must produce the heir."

"Aye, and I'm sure your father gave that much thought." Barto's gaze found Diego's. "Yet in one thing you and your father are alike. You're both men of conscience. You both do what is most honourable, even if not most expedient. So Alejandro decided in Celeste's favour. He sent her to you."

Diego choked. "You're saying my father *wanted* Celeste to fall in love with me?"

Barto shrugged. "Just an idea of mine. But when I saw her in your arms it all suddenly made sense. Your father meant her for you."

"I'm a priest."

"He didn't know that. All he knew was that he loved Celeste and wanted a grandchild by her. And while one son is not fit to be her mate, the other son most definitely would be."

"And he knew I'd fall for it, since I seem to have the unerring ability to feel desire for my brother's betrothed."

Barto frowned. "Nay, it wasn't like that. He never blamed you for Leonora. He never—"

"He sent me away."

"For your own protection. You must remember that."

"I never heard from him."

"Damian had spies everywhere. Alejandro knew it. He trusted only one servant enough to send him to you, and Damian used even that to make an attempt on your life. By the time your father could find a way to communicate with you, you were gone and he knew not where to find you. Only by the whim of fortune did Capitán Pérez see you in Caparra eighteen months ago."

Diego breathed in deeply and looked up at the creaking mast above them. "Sweet mercy," he said. "What a mess."

"It doesn't have to be."

"How can it not be? I can't take my brother's betrothed."

Barto raised one eyebrow. "It looked to me like you could," he said dryly. "You two seemed rather compatible."

"I was wrong in what I did. It will not happen again."

"Your priestly vow means that much?"

"It does."

"Celeste's happiness matters naught to you? The happiness of your parents?"

"Aye, they matter. But I've made a vow to God—"

"Men leave the priesthood all the time. Sometimes it's discovered they've fathered bastard children already, and sometimes they marry and father legitimate children afterwards, but—"

"Listen, Barto!" Diego's voice shook with anger. "I didn't ask my father to play matchmaker. I didn't ask you and Padre Francisco to intrude in my life and play games with my sanity. Still, I *have* left my home and my life to do as you asked me. Why? So I can know I've made amends to my parents and my brother and go on about my life in peace. Don't you change the rules in the midst of the game. Celeste is to wed Damian. She's to lie with him and give him an heir." He took a deep breath. "How could it be otherwise?"

"She could lie with you. She could bear your seed. From what I saw, I think she'd like that."

Diego tried to keep his voice calm, but he wanted to shake Barto to pieces. The worst part was having to resist the thing he himself most wanted. "I cannot leave the priesthood. And I'll not lie in sin with her. Dear God, do you not remember how it was after Leonora? Can you imagine for one moment that I'd be fool enough to—" Diego forced his fists to unclench, forced his voice into calm, drew in a breath. "I never thought you a foolish man, Barto. Yet you speak foolishness at this moment. I did *wrong*. I'll not do wrong again."

"Maybe it was not wrong. Maybe it was not foolish. Maybe your two hearts have a logic both sensible and right."

"Fornication is a *sin*."

"So is coveting your brother's wife."

Diego was silent, scowling. The words struck him, the raw truth. Diego flung his sea cape over one shoulder and strode away, not looking back.

Barto watched him stalk away, an odd, almost amused expression on his strong features. Well, so he'd angered Diego. He hadn't meant to, but that ought to give the good Padre some food for thought, anyway. Perhaps, with time, Celeste might find the love her heart craved. If so, Barto thought, he'd be mighty glad of it. She deserved it if anyone did. She alone was innocent of all the mistakes and sins of the Castillo family's past. She deserved a good man and beautiful babes. And Diego Castillo, were he to cease being so stubborn, could give her both.

Barto smiled and stroked his chin thoughtfully. Perhaps he ought to pray about that—and if God seemed reluctant to hear the prayers of a heathen, he'd get Padre Francisco to help. Maybe even right away, if he could find the priest alone.

He turned away and, whistling a sea ditty he'd heard a seaman sing with his guitar the night before, moved towards the quarters in the castle where he knew Francisco often played chess with a young officer named Jorge.

Chapter Six

A week passed, and Diego knew tension both fierce and subtle. Fierce, because thoughts of Celeste consumed most of his waking moments and all of his dreaming ones. Subtle, because the struggle was internal. Only those who knew him well might detect the anxiety that tinged even his smiles.

To ease the distress he put his hands to work. He was experienced at sea, and Captain Jones had not been reluctant to assign him duties during the night watches, since the officers were shorthanded and several were sick in their cots. Diego enjoyed working among the seamen. The evening air was cool and invigorating, and he liked the quiet and solitude of sailing at night. The darkness held its own sensual delights—the smell of sea and rope and tar, the dampness of his hair in the breeze, the rolling of the deck beneath his feet, the creaking of riggings and snapping of canvas. Those things were seldom noticed in the busy hustle of daylight, but in the silence of the sleeping ship they were stolen treasures for him to enjoy.

In the darkness he thought of Celeste, but at least the work tired him so that he slept in his cot during the heat of day without torment. And each day that passed brought him closer to Spain, closer to the time he wouldn't worry about rounding a corner and seeing the startled longing in her brown eyes.

Another week, perhaps two, and he'd not have to endure the agony of her nearness.

That thought comforted him. Terrified him, too. He ached for her presence and fought off thoughts of Celeste in his brother's arms. How he'd find the strength to do the right thing when the time came, he knew not.

Now he faced the dawn of a new morning. Captain Jones stood with him beside the whipstaff. They were talking in muted tones when the watch aloft suddenly called down. A ship had been spotted on the horizon.

Captain Jones brought out his spyglass. "She's a caravel," he said, squinting against the slanting rays of the rising sun. "Not flying any flag I recognize. A gold falcon head on a field of crimson." He lowered the spyglass. "Not a good sign."

"Pirates?"

"Most likely." The older man cocked his head. "Seems I've heard of a pirate lord called El Halcón—The Falcon. I'm afraid, sir, that we've chanced upon him." He looked around to the boatswain, who had joined them and frowned as he understood their conversation. "Señor Lorca," said Captain Jones, "rouse the men. Hoist all sails and outrun them."

José Lorca went into action. Soon the deck scurried with seamen who, despite being jerked roughly from sleep, understood the situation and went about their business with grim-faced resolve, all the while keeping their eyes towards the ship that was a dot on the rose-tinged gold of the horizon.

After the first hour it had become apparent, even without the spyglass, that they were gradually being overtaken. "Damn them to hell," muttered Captain Jones as he lowered the spyglass again. "Diego," he said. "They will overtake us within a short while. You know what to do, you and Lorca. Start the preparations. I doubt we'll escape a battle."

Diego's first thought was of Celeste. She didn't know the danger into which they now sailed.

Hettie opened on his third insistent knock, her grey hair dishevelled and eyes puffed from sleep. "Padre Diego!" she cried. "Why are you here? Is there a fire? Some other problem?"

"No fire, Hettie," he said. "But, aye, a problem. Please wake your mistress and tell her to dress. We're being pursued by pirates."

"Pirates!" Hettie's screech raised the hackles of Diego's neck.

"Now, Hettie, don't panic. Just do as I've asked. Wake Celeste and get dressed. I'll be back to take you both to a safe place in the hold."

He heard Celeste's voice behind the maid. "Hettie?"

The maid turned towards her mistress and Diego got a momentary glimpse of Celeste, upright in bed, her hair loose and tousled over breasts that were unbound and glorious beneath the soft linen of her nightshift.

His throat suddenly tight, he nodded to Hettie. "Get her up. Get dressed." He turned and bounded away, taking the stairs two at a time, leaving the maid to follow the terse command.

If there was one thing to be said about sailing on the ships of Don Alejandro Castillo, it was that they were well prepared to battle pirates. And Diego, like all the others who'd sailed on them, knew what to do to protect their vessel.

First the men had been brought breakfast—a full ration of food and drink, since many hadn't eaten. They would need every bit of their strength for the day ahead. To Diego, sipping the wine provided, it felt suspiciously like the last meal given a condemned man. As the men ate, quickly and in silence, Captain Jones appeared. He seemed the epitome of courage and cool-headed command, exhorting them to fight with honour, to distinguish themselves as men, remembering always to commend their souls to the grace of God.

Privately, however, he looked concerned. He took Diego aside. "I need your help," he said. "These men are good seamen and will fight bravely. But I have no well-trained gunners. In the heat of the fighting, their anxiety might lead to the firing of harmless salvos. I need you to remain with our heaviest artillery and make sure that my crewmen stay calm and focused. Are you willing?"

"Of course, Captain. Ricardo can help. He's trained in artillery. We'll do all we can, but, with your leave, I'd like first to secure the *señorita* and her maid in the hold."

"Oh, no," said the Captain. "I'd forgotten about the women." He frowned, suddenly realizing the danger pirates posed to the females. "Certainly, Diego. See to their safety first of all."

A short while later, Diego felt the shuddering motions of the ship as the rudder was used to reposition the vessel upwind, so the smoke of the firearms would blind the pirates and not *La Angelina*'s crew. The pirate ship was almost within firing range. Diego and Ricardo stood alongside the gunners, giving them commands in calm, clear voices. He could see men scurrying about on the pirate vessel and hoped their guns were of shorter range than the ones his father had ordered placed aboard this ship.

A soft tug at his sleeve made him turn. Celeste stood beside him, dressed in a simple gown of gold silk. Even though Diego's mind was occupied with the impending battle, he could not help but admire the woman, all gold and copper against the golden haze of a late summer's morn. He must be a madman. Death by pirates breathed down his neck and all he could think of was how he loved her. He took her hand and led her towards the ladder to the hold.

Her eyes were wide and worried. "Diego? Will you be all right?"

"I'll be fine. I've been schooled to engage pirates." He raised a hand to caress her cheek.

"I know. Barto told me your father was a pirate."

Diego's expression held momentary surprise. "He was not as ruthless as some. Yet he knows how to provision and defend his own vessels. Captain Jones told me that since he's been a captain for my father he's battled corsairs in the Mediterranean on several occasions and bested them all but one time."

Celeste's eyes widened. "All but one? And what of the time he didn't?"

"He ended up imprisoned in Tunis. Father sent men to get him and his crew out." Diego motioned for Celeste to start down the ladder, helping her with a hand about her waist until her footing was secure. "Truly, Celeste, you needn't be worried. We'll hide you well."

"I'm not worried for myself." She looked up with a worried expression as Diego started down the ladder behind her. "I don't want to lose you. Won't you let me stay with you? I could...I don't know. Treat the injured, maybe?"

Diego reached the bottom of the ladder. Her expression was intent, full of forbidden longings he could not acknowledge, feelings he recognized immediately. He'd lived with them and slept with them for weeks now himself.

"Hettie," he whispered absently, his gaze unable to leave the darkness of Celeste's eyes. "I must get Hettie."

A voice spoke from the darkness beyond them. "Nay, sir. I'm here already. Captain Jones sent me down."

Diego was relieved, not because the maid's presence saved him the trouble of climbing to the upper deck again, but because he'd be able to keep his hands off Celeste with her chaperon nearby. He'd been dangerously close to crushing her to him and tasting her lips.

"Come with me," he directed, pulling a lantern from the wall and lighting it. After they were secure, he'd take the lantern away. Any pirate entering the hold would have to either provide his own light or stumble around in darkness. A small measure, to be sure, but something.

The hold was not filled with cargo, but there were crates and casks of provisions. Diego found a small cranny between the stores and helped the women over some large crates until they were within it.

"When you hear the noise of battle above you, get down and cover the crack above your heads with this crate of lemons," he said. "Whatever you do, don't move or give away your presence. Stay put until I return."

They nodded. Diego took a pistol from his belt. "Here," he

said, handing it to Celeste. "It's already loaded. You'll have one shot only. Should you be discovered, shoot to kill, not to maim. Believe me, if they find you, they'll show no mercy." He drew a dagger from his boot and handed it to Hettie. "I haven't another pistol. Let's hope there's no need to use either weapon." Diego turned to go, but Celeste grasped at his sleeve.

He halted, turning to face her.

She looked uncertain. Then, without warning, she grasped the front of his linen tunic, pulling him hard to her. He thought he'd die when their lips made contact—such sweet, sweet death. She ravaged his mouth. Her tongue parted his lips, not gently, not patiently. She devoured him as if she'd never taste him again.

His crazed brain registered Hettie's gasp. The maid tugged at her mistress. "Lady Celeste!" she said hoarsely. "Whatever are you thinking, putting yourself on the man that way? And him a priest and the brother of your own betrothed!"

Celeste ignored her. She wrapped her arms around Diego's neck and brought him yet closer. Her breasts pressed into his chest, nipples taut beneath silk. He stifled a groan.

Only after she'd thoroughly tasted his mouth did Celeste let him go. He stepped back, his heart hammering, blood pulsing through every part of him.

Celeste licked her lips as if she savoured his taste. *"Vaya con Dios,* Diego. I will pray for your safety."

Diego could barely talk. "And I for yours, my lady. Please remain here. I'll return when I can."

"Damn! Damn! Damn!"

Diego heard Ricardo swearing with nearly every breath and wondered how his friend could find enough air in the acrid smoke of the firing artillery to curse so soundly.

He understood his friend's frustration, though. Their gunners were working as hard as men had ever worked, but they were clumsy and inept. Their timing was ill-managed, and so far the barking guns had failed to take down the masts of the other vessel or to blow a hole into her below the waterline.

The pirates, on the other hand, had already shown themselves as well equipped as they. They'd been first to fire, and their gunners were more skilful. Their first salvo had taken out the foremast, and while following blasts had fired harmlessly, Diego had felt the shudder of their ship with the last.

The decks were pandemonium. Sailors hustled into the nether realms of the vessel with huge plugs of tarred canvas to repair the damage. Others doused blankets with water to put out fires.

Ricardo still cursed with every breath, and tried to aim the largest gun himself, bracing himself against the rolling deck. He sighted in the weapon and stepped back. "Fire!" he yelled. A seaman touched fire to cord. The big gun barked.

An eternity passed in but a few seconds; the entire crew sent up a rousing cry when a mast aboard the other vessel convulsed and slowly toppled, billowing canvas into a tangle of rope as pirates scrambled from beneath it.

Pirate guns sounded again. Another blow rattled *La Angelina*. Diego focused on the guns before him, sighting the heavy pieces, desperate to send a cannonball true enough to open a breach in the hull of the pirates' vessel. To his right, Captain Jones directed men with frantic gestures, his face taut. The set of the man's jaw told Diego the battle wasn't going well for them.

Again and again their guns sounded, until Diego realized most of their shots now sailed harmlessly over the pirate vessel as the other ship neared. The pirates were now intent on boarding *La Angelina*. He glanced towards Captain Jones. The Captain had realized their intent as well, and was already making preparations, putting seamen to the smaller guns on the castle—twin falconets and a small culverin. Other men passed out muskets and crossbows. Yet another emerged from the hold, his arms loaded with an assortment of swords and sabres.

Diego ordered his men to stop firing and they took up arms. Diego chose a pistol and a sword, grateful now for the instruction his father had insisted upon. But never in practice had he felt the tension he felt now. His muscles tightened as he swung the sword in a graceful arc, testing the balance.

When the pirate vessel was so close that Diego could see the powder-blackened faces of their gunners, Captain Jones barked out an order and seamen who'd climbed atop the mainmast began to barrage the enemy with projectiles. Diego couldn't see what they threw, but he knew their purpose was to maim as many of the pirates as possible. They might be using anything from javelins and flaming arrows to simple rocks. But when he began to hear booming blasts and the screams of injured pirates, he realized Captain Jones had equipped his vessel with acacias, small clay vessels filled with an incendiary mixture of gunpowder, tar and oil, lit with a match and tossed onto the other vessel to explode.

Diego's father had taught his sons about them, and about other weapons as well. He knew the seamen likely would throw containers of lime to blind the enemy. They'd throw soap or oil onto the deck of the pirate vessel to cause slips and falls. Worse yet, they'd litter the enemy's deck with *abrojos,* pieces of iron with four sharp points projecting out at equal angles— very hazardous obstacles indeed to any unwary pirate who stepped or fell onto one.

Diego prayed. The seamen above him were working furiously to lower the numbers who'd swarm upon them shortly, but those who survived would be filled with rage and blood-lust. And soon now, too soon, he'd feel the jarring as the pirate vessel came alongside theirs and grappling hooks were thrown over to secure their sides.

The pirates would still be vulnerable, though. Men already awaited them under the wooden grating between the forecastle and the aftcastle, not clearly visible to the attackers. As the pirates crossed it, they'd be perfect targets for those shooting at them from below. Only those who managed to survive that last assault would have to be fought man to man. Diego prayed they'd be few.

He heard a wrenching scream from above and looked up just as a seaman high on the mainmast toppled forward and fell, landing with a sickening thud onto the deck. A young apprentice ran forward to grasp his lifeless arms and drag him away, down into the hold. At the same moment Diego felt the shuddering of the collision and shouting—of their men or of the pirates? He knew not.

He drew a breath and looked around. Ricardo was behind him, still cursing under his breath as he strapped on a sabre. Barto was on Diego's other side, closer to where the pirate horde would enter. The African's dark muscles bulged with tension.

Time became confused, running in disorderly streams, running fast and slow, slow and fast. Running so swiftly that the pirates were upon them with no prelude at all. Running so slowly that all Diego's actions seemed dreamlike and bizarre. He saw details—the glinting of gold in a pirate's ear, the man's tight-lipped visage, the eyes that widened when his chest spurted blood.

Time, moving fast again. Diego threw down the smoking pistol and swung his sword.

Time, moving slow, as he parried and thrust, parried and thrust, again and yet again, seeking any opening in the pirate's defences. Time, so slow now. His forearm ached. The pirate's blade hammered at him, his wrist feeling each forceful blow.

Time, hurtling forward. Diego buried his sword into the pirate's chest.

Breathing hard, he looked around. Ricardo fought two men at once, slowly being pushed backwards beneath their combined attack, his blade flashing as he barely maintained his defence. Diego reacted instinctively, hurling his dagger into the throat of the most burly of the two, satisfied when the man gurgled and fell. Ricardo's gaze found him for a brief, grateful moment, before his blade began a furious new rhythm and the other pirate fell back in surprise. Moments later, that enemy lay dead at Ricardo's feet.

Then Diego saw her. Past Barto, near the opening of the
hold, Celeste hunched beside a wounded seaman, the gold
silk of her gown up around her knees as she tore at the hem of
her chemise. Sweet merciful heavens!

"Barto!" he yelled over the din of the battle. Barto heard
him and looked around. Diego gestured towards Celeste. Barto
had barely time to turn before another pirate appeared from
nowhere, brandishing a broad-bladed scimitar. Barto smiled
wickedly and raised his own weapon.

Diego would have to get her to safety. He raced across the
deck, leaping over the bodies of fallen men. He reached her
side and snatched her slight body up into one arm, the other
still holding his bloody sword.

"Nay, Diego!" she gasped. "Put me down! I must attend that
man's injuries!"

He didn't answer, just headed for the darkness of the hold,
holding her more tightly as she began to squirm. "Be still,
Celeste, for heaven's sake!" he commanded. "I told you to stay
put. Now, be still before I drop you down this ladder."

"Nay, Diego! I can be of use up here!"

He ignored her and carried her down the ladder, breathing
heavily, his heart hard as flint. He lowered her to her feet when
they reached the bottom. "You can be *dead* up there!" He
pushed her towards the darkness. "Get yourself back to your
hiding place! Men are fighting up there. Men are dying up
there. Think you those pirates will have any honour should
they come upon you? They will not!"

She turned to face him, but he spun her back round and pushed
her forward. "Don't even think to argue with me!" he roared.

He reached for the lantern. There was no lantern. He'd
taken it to slow the pirates, and now it was he who was slowed.
He wanted to curse. They left the sunlight at the opening and
bumped through the darkness.

"Hettie?" he called softly. "It is I, Diego. Where are you?"

"Here," she said. Diego followed her voice. "Is it over?" she
asked. "Is my lady safe and unharmed?"

"Nay, the fighting continues. Your mistress should never have left your side. Don't let her leave this place again."

He touched something warm and soft and knew he'd found the maid. He felt around more, hearing Celeste's gasp as his hand made contact with what must have been her breast, so warm was it, and so full and fitted perfectly to his hand.

The lust which speared him only angered him. He lifted her over the crate and heard her thump into the darkness. "Hide yourself," he growled. "Do not *dare* show your face again."

"Aye, listen to the priest," Hettie said, her voice full of disapproval. "Those wicked men would kill you, my lady."

Diego was angry. More than that, he wanted to frighten Celeste so she'd not be so foolish again.

"No, they'll not kill you," he said. "They'd have no use for a dead woman. What they'll do is strip you naked in plain sight of all and spread your legs and ease their lust on you—one nasty, stinking man at a time—until you lie bleeding and torn and filled with pirates' seed."

Celeste gasped.

Maybe it was enough, he thought as he made his way back towards the opening where sunlight filtered in. *Oh, God, please let it have been enough.*

He had only just reached the ladder when a pirate stepped out of the shadows beside it, sword in hand. "Die, you worthless Spanish dog!" the man yelled, in what sounded like the accent of a Frenchman.

Diego raised his sword. The man who faced him looked down at it, raising an eyebrow. He cocked his head slightly and laughed. That laugh made Diego's blood run cold.

It was the last thing he remembered.

He was being hauled somewhere roughly, his hands bound. Diego heard himself groan, an involuntary reaction to the pain that split his head, especially now that sunlight tried to penetrate his shuttered eyelids.

He forced himself to open one eye slightly. He was being

half carried, half dragged across the upper deck by two pirates. They grunted with their exertions; Diego was no small man. As dead weight, his tall frame caused them considerable problems. At such close range, Diego's nose burned with the smell of their unwashed bodies, now perspiring heavily.

There were two of them. Even as he had earlier faced his attacker, the other had waited in the darkness behind him. That explained the pain in his head. They'd hit him, bound his hands, and now carried him to…where?

He surveyed his surroundings through the slits of his barely raised eyelids. The sunlight was ferocious. He wanted to groan again, but stifled the sound. One brief glimpse had told him enough. The battle was done. The decks were quiet and littered with dead. The pirates had won.

He was heaved forward and thrown against something both hard and soft. Bone and flesh. Hands reached out for him, many hands at once. He heard his name, the voice familiar.

"Ricardo?"

"Aye, I'm here." Ricardo's voice was low and guarded.

Diego squinted, trying to make out his friend's blurred features. Sweet mercy, his head hurt. His eyelids fluttered down.

"Are you all right?"

Diego nodded. His eyelids lifted again. "Are you well, Ricardo? And the others?"

"We're here. Barto's shoulder's been sliced open to the bone, but he lives. Francisco and you and I…we yet live."

"Captain Jones?"

"Nay. He took a bullet in his chest. He lies yonder, beside the capstan. The pirates carried the day. We're surrounded by them now, so be careful. They have weapons trained upon us even as we speak."

Diego sat up and raised his bound hands to his head. "Ricardo," he whispered. "Do they have the women?"

"Not yet. But they're searching the ship now. Some are going through the upper decks and others are below. Pray, _

Diego. Pray as you've never prayed before. It can be but a matter of time."

"Untie my hands," Diego said. "I have to—"

A hideous shriek rent the air.

Celeste. They had found her.

"Hurry, Ricardo!" Diego urged.

"Hell and damnation." Ricardo cursed as he loosened the bindings. "There's not one blessed thing you can do for her now. You're a prisoner, just like she is. We're surrounded by pirates with pistols. What are you going to do, you madman? Charge them all and end up with lead in your chest?"

Diego stood on weak legs and forced his eyes fully open. The sunlight was like daggers piercing. He could not help the groan that escaped.

But they had Celeste.

They brought her up screaming and flailing, a frothing bundle of swirling gold silk and petticoats. Had the situation not been so grim Diego might have smiled, for it seemed that five pirates were needed to contain the one small woman.

They dumped her unceremoniously before their captain. Celeste, squinting in the sunlight, jumped immediately to her feet and launched herself at him with all the fury of one demon-possessed.

It took several of the others to get her off the man, and by the time they did she'd landed some vicious blows with her small fists. Diego noted, too, that the pirate captain pulled a cloth from his doublet to wipe blood from the claw-marks her fingernails had raked down his face.

The slow, thoughtful manner in which the pirate did it, all the while studying the woman who writhed and fought the grip of his strongest men, made Diego wary. The man's eyes were cold, narrowed slightly as he sized up his petite adversary, lingering much too long on her heaving chest. Without enough warning, the pirate stepped forward and drove his meaty fist into her face.

It landed with a sickening thud. Diego stepped forward, fists clenched..Celeste slumped, unconscious.

The pirates surrounding him cocked their pistols. Diego froze in mid-stride, wanting to curse, wanting to fight, wanting to vent his rage to the heavens. Ricardo pulled at him, but he shoved off his friend's hands.

"You—Captain Swine!" Diego yelled out, gesturing angrily at the pirate who stood, smiling now, above Celeste's unconscious form.

The Captain turned in his direction.

"Most impressive, Captain. It takes a brave man to strike a woman so, with five men holding her so you might force her submission. What do you do to get the wenches to bed you? Tie them to your bed with chains and beat them into spreading their legs for you?"

His words evoked the desired reaction. The pirate's eyes narrowed dangerously. He moved forward towards Diego. The man made only two steps, however, before he stopped dead still, his eyes widening.

Then, inexplicably, the pirate captain swept off his hat and bowed before Diego. He lowered himself onto one knee, seemingly heedless of the blood smearing the rough planks.

"Ah, m'lord!" he said, lowering his eyes. "You must forgive your poor servant his failures. I had no idea you were aboard this vessel."

The pirate looked upward, a frown creasing his brow. "You sail under the flag of the King of Spain? How was I to know this ship was that of El Halcón himself?"

El Halcón? Diego's mind spun crazily. How did the man think that *he* was El Halcón?

Suddenly, he knew.

Ignoring the weapons of the pirates around him, lowered now as confusion touched their faces, Diego strode forward and yanked the man up by the front of his leather doublet. "You scurvy bastard!" he gritted out. "I should kill you like the cur dog you are."

The pirate's eyes showed a brief moment of fear, covered quickly by a colder cunning. "You will not kill me, my lord," he said, half smiling. "You are angry, no doubt. But you know that Felipe Cristóbal de Eraso has been for you a most worthy captain. Have I not captured more ships and gold than all your other captains put together? For you, my men and I have risked our lives. We've made you a wealthy man."

Diego lowered the man. He looked around. Most of the pirates wore grim frowns.

Their prisoners looked stunned. Diego's gaze found Barto's and a look of wordless communication passed between them.

Barto stepped forward, his free hand holding a bloody rag against his shoulder. "Shall I handle this, my lord?" he asked Diego. "Should I kill him outright…or just make him wish he were dead? What shall it be? Do I slice out his tongue for his impertinence or cut off his balls so he'll never mistreat a woman again? Tell me, and it shall be done."

Captain Felipe looked at the huge man and frowned. He looked around at his own men, more in number than those of his erstwhile lord and now adversary, but he seemed unsure of whether they would fight.

At just that moment Celeste groaned, and Diego felt his heart lurch. It was all he could do not to shove the man aside and race to her. Yet he held his ground.

He crossed his arms and studied the Captain with narrowed eyes. "I sail under the flag of the King of Spain because I am on official business for the Crown, Capitán. The English-woman who now bears the imprint of your ugly fist is my be-trothed, sailing with me to Spain for our wedding. You have heard, have you not, that I am to be married shortly to effect a political alliance between the royal families of Spain and England?"

"Aye. Some of my seamen have spoken of this."

"That lady lying yonder is the kinswoman and ward of King Henry of England."

Diego watched the words sink in. The man's face remained carefully blank, but the way his Adam's apple bobbed as he swallowed was enough. The fear was there.

Diego turned. "Ricardo," he said. "Please see to Lady Celeste."

"Aye, my lord," his friend answered. Diego wanted to smile. At any other time he'd find humour in Ricardo's subservience, but this was no mere game they played.

And right now the most precarious part of their situation was that Celeste was beginning to groan and move. Any moment now she would awaken and see him. She'd say his name and the game would be up.

Ricardo understood and moved quickly into position, shielding her line of sight with his broad shoulders.

Diego's gaze returned to the man before him. "I will allow that an honest mistake has been made, Capitán. I will allow that the flag of El Halcón did not fly, and that as such *La Angelina* was fair prey."

The Captain bowed slightly and glanced again towards Barto.

"I will allow that you've served me well heretofore and that your men fought bravely. For those reasons you shall live to serve me another day. For those reasons I'll allow you to keep your eyes. Your tongue. Your manhood." Diego's eyes met those of the other man unwaveringly. "However, I will not abide the abuse visited upon my future bride." He stepped backwards. "Barto?"

Barto captured the Captain by the throat. With his powerful grasp, he squeezed the man's neck, tight and tighter still, until he lifted him nearly off the floor. They heard the soft, reedy sound of the man's escaping breath, saw his hands come up to grasp futilely at Barto's, saw his face change through four shades of colour, from red to white to purple to blue.

When the pirate was on the verge of losing consciousness, Diego gave a quiet command. Barto's hand opened. The Captain dropped to the deck, his breath rasping.

Diego moved to stand over him. "I am now in command, Captain."

The man nodded, still gulping.

"I feel by the slight listing of our vessel that she's taking on water. What is the condition of your ship, Captain? My *other* ship?"

The Captain raised a hand weakly. He could not yet talk.

Another pirate stepped forward. "She's lost a mast, sir, but she's otherwise seaworthy. She didn't take no hit below the waterline."

Diego nodded.

He turned to the men around him. "Move all foodstores and provisions from this vessel to the pirate ship immediately. We've little time. *La Angelina* will be at the bottom of the sea in another hour. Move!"

The men bustled into action. Diego watched them grimly, his chest tight. He let the Captain rise and stumble away.

Barto moved to stand beside him. "That was one hell of an acting job," he said.

Diego nodded.

"You do know what this means?"

Diego closed his eyes and drew in a long, shaky breath.

Barto laughed—a short, too bright sound. "Aye, you do know. It means our God-fearing priest has just become a godforsaken pirate."

Diego felt the truth tighten his gut.

Chapter Seven

The first sensation to break through the grey was that of someone bathing her face with something cool and wet. It helped relieve the throbbing, but as soon as the delicate stroking stopped, the pain returned anew.

She heard the swishing of water, then the trickling into a basin. The cool cloth returned. She sighed, reluctant to open her eyes. It seemed more effort than she could comfortably expend, and as long as Hettie didn't mind continuing her gentle ministrations, Celeste wanted more time to pull the scattered pieces of her head back together.

She wasn't sure what had happened and reached backwards into memory.

Pirates. She sat up. "Hettie!"

Her vision cleared. Hettie was not before her. "Don Ricardo?"

He answered in Spanish. "Aye, *señorita*. I am here. Lie back. 'Tis not good to make such sudden moves."

"There were pirates! They captured the ship. And Diego... I know not where he is." She swung her feet around and made as if to stand.

Ricardo pushed her gently back down. "Nay, my lady. You must rest. All is well."

"What happened?" She looked around. "Where am I? And why does my head ache so?"

"The pirates captured you. When you resisted, their captain struck you."

"We're prisoners?"

"Nay, not prisoners." He stroked her cheek with the cloth. "Not exactly. We are being treated well. You rest now upon the bed of the pirate captain himself."

Celeste gasped. "Oh, no! He doesn't mean to—"

Ricardo hurried to allay her fears. "Nay, nothing like that. You are safe."

"And the others?"

He shot her a sharp glance. "They're well. Barto has an injury, not fatal. Hettie's gone to see to his wound."

"And Diego?" Celeste held her breath.

Ricardo smiled. "He's fine. You'll see him for yourself very shortly. You are in his bed, after all."

"His?" Her head jerked around. "But you said it was the bed of the pirate captain!"

Ricardo's smile widened. "Oh, but it is."

"So how can it be Diego's bed, too?"

Ricardo shrugged and picked up the basin of water, turning away. "A good question, *señorita*. One I wish I had the answer for myself. I'm sure he'll explain it all in good time, but somehow Diego now leads these pirates."

"He *what?*" Celeste looked up in disbelief. "But he cannot! He's a *priest!*"

Ricardo's lips twisted into an odd grin, his gaze finding hers and holding it. "Funny thing about that. I do seem to be reminding him of it an awful lot lately."

Celeste felt her skin tingle. She looked away.

Ricardo laughed. "Don't be embarrassed, *señorita*. Of all people in the world, your secrets—and his—are safe with me."

Celeste looked up sharply, but found no reproof in his eyes. "You know what has passed between us?"

"Just a bit. Diego is a gentleman, and gentlemen do not boast of their conquests."

"There has been no conquest. Diego has been true to his vow to God."

"Aye, I doubt it not. Diego is the most honourable man I know."

"Then rest assured that I've no desire to change him." She looked down at the hands in her lap. "I didn't know he was a priest, not when first we met."

Ricardo cleared his throat. "Never mind. You don't have to share such confidences with me."

"And yet I wish to be understood. I am no wanton seductress."

"I know that."

"It grieves me, Don Ricardo."

"What, Celeste? That you have desire for a man?"

Celeste could not meet his gaze. "Aye. And that my desire is for a priest. But I didn't know. I truly didn't know."

Ricardo reached up and gently stroked her hair.

"By the time I knew, I had already lost my heart to him. And now…." Her voice cracked. "It hurts so badly."

Ricardo looked down. "I wish to ease your pain, but my poor words are feeble balm for such a wound. Perhaps it would help to know you've not suffered alone. Diego is hurting, too."

"We've made an agreement to stay away from one another. It's the only way we can remain true to the vows we've made."

"A wise choice, my lady, though a painful one."

Celeste gave a bitter little laugh. "Like nothing I've ever experienced. It would be easier to carve out my heart with my own hand. I cannot rest. I cannot eat. I cannot stand to be near him, but I cannot stand to be apart from him. Have you ever experienced anything like this?"

"Nay, though I have always longed to love in such a way."

"Don't wish for it. 'Tis the closest thing to hell on earth there could be."

He nodded. "I've seen the loneliness in Diego's face. His prayers surely give him peace at times, but…" He stood and walked to the door. "Prayers are a far thing from the soft touch of a woman."

He looked back towards where Celeste sat, motionless and silent. "I don't have answers, my lady. And I fear your situation will soon grow yet more painful. I heard Diego give the order to move all your possessions into this room along with his. It would appear you and he are to share these quarters."

"Nay! We cannot! It would be unseemly!"

Ricardo shrugged. "Unseemly for a priest, most certainly. But not, I should think, for a pirate."

Celeste, pondering the words, could not decide whether to feel pain or excitement. Whenever she thought of Diego, her emotions became a confusing mixture of both.

Diego was tired. Exhausted. The odd buoyancy that came from nervous energy could only last so long. Now it was gone and he wanted nothing more than to sink down onto his bed, freshly made with clean linens, and collapse.

But first he had to explain everything to Celeste.

Hettie had answered his knock. Diego could tell from her pursed lips and tight expression that she'd heard what he'd done. She hadn't confronted him, though, choosing instead to slip out after muttering some hasty excuse.

Diego let her go. He was too tired to battle the both of them, and he had no doubt that he'd battle Celeste—in one way or another. Either she'd be horrified that he'd compromised her reputation so profoundly or…she wouldn't. And, to be honest, it was the *she wouldn't* possibility that scared him.

He'd had to do it, of course. The pirates expected no less of their notorious leader, El Halcón. And, since he was now that man's impostor, he needed to give a convincing performance or they'd all be in jeopardy. Their continued safety depended on how well he—and Celeste—played their parts.

So now he stood before her, silently praying that she'd understand. That she'd forgive him. And most of all, that she'd be one hell of an actress.

But, goodness, it was difficult to concentrate on explanations when she looked up at him with those beautiful eyes.

When just the thought of having her and a bed in the same room made him hurt.

"We must pretend to be lovers?" she asked.

"Aye," he answered. "*Intimate* lovers."

She went red and then white. Her heart must be beating as quickly as his own; her left hand kept coming up to pat her chest, as if she had to force breath to come.

"I'm sorry. I would never have compromised your reputation in such a way unless I truly believed our lives depended on it."

She nodded, still pale.

"Our lives, and that of the others. Hettie's and Barto's and Padre Francisco's and all the seamen who sailed *La Angelina*. Everybody, Celeste. They're depending on us."

"Dear God," she whispered.

That was all she said.

He wished she'd say more, so he could know which one of all the disturbing problems troubled her most. Whether it was that her future husband was really El Halcón, the infamous pirate lord. Or whether it was that Damian's brother—the priest—was having to play his part a little too early. Or whether it was that after this voyage all the world would think he and Celeste had slept together nightly in that bed yonder and that she'd spread herself for a pirate lover.

Or could it possibly be that she was as frightened of their forced companionship as he was? Neither of them seemed strong when it came to resisting the attraction. She might just now be realizing what he'd already considered—that it could well be true she'd be a compromised woman by the end of the voyage. Only Damian Castillo, the pirate El Halcón, would not be the man responsible. His brother, Padre Diego, would have done the deed.

What a mess. What a terrible, titillating mess.

Padre Francisco's scowl was worse than Barto had expected.

"I can't believe you have just asked me to do that," the priest said. "I know you're a heathen, Barto, but I can't believe even you would have such a thought."

"Oh, have done with the pious religious bit, Padre. If your religion can't help worthy people through their unworthy situations, then what's the use of it?"

Francisco shook his head vehemently. "One does not pray for someone to yield to temptation. Especially when that someone is a priest and that temptation is *carnal.*"

Barto sighed and looked up at the ceiling. "I knew you'd say that. I knew you'd argue. That's why I waited so long to come to you. You make my request sound sinful."

"It is sinful."

"Nay, it's logical. Diego wants Celeste and Celeste wants Diego."

Francisco crossed his arms over his chest. "They've both made vows to others."

"Vows made for the wrong reasons," Barto countered. "Even you believe that, don't you? Diego's not meant to be a priest and Celeste isn't meant to be Damian's wife."

Ah, the good Padre hesitated a bit on that one. Barto realized he'd hit on something then, even as the priest struggled to find some new argument. The big man drew in a deep breath and decided that if he held out long enough maybe Francisco would wear down.

"Still, to pray that they might yield to their desire, and that a child might be conceived of that union... Barto!"

"I'm thinking of Alejandro and Anne, though I don't doubt Diego and Celeste would enjoy themselves a bit."

"Barto..."

"I'm just being honest. You didn't see them together like I did. That kiss was enough to reduce them to cinders. The answer's so simple, Francisco. Diego and Celeste need to couple and make the Castillo heir."

"Diego's not the eldest son. He can't make the heir."

"Well, we can always pray that Damian isn't found."

Francisco scowled fiercely. "Good heavens."

"I'm not asking for him to be dead or anything. Just gone for a long, long time. Permanently."

Francisco scowled even more fiercely. This wasn't going nearly as well as Barto had hoped. "You're a wicked man," Francisco said.

Barto snorted. "As if you haven't wished the same thing for the slimy bastard."

Francisco was silent for a moment. "All right, I confess it. 'Twould be better if Diego were the heir. But he isn't. He's a *priest* and they don't—"

"Well, then, pray he'll leave the priesthood."

Francisco was silent. Barto glanced over, surprised by the strange expression on the other man's face.

"I already have," Francisco said.

"You've already prayed he'll leave the priesthood?"

"I have. And I've tried to talk to him about it."

"You, Francisco? Why on earth?"

"Because you're right. Diego's not meant to be a priest."

Barto tried not to smile.

"He wouldn't listen to me. I told him his guilt couldn't be absolved that way. I told him he'd never find the peace he sought. But he wouldn't hear me."

"Well, then." Barto rubbed his hands together. "Light the candles, or whatever you have to do, and let's get on our knees and ask God to take care of it."

Padre Francisco hesitated. He looked uncomfortable, as if the thoughts he considered were forbidden fruit, as if he half expected a lightning bolt to put an end to his waywardness. But that was good, Barto thought. At least the priest hadn't outright disagreed.

"Barto, you know prayer is a very sacred thing."

"It is," Barto agreed solemnly. "That's why I came. I thought about praying on my own, but God might not want to listen to me, given my ways. I'm not just twiddling around. I want you and me to get down and beg for a little divine intervention here."

"I won't ask God to lead them into sin, Barto. Only that they might see the true path."

"Good enough, as long as the true path leads to a baby."

"We can't be selfish."

"I'm not being selfish. I hate babies."

"You know what I mean."

"Aye, I'm not a stupid man. So you will pray with me, then?"

"Only if I do the praying."

Barto raised one eyebrow. "Agreed. You lead; I'll follow."

Barto dutifully knelt down by the priest's cot, resting his elbows on the thin mattress. The priest joined him, his knees creaking as he eased into place.

"Dear Lord God," Francisco began, "we come to you on behalf of Diego and Celeste—"

"And Alejandro and Anne," interrupted Barto.

Francisco looked up with a scowl. "Hush, Barto. I said I'd do the praying."

"And I said I'd help. You don't mean to tell me I can't pray, do you?"

Francisco had no answer for that. He bowed his head again. "We've come to ask you to lead them in whatever path you've chosen for their lives, for it seems to us that they'll be unhappy if they continue on the present course—"

"They're already unhappy, Lord. They're burning up with need for one another. It might be good if you'd let them work some of that out—"

"Barto!"

Barto shifted his large bulk uncomfortably. "Sorry, Padre. Please go on."

"And, Lord, we also pray that the course they choose might be a righteous one—"

"And that they might make a baby together—"

Francisco jumped to his feet. "That's enough, Barto! I'm not going to do any more praying with you. You're going about it all wrong!"

"I didn't know there was a right way and a wrong way to pray. I thought any man was free to come to God at any time with any need."

"But not to pray for things that are sinful! You're asking God to have them fornicate!"

"Then *you* ask God to let them marry!"

Francisco stopped dead still. "That's it."

"What?"

"That's the prayer we should be praying. That's it."

Barto raised one eyebrow.

"I felt it spear my soul when you said it. That's the will of God. They should marry."

"All right, I can agree with that. Marry, then make the baby." Barto rubbed the tension out of the back of his neck with a large hand. "Only...*how?* There's still Damian. And Diego would have to leave the priesthood. And Celeste would have to risk angering the King of England."

Padre Francisco frowned. "Aye, the obstacles are great, but God is surely greater. I say we just pray the prayer and let Him figure out the way round all the problems, shall we?"

Barto raised both eyebrows, rather impressed. "So that's the way it works, is it? Well, if I'd known that I would've been at this praying business long 'ere now."

Padre Francisco sighed and knelt beside Barto again.

Later, as they rose from their places beside the cot, Barto stretched out his cramped legs and grinned. For once he and the good Padre had agreed on something important. Profound, in fact.

It only remained to see if the good Lord would hear the heartfelt prayer of one lowly priest and one wayward, mostly unrepentant sinner.

Celeste awoke slowly, lulled by the rocking of the ship and by the softness of the mattress that cradled her aching body. She stirred and let awareness overtake her. She sat up suddenly with a gasp.

Diego!

She relaxed when she saw he was not beside her in the bed. She'd almost expected to find him there, his lean form barely clothed, his tawny hair tousled, warm with sleep. She'd almost *wanted* to find him there, and that disturbed her most of all.

He wasn't in her bed, but he was in the room. A hammock had been strung across the other side of their cabin and he was in it, asleep, his breathing deep and even.

Celeste studied him. He slept fully clothed. One arm dangled down outside the sheet, garbed in the soft linen of his tunic.

She eased out of the bed and moved nearer. As she did, Diego shifted beneath the thin sheet. It fell to his waist and Celeste's throat tightened. His chest rose and fell in a deep, even rhythm, but there, above the warm flesh and the warm breath, was a pistol. And on that pistol, loosely curled around the smooth wood of the grip, were Diego's lean, brown fingers. It reminded Celeste immediately that their situation was most precarious.

She glanced towards the door. It was locked, the key still within the keyhole, her heavy trunks stacked before it. On top of them was a bell, small and made of brass, balanced gingerly on the edge. No one would enter without Diego becoming aware of his presence.

The sight made Celeste frown. Thankful as she was for the precaution, it hindered her from leaving the cabin. And she had…well…*needs*. She bit her lip and looked around the room. She jumped when Diego's voice sounded in the stillness.

"What is it, Celeste?"

Oh, good heavens. What did she say now?

"It's…nothing. Go back to sleep, Diego. I'm sorry I disturbed you."

He sat up in the hammock, setting it to swaying slightly, and regarded her in the dim light. For the first time, Celeste considered the impropriety of their situation. She stood before him clad only in her chemise, her hair loose, her breasts unbound beneath the thin cotton of her garment. She suddenly wanted to run back to the narrow bed and hide beneath the sheets.

"There's a chamber pot in the corner," he said quietly. "And a sheet to drape over the hook there as a makeshift screen. It was the best I could do in the dark last night."

She flushed scarlet. Surely he didn't think she'd do *that* with him still in the room?

As if he sensed her predicament, Diego sat up, drew on his boots, then went to the door and moved aside the trunks. "I'll return shortly," he said. "Keep this door locked while I'm gone. Don't open it until you hear my voice."

Celeste nodded. Then Diego was gone.

He was gone so long that Celeste began to fret.

She used the time to wash hurriedly and dress, though doing so without Hettie's assistance was difficult. She couldn't risk being in her nightclothes when Diego returned.

She combed out her long tresses and arranged them in a simple coil atop her head, covering them with a soft veil. She felt more comfortable, and very chaste.

She straightened the room, pulling up the bedclothes quickly lest her imagination start on wayward fantasies of Diego's magnificent nakedness lying against the crispness of the sheets.

She found a cloth and used it to dust the sparse furnishings. Although Captain Felipe's personal belongings had disappeared hastily, there was a veneer of filth that was becoming more apparent now as the sunlight grew stronger.

She pulled back the curtains at the window, and a cloud of dust billowed out. Ugh. She wiped her hands and studied her surroundings, tempted to close the draperies again when she saw how deplorable the situation truly was.

When Diego returned she'd ask him about water and soap. She might not be able to help the situation in which she now found herself, but she'd be a little more content with it if she could just enjoy being clean.

Where was Diego, anyway? Hadn't he said he'd return shortly?

Celeste straightened, rubbing the tension from her back

with a firm hand. She hated being confined, though she understood the necessity. Diego had told her that a woman as lovely
as she would be a temptation any man would find difficult to
resist. Any man? Had he considered himself when he'd said
it?

Yet she had no desire to stir up the lusts of the pirates, and
so she sighed at her enforced imprisonment. Soon they'd come
to land and could escape and make their way to Spain. In the
meantime, she had to keep out of the way. She could walk on
deck only when accompanied by Diego or Ricardo or Barto.
Even then they'd have to limit her appearances to avoid trouble.

But where was Diego? He should have returned by now.
Had something happened to him?

Celeste frowned. She hadn't let herself think freely of their
danger, but now she'd run out of anything to occupy her hands.
Her mind had nowhere else to go. So much depended on
Diego, on his ability to play the part of El Halcón.

El Halcón. It hardly seemed possible. The man to whom she
was betrothed, the overdressed rake who was heir to the
Castillo fortune, was also the infamous pirate.

In another way, though, it did make sense. It explained his
arrogance and the subtle undercurrent of cruelty.

What this would mean to her now, Celeste could not say.
She didn't wish to be wife to a man who'd be hanged as a
criminal if caught. She had no wish for the stain that would
blacken the reputation of any children she'd bear him. And she
most certainly had no desire to lie with a man who'd done
vicious murders and sated his carnal appetites with forced at-
tentions on innocent women.

She couldn't marry Damian now. Not for any reason. Don
Alejandro and Doña Anne would be saddened by her decision,
she knew that. And King Henry might lose the political
alliance, though he'd understand. He was known to despise
piracy.

Worst of all, Jacob would be disappointed. Hope had flick-
ered so briefly in his eyes when she promised they'd soon be

a family again. Now she'd have to crush that small flame, at least until she could return to England and find another husband.

Even though she wanted Diego.

She had to be the most unlucky woman alive. She couldn't believe the irony. All her life she'd thought herself somehow above wayward passions, and when she finally discovered that she was indeed a woman of strong emotions, she was unable to consummate her desires.

Well, not exactly *unable*. Diego was a priest, but priests were men. And men could be seduced, especially when they shared some feeling for the woman.

Truth be told, she'd let herself wonder what it would be like to follow her heart in that direction. She'd let herself fantasize about it. More than once.

To make love to Diego Castillo would have to be thrilling beyond anything she'd ever imagined. Even his gaze could warm her.

But was she the kind of woman who could seduce a priest?

Sadly, she knew the answer, and that it determined her destiny contrary to the whispers of her heart. She was the child of honourable parents who'd shown her by example what was good. They'd taught her decency and respect for God and others. She could not destroy something sacred.

She felt lost and forlorn, like a ghost haunting a place of former happiness. If only there were a way she could find peace with her situation.

Maybe when she returned to England. Maybe then she could gradually forget and the pain would lessen. Perhaps she'd eventually be certain she'd done the right thing to have kept Diego pure.

Eventually.

Right now, it hurt.

A knock at the door intruded upon her thoughts. Celeste jumped up, returning abruptly to the present. She moved to the door. "Who is it?"

It wasn't Diego's voice that answered, but one with a coarser, thicker sound, speaking English. "You must come quickly, miss. Yer man's been in a fight. He's hurt bad and callin' yer name."

Celeste reached to open the latch but drew back suddenly. What if this were a trick? Diego had told her not to open the door unless she heard his voice. But if he were injured...

"How do I know you're to be trusted?"

"Well, now. I don't reckon you can be sure. There ain't no way I can prove that, and no time to spare fer it. 'Tis your choice. Come with me now or let yer man bleed ta death without the comfort o' yer pretty face or yer hands ta tend his wound."

Celeste bit her lip. Surely Diego would have sent Barto? Or Ricardo?

But what if he'd been frantic with pain? What if he hadn't been able to think clearly? What if he needed her?

She turned the key and swung the door open, praying she'd made the right decision. The man standing before her was small-built and clean, dressed neatly in simple clothing. His face held concern that changed to relief when he saw her.

"Thank the Lord," he said. "Come quickly."

He led the way out of the shadowed doorway and across the deck. She hesitated when he stopped at the hatch that led to the lower decks and hold. "Down there? He's down there?"

"Aye, miss. That's where they got into the scrap."

Celeste hurried down the ladder. The darkness engulfed her, but she could see a lantern's glow around a corner. She wanted to hurry towards it, but waited for the man to descend the ladder and lead the way, almost afraid of the sight that would meet her eyes when she found Diego. She could already envisage him lying pale and wounded, his linen tunic stained crimson where a sword's blade had entered his chest.

"Hurry, miss," the man said, pulling her forward. "I hope he ain't passed on already. He was wantin' to see ya awful bad."

There was a crowd of men around Diego. Celeste couldn't see him.

"Move aside, lads!" The man with her pulled at them and pushed forward. "Move aside, I said. Let the little miss get to her man."

They let her through, then closed ranks again behind her. Celeste choked at the sour smell of so many unwashed bodies. Still she pushed forward, steeling herself to be strong for whatever sight would greet her. She pushed past the last huge man, finally at the centre of the circle.

Diego was not there.

Instead, Captain Felipe faced her, seated with casual nonchalance on a barrel of wine, arms crossed, smirking at her with a too-intense light in his grey eyes. "Welcome, my lady," he said in heavily accented English. "So kind of you to join us."

"Where is El Halcón?" she asked, her voice betraying her anxiety.

The pirate captain grinned. "Ah, now. Don't tell me you're disappointed to see me instead of him. A man doesn't like to feel bested by his competition."

"El Halcón is not your competition. He owns this ship and pays your wages. And I am his betrothed, while you...you mean nothing to me."

The pirate's eyes grew dark. Celeste backed up a step, not forgetting the blow he'd given her before. Her retreat made him smile. "I may not mean anything to you now, but soon I shall mean more. Much more."

"Where is he?" she demanded.

He laughed, a short, unpleasant sound, and shrugged. "He's gone. Do you think I'd claim you for myself without first taking care of him?"

"What have you done?"

"I killed him, of course."

"You didn't!"

He smiled. "Well, no. Not personally. I didn't have to do it myself. My men are more loyal to me than to a ship's lord they rarely see. It wasn't hard to find someone willing to make fish food of him."

Celeste fought panic. Diego hadn't returned. Now she knew why. He was dead.

Pain didn't come in the form she'd expected. It wasn't sharp as a sword's blade, skewering her through the heart.

It was a dull knot in her gut.

It was the slow hammering of blood in her ears.

Diego was gone.

The pirate captain watched her. His steely eyes glinted with reflected light.

She raised her chin and faced his gaze squarely. "You, sir, are a worthless bastard."

He laughed. "Aye, I am," he said. "Truly, I am."

"I will die before I yield myself to you."

He stepped forward. "No. You will not die, though you might wish to." He reached up with a thin finger and traced the delicate curve of her jaw. "I will persuade you to lie willingly beneath me."

"With something akin to the blow you gave me at our first encounter?"

His expression hardened. "If you wish. Though I'd prefer to be more gentle. I'd rather pleasure you than punish you."

"Lying beneath you would be punishment enough, Captain."

Her words met the mark. He raised a hand to strike her, then restrained himself at the last moment.

A voice came from above them. "It's a good thing you held your temper, Captain. I'd not have failed to kill you for hurting her a second time."

Diego! Celeste's heart gave a wild leap of joy.

He lived. He'd found her. He'd entered the crowd without being seen and now stood above them all, casually relaxed, his sword winking with wicked intent in the dim light. He looked down at them from a large wooden crate, as arrogant and self-assured as any pirate.

The pirate captain studied him with cool deliberation. "So. You did not feed the sharks today."

"Sorry to disappoint you. I let that task go to the two men you sent to kill me."

Captain Felipe dipped his head in acknowledgement. "Well done, my lord Halcón. You have survived. For the time being."

He gestured to his men and Celeste was suddenly caught up into rough hands, her body pinned against the firm muscles of a huge chest. The grip was unyielding, though she fought to free herself. "But, as you see, I am not without resources of my own. I do not think one lone man can do much against this number. Not when I have the girl, too."

"Oh, but I'm not alone."

As if on cue, several men rose from the shadows surrounding the ruffians. Celeste immediately recognized the huge bulk of Barto and, near him, the robed figure of Padre Francisco. The rest were the remnants of the crew of *La Angelina*. She felt the immediate surge of tension in the pirate crew.

Captain Felipe laughed. "Again, I commend you. I should not have underestimated the abilities of one with your reputation."

Even in the weak light, Celeste could see the hardening of Diego's features. "Save your flattery, Captain. It will do you no good. I'll not be challenged by one of my captains. You've attempted to take what is mine—my ship, my woman, my life. For this you will die."

"Oh, I think not," sneered his adversary. "Look around you. You are still outnumbered and I, my lord Halcón—" He stressed the title with biting sarcasm. "I have the girl."

Diego's eyebrow lifted. "I don't intend that our men should do battle, Captain. I value those who serve me, and I would that each of these…" he gestured towards the pirate crew with his sword "…should live. You are another matter, however. You, Captain… You will die."

"Oh? And how do you intend to accomplish such bold threats?"

"Not threats," Diego said. "Promises. For I do, here and

now, and before all these men as our witnesses, challenge you to a fair fight in accordance with the code of pirates."

Celeste felt the tension rise higher. What Diego had just said was serious to the pirates holding her.

The look on the Captain's face told her it was serious to him, too. He lowered his eyelids quickly. His expression was guarded, but Celeste was certain she'd seen a flash of fear.

"When and where?" he asked.

"In two days' time we'll be near La Isla de Caballos," Diego answered. "We'll anchor there to make repairs to the damaged mast before sailing on to Spain." He waited until the pirate captain nodded. "We'll take the ship's boat ashore—you and I, your men and mine in equal number—and there on the beach we'll do our business in plain sight of all."

"With weapons?"

"With or without. The choice of weapons is yours, Captain, in accordance with the traditional rules of such engagement."

Captain Felipe nodded, his expression taut. "And the girl?"

"She will be present as well. In the meantime, she is mine. Any further attempt at taking her will be in violation of this challenge." He looked around at the men. "Even pirates understand such betrayal to be wrong."

The pirates around Celeste muttered their agreement.

The Captain moved forward until he was before the crate on which Diego stood. "Agreed, then."

The man holding Celeste immediately released her. She stepped away from him with a baleful glance in his direction, rubbing her arms where his grip had hurt her.

"Barto, take Celeste back to my quarters and lock her in."

"Nay, I don't—!" Celeste protested.

Barto grabbed her arm, leaning low to whisper harshly in her ear. "Don't argue. Come. Come *now*."

She followed, casting one nervous glance back in Diego's direction before she rounded the corner and he was lost to her sight.

Chapter Eight

Celeste stood beside Barto on deck, grateful for his huge bulk that overshadowed her and blocked out the full strength of the sun's rays. She squinted as she looked out over the deep blue of the waters, sunlight shimmering off the waves like stars in a dark constellation.

"I don't understand," she said, turning to face her friend. "It's as if we've entered some ephemeral dream and life aboard this vessel has changed so that it's hardly recognizable any more."

Barto raised an eyebrow.

"After Diego confronted the pirates, and you took me back to my quarters, I was worried he'd be angry with me, that I was somehow responsible for the whole encounter."

"Because you left the cabin?"

"Exactly. Well, Diego returned later but, surprisingly, he wasn't angry. In fact, there was a gentleness in him that was rather pleasing."

Barto smiled. "He kissed you, did he?"

Celeste felt her face grow warm. "Nay, Barto. He didn't touch me, not in that way. But he was *different,* somehow. More peaceful, as if he cherished time with me. He had a meal brought in, with fine china and good wine. We ate and we talked about…oh, everything. Our lives. Our families. Our dreams."

"What is so peculiar about that? Such behaviour is perfectly normal for a man in the presence of a beautiful woman."

"Perhaps. But then he did the most unusual thing. He opened one of his chests and took out paper and pen and ink."

Barto smiled. "And let me guess. He drew pictures for you. Pictures that took your breath away with their fineness of detail, their loveliness of execution."

Celeste turned to him. "Aye, he did."

"What did he draw for you?"

"He told me he wanted to give me memories of my adventure, memories to keep for ever. First he drew *La Angelina,* skimming over the ocean with wind in her sails. Then he drew a sketch of you and Padre Francisco—a sketch so good it looked as if you were standing before me. A sketch that captured not only your likenesses, but even the very essence of who you are."

"Aye, I doubt it not. I've seen his drawings before. Diego has a wondrous talent."

"Then he drew two sketches of himself, one as a priest and one as a pirate."

Barto looked at her curiously. "And which of the two did you prefer?"

She glanced up. "They were both equally well done, of course. But the one of Diego the priest… I know not how to express this. It seemed *wrong,* somehow. There was a sadness about his features that he unwittingly captured. When I commented on it, Diego merely shrugged and said that a priest carries many burdens, those of others as well as his own." She smoothed her hands down the folds of her gown before looking up again. "But the sketch of Diego as a pirate…ah, it was magnificent."

"There was no sadness in that drawing?"

"None. His stance was relaxed, leaning on his sword. His head was cocked at a rather jaunty angle, and there was the most intriguing half-smile upon his lips. 'Twas done with such realism that you'd almost expect him to raise his blade and laugh wickedly at any moment. And the eyes—they were particularly engaging. Full of challenge, and yet full of longing, too."

Barto stroked his chin. "Then the pirate sketch captures everything Diego most certainly feels at this moment."

Celeste glanced up. "Aye, I think it does."

"Did he draw you?"

She looked away. "Aye, he did. But it was different from the others. It was most fanciful and unique. He portrayed me as a woodland nymph."

"A woodland nymph." Barto's lips twitched. "I've read of your English nymphs and fairies, and seen drawings of them, too. In Diego's sketch, you *were* clothed, weren't you?"

"Barto!"

He smiled. "Well, were you?"

She flushed crimson. "Only partially, although my hair… It covered the parts of me that would have been indecent to portray."

Barto nodded and looked out over the water. "Poor Diego. His very soul wars with itself."

Celeste looked away, swallowing hard. "Aye, I know it does," she said. "I know his pain. I feel the same."

Barto sighed. "At least you two had one beautiful day together."

Celeste smiled. "A most beautiful day. And a beautiful night, too."

Barto's head jerked around. "Did you…? Did he…? Were you lovers then?" At her shocked expression, he held up a hand. "Nay, forgive me for asking. I forget myself."

Celeste shook her head. "Nay, Barto. We did not…consummate. Diego was a perfect gentleman, but he did ask that he might hold me through the night as we slept. Do you think that improper?"

Barto regarded her quizzically. "Do you?"

"I don't know. Ordinarily, I'd be aghast at such a request,

and equally aghast at any young lady who'd allow it. But with Diego…"

"Aye. When Diego promises he'll not compromise your virtue, 'tis easy to believe. And if he says he will not, then he won't. His word is always true."

"You respect him, don't you?"

"I do. He is without equal, the pride of the Castillo family."

Celeste nodded and was silent for long moments. Finally she turned away with an apologetic expression. "I must return to the cabin now. I'm still reluctant to be out here among the pirate crew for long, despite what Diego said this morn."

Barto raised a questioning eyebrow.

"He said we'd have no further trouble with the pirates, not today, and that I might relax my guard and venture into the sunshine, as long as you or Padre Francisco or he accompanied me. And that furthermore he and Captain Felipe were to have a sumptuous meal together tonight. I am to be present, dressed in my best gown."

She shook her head. "I don't know what to make of that. Yesterday they were enemies, and tonight they dine together."

"You don't understand, do you?"

"Understand what?"

Barto's face tightened into a scowl that was almost painful. "My God. You don't know."

Celeste felt suddenly cold. "Know what?"

"The challenge that Diego issued the Captain. 'Twas a challenge to fight by the pirates' code."

"So?"

"A fight to the death, Celeste. Winner take all."

Celeste could not breathe. She could not think. Time must have stilled, for she was unaware of anything save the heavy thudding of her own heart. Barto reached across and took her hand. "Lady Celeste? Are you all right?"

All right? How could she be all right?

It suddenly came to her what last night had meant. Diego's softness of manner, his beautiful sketches, his holding her against his warm chest as they slept... It had been a goodbye.

Without a further word, she turned and fled.

Diego sank down into the warmth of the bath and sighed. A bath. A real bath. It had been weeks since he'd known such luxury. Hot water baths aboard a sailing vessel were almost unheard of. But Captain Felipe was full of surprises. He'd sent up the tub and buckets of heated water with an almost cordial note. Diego sighed and relaxed against the tall back, letting his lids drift down over his cheekbones.

He heard the door open and close. When he raised his eyelids Celeste stood over him, her face contorted with some strong emotion—and it wasn't desire.

"You! You didn't tell me!" she said, her chest heaving as if she'd run.

Jolted so suddenly from his languor, Diego had no idea what she was talking about. He looked down at his naked body, the form blurred beneath swirls of water and soap. "Tell you what?" he asked. "That I was bathing? I'm sorry, but I didn't know I would be until—"

"No, not that, damn you!" Celeste clenched her fists. "You didn't tell me you were fighting to the death with that pirate!"

"Oh." He thought she'd understood, but then...how could she? She hadn't been reared by a pirate family as he had. Indeed, the closest Celeste Rochester would have ever come to a pirate might have been the villain's public hanging. She wouldn't understand their ways and their own time-honoured codes of justice.

So she'd just discovered what his challenge meant.

That had to be the cause of her distress. She'd just realized that, should he die at the hands of the pirate captain, all he owned, or all the pirate *thought* he owned, would become the other man's property. Including Celeste.

But Diego did not intend to die.

He raised his gaze to meet her dark, angry eyes. "Celeste, show some faith in me. I will not lose."

"*Why?* Why did you do this?"

He shrugged. "It was the only way. He tried to kill me. I only barely escaped. Then I returned to the room and found you gone…" Diego closed his eyes, his throat tight at the memory. It had torn him in half. They'd taken her. She'd been his to protect and he'd failed her.

Silence stretched between them. Diego did not know what to say. He'd done the only thing he'd known to do. He could not apologize for the gamble. It had been his only option.

"Diego. Diego, look at me." Celeste's voice was no longer angry. It was as soft as a caress.

He opened his eyes…and lost his breath. Celeste's gaze had shifted away from his face and onto his bare form. When their eyes met again, the desire in hers was unmistakable.

More long moments passed, with no words between them. Diego felt his muscles tighten.

He decided to do the honourable thing. "Turn around, Celeste, and let me get out of this bath. We'll both be better off if I put on my clothes."

"Nay, Diego."

He looked up in surprise.

"I will not turn away from you. I want to see you. I want all this day has to bear, in case—" She broke off, her voice choked on a strangled sob.

Her tears made his chest ache. He wanted to comfort her, to draw her against his body and hold her tightly so the pain would cease. But if he did…

Curse it all. How much temptation was a man supposed to endure?

He rose from the tub and towelled himself, knowing her hungry eyes followed, knowing they traced the leanness of his form, the firmness of his erection. Just knowing she watched him as he drew on his hose made him so hard he thought he'd burst.

When he was fully clothed, she sighed. "Yesterday, last night. It was a goodbye, wasn't it?"

He turned. "Nay. How could it be a goodbye, Celeste, when I don't intend to die?"

She sat down on the bed, her face etched with sadness. He wanted to go to her, to caress the soft curve of her jaw as he'd done a thousand times in his dreams.

"You're a mortal man, Diego. Your adversary is a pirate. He fights often. You...you've been a priest, devoted to giving succour to those in need. A worthy task, an important one, but hardly preparation for what is to come tomorrow."

Diego sat down beside her. "You have so little faith in me." She looked up into his face. Diego was surprised at the tears in her eyes.

"I want to believe," she said quietly. "But I'm so afraid."

Diego took her hand. It trembled against his fingertips. Unable to help himself, he lifted it to his lips. He felt her shiver.

His tongue touched her palm, a touch as gentle as dew. She drew in her breath and closed her eyes. "Believe in me," he whispered. "Believe."

His arms went around her. She whimpered and waited, lips slightly parted. Diego kissed her, trying to remain gentle so she would be comforted. But, oh, how his body responded to her, especially now, when there was so much warm feeling between them, when she seemed to care for him and he knew, he *knew* how much he'd come to cherish her.

"Don't die," she whispered. "Come back to me."

"I will."

The kiss he gave her was firmer, an answer to her plea, a promise. When it ended, they both breathed much too hard. Diego fought the urge to lay her back against the pillows. Her eyes were full of longing, softly edged with languorous desire.

"I should go," he said. "If I stay..." He ran lean fingers through his hair, leaving it tousled. Celeste reached up to brush it back into place. He captured her hand and kissed it. "Thank you."

She smiled. "It was merely a stray curl, my love."

My love. The words hit him with force. It was hard to speak, hard to turn away from the one thing he most desired in the world. If he didn't go now…

"I'll return later. When my blood has cooled and I can look at you without wanting to make love to you."

She drew in her breath at his honesty. Her eyes widened. "Do you want to make love to me, Diego?"

His jaw tensed. "Aye."

"Would you? If I were willing?"

Long seconds passed as his conscience waged war with his body. "No, I cannot," he said in a tight voice. "Please don't ask it of me. I am so close to…I fear I can deny you nothing."

Her tongue flicked out to lick at her lips, the provocative display an unwitting one, but devastating. His hands clenched. He forced himself to look away, then stood up to leave. He had to leave. *Now.*

"Don't go, Diego. Stay with me. We could…talk, if you wish."

He made a sound somewhere between a growl and a groan. "You don't understand, do you, Celeste? You've never before had a man. You've no knowledge of what might happen between us."

Their gazes met, tension racing between them. "I want all this day has to bear, Diego. If you walk away from me now, I'll grieve the loss of this moment for ever."

Diego's mouth went dry. "You are a virgin. Your purity is a special thing."

"Aye, it is. But it's mine to give to the man I love. I don't wish to find out I've withheld myself from you only to have it stripped from me later by another less worthy."

Diego frowned. The thought of her beneath the rutting pirate captain made him hurt. Or would Damian be the one? The pain was nigh unbearable. He ached to be the first to love her.

"You are betrothed," he said quietly. "My brother—"

"I won't wed Damian. Not now. Not knowing what he is. I

can't wed you, so I'll return to England. To what future I know not."

She stood and came to him, placing her palm against the erratic thudding of his heart. "Give me today, Diego, and a memory I might always cherish. Teach me what happens between a man and woman who love."

Whether Celeste came into his arms or whether he pulled her into them Diego did not know. Suddenly they were together, their embrace a terrible agony of need, their lips only inches apart. "God help me," he rasped. "I can't fight what I feel for you."

They came together, their tongues searching out the depths of the other in a breathless foreshadowing of the joining they craved.

They fell together into the bed, arms entwined and loins pressed together. Celeste gasped, feeling his hardness firm against her softness. She moaned against his mouth. "I love you. From the moment I first saw you I've loved you."

His lips stilled the words, then left her mouth to taste other, more tantalizing places. The shadows of her neck, the creamy skin of her shoulder, the fine bones of her collar. When his hand stroked across her hardened nipple, her strangled cry made him throb. He was suddenly in a hurry to push aside the silk of her gown, to taste her flesh, to hold the delicious weight of her breasts against his palms.

No woman should be as responsive as she. Each tiny motion of his tongue, the most tender tracing across her nipple, caused her to groan and move against him. He suckled her; her hands speared into his hair and fisted, pulling him hard against her.

It was almost more than he could bear. He was as close to losing control as he'd been since he was a green boy. He had to calm down, to relax and make it good for her, too.

He pulled back, his fingertips replacing his lips at her nipples, circling and then squeezing with infinite gentleness. But, oh, she liked that, too.

He wanted to see all of her. Her eyes had opened, the dark

pupils wide and cloudy and confused. His palms slid across her shoulders, pushing aside fabric as they slid back down. The gown fell to her waist.

With gentle movements he unhooked her and unlaced her, and pushed gown and chemise further down to pool at her feet. She lay beneath him now clad only in garters and hose. He feasted on her delicate proportions. He marvelled at her petite beauty.

Their eyes met. "You are a vision for a man to behold, my sweet Celeste," he whispered, hearing the awe in his own voice. "A tiny woodland fairy, too perfect to be anything but a dream."

She smiled. "Nay, Diego. No dream lover would want a consummation as physical as the one I desire."

The words pierced his gut with sweetness. He wanted to die within her.

She gasped when his hand slid across the softness of her thigh, removing the garters and hose. She lay naked beneath him.

He began to remove his clothes. It was quickly done, for she was eager to help. When they came together again, warm skin against warm skin, the curling red hair of her feminine mound straining against his blade, Diego throbbed so forcefully he feared he would spill his seed too quickly.

She reached for him, curious to know his form. Oh, mercy, how he wanted her to touch him, but he gently pushed her hand away. "Nay, my love," he said. "I'm nigh to bursting now. If you want to be pleasured, give me time to calm myself."

She smiled and withdrew, then arched hard when his hand cupped around her most sensitive parts. "Oh, Diego!" she gasped. "I never knew…! Oh, God, it feels so good!"

Diego pleasured her, taking his time, finding enjoyment in the increasing tension of her body, in the way her hips began to dance in sensuous rhythm against the movements of his palm, in the way she grimaced and bit her lip as she raced towards her climax. He memorized the feel of her, the smell of her, the sight of her.

He found enjoyment in watching her lose control as she surrendered to her first experience with that intense pleasure. He revelled in learning of the way it overtook her, rejoiced in the shuddering that spasmed through her whole body and made her shriek his name.

No woman should be as responsive as she. It made him want to explode, just watching her go mad with desire.

And yet she was still a virgin—a sweet, untouched virgin. He drew in a long breath and tried not to think how it would have been to have her respond so wildly beneath him, with his hardness sheathed within her, when her climax came. Diego swallowed hard. He held her closely, stroking the softness of her hair as her breathing returned to normal.

"Diego?" she asked.

"Mmm?"

She hesitated, now a young maiden again, sweetly timid. "Thank you," she whispered. "I have never been so...so *shattered* before. Is it like that every time?"

"More or less. It's always wonderful."

"But that wasn't all, was it? I mean, you didn't... You weren't..."

He laughed, enchanted by the blush that crept up her cheeks. "Nay, that wasn't all there is. And, no, I didn't find my release."

"But you will, won't you? I mean, you will teach me everything...won't you?"

Diego breathed in deeply. He wanted to. Oh, how he wanted to.

He didn't answer, only kissed her until she groaned, her desire slowly building again. Again he tasted her, licked her skin, teased her nipples, made her hungry, until she lay panting all over again. "Now, Diego," she moaned. "Teach me the rest. I want it all. I want you within me."

He rose over her and stroked her swollen moisture with his smoothest skin, stroked her until she was nigh to the pinnacle again. She arched wildly against him, begging him for something more with the crazed dance of her hips.

He stretched his body out over hers so that she felt his weight pressing her into the bed. She moved beneath him, trying to ease his body into hers. She was so slick and swollen that it was almost too easy to slip within her. His throat tightened. "No, Celeste," he ordered, his voice sounding harsh. "Don't move like that. I cannot enter you."

She stopped dead still, looking so hurt and vulnerable that Diego wanted to curse.

He stroked her brow with a finger, smoothing out the creases of her disappointment. "I cannot. I love you, Celeste."

He laid a finger across her lips and let his hips glide ever so slowly, ever so smoothly, against her flesh. "I want to make love to you. God knows I do."

"It's because of your vow, isn't it?"

Diego was silent.

"Oh, Diego, what have I done?" Her voice cracked. Tears filled her eyes. "I should leave you. I should. But I cannot. Oh, God!"

"Shhh." Diego laid his finger again across her lips. "Hush, now. Just close your eyes and enjoy pleasure."

Sweetly trusting, she did as she was told. Diego moved against her, his hips engaging her in a slow, circular dance.

She shuddered against him. "Oh, Diego," she breathed. "That feels wonderful."

It did feel wonderful. Almost too wonderful. Diego knew he must pull back soon, before his own needs became too powerful. Only a bit more, another deliberate move against her, so that his male blade stroked hard against the softer mound of her flesh.

Desire shafted through him. He nearly gasped with the pleasure. It would be so easy to give himself up to that feeling, to the sliding of his heat against the warmth and wetness of hers, to the firmness of her gently twisting hips as she rose against him.

For a moment he considered how near he stood to the edge of the precipice. An inch more and he would plummet over it.

Half an inch more and he would no longer resist the fall. He had to stop. *Now.*

He wanted to growl with displeasure when he forced his unwilling body to pull away from her. *Only his hands,* he told himself. Only his hands could touch her from this moment on.

But even that new restriction could not ease his torment. Not when her womanly musk pervaded his senses; not when her groans at his lightest touch scored his heart with lust. He imagined all he could not do, saw himself buried within her, savoured their mingled scents filling the air, imagined his guttural cry at the moment of deepest pleasure, and his thick flesh pulsing in climax, filling her full of himself.

Diego pulled away with a low snarl of distress.

Celeste opened her eyes, tormented by desire and confusion.

He looked down at his clenched fists and shook his head. "It's too much," he whispered in an anguished voice that he scarcely recognized as his own. "I dare not touch you. God above, I dare not even touch you."

She sat up then, tears filling her eyes. Diego glanced at her and forced himself to look away again, not sure he could endure the loveliness of her body. Her breasts...*sweet hell.*

"Don't leave me," she said quietly. "Don't leave me."

He drew in a ragged breath. There was a long silence as he considered his limitations. Finally he relaxed and eased into place beside her, drawing her into his embrace. "I can't leave you. And I can't make love to you," he whispered against the fragrance of her hair. "But for now, I do need to hold you."

He knew she understood when she snuggled more tightly into his embrace, her body fitting far too perfectly against his own, skin to warm skin.

It was a compromise, the best compromise he knew how to make. On the one hand was his love for her, a love as real and intense as anything he'd ever felt. A love that wanted all of her to know all of him—not just in body, but in spirit and soul and throughout eternity.

On the other hand was his vow to God. That vow, and his own sense of honour towards his brother and the betrothal Celeste had made with him.

But it *was* a compromise, and as such, neither part of Diego's heart could feel satisfied. As he held her through the long afternoon, drifting in and out of the shadowy dream of her softness and her fragrance, he knew the uneasy feeling that he'd done wrong. Both to himself and to her.

Chapter Nine

❦

Evening had come, and with it the slanting rays of a sunset piercingly beautiful, so breathtaking it exhausted nature's palette of colours in a grandiose display of reds and oranges and purples edged in gold. Diego stood with one arm around Celeste's waist, his hand warm through the thin silk of her gown. She sighed and leaned her head back against his chest, enjoying the unexpected freedom that came with this charade they played, even knowing it was purchased at the expense of her reputation.

"It's almost time," Diego whispered into her hair. "The food is being brought out and the pirates are gathering beneath the pavilion they've erected on deck for our feast. We must not disappoint our host and arrive late."

"I know," Celeste sighed, reluctantly pulling away. "But how I would that this nightmare were over."

Diego traced a finger down her nose. "Believe," he whispered.

The Captain saw them coming, and stepped forward with an effusive bow. "Ah, Lord Halcón!" he said. "How fine a gentleman you look in your elegant clothing! And how lovely is Lady Celeste!"

Celeste did not like the way he looked her over so intently.

She wished she had her lace shawl draped over her bosom now. Her neckline showed only a small amount of creamy skin, but she flushed beneath the Captain's hawk-eyed stare. She withdrew her hand from his quickly, wiping it down the side of her skirt without realizing she'd done so—until she saw the man's eyes harden.

Well, at least they weren't outnumbered. Captain Felipe stood with the four officers of his pirate crew, but he'd also invited Padre Francisco, Barto, Ricardo, and José Lorca, the only remaining officer of *La Angelina*. Diego's eyes swept the scene, noting the evenly matched numbers, and that the pirates were not armed. His tight muscles relaxed beneath her fingertips.

Makeshift tables awaited beneath a pavilion of canvas sail. The Captain hurried them forward, talking excitedly of the excellent fare which awaited. Even Diego seemed impressed, for rations at sea were often scanty and of poor quality.

However, this evening's meal was exceptional. As might be expected, freshly caught fish was the main course, but prepared in a sauce rich and succulent. It was accompanied by generous helpings of fruit preserves, cheese, sea biscuits softened in honey, and good French wine.

The conversation during the meal was what Celeste found most surprising, though. She'd expected the two enemies to accommodate one another's presence only grudgingly. Instead, they seemed as old friends, sharing stories of the sea and humourous tales of their adventures in an easy camaraderie that amazed Celeste. Even more stunning was how perfectly adequate Diego seemed in his role as El Halcón, lord commander of a pirate fleet. His stories were surely fabrications, but they were imbued with such realism and detail that Celeste could almost believe he'd spent time aboard pirate vessels and captured his gold and silver at the expense of others' lives.

The pirates believed as well; they laughed with raucous humour at Diego's imagined exploits. In turn, they spun tales of their own adventures, tales which occasionally made Celeste flinch when grisly details were particularly emphasized. Only the tightening of Diego's fingers against her knee warned her to remain calm.

Somehow they made it through the meal without mishap. Indeed, as Diego finally led her away towards their shared quarters, she admitted with some surprise that the evening had been almost a pleasant one. Captain Felipe had comported himself as a gentleman. He'd talked with ease about many topics, and had shown himself a man of learning, knowledgeable about books and ideas and the politics of recent world events. Only when Celeste's eyes had inadvertently met his had she seen the underlying savagery of the outwardly civilized Captain. His dark gaze had chased a shiver down her spine. It reminded her that in the morning Diego would meet him and fight until one of them spilled blood on the sand of a deserted beach.

She prayed Diego would not die.

Yet she feared. The pirate captain had survived by being ruthless. He would be cold. He would be cunning. Celeste doubted the fight would be fair.

Diego was not ruthless. He was a man of honour and virtue. The Captain would inevitably use it against him.

She was in a dark mood when they returned together to their cabin. Diego watched her cautiously as she uncoiled and brushed her hair. His efforts to converse with her were met with short, impatient answers.

Finally Diego sighed. "You're in a black mood tonight. You still don't believe in me, do you?" He ran dark fingers through rumpled hair. "Set your fear aside. I will best him."

"How can you be so sure? You've been a priest—"

"Aye, I have. But my father was a pirate. He made sure I was trained in warfare. Trained well. Trained by the best."

"But years have passed—"

"Ricardo and I practise swordsmanship together. Knives and bare hands, too. I can hold my own in a fair fight."

"But what if it's not a fair fight, Diego? Perhaps you're too trusting."

"Then I can only hope God will somehow work on my behalf."

Just as she'd feared. Diego was too noble. Tears filled her eyes. She swiped at them in anger.

Diego heard her sniff and turned, studying her for long moments, his blue eyes glittering with some deep emotion Celeste could not read. Her stomach tightened, her senses aware of his maleness in their confined quarters.

He came to her and stroked her cheek with one fingertip. "Don't cry. All will be well. By this time tomorrow evening I will be undisputed lord of this ship. You'll see." Celeste tried to hold back a sob. Diego smiled at her gently and turned away.

She was disappointed. She'd wanted him to come even closer, to trace that lean finger into the dark shadow between her breasts, to pull her lips to his, to enfold her within his embrace. To do again all he'd done with her earlier, and perhaps even more.

Instead, he shook out the canvas hammock and strung it across the hooks he'd screwed into wooden beams. He eased his boots off and climbed into it, fully dressed.

Celeste stood and wandered the room, nervously straightening the bedclothes, then the stack of books beside Diego's trunk. Her fingers brushed across the sketches he'd made. She pulled them out and studied each one.

He'd said he wanted to give her memories. Well, he had.

She saw again the lean stranger with tousled damp locks who had pulled her from the rapids. She saw eyes of deep blue-green, eyes lit with desire, and a manly form both majestic and beautiful.

She remembered the compassion in his voice when he'd listened to her secret confession, and the anguish later, when he'd admitted that a priest could feel lust.

And then there had been that which they'd shared in this room. Just thinking of it made her stomach feel strange. He had given her something beautiful and precious.

She only hoped that the morrow wouldn't snatch it all away again.

* * *

Diego did not know why he'd allowed Celeste to come. It had been a spur-of-the-moment decision, and a rash one. He realized that now, as they rowed to the pristine shore of La Isla de Caballos. She was gently born, and a woman, and should never have to see the grisly work of bloodletting.

He hadn't considered his decision carefully enough, acting on instinct and weighed by the fear that she'd be too vulnerable if left on the ship alone. Even locks on doors wouldn't have withstood the onslaught of determined pirates. So Diego had decided quickly in favour of her presence at his side.

Yet now, with her loveliness seated beside him in the small boat that carried them to shore, he wondered if he'd done the right thing. Either way he went, she'd see him in less than a virtuous light this day.

Not that he had a single qualm about killing Felipe Cristóbal de Eraso. The man was a black-hearted knave and deserved to die. Diego had gleaned enough information about the pirate to know the full extent of his ruthless depravity, and though Diego had carefully kept most of it far distant from Celeste's virginal ears, he understood well the cost to her if he should not survive this contest.

For himself, he had no compunction about skewering such a rat on his blade.

But women were soft-hearted creatures, easily become emotional and anguished by human pain. Celeste might later despise him for what he must do this day. Would she?

Such anxious thoughts made him pull her more tightly into his embrace. Only when she turned her delicate face towards his did he realize he'd brought her body into scandalous contact with his own. Her lips were mere inches from his, her eyes sweeping his face with a hunger and intensity that made his chest tighten. He would have kissed her, but the others in the boat watched them with avid interest, especially the pirate captain. His eyes were dark with lust.

"Go ahead and kiss her," Captain Felipe said in a voice loud with derision. "Let me see how the Falcon captures his little dove. Then I'll know better what to do when she is mine. Tell me, Lord Halcón. Does she like to play sweetly, or does she prefer her tumble a bit rough?"

Diego's eyes narrowed but he refused the bait, which caused the three pirates with Captain Felipe to laugh.

"Pay them no heed," Diego murmured near Celeste's ear. "They seek only to anger me. An angry man will not fight with cool precision." He met her gaze. "I know the game and refuse to play it."

"Oh, Diego. I fear for you," she whispered.

"Shhh," he cautioned. "All will end well."

He did believe this. His early-morning prayers had brought him some measure of peace. It seemed contrary to the ways of the Almighty to fail an honourable man in a righteous cause.

But it was the Captain's choice of weapon which had brought Diego the most recent reassurance. Barto had also smiled when told of it.

"Blades, then." Barto had chuckled. "I could only have dreamed of such good fortune, knowing your skill as I do. Still, you must not underestimate your adversary. The crew say he's wicked with cutlass, sword or dagger."

"I doubt it not. Pirates do not usually survive as long as he. That does attest to some measure of ability."

"Aye, but he's overconfident. Strength and speed, but no finesse. And his weapons are lacking."

Diego turned in surprise. "How would you know?"

"I bribed his cabin boy. Slipped into the Captain's quarters and took good measure of the toys with which he plays. Not bad, but not particularly *good,* either. And the weapon oft makes the critical difference."

"I agree, all other things being equal." Diego sighed. "But in this he has me. I lost my own in the fighting aboard *La*

Angelina. I must now rely on his offering and trust only to my skill."

Barto surprised Diego with laughter. "To your skill I can attest, and to your grim intent, too. But trust me, *hijo.* I've gone further and used a bit of gold to outwit that wily bastard." Barto moved to one of Celeste's large trunks and opened it.

He shook free a long swath of silk chemise from around a leather scabbard and smiled as he handed it across to Diego.

From the moment the weapon's hilt fitted into his palm Diego knew Barto spoke the truth. The sword was a work of art. He stepped back and tested it, swinging it in a delicate arc to determine its weight and balance. It was perfect, made for both cutting and thrusting, the length short enough for easy manoeuvrability, but long enough to reach the pirate captain's black heart. He smiled up at Barto as the fine blade winked wickedly before him, sharp and savage.

"Beautiful," he breathed. "Absolutely beautiful."

"Even more so when you see that cur-dog's blood on it."

Diego smiled as he envisaged that, breathing a prayer that it might be so, and quickly done.

Now he breathed another prayer for the same thing as he dropped a light kiss onto Celeste's brow. Her hair was soft beneath his lips, her fragrance enticing.

The boat bumped as it made landfall. Two wiry sailors jumped out to haul it up onto the beach. The pirate captain leaped with agile grace onto the wet sand, followed by Ricardo, Francisco, and Barto. Diego lifted Celeste into his arms and carried her easily over the dampness that would soil her slippers. He put her down several feet away from the men, smiling at her light gasp when their bodies made unexpected but very pleasant contact in all the right places.

The soft sound wasn't lost to Captain Felipe. His laughter was low, tinged with envy. "So the little woman enjoys the feel of your sword, eh, Capitán?" He stepped forward and captured Celeste's hand without warning, bringing it towards his wickedly smiling lips in a firm grasp she could not escape.

"We'll see how she reacts when she experiences *my* blade. No doubt she'll gasp with surprise at that one, too."

"You! You *perverted,* sinful wretch!" Padre Francisco sputtered behind them. "Take your hands off the lady or I swear by all that's holy—!"

The pirate captain glanced around, eyes glinting with amusement. "That you'll do *what,* Padre? Excommunicate me from the fellowship of the saints?" He laughed and returned his attention to Celeste, his lips touching down on the delicate skin of Celeste's wrist.

Francisco snarled, and would have moved forward, but Ricardo restrained him with a firm hand on Francisco's shoulder. "Hold off," he said in a low voice. "I dare say—"

A sharp crack rent the air.

The three pirate seamen with Felipe made a collective sound of disbelief as their leader jerked upward and backwards, one swarthy hand flying towards his jaw, which now was an angry scarlet patch beneath his enraged eyes.

Celeste shook out her wrist and rubbed her palm, soothing the sting of the slap she'd delivered.

"You bitch," Felipe growled. "You nasty bitch! I'll teach you—!"

"Nay, you will not." Diego's voice was dark with menace. "You'll not touch her. Not until you're done with me." Diego moved, using his body to shield Celeste. Outwardly, his manner was calm, but inwardly he seethed with the desire to twist the man's throat into fine knots. With slow deliberation, he planted one fist in the centre of Felipe's chest and applied the necessary pressure to drive the smaller man backwards.

Felipe's forearm came up to knock Diego's wrist away. "Don't touch me," he snarled. "You've always thought you could push me and pull me, you with your high-born, lord-of-all-pirates ways! Oh, how I've hated you, you disgusting faggot!"

The accusation stunned Diego, until he remembered that it was his brother of whom Felipe spoke, his brother who was the hated one. Even so, it served his purposes now to see Felipe growing agitated, so he pressed for the advantage.

"My high-born ways?" Diego curled his lip in a sardonic sneer. "Oh, of course you'd notice that, having crawled from the slime-pits yourself. Careful there, lad, that your envy doesn't show. Or might it be more a case of *lust?*"

Felipe took but a moment to register the soft-spoken taunt, before he launched himself at Diego.

Diego had been expecting him, but even so he'd barely enough time to move away from Celeste before the pirate captain slammed into him, bellowing with rage.

His quick sidestep kept Felipe from locking him into an unbreakable vice, and Diego was able to use his superior size to loose himself quickly and thrust the man away.

Felipe fell hard onto his backside in the sand, where he waited for a moment, stunned by the force of the move that had repelled him, before vaulting up again onto his feet, tearing at the fastening of his short cape. "Come on, then!" Felipe screamed. "Let's do this! Come on and fight me!"

Barto stepped forward. "Hold up. Your man and I must insist that this affair be conducted in accordance with the rules of the code."

Felipe cursed, disgust evident in every taut line of his body as he flung his cape away behind him.

A man named Leon from the pirate's crew stepped forward and held out his hand to Barto, who shook it in civilized fashion. "My captain ain't no real patient man," the short, round fellow said in an amiable voice. "'Tis best we git on wit' checkin' the weapons and move along wit' this business."

Barto nodded. "Who stands as second to each of these men?" he asked, in a voice loud enough that all present could easily hear. Ricardo stepped forward for Diego, and a ruddy-faced lad of perhaps eighteen moved into place at Ricardo's side.

"You have the weapons of combat?"

Both men unsheathed and held out their masters' blades.

Diego saw that the pirate captain would match his sword with a cutlass. Its short, curved blade looked strong and capable of inflicting pain. He wondered momentarily how many had lost their lives beneath its vicious edge. He did not intend to be among them.

"Draw them blades across yer palms until th' blood flows," Leon ordered. "Forte to foible, the whole damn length of it."

Both seconds did as they were told.

Diego watched the proceedings carefully from his position a few feet away. Celeste came to stand beside him, her face a mixture of bemusement and fascination. "What are they doing?" she asked.

"Checking for poison." Diego glanced sidelong at her before returning his attention to the slow pull of metal against skin and the bright trail of blood which followed it.

"No!" She gasped. "They wouldn't dare!"

Diego met her gaze for a brief moment before returning his attention to the grim play before him. He felt her shudder as full truth entered.

"Can we not halt this now?" she asked. "Is there no other way? Diego, is there no other way?"

"No," he said quietly. "There is no other way."

There was a brief wait in silence. When neither second fell victim to tainted steel, Barto and Leon were at last satisfied and nodded at the two men whose blood dripped slowly onto the sand.

Barto uttered some low-voiced comment to Ricardo before drawing a pristine handkerchief from his clothing and closing his friend's blood-soaked palm around it.

Leon looked up at his fellow crew mate with a sheepish expression and shrugged, ignoring the younger man's curse. The seconds took the weapons to their owners and withdrew.

Diego stepped forward to take the hilt of his weapon, meeting Barto's gaze momentarily. "Celeste," he said quietly, trusting his friend to understand the request conveyed in the one word.

"Aye, lad," Barto answered with a curt nod. No more was said.

That important bit of business done, Diego made eye contact with his adversary, who also had come forward into the centre of the newly formed circle of men, his stance still angry, his grip too tight upon the leather-wrapped hilt of his cutlass. The gaze which met Diego's was cold and intent, eager for the kill to come.

Diego took his guard, concentrating on those cold eyes, on his own breath, on the deceptively light stance of his eager muscles, on the feel of the smooth grip in his right hand.

Come on, you slimy rat, he silently urged his adversary. *Come on and let us have this done.*

Silent though the command was, he knew the pirate captain understood it when his eyes hardened and he launched himself forward, coming at Diego with a rush and bellow of noise. And Diego, meeting the hungry intent of the pirate's blade with hungry intent of his own, tasted bloodlust for the very first time.

Celeste could not take her eyes off Diego. He was her lover, her dearest champion, her very heart—and in one swift riposte, he could be dead. This was a cruel nightmare, this moment when steel rang out against steel. The cold noise chilled her.

She felt Barto come to her side, felt him take her hand and pull at her. She resisted, unable to tear her gaze from the battle before her, not even when Barto wrapped one arm around her waist and pulled her backwards away from it.

"No!" she protested. "I won't leave him!"

"I'm not asking you to leave him," the big man said. "But Diego knows his business and it's a damned dangerous one. One hook or one good glide and that pirate's cutlass will go sailing out of his hand into the great blue sky. Do you want to be in its path when it comes back down again?"

Celeste's eyes darted to Barto's black face. "Diego will win, won't he?"

"Of course," he said. "He was trained by the best."

The arm about her waist supported her now, giving her comfort and strength as they watched from what Barto deemed a safe distance away.

"Good, that is good," Barto murmured approvingly as Diego met his opponent's attacks with restraint and skill. "Already the pirate shows a foolish penchant towards excess. He should attack slowly, feeling out his opponent with caution. Instead he commits himself too completely, letting emotion sap his energy."

As Celeste watched, Diego parried each one of the pirate's thrusts with seemingly casual grace. After a few minutes, they pulled back to circle one another.

"You fight with more skill than I expected," the pirate captain sneered at Diego. "I thought a coddled nobleman such as yourself would have little time for learning to fight like a real man."

Diego lifted an eyebrow. "A coddled nobleman such as myself never knows when he might have need of the skill. I might even some day run into one who knows how to fight like a real man."

The pirate's laughter was not pleasant. It made the hackles rise on the back of Celeste's neck. "And what would you know of real men, Capitán? You are too busy with your sweet-faced little boys."

The pirate captain struck out at Diego, cutting towards his right knee with a powerful stroke that belied the softness of his words. Diego beat the blade back and pushed forward a swift attack of his own. By the time Felipe had successfully countered it the pirate was sweating profusely and his breathing was laboured.

He wiped at his brow, his dark eyes never leaving Diego's intent face. "I admit to some surprise that the pretty *peliroja* caught your attention. But then, she has money, doesn't she? Perhaps we can work out something. You keep the bitch's money, Capitán, and let me have her to warm my bed."

Beside Celeste, Barto heard Diego's low curse. "Stay calm, Diego," he murmured. "Don't let that piece of murdering trash break your concentration."

"The girl is mine," Diego said with careful enunciation. "She is mine, the ship is mine, the wealth is mine. And you, Captain Swine, *you* are mine. Come, let me sink my blade into your filthy heart."

"Aye, try to do it, then!" Felipe sneered. He plunged into immediate attack, but Celeste saw that Diego fell into a comfortable stance and easily parried every one of the Captain's forceful thrusts. His movements were as graceful and beautiful as a dancer's, and, despite the fact that this ballet was a duel to the death, Celeste could not help but admire the athletic agility of the man she loved. Only when she looked into his face did she completely realize the grim reality of this contest. His expression was cold and dispassionate, and Celeste understood that Diego meant to kill the pirate captain if he could.

Her heart beat wildly in her chest as, again and again, Captain Felipe attacked and Diego defended. Her nerves stretched taut as the fight seemed to go on for ever.

"Diego's wearing him down," Barto said quietly. "It's a good strategy."

Before long there was a subtle shift in Diego's stance, and Celeste imagined that his sword became more aggressive. Barto's small grunt of approval soon told her she wasn't imagining things. Her interest became more intense.

The pirate captain was no neophyte, no fledgling youth in his first pitched battle. He was determined, and physically adroit, but even to Celeste's untrained eye his movements were beginning to show signs of strain and weariness, in addition to his general lack of finesse.

Again and again Diego's sword flashed. Each time the pirate blocked, but without enough force to effect either a counter-attack or further defence. A quick quartet of moves and a small gap appeared in Felipe's tunic. Diego took it, ripping through the loose cloth. With a small cry of surprise, the pirate jumped backwards, both arms raised. He landed gracefully on his feet, staring down at the spot where a spreading spot of crimson stained his chest.

"Diego stabbed him," Celeste breathed, half expecting the man to fall dead where he stood.

"A slash, not deep," Barto said quietly. "Not yet. But Felipe tires, while Diego has hardly begun. The pirate's cutlass is able to kill or maim, but it's heavy and cheaply made. His weapon is literally wearing him out."

Celeste began to notice that the weapon's edge caught frequently on Diego's smoother blade. Often the pirate had to jerk it free in order to parry Diego's increasingly more powerful thrusts. Felipe's face now began to show frustration—and true fear.

When another slash of Diego's blade brought blood from Felipe's shoulder, the pirate jerked himself backwards and circled his adversary. Diego moved opposite him, watching with hard, wary eyes. Felipe rushed at him with a roar of desperation; Diego beat back the assault, but just as he would have counter-attacked, he stumbled.

Celeste gasped as Diego fell to one knee.

"No!" Barto's body tensed. He would have surged forward, but caught himself. "Get up! Diego, get up!"

Felipe's cutlass was little more than a flash of light around Diego. By some miracle Celeste would never completely understand, Diego managed to rise, his own weapon moving in constant defence while he shook off the offending piece of blue sea cape that had shackled his left leg. Felipe's sea cape. The wicked pirate must have known it was there, and reversed positions with Diego for that very reason.

Once free of the offending cloth, Diego immediately went on the offensive, punishing Felipe with a brutal, almost constant attack. Felipe struggled, easing backwards with every thrust, barely able to maintain even a reasonable semblance of defence.

"Yes! Yes!" Barto urged under his breath, when he saw

Diego's muscles bulge and push in very near to the pirate's body. Celeste didn't understand what had excited Barto, only that Diego's blade and the cutlass blade had touched and crossed and that both men strained and pushed hard against the other. There was the sound of a long, metallic slide of metal as blade scraped along blade, and in another moment she flinched as the pirate's weapon flew out of his sweat-dampened hand to land somewhere in the dense vegetation of the nearby jungle.

When she looked back to Diego, he stood, muscles tight, his blade pressing deep into the soft flesh of the pirate's throat.

Celeste had never seen a man die, and the sudden fear of it made her cry out. "No!"

Diego's head jerked upward.

Barto grabbed Celeste's arm. "Don't be foolish, woman! Let Diego kill him!"

But Diego had already stepped backwards, breathing hard, the tip of his sword still pressing into Felipe's skin. He gave an angry nod in her direction. "I should kill you," he told the pirate with a low growl. "But the woman doesn't want you dead."

"I don't want her pity, or yours," the Captain gritted out through clenched teeth. "Kill me if you dare, Capitán, but never let it be said that Felipe Cristóbal de Eraso needed the defence of your redheaded slut."

There was a long moment of silence as Diego struggled with his emotions.

"Kill him, Diego," Barto said. "He's a filthy pig. Don't make a mistake you'll always regret."

Ricardo seconded that, adding a few choice profanities of his own.

Diego shook his head and backed away, lowering his sword. "No," he said, pivoting a half-turn and pausing before starting in their direction. "It's not God's way. He would have mercy and not sacrifice. He would—"

Celeste's scream alerted Diego. His head snapped around just as Felipe's dagger cleared the top of the pirate's leather boot.

The next few seconds were a nightmare of blurred motion, with each movement somehow slowed into an eerie, macabre dance.

Celeste saw Diego pivot and whirl, his hands splaying out, his body pitching forward towards the pirate even as Felipe's hand lifted to send the dagger flying straight to Diego's heart.

The scream that tore from her throat had nothing to do with her fear of watching a man die. It had everything to do with her fear of watching Diego die.

In that moment Celeste would have taken that blade for him. She would have died in his place.

She understood love.

Thankfully, Diego reached the pirate before she did. The blows that he delivered to the man's face without mercy, punishing him until the man's head lolled back, doubtless lessened the pain of the pirate's own dagger and made the death that came to him by Celeste's hand a merciful one.

Chapter Ten

Diego hated it when Ricardo looked at him like that, with that sly, knowing look that said his friend could discern his soul.

Ricardo shook his head. "Let me see if I have this straight," he drawled, a curious expression somewhere between pain and humour upon his handsome features. "You want to move in with Barto and me for the rest of the voyage. You do know, of course, that our quarters are not nearly as spacious as those you've shared with Celeste?"

Diego frowned. "Aye, I know it."

"And you know we've only the most narrow of pallets upon which to sleep. Certainly not the comfortable mattress you've been sharing—"

"Watch it, Ricardo!" Diego growled. "You know I've not slept with Celeste."

"Tsk. Tsk. The tension must be terrible, if it causes my priest to become so crotchety."

Diego did not reply.

"It must be *agony,* in fact." Ricardo stroked his chin thoughtfully. "Such a lovely woman. With such beautiful, fine-boned features, such dark and expressive eyes. And her body. So delicate, but yet beautifully rounded, with breasts high and firm—"

"Ricardo!"

Ricardo grinned. "Indeed, the tension is killing you. You're as foul-tempered as ever I've seen you."

"Are you going to let me stay with you or shall I seek another place?"

"You truly don't intend to stay where you are?"

"I cannot."

Ricardo stared at him intently for a moment, all humour fleeing his face at the anguish he read in his friend's blue eyes. "Has it come to that? What will you do now that you love her?"

Diego sighed and looked away—at the billowing sails above their heads, at the rolling ocean past the ship's rail, at the waning rays of light that would soon give way to dusk. "I don't know," he said. "I didn't mean it to happen. I thought I could control my feelings, could keep it from turning out like this again."

"But you couldn't."

"Nay, I could not." Diego looked away, his eyes burning. "I love the girl. I wish to Almighty God that it were not so, but I love her."

"And she's betrothed to Damian."

"Not for long. Celeste says she'll not wed him." Diego laughed dryly. "I suppose that's the one good thing to have come out of this whole wretched mess. At least I can always take comfort in knowing she'll not be abused by my wicked twin."

"I always knew the girl had too much good sense to allow that. So what will happen now? Will you leave the priesthood and marry her yourself?"

Diego frowned. "Once a priest, always a priest. That's the Church's view. Only a special Papal dispensation allows a man to revoke his vow, and such is rarely given. Even so, the Church's Law of Affinity would prevent our marriage. It forbids union to anyone formerly betrothed or wed to one's own family. Celeste is legally betrothed to my brother. So there'd have to be a special Papal dispensation to allow exception to that, too."

Ricardo cleared his throat. "Pope Leo has great need of funds, Diego. The Church is selling more and more indulgences to finance his renovations to the Vatican. Your family has the wealth to buy those dispensations."

Diego shook his head. "One miracle might be accomplished—but two? I doubt it. And, besides all that, I've made a solemn vow. A vow to *God,* Ricardo. Not something for a man to take lightly."

His voice softened and he looked away. "I've already come far too close to carelessly disregarding it. I can only pray God will be merciful to me in my weakness."

Ricardo regarded him in silence, his brow knitting together. "I, of all people, am not an expert in the ways of the Almighty. But I wonder if you might be wrong. Perhaps God is leading you in another direction."

"A priestly vow is made for a lifetime of service."

"I know. I know. But what if you misunderstood? We're all human and riddled with error, our very weaknesses blinding us to God's perfect ways." Ricardo drew in a deep breath. "I don't think you're meant to be a priest, Diego." He held up a hand to silence forthcoming protests. "Nay, let me finish. I'm not saying it wasn't right for a time. You've been a good priest. A very good priest. Far better than I could have been. The people you've served, they all love you. Hell, even *I* love you. If it weren't for you, I'd still be living in debauchery today. You helped me make something of myself and become the decent, compassionate *encomendero* I should be. If not for you I'd still be a damned drunk who'd have sired half a dozen bastard children by now, wasting my life in the shortest route to the fires of Perdition."

He squeezed his friend's shoulder in a gesture of respect. "You, Padre Diego, have been good for me, and good for the people of San Juan Bautista."

Diego raised an eyebrow. "But…"

"But God may be leading you another way now."

"Or perhaps I'm being tempted to leave my calling."

"Were you truly called, Diego? Or were you just seeking a way to ease your guilt over Leonora's death? Maybe trying to find in your love for God the love of the family you had to leave? Was your entering the priesthood God's plan for your life—or your own?"

Diego looked away. "I don't know."

"*Pues, mi amigo.* When you find the answer to that question, then you'll know what to do." He moved away, pausing to look back over his shoulder. "I'll ask Barto to bring your hammock to our cabin. But I doubt our snores will make for the same pleasant company you've had of late." He walked away, leaving Diego standing at the rail, washed in the burnished colours of sunset, his face towards the dark, mysterious ocean as he contemplated the dark, mysterious depths of his soul.

Hettie carried the bundle of clothing towards Celeste's door where Barto stood like a mountain of muscle.

Her hand on the latch, Hettie heard muffled weeping from within and glanced sharply at Barto. He shrugged, his dark eyes filled with concern. "She's been like that all morning. Nothing I've said has made any difference. She won't cease crying and has taken naught to eat or drink."

"Ah, my poor little lamb," Hettie sighed, pushing open the door.

Moments later the older woman held the younger in her arms, smoothing copper curls beneath her work-worn hand.

"I must have made Diego angry, Hettie," Celeste said. "But I only meant to keep him from being killed."

"I know, love. Give him time. He'll come round and see things your way."

"He's left me. He moved his things out this morning."

Hettie placed a kiss on the heated brow of the girl she'd reared since infancy. "Don't blame yourself. His action was probably taken only because there's no longer any need for the charade."

Celeste lifted her red-rimmed eyes.

"The pirate captain's gone. Diego's in full command of the ship. He's out there right now, giving orders like he knows his business. None dare question him or what he does. So there's no longer any need to pretend he's a wicked, murderous pirate, is there?"

Celeste sniffed and wiped at her nose with a crumpled handkerchief. "What has that to do with me?"

"Ah, lamb, the Padre's a man of fine integrity. Doubtless it's rankled him sorely that he compromised your reputation as he did, making it seem you two were lovers. I can't say I liked that too much myself, though I understand why it was necessary."

Celeste sat back, her face thoughtful. "Diego's left me because he wishes to maintain propriety?"

"Aye, love, I do think so. He's a fine man, the Padre is. And had it been any other man but he who'd moved himself into close quarters with you I'd have gelded him myself, make no mistake of it!" She wiped at the trace of a tear as it dripped from Celeste's chin. "Don't weep any more, sweet lamb. All will be well, you'll see."

Hettie hoped her words would bring comfort, but instead she saw the dark eyes tear up once again. "Nay, Hettie. It won't be well. It can't be."

"Why wouldn't it be? Diego's in charge of this ship now. He's taken down her pirate flag and has her headed straight for Seville. A few more days and you'll be a lovely bride. Then you can send for Jacob and—"

Celeste burst into tears. "Nay, Hettie. I'll *not* be a lovely bride. I cannot wed Damian Castillo."

Hettie gasped, her hand flying involuntarily to her bosom.

"I don't love him. I will not marry him."

Hettie stared at her. "Love has nothing to do with it. You know that; you've always known that." Her eyes narrowed. "What's the truth, now? I know you, just like the wrinkles of my own face. What's changed your mind?"

Celeste turned away. "Nothing in particular. Only that I've heard enough about my betrothed to know he's not the man for me."

Hettie studied her charge. "That's not all there is."

Celeste seemed to crumple before she fell backwards onto her bed and unleashed another torrent of tears. Hettie, chagrined, moved to comfort her. She patted Celeste's back as the girl's fragile frame shook with great sobs. "There, there, love," the maid murmured. "All will right itself."

At length the sobs subsided into whimpers, then into little catches in Celeste's breathing. Still Hettie soothed her, stroking Celeste's hair and massaging the tense muscles of her back and shoulders. "When did you fall in love with Padre Diego?" she asked.

Celeste twisted around and stared at her. "You know?"

"I'm old, but I'm no fool. 'Twas the most likely reason for your sudden change of heart."

"Oh, Hettie!" Celeste whimpered. "What am I going to do?"

"What *can* you do, love? The man's a priest. He's married to the Lord."

"I know," Celeste said. "I know! Oh, Hettie! I never meant to fall in love with him. It just happened, before I knew he *was* Padre Diego. What am I going to do?" The tears were gathering in Celeste's eyes again, and Hettie didn't know if she had the stamina for another round of the girl's weeping.

"Take heart, my lamb," she said. "Soon you'll be back in Seville and—"

"I want to go home. Back to England."

"As you wish, love. That would be even better to help the memories pass away. You'll find another handsome man soon enough. One who *can* be your husband. And then you and I and Jacob can—"

"I don't want another man," Celeste said firmly. "If I can't have Diego Castillo I'll die an old, withered spinster with my maidenhead intact."

Hettie frowned. "You can't mean that. What of Jacob? The King will never grant him to your care without a husband to be your protector. He'd never see you as a fit guardian by yourself."

Celeste bit her lip. "I don't know yet exactly what I'll do, but I do know one thing. I love Diego Castillo. And no matter what my future holds, whether I must wed to secure a home for Jacob or not, I'll never give my heart to any other."

She buried her face in her hands. "But how could he leave me? After all we've shared?"

Hettie raised an eyebrow. "All you've shared? And just what have you shared? You didn't…? He didn't…?" Her face grew warm. "Did you make love with him?"

Celeste shook her head. "Nay, but it wasn't because I did not want to."

"You didn't attempt to seduce him!"

"No. I've enough of my lady mother in me to keep from flinging myself upon him, wish it though I may. But Hettie, I have learned that there are some fires which cannot be kindled, and others which cannot be put out. For Damian Castillo my fire will never burn. And for Diego, my love, the fire will never be quenched. I know little else, but of that I am most sure."

Hettie drew in a deep sigh. "Then perhaps you need to make things right with the Padre before we reach Spain and you depart from him for ever." She gestured towards the door. "Reconcile your differences and your feelings. Then perhaps you'll be content to return home and find a good Englishman to wed you. Aye, love. Go and find the Padre and make things right. 'Tis likely he'll need the comfort of that in the coming days as well."

Celeste frowned. "What do you mean by that?"

"The lad loves you, too. It will rip his heart in two when he must turn aside from you to remain true to his vow."

"He loves me? Oh, Hettie, I do hope so!"

"Better to wish it undone. The pain will render both your souls in torment."

Hettie shook her head and left the room, leaving Celeste to stare at her departing back and frown at her words.

Diego stood watching two young seamen splice a section of rope when he heard a soft clearing of the throat behind him and turned to find Celeste. Immediately his breath left his body.

She had to be the most beautiful woman he'd ever laid eyes upon, her gown of turquoise silk catching the morning sun's rays and shimmering with intense colour, as if radiating the vitality of the woman herself. The clothing was simple and well-tailored, with a contrasting stomacher of cream embroidered with dainty gold flowers. The square neck only hinted at her ripe curves before rising into a collar of stiff lace that made her appear as regal as a queen. Her auburn curls were elegantly coifed, the braids entwined with turquoise ribbon and pearls and covered with a veil so soft and sheer that he could almost feel its delicacy against his lips. He imagined pushing back its folds to taste the curve of her ear. *Madness.*

Unable to speak, he reached out his hand. She laid her own within it and Diego bowed low, touching his lips to it in a lingering caress. Then, because the madness had not yet left him, his lips parted against the softness of her skin. His tongue flicked out to tease the warm place where his lips tasted her. Her hasty indrawn breath made his pulse quicken. He straightened, reluctantly. Too many eyes of too many seamen watched them.

"Celeste," he said. "You're lovely this morning."

She smiled. It was like the sun breaking through clouds. Her lips were beautifully formed, curving into a shape that tantalized him without any intention to do so. They were the most perfect shade of pink, and as moist as an English rose after a summer shower. He could hardly rip his gaze from them.

"I need to speak with you, Diego. In private, if you please."

He glanced around the deck.

Celeste shook her head. "Not here. My cabin or yours,

whichever suits." Something in her voice bespoke hurt, and Diego turned to her. Tears had come to her eyes and made the dark depths glitter. She turned away in a sharp, angry motion, as if frustrated by her inability to control the emotion.

"Ah, Celeste," he said, his hand capturing one of hers, tightening upon it. "I never meant to make you cry. God knows…"

He drew her away quickly, towards the cabin which they'd occupied together.

Once within it, he shut the oak door, facing her with his hands clasped tightly together behind his back so he wouldn't touch her, so he wouldn't draw her as close as his own skin and do all he wanted to do with her. But there was that bed there yonder, and the whispered memory of their soft intimacies within it.

"Why did you leave me?"

He glanced at her, then away. "Because I love you."

Celeste gave a small snort of derision. "You have a most odd way of showing it."

"Aye, it must seem so."

"Most men would take a different approach."

"No doubt."

Celeste seemed suddenly unsure. Her fingers played nervously with one of the ribbons adorning her gown. "You're angry with me?"

"Nay, never that."

She visibly relaxed. "Then can you not return to our cabin? We'll be in Spain soon, and I would spend each precious moment of our remaining time—"

"Nay, I cannot. Please don't ask it of me."

She raised her chin. "Yet I *do* ask it of you. Come back to me, Diego. I miss you. These small quarters which were so pleasant and cosy when you were here are now bleak and cramped. I try to occupy my mind, but nothing helps. I cannot read. I cannot sew. I cannot sleep. My every thought turns to you—to the way you sat here and pulled your boots on every morning, to the way you stretched your form upon the hammock there, to the way you loved me in that bed—" Her voice broke.

Diego could not miss the glittering of her tears. He hesitated, wanting to go to her and pull her trembling body into his arms.

"I'm sorry," he said quietly.

She crossed the room and fished about in a small trunk for a handkerchief, took it out and blew her nose loudly and without the delicacy he'd expected of such a tiny woman. It almost made him smile. Almost.

"Celeste, please understand. If I stay, I will make love to you."

She closed her eyes and swallowed hard.

"I love you," he said. "It torments me."

There was silence. A tear slid out of the corner of her eye. He reached out and captured it with a fingertip. "Don't cry, my heart. I cannot help what I am. I cannot help what I feel. I can only help what I choose to do. To leave you will keep me from weakness. It will keep me from dishonour. Please understand. I am only a man, a mortal man. You may not comprehend all that means, but I do."

Her dark eyes searched his face. Long moments passed. He waited, scarcely breathing, oddly mesmerized by the slow sweep of her gaze. "What *does* it mean? Tell me your secrets."

Diego felt strangely light-headed. Celeste's whisper seemed to take on strange properties, as if it could move the air all around him. It breathed across his eyelids, sighed through his hair. It pulsed with a sinewy energy and wrapped him in a strange mist that appeared from nowhere, a mist of charcoal velvet, lightly touched with dew that clung to it like tiny prisms, each petite diamond of light growing larger before exploding into darkness.

His blood pulsed against his eardrums, driving and relentless. There was so much darkness, a tunnel full of darkness; he was slipping towards it.

"I dare not," he said.

"Dare," she whispered. "Dare to give me this piece of yourself."

His eyes closed.

"You have bewitched me."

"Aye," she whispered into his ear. How had she got so close that their two bodies touched, that her breath was soft and feathery against the throbbing pulse of his throat?

"What do you want of me? Would you destroy me?"

"No," came the whisper. "I would heal you."

"Your love will wound me beyond all help."

"Diego. Let go your fear. Trust me with your secrets."

"I cannot."

Diego closed his eyes and fell into the abyss. He hadn't wanted to feel this pain, not ever again. He hadn't wanted to live again the hell through which he'd once walked.

He hadn't wanted Celeste to know the utter truth of the evil he'd done, but now the time had come and that truth was upon him.

He opened his eyes. He was in Celeste's arms. Her worried gaze raked his face.

"Diego?" she asked. "Are you well? You seem not quite yourself."

He pulled away and sat down on the bed, cradling his head in his hands. "I don't know," he said. "I don't know who I am any more. I don't know what I want. All the supports have been pulled from my life and I am adrift, without any idea of where I am headed. I feel so *lost.*"

Celeste sat beside him and took his hand, just a touch, with nothing of desire to mar the soft intimacy.

"I'm sorry," he said. "I should have explained everything before I removed my things. But after all that's passed between us…"

Celeste smoothed the furrows from his brow.

"There is so much you don't understand. About my family. About my past." He rubbed a hand across his tired eyes. "About Leonora."

He met Celeste's gaze. "Leonora was my brother's be-trothed. Ten years ago, when he was eighteen and she was twenty."

Celeste frowned. "Damian's betrothed? Yet he didn't marry her?"

"Nay, he did not. She died."

A look of true distress crossed Celeste's features, then a fleeting fear. "He did not...Damian didn't kill her, did he?"

"Nay, he did not," Diego said. "I did."

He'd expected the gasp, and the way her hand flew to her bosom. He'd expected the silence that stretched between them.

He did not expect her to fling her arms around his neck and claim his mouth in the fiercest kiss he'd ever experienced. At first he could not react, only clench and unclench his fists as he struggled against the need to touch her. She groaned when he gave up and drew her more firmly into his embrace. For long, long minutes they tasted one another in a frenzy of wanting.

Finally they drew apart, staring fearfully into eyes dark and intense, their breathing ragged and harsh.

"You did not kill her," Celeste said. "I know you did not. You are incapable of such a deed."

"My love killed her."

"Your love? But she was betrothed to—"

"She was my lover." Diego closed his eyes, not wanting to see the pain his words would cause. "And the mother of my child."

"Sweet merciful Saviour."

Diego said nothing.

He stared down at the floor and let weariness overtake him, the weariness of ten long years. His mind was numb, blessedly numb, but still he knew what he'd done. He'd lost Leonora. Now he would lose Celeste, too.

Celeste stood rooted in place, letting the words sink in. Leonora had been Diego's lover. They had made a child together. Yet Leonora had been betrothed to Damian, as Celeste now was. And somehow, because of that, Leonora was dead. Suddenly all the pieces came together. Celeste knew why Diego held himself from her.

She looked at him. The sight wrenched her heart. His face, his slumped shoulders, everything about him seemed anguished. Fearful of facing again the nightmare of his past, fearful of his brother, fearful of *her*.

She took his hands into her own, letting her warmth soothe his chill. "Tell me, Diego. It's time you let go of this pain. You cannot bear it much longer."

He nodded. "It has long devoured me."

She bent and kissed his lips. A soft kiss, a tender kiss. A kiss that comforted. Diego sighed and looked down at his boots. The muscle in his jaw worked, but words did not come.

"Did you love her very much?" Celeste asked, after the silence had stretched long.

"I did," he said. "As much as I knew how to love at eighteen years old." His eyes raised to Celeste's face. "I was young and I was foolish, but I truly cared for Leonora."

Celeste nodded.

"It was not like the love I bear you now, Celeste. I am a man now. Grown older, grown wiser. I know now that love cannot be selfish. It must always do what is best for the beloved." He looked away. "That is why I left you. Because I have learned these things."

"What happened to Leonora?"

Diego grew silent again, his brows drawing together in a fierce scowl. Then finally, as if he realized the truth was inevitable, he began to speak in a voice so quiet that Celeste strained to hear all the words.

"We didn't mean to fall in love. We resisted our desires for long months. But it seemed without cure. We became lovers, torn by the guilt of what we were doing and yet powerless to hold ourselves from one another. I didn't consider the consequences."

He sighed. "I didn't know about our child. Leonora kept that secret, and I was too ignorant of the ways of women to realize her monthly time had not come. We continued our trysts, but Leonora seemed strangely preoccupied. She worried that Damian would soon discover our secret. She had a terrible sense of foreboding, and she feared what the knowledge would do to my family."

He shook his head, a grim expression on his face. "It turned out she was more right than she knew."

"Damian discovered the truth?"

"Nay, not immediately. Perhaps he suspected. I've always felt that he probably did suspect us. Damian didn't love Leonora, save that she was a wealthy heiress and the match would have brought him money and influence at court. But had he discovered that she carried my child…"

"Then her child would not have been the Castillo heir, and the betrothal would have been set aside."

"Aye, and Damian would have borne the public shame of being cuckolded. And he would have never endured such without reprisal."

"So what happened?"

"Leonora took matters into her own hands."

Celeste waited. Diego's eyes took on a distant, faraway look, and his face mirrored so much pain that she wanted to stroke his soft hair and hold him like a child.

"There was a woman in our town. It was said she could rid a woman of an ill-conceived child—" He broke off, his voice strangled. "I never knew about the babe, Celeste. Dear God, if I'd only known!"

He swiped a sleeve across his eyes. Celeste waited.

"I was exercising my horse one morning when one of the grooms rode out to meet me, bearing a note from Leonora in her own hand. I was struck by the strangeness of that; usually we were cautious and circumspect in our contact with one another. When I opened it, though, I understood the urgency. Leonora begged me to come to her. She was ill and in pain.

Her maid was waiting," he said, "and as she hurried me up the back stairs she told me what Leonora had done. I cannot tell you how I felt in that moment, to know what my sin had wrought. I saw it all in a flash of hideous insight—my base enjoyment of lustful pleasure, all at Leonora's expense. To have thus made a child, a tiny human life, and to have driven the babe's mother to so great a shame she'd do something as desperate as that."

He drew a breath and raked his hand through his hair. He looked up at the ceiling. Tears glittered in his eyes.

"I found Leonora moments later, already dead. Her gown, her sheets, the floor…everything soaked in her blood." His voice cracked. "I'm sorry, but I can tell you no more. I remember little of what followed. Somehow I made my way to Padre Francisco. He tried to comfort me—but what comfort was there for a wretched sinner such as I? He brought my parents to me and they conceived some plan to hide me from Damian's anger. They gave me gold and a horse. They sent me away."

"They were thinking of your safety."

"Aye, I know that. Some weeks later, however, Damian discovered my whereabouts and sent a hireling to murder me in my sleep."

"He didn't!"

"He did. Lucky for me, the black humour of those days made sleep a stranger to me, and I managed to hear the assassin as he slipped through the house and into my room. I was prepared and surprised him. Before the night was done he'd confessed all. I sent him back to my brother two days later, with a note explaining that while I appreciated his help in facilitating my journey to Hell, I was not yet prepared to make such an arduous trip."

"You wrote that? To Damian?"

"I was a different man in those days. My mood was very dark. Life held scarce value to me."

"It was foolhardy to so rashly tweak Damian's ire."

"Agreed. However, I was not completely without wit. By the time Damian received the message I'd fled the country. I travelled aimlessly for a while—to France. Italy. Even to Africa. During that time I began to seek the solace of God. I spent time in a monastery and finally joined the priesthood. I met Ricardo. We became friends and later, when he and his brother were granted the *encomienda* in the Indies, he asked me to minister to the people there."

Celeste was thoughtful. "I understand now. I see why you'll not let yourself love me."

Diego stood and pulled her into his embrace. "Nay, Celeste. You have wrongly said it. I cannot help the love I feel for you. There is no 'letting' or 'not letting' myself feel it. I can no more control it than I can keep the sun from rising in the morning. I've loved you from the first moment I saw you. I always shall love you."

She raised an eyebrow. "But…?"

"But I cannot, in good conscience, consummate that love with you."

A sharp rap at the door forced them apart, just before Barto flung the door open and filled the entry with his great bulk. "Diego. You're needed on deck. A ship's been sighted and she's…well, you must come see for yourself."

Diego bowed before Celeste. When he straightened, their eyes met and held. Celeste could not still the shudder which raced through her, hoping against all hope that she was wrong in what she saw there. Diego's eyes had told her goodbye.

José Lorca lowered the spyglass as Diego and Barto approached. His frown was ominous as he handed it across. "Damned bastard. How many ships does he own, anyway?"

"Who?" Diego asked.

"El Halcón. That vessel flies that pirate's flag."

Diego looked through the spyglass. It was true. The ship was making straight for them, all sails hoisted to catch the wind, all hands on deck scurrying with preparations for battle.

"She's a *nao*. A large one, perhaps one hundred and six *tone-ladas*." He scanned the deck. "Well armed, too. At least three large bronze cannon, each with a crew already in place. They're preparing for attack. At the rate they're gaining, they'll be within range in another half hour."

"What do you want me to do, Capitán?" Lorca asked, his expression dark. "I have all sail out. We're already running as fast as we can."

Barto cleared his throat. "Take down the King's flag, Diego. Hoist the one of El Halcón in its place. Surely the Captain won't attack another of his master's ships."

Diego didn't acknowledge him. He lowered the spyglass and turned to Lorca. "Lower the sails and bring her around. Let them overtake us."

Barto's jaw dropped. *"What?"*

He studied the younger man for a long moment. Suddenly he smiled. "Ah, I see your plan now. You'll play the pirate's part once again. It worked before."

"Nay, Barto," Diego said grimly. "It won't work this time."

"Sure it will. You're the very image of your brother now. Why wouldn't it?"

Diego handed Barto the spyglass. "Look to the right of the capstan." Barto took the spyglass with a frown and raised it.

As if he sensed their gazes upon him, the well-dressed Captain of the pirate vessel turned just then to peer towards their ship. Perhaps contemplating the easy capture of the vessel he saw before him, a vessel much smaller and less equipped with cannon, Damian Castillo smiled a tight-lipped smile and nodded towards one of his officers.

Barto lowered the spyglass. "Damn."

Chapter Eleven

Celeste had stooped to open one of her trunks, looking for a new ribbon with which to tie on her sleeves, when she felt the first shuddering movements of the ship and knew that the rudder was being used to turn the vessel. She'd already sensed the slackening of its speed, and that worried her. After their desperate battle with the pirates it was hard for any of them to feel secure. Even knowing that Diego was on deck, that he directed the seamen with an experienced hand, did little to calm her fears. Perhaps knowing he was there made them worse.

Hettie knocked on her door. Celeste let her in, wondering how the little woman could talk so quickly and in such an incessant stream, the words tumbling over themselves in their haste to come to air.

"Oh, m'lady," Hettie said. "Padre Diego says we're to hide ourselves in the hold and be quick about it. There's a ship approaching, another one of those Falcon Head pirate ships. We must hurry." She grabbed Celeste's hand and pulled her towards the door.

"A pirate ship? But we're slowing, not trying to outrace it."

"I know only that Padre Diego told me to get you quickly to a place of safety. Don't be a stubborn lass. Come along with me."

She pulled her charge out of the cabin and across the deck towards the opening that led down to the nether parts of the ship. Celeste paused at the entrance and looked around the upper deck.

The sight was not what she'd expected. Instead of the hustle of men preparing for battle, she saw seamen standing still, watching with dark expressions as the oncoming vessel sliced through deep water like the dorsal fin of a shark. It would soon be upon them. Already it was so near Celeste could see sailors on her decks preparing for battle, big guns aimed towards the deck on which she stood.

Whatever was Diego thinking? It seemed sheer madness that he would let this ship be overtaken by pirates. Sheer dangerous madness.

"Wait!" Hettie cried out, trying to snatch her mistress's hand or snag some portion of her fleeing skirts. "What are you doing? Diego said you must hide. We have but little time!"

Celeste was halfway across the deck before Hettie had finished speaking, headed for the poop deck, where Diego paced back and forth, calling out orders to Lorca and the other officers as they directed the seamen in their labours. Her voluminous skirts slowed her climb up the short ladder to where he stood, but they did not stop her.

Diego was not happy to see her.

"Why are you slowing this ship?" she demanded. "What are you doing?"

"I'm doing what I must. Now, will you go below and hide yourself as I asked, or will I have to endanger these men by leaving my post and carrying you down there myself?"

"I'm not a child. I do not take orders."

"*Everybody* on this ship obeys my orders. It has to be that way."

"Not if your orders aren't sensible. And Diego…" she shook her head "…giving this ship over to those pirates is *not* sensible!"

"I'm not giving the ship over to pirates," Diego said in a low voice. "I'm giving it over to my brother."

Celeste froze, heated words dying before they crossed her lips.

"Your brother? Damian?"

"Aye, Damian. What other brother have I?"

"Damian is aboard that vessel yonder?"

"He is." Diego turned and Celeste noticed for the first time the taut lines in his face. "My days as El Halcón are at an end. The game is up."

"What will happen now?"

"I don't know. But I cannot in good conscience order these men to fight. I cannot ask them to die."

"You can't mean to give yourself up to your brother?"

He did not answer.

"Sweet mercy, Diego! You do, don't you?"

"Let me take you below. I cannot know the outcome. It will be a comfort to me if you're safely—"

"Nay, I'll not be apart from you."

"You will go below."

"I'll not go! I'll stay here. I'll fight at your side, if need be."

Diego's whole body tightened with frustration. "Celeste, you have got to be the most... I don't even have words for what you are!"

"Stubborn," she offered.

"Aye, stubborn."

"Tenacious."

"That, too."

"Uncompromising. And passionately in love with you, Diego Castillo. I absolutely refuse to leave your side. If Damian wants to harm you, he must cut me down first."

Diego studied her for a long moment. His expression was unfathomable, his eyes as dark as turbulent seas. He reached up and caressed her cheek, then moved his hand lower, stroking the smooth skin of her neck. "I love you, too, Celeste Rochester, more than 'tis possible for you to know."

"Good. Then we're agreed—"

"Barto!" Diego's gaze looked past her to the huge African,

who had come up to stand behind her. "My brother is doubt-less watching this deck through his spyglass. Celeste needs to go below."

"I do not!" she protested as Barto's large black hand came to rest heavily on her shoulder, very near her neck.

"You do," Diego said softly, nodding at Barto. The hand tightened on a muscle in her neck, making Celeste gasp.

That was the last thing Celeste would remember—the un-relenting grip that hurt and yet did not hurt, that grip that made her desperate to breathe and yet unable to breathe—before light exploded behind her eyelids and oblivion descended like a huge dark angel.

Celeste awoke in Barto's arms, her nose pressed against the soft napped velvet of his doublet. The first thought to strike her brain was how clean the big man smelled, despite weeks of living aboard ship with little access to water and none to do his laundry for him. The second thought was that he was carrying her somewhere into the interior of the ship. The light was dim about them and he held a lantern precariously in one hand. He shifted uncomfortably before a portal to hang it on a nail.

"You can put me down now, Barto," she said. "It will be much easier to unlatch the door if you have your hands free."

His chuckle was a deep rumble. "Nay, *señorita*," he said. "Forgive me, but Diego said I was to give you no opportunity for escape."

"Explain how I came to be in this state, then. I would accuse you of striking me, but I don't feel the after-effects of such abuse. My head doesn't hurt like it did when the pirate captain hit me."

"I merely rendered you unconscious with something I once learned from a merchant who'd spent time in Cipangu."

"You churl! And now I am here with you, and neither of us do Diego any good! Barto, turn your huge bulk around right now and march back up to that deck!"

"Nay, my lady. Diego would flay us both. He values you

above even his own life. So you, my little English hellion, will remain here until matters are settled."

Celeste grunted her frustration. "I am a lady. This places us both in a most undignified—"

"A lady you are, *señorita,* and a beautiful one. But you're also a hellion when you wish to be. Diego is well advised to secure your safety, even though it be against your wishes."

"But you don't know what he's about. He's giving himself and this ship over to Damian!"

"I know that."

Celeste gasped, then grunted as Barto shifted her lightly in his arms to unlatch the door. It opened with a creak. He eased within it, balancing his struggling burden carefully as he closed it with one foot. Only when he firmly rested his back against it did he ease Celeste to her feet.

She shook her skirts into place and stood, arms akimbo, glaring up at him. "Move aside, Barto. I'll not be kept prisoner here while Diego needs me."

"Aye, you will. I shall see to it."

Celeste shoved at him. "Move, Barto! Diego will be killed!"

"Nay, he'll not. He knew this moment would come. He told me several days ago. God revealed it to him."

Celeste was taken aback momentarily. "Diego knew this?" Barto nodded.

"And does he know the outcome?"

"Only that he'll not die."

Celeste paced the small room, stopping to push aside crates in her path. Barto watched her, a curious expression on her face.

She stopped and frowned at him. "What are you looking at? And where are we, anyway?"

"The steward's closet. Used to lock up the ship's most precious stores."

"A convenient prison, then."

"Aye, it is. For Diego's most precious treasure."

Celeste paced some more, stopping occasionally to fling murderous looks at her captor.

"I can't take this!" she finally said in exasperation.

Barto watched her pace for long moments, then cleared his throat. "It does occur to me that you might show some faith in the man," he said. "He's not without wit, and he fights with some measure of skill."

"Aye, I recall. But better than his own brother?"

Barto chuckled. "If not better, then at least as well. Where do you think they learned?" He thumped his chest. "From me. *I* taught them. And, if I remember correctly, Diego was always the better of the two. So ease your mind about his safety."

Celeste sat down on a keg of nails and sighed. "I hope you're right."

"All will be well. Francisco and I have been praying for some very specific things. And since they haven't happened yet, we have to believe that somehow all will yet come to a worthy end."

Celeste lifted a delicate eyebrow. "You've been praying? You, Barto?"

He looked sheepish. "I admit I'm not very practised at it. But aye, I've bent the knee to make a request or two of late."

"What did you pray for?"

"Now, that I'll not say. A man's prayers are his own."

Celeste's lips twitched. "I hope they have something to do with getting us safely to Spain."

"You might say that."

Celeste looked up into his face just then, and would have almost sworn his eyes glinted with mischief. But when she looked again she saw nothing amiss and wondered if the flickering lantern played tricks on her overwrought mind.

Diego was surprised at his own calm as he faced the approaching darkness of the other ship, a larger ship than the one on which he stood, painted the same deep blue as the ocean, with trim of red. Blood-red. Its crew was lined up at the rail, weapons in hand, preparing to board. His brother was above them on the raised deck, very still, his face inscrutable.

"Damn your brother for the bastard he is," Ricardo said. "If he tries to harm you, Diego, I'll skewer him. I'll not let him take you without a fight."

Diego smiled. "You've always been true to me, Ricardo, but I hope your valiant efforts will not be needed today."

"Well, at least know that I'm here. Padre Francisco, too. The good cleric has an entire arsenal beneath that robe."

Diego turned to the slight figure of the priest, who stood on his other side. "You, Padre? You would fight my brother?"

Francisco turned a fierce countenance in his direction. "There's a time when a man has to stand for righteousness with more than just a word and a nod. If your brother means to harm you, he'll not do so without resistance from me."

Diego clasped the priest's hand. "Padre, I'll always affirm that you're a true man of God. If I've learned aught of being a loving shepherd, I learned it first from you."

Francisco's eyes misted over. He started to speak, but the words were cut short by a jolt as the two ships collided.

Diego's seamen appeared restless and tense as grappling hooks were thrown over. Their tension increased as the bridge of boards soon followed. Only Diego's harsh command to remain still kept them from drawing their weapons, although some rested their fingertips lightly against the hilts of the swords they wore.

Yet the seamen of the other ship did not swarm aboard, as Diego had anticipated. Instead they began to murmur, in a strange burble of discontent, and when Diego looked round he saw only his brother cross the makeshift bridge.

His brother alone.

"What's he doing?" Ricardo muttered beneath his breath. "What's he up to?"

Diego stepped forward. His brother strode across the deck towards him. Only when the two stood before one another did realization come to the crews of both ships. Their gasp was almost a collective sound, followed by a buzz of confusion and question.

Diego did not take his eyes from his brother. He noticed a myriad of details in the space of only a few seconds. He saw Damian's clothing—of costly silk, richly embroidered and ruched with expensive Naples lace. A heavy gold medallion hung about his neck, and jewelled rings adorned several of his fingers. He carried a gold-tipped cane carved of mahogany.

And his eyes. So like Diego's own, but unlike them, too. Eyes of deep blue-green set in a tanned face. But they drew no warmth from sun above or seas below. Eyes that pierced a man through with neither mercy or compassion.

There was silence between the two men.

Damian glanced up towards the ship's flag. "You fly beneath my banner, brother. You know my identity."

"I know it."

"How come you to be on my ship? And, it would appear, acting as her captain?"

"I sailed aboard *La Angelina*. This ship overtook her and engaged in battle. Your crew won the engagement, and we were taken aboard this vessel."

"*La Angelina?* Our father's caravel?"

"Aye."

"My captains do not take prisoners. I assume they did so because they thought you were me."

Diego nodded.

He didn't know how Damian's eyes could become harder than they already were, but they did.

His brother pivoted sharply and called to one of the crew. The seaman trotted over. Damian spoke something low and inaudible in his ear. The man nodded and hurried off towards the quarter-deck.

Damian turned to Diego again, studying him with a tight-lipped expression. He frowned when he noticed Padre Francisco beside his twin.

"You, Padre. What business led you to forsake the comfort of your pastoral duties for the open sea?"

"Your father sent me to find Diego."

Damian's eyes narrowed. "My father?" He glanced around, his gaze halting long on Ricardo, whose squared jaw and whose hand resting firmly upon the hilt of his sword bespoke a determination to fight. Damian smiled, but the smile didn't quite reach his eyes.

He turned to Diego. "We'll talk in private. I dare say we can find a quiet place to discover this matter."

Diego motioned him towards the *toldadilla*, towards the chamber he'd shared with Celeste, regretting that he'd not had the foresight to inspect the small cabin beforehand, in case she'd left any evidence of female occupation. He breathed a sigh of relief that Celeste was safely ensconced with Barto, although he could only imagine the disagreeable mood she must be in by now.

Damian frowned when Padre Francisco and Ricardo followed them to the door. "Your lapdogs, brother? Call them off. I give my word that I mean you no harm."

Ricardo snorted. "As if your word can be trusted."

Diego shook his head. "Keep silence, Ricardo. There are times when it's better not to provoke with a wayward tongue."

Ricardo's eyes narrowed at the gentle rebuke, but he stepped backwards, flashing Damian a challenging look.

"If it will help you be at ease, Ricardo," Diego said more gently, "you may wait just outside." Ricardo nodded.

Diego eased the door closed and stood in place while Damian's eyes swept the room. His brother moved towards the nearest chest and pulled it out, seating himself with an air of haughty indolence.

"Well?" he questioned. "I'm awaiting your explanation. Why were you aboard *La Angelina?* Why did Father summon you?"

Diego met his brother's cold gaze. "Because you'd been captured."

Damian snorted. "Is that what he told you?"

"Aye, that's the story I received from Barto and Padre Francisco."

Damian's lips twitched as if he were slightly amused. He

looked away. "All right, then. I was captured. But what has that to do with you?"

"You left a betrothed waiting to be married, I believe?"

Damian raised an eyebrow. "And what has *that* to do with you?"

"It was decided that the wedding would be performed by proxy, with me placing the ring on her finger in your stead."

Damian took a moment to digest that information. "I see. And what did Father promise, should you return to Spain?"

"Promise? Why, he promised nothing."

Damian snorted. "Oh, come now. Surely he promised something. You would not have returned without something being offered."

"But I did." Diego walked nearer. "You'll not understand what I'm about to say. You and I have ever been at odds in matters of the soul. But I thought to make restitution for the wrong I did you ten years ago."

Damian's lips tightened. "I see. And this proxy marriage was to have done that?"

"This marriage was meant to make you a wealthy man, and a powerful one."

"Aye, it shall. And Lady Celeste is pleasant to look at."

"You desire the match?"

Damian laughed. "Hardly. What man *wishes* to lock himself into the chains of matrimony? Yet I have resigned myself to it, since I shall profit withal. I'll bed the wench and get an heir, and enjoy the pleasures of her money and royal connections for the rest of my days. A fair exchange, I'd say."

Diego tried to ignore the surge of anger. Unsure if he could keep the emotion from his voice, he merely nodded.

Damian's gaze met his. "So you were returning to Spain merely to do me this wondrous favour of wedding me to my bride. You know, of course, that a wedding could have been performed by proxy without your help."

"Father deemed it important that nobody know you were missing."

Damian frowned. He shifted forward on his trunk, losing his indolent pose so quickly that Diego was reminded of the sudden strike of a serpent.

Damian leaned towards him now, his face intent, his eyes filled with an odd energy. "Perhaps Father meant for *you* to wed the girl." Damian held up a hand to still Diego's protest. "Don't be a damned fool, Diego. Shut up and listen." He frowned and stood, pacing the small confines of their quarters for a moment before halting in agitation. "Father's trying to kill me."

"Father? Nay, he would not."

Damian wheeled about. "I said to listen, damn you! I don't need your sweet-mouthed platitudes. You don't know him like I do. You never have. To you he showed his best side. You were the son he admired, the one he reserved his smiles for, the one who soaked up his praise. He never had a kind word to say of me, but he sang long and loudly of all your virtues. You could ride. You could dance. You could paint and fence and shoot. You, you, you!" He clenched his fist. "He loved you. He despised me. He still does."

"No. You are his heir."

Damian smiled. "Aye, I am. At least until my death."

"Father would not murder you."

"He has already tried."

Diego said nothing.

"My 'abduction' was nothing but another of his attempts to rid himself of me. Oh, the men who captured me played their parts well. They acted as if they were trying to prevent the union for political reasons. They made much of hating the English. The whole dramatic bit was well rehearsed. They took me out with every intention of murdering me, but I escaped and made my way to one of my ships. I've sailed for weeks now so Father wouldn't know I yet lived. He probably thought his scheme was perfect, that it would work this time. He sent for you on some convenient pretext so you'd be in Spain when my death became known. How grieved you all would be! How many tears Father would shed as he walked to the chapel yard to inter my bones. And how quickly he'd install his younger son in my seat. Would you have liked that, Diego? Would you have rejoiced to know that finally you'd gained the wealth and honour that should have been mine?"

Diego's eyes narrowed. He was uncomfortable with the gleam of madness in his brother's eyes. "I care nothing for your wealth or your position."

"Like hell you don't."

"I speak the truth." Diego met his brother's hostile gaze. "I am a priest, Damian. All that I own in this world would belong to the Church."

The words seemed to take Damian aback. Surprise flitted across his features. "You're lying," he said. He gestured to the clothing Diego wore. "Where's your robe? Your crucifix? Your book of holy writ? If you're a priest, you've no appearance of it."

"I've been affecting your dress and appearance. I confess I've used it to full advantage. Playing your part kept us all from being killed. But I *am* a priest, Damian. Sworn by Holy Vow to serve the Lord."

Diego walked to his trunk and opened it, moving aside his sketches and a sheaf of unused paper. "Here," he said, withdrawing his coarse robe. "If you distrust my words, then trust this." He drew the garment over his head and shook it down into place, belting it with the ease of one long-practised.

Damian studied him, his eyes dark. "You are a priest. Strange to imagine it."

"No doubt."

"You must have changed. You're not the man you were when you left Seville."

Diego looked away. "Nay, I'm not. I hope to God I am not. I'd like to believe I've learned from my mistakes."

Damian seemed lost in thought for long moments. Then he startled Diego with abrupt laughter. "Father doesn't know?" Damian said. "Oh, that will be sweet, the irony when he discovers you're a priest."

Diego lifted an eyebrow.

"He thinks to murder me and make you the heir. He thinks to marry you to the Englishwoman." Damian laughed again. "And you're a *priest* and can't fulfil any of his expectations. Truly, that's delightful."

"Then perhaps you'll put aside this notion that he'll murder you. Perhaps you can return to Spain and—"

"Of course I'll go back. I wouldn't want to miss the expression on our sire's face when we walk into the room together, when he realizes his beloved Diego is nothing more now than a dead branch, a worthless eunuch who'll never fulfil his hopes. I want to be there when he has to admit that I, Damian Castillo, am the sole heir to the fortune he's built and to the honoured name of which he's so damned proud. I'm going to enjoy that moment. I don't think I shall miss it for aught."

"Then you'll return to your ship and let us progress onward to Spain?"

Damian smiled. "I'll let you return to Spain. But as far as returning to my other ship, I don't think so."

"Why not?"

Damian shrugged. "Because I've already sent her on her way."

"Then you intend to sail with us?"

"Aye. This is my ship, after all. My trunks, my charts…all await me on deck now. You'll vacate these premises forthwith; I intend to use them." He turned a sardonic smile in Diego's direction. "You realize that I am now in command of this vessel."

Diego tried to ignore the sudden sickness in the pit of his stomach. He turned away, afraid of what his face might reveal. There remained at least three more days of sail time before they reached Sanlúcar. Another day more before they might expect to see Seville.

And there was absolutely no way he could keep Celeste Rochester's presence a secret for that amount of time.

Chapter Twelve

Celeste awoke to stifling darkness, feeling panic for a brief moment before she remembered where she was—the black, airless storeroom in the hold. No wonder she was hot and rivulets of sweat trickled down between her breasts. No wonder her body ached. The pallet Barto had made for her on the floor lacked much in the way of comfort.

Barto—where was he? She listened in the darkness. He was there, asleep. His breathing was deep and even, his snoring softer than she would have figured for one of his size and depth of voice.

Judging from the sound, he was still positioned in front of the door. Of course he would be. Diego and Ricardo had come down only once, to bring her food and wine and to escort her to the jakes, moving warily through the darkness without even a light. Such behaviour was odd. Celeste was immediately suspicious, questioning them in hoarse whispers and receiving little more than a too-quick assurance that all was well, but that she must remain where she was for the time being. It had done nothing to relieve her anxiety. She'd tossed restlessly on her pallet for hours.

Something had to be very wrong, for when Barto had returned to his guard duty after a hasty conference with Diego he'd worn an expression more grim than before. She'd begged him for information, but he had merely shrugged and pasted on a weak smile. "Naught is amiss," he'd said soothingly. "Damian was content to put aside the past. Diego's life is no longer in danger."

Celeste had asked a multitude of questions, but Barto had declined further response until finally Celeste had flounced down on her pallet and growled her frustration. "I'll remember this, Barto, don't you forget. If all be as well as you say, I'd be back in my cabin sleeping comfortably tonight. Something is still askew, or I'd be free of this horrible little prison."

"Go to sleep, *señorita*," he said. "Truly, naught is amiss. Diego's merely being cautious with that which he values most in this world." His voice softened. "He loves you, you know."

"Loves me?" She snorted. "Usually when a man loves a woman he plies her with gentle words and brings her flowers and jewellery and gifts. What has Diego done to prove his love? He sets me away from him at every opportunity, and when I am most desirous of being at his side he locks me into this stuffy room with rats and cockroaches. If that be Diego's love, I have no great wish for more of it."

Barto laughed. "You are such a little liar. You wish for his love like you've never wished for anything else in your whole life. Indeed, you'd crawl to Cathay on your knees if you thought it would unravel the coil."

Celeste could not answer. Her chest ached with the truth.

"Mercy, Barto! What are you saying?"

Barto shook his head. "I'm only bringing to light the thoughts you've denied these many days. You love Diego Castillo and want to be one with him in all the ways a woman can know a man."

Celeste stared at him. For long moments she was unable to speak, unable to think. Finally the tears came, filling her eyes and overflowing to trail down her cheeks. Barto reached up with a gentle hand and wiped them away.

"Aye, I confess it," she whispered. "Oh, Barto, it's wicked

of me. I know it is. But you do know my very heart. I want Diego like that. What am I to do?"

Barto looked as if he wanted to speak, but he hesitated. "I know not," he said finally. "I wish I could give you ease. I've always loved Diego, and now I love you, too. But I'm beginning to understand that love is not what I thought it was."

He smiled wryly. "I'm learning from Diego. Love's not merely enjoying a lover's touch or a passionate kiss, as wonderful as those things are. Love's also…" he quirked an eyebrow "…locking a woman in a tiny closet to keep her from rash action, even though you know she'll scratch your eyes out for it later. It's agreeing to marry her to your brother if she wishes it, even though you're dying inside because you want her for yourself. And, perhaps the hardest of all, it's setting her aside when your heart most desires that you lie with her."

He looked down, as if embarrassed at his own forthrightness. "I'm sorry, *señorita*. I'm grieved by the pain I see you both experiencing, but I know not how it can be resolved. It would be the easiest thing in the world for you and Diego to consummate your desires. And yet it would be the hardest thing, too, for later there'd be immeasurable hurt. Worse, I think, than even that which you now feel. And I'm so sorry."

Celeste sank down onto her pallet, not wanting Barto to see her tears. It was truth, every word. She lay still, letting her heart seek out its own truths, knowing she would not be happy with the path it would probably find. She loved Diego so much she could scarcely contain it, but she loved him so much that she *must* contain it. Never in her whole life had she wanted something so badly and yet failed to pursue it.

Barto was still sound asleep now. Celeste was wide awake, reliving all that had been said. She knew she should rest, but her heart was uneasy. She didn't trust Barto's assurances that all was well and Diego was safe. If only she could somehow slip out of the door and find out.

She sat up and pushed aside the blanket, her fingers stretching out into the darkness towards the rough splinters of the floor and the softer fabric-covered flesh of the man who snored softly near her.

Barto had told her that years of fighting enemies had made him wary, even at night, and she fully expected to hear his deep voice question her at any moment. But as she eased off her pallet and crawled over him to the door his breathing remained deep and even, without even a hitch to indicate that he was disturbed.

The latch was locked. There was a padlock and a keyhole. No wonder her warden could sleep soundly. He held the key.

Suddenly she remembered Roberta Jiles. Roberta had come to the convent at about the same time as Celeste, but from a much different background. Roberta had been a foundling of the London streets, a tough and gritty survivor who'd already encountered more raw life in her ten years than most people would in an entire lifetime. Her rough existence had taken a turn for the better when an elderly woman of wealth had discovered the child digging for food through piles of refuse and, enchanted by the child's hauntingly beautiful visage and world-weary eyes, had taken her in. Thus Roberta had come to be educated at Celeste's convent school.

What an education Roberta had been for Celeste and the other girls there. Within a few weeks the lucky street urchin had taught them all the fine art of picking pockets, as well as everything she'd ever learned about scamming, bilking, and swindling the unwary. It had seemed great fun at the time, and they had all been truly and vastly disappointed when the nuns had discovered their new entertainments and called for Roberta's patron to come and retrieve the girl.

Now, cloaked in the darkness of the stifling closet, Roberta's lessons came back to Celeste. She could pick Barto's pockets and find that key. Moving with great stealth, Celeste eased her way alongside the sleeping giant, her fingertips no more than a whisper against the rough cloth of his doublet. She moved slowly, deliberately, almost afraid even to breathe. In no more than a minute she held the warm, smooth metal of the key firmly within her clenched palm. She crawled around Barto's prone figure, making straight for the door.

Even the click of the lock as it released did not disturb Barto's slumber, nor the muted squeak of the hinges as Celeste inched out through a crack barely wide enough for her small body. Only when she stood in the darkness on the other side did she allow herself to breathe again.

After the airless murk of the hold, the main deck seemed cool and refreshing, bathed in enough soft moonlight that she could see without bumping into anything or tripping over the huge coils of rope that lay here and there on the sea-washed planks.

Now to find Diego. A young apprentice that she recognized as having been aboard *La Angelina* passed nearby. She hissed at him. He turned. *"Dónde está el Capitán?"* she asked.

He gestured towards the quarters she and Diego had shared. *"Allá,"* he answered. She nodded her thanks and gathered her skirts, stepping over a seaman who slumbered on deck as she dashed towards the room.

The door wasn't locked, which made her frown. She eased into the room, making a mental note to warn Diego later to be more wary.

Moonlight filtered in through the curtains. She could make out the rough outline of Diego's form amid the bedclothes. She moved to his side. He lay sprawled out upon the mattress, the sheet covering his loins but little else. At the sight of that firm expanse of chest, she felt her pulse quicken. She wanted badly to reach out her finger and stroke the warm flesh, to feel the crisp curl of his hair beneath her touch. She wanted to trace it down his waist, down to where the twisted sheets tantalized her with their hidden secrets.

For a moment she debated, imagining his reaction if she were to slip quietly into the bed beside him. She could almost taste the soft, languid response of his lips as she coaxed him from his dreams, then the tightening of his muscles when he realized that it was no dream.

Her conscience intruded, marring the lovely image.

If she awoke Diego like that, he'd be in his weakest, most vulnerable state. Heavy with sleep, warm with desire, he'd be little able to resist the overwhelming tide of feeling. Their love would be consummated.

When she thought of his hips against hers, his body pushing into hers, her blood flamed and her breasts fairly throbbed with anticipation. All her wishes for proper behaviour, all her training in a lady's virtuous conduct—they fled beneath that primitive longing. She wanted Diego's heat within her.

But what then? How would Diego feel once the storm was spent and he realized he'd just placed his seed within his brother's betrothed? That he'd broken his vow to God?

He'd blame her. He'd know she caused his fall, leading him to it with soft kisses made of dreams.

Celeste wanted to growl her frustration, standing there in the silvered pool of moonlight, gazing at his tall, lean form against the crisp sheets. Why did love have to be so difficult? Why did Diego have to be right in saying that love did what was best, not what was easiest?

How long she stood there, warring with her soul in the darkness, she could not say. Everything within her wanted to reach out, to stroke Diego's skin, to lift the covers and feel his manhood grow larger and firmer beneath her gentle caresses. Only the thought of the regrets which would come later kept her rooted in place, hands clenched lest they betray her and move of their own volition towards Diego's sleeping form.

No one heard her soft groan when she turned from him. No one heard the whisper of her skirts or her stealthy footfalls when she eased out of the moonlight and back to the darkness, back to an uncomfortable pallet in an airless storeroom in the hold.

It seemed only a few moments later that Barto was shaking her awake. Her body did not want to respond, exhausted as she was from the long hours of fitful tossing before she'd finally succumbed to the sweet succour of rest.

But Barto was insistent, and Celeste's numbed brain finally comprehended that he was upset with her, that he'd discovered the storeroom door unlocked and the key missing from his pocket.

"What have you done?" he was saying, his brow furrowed. "Diego gave me orders to keep you safely, and you've done…*what?* Slipped off to him in the night and made me the buffoon? He'll never trust me again, even after all my years of serving the Castillo family with my lifeblood!"

Celeste groaned and sat up. "Nay, there's no harm done."

"You slipped out last night, didn't you? Tell me the truth before I grow mad with worry."

"Yes, I slipped out," she said. "I could take no more of this oppressive little room. No more of my worries for Diego's safety. I went to find him, to assure myself that all was well with him."

Barto slumped against the door. "And so now he knows I failed in my charge, that I did not guard you well enough."

"He doesn't know. He was asleep and I did not wake him. It was enough to know he rested peacefully in the Captain's quarters and that no harm had come to him."

"The Captain's quarters? You went to the Captain's quarters?"

"I did. And he was there, sleeping soundly."

Barto stared at her for a long moment and then laughed. "Nay, *señorita*. That was not Diego you saw. He sleeps with Ricardo, not in the Captain's quarters."

Celeste's heart skipped. "Then…?"

"That was Damian who slept so peacefully before you."

Celeste gasped. "Damian is still aboard our vessel?"

"Aye, he's now in charge of the ship and will be with us until we reach Seville. So—"

"And why has no one told me this?"

"Diego didn't wish to frighten you, but now you see the reason for your imprisonment. Diego's determined that his brother does not discover your presence. Damian is a frighteningly odd fellow, and none of us can be sure of his reaction should he find you."

Celeste shuddered, realizing for the first time how close she'd come to letting Damian know of her presence in the night.

"But how am I to endure this?" she moaned. "We've yet three or more days to Seville, and already I'm nearly mad with boredom!"

Barto glanced around at their surroundings and nodded. "I know. I grow weary of this place myself. One can only play so many hands of cards or read so many books before the body craves physical exertion. So I've devised a plan. It will have to be our secret, and we'll have to be wary of Diego, for he'll not approve it."

Celeste raised an eyebrow.

"Suppose we pass you off as an apprentice?" Barto said with a sly half-smile. "You do still have the seaman's clothing I found for you?"

Celeste nodded, her excitement growing.

"We'll have to find some linen cloth to flatten your bosom and your backside." He shrugged awkwardly. "And you'll have to take great care to stay near me and far away from both Damian and Diego. But if we're careful at least you can get out of here and let the sun warm your cheeks and the wind kiss your lips with salt spray. You can easily do the work of an apprentice by now. You know the ropes and the knots and the calls of the boatswain. Are you game for a little adventure?"

Celeste nodded, her spirits lifting already. "Aye, Barto, anything to escape this drab little room!"

"Well, then. It's settled. Today we'll attempt it, but only for a short while, and only after Diego comes with breakfast and an escort to the jakes."

At just that moment there was a soft rap on the door.

Barto grinned. "Speak of the devil…"

"…and he's sure to appear." Celeste stifled her grin. Diego, were he to see it, would surely wonder what mischief she contemplated, to smile so wickedly when there was so little to smile about.

Two days later, Celeste and Barto were still congratulating themselves. They'd escaped their restricting confines several times and nobody had been the wiser. Of course Barto had been careful. They'd waited until Diego had been occupied with other things, either studying or sleeping in his hammock. It helped that he preferred the night watches. He'd bring her the morning meal, escort her to the jakes, and then disappear to sleep. It was then that Celeste and Barto could make their way to the main deck, working alongside the other seamen as the boatswain directed the labours of the crew.

Only José Lorca had discovered her secret, but they'd sworn him to secrecy. He'd acquiesced with a chuckle and an incredulous shake of his head. Indeed, the boatswain had seemed to delight in her presence after that. He'd often set aside his own duties temporarily to work beside her, entertaining her with embellished tales of the latest gossip. With her safety assured, Barto had occasionally relaxed enough to let himself be cajoled into games of chess or poque with some of the idle mariners, or lean against the rail and smoke his pipe.

On the third day, he realized he'd relaxed a bit too much. Celeste had disappeared with José Lorca, but the boatswain reappeared without her, striding towards Barto with a grim expression.

Barto met him near the rail. "Where is she?"

"With the Captain." Lorca grimaced. "I'm sorry. I swear I didn't see him coming. We just turned around and he was there."

"The Captain? Celeste is with *Damian?*"

"Aye, she is. He was behind us, and when we turned he crooked his finger and called for the apprentice to come with him. Said he had some task to be done in his quarters."

Barto's gut twisted.

"I swear I didn't mean for such a thing to—"

"I know, I know," Barto said, already beginning to stride away. "But she can't be alone with him. If he discovers who she is, we're all fit for the Devil."

Lorca stared after him, crossing himself frantically and muttering what sounded like prayers, understanding that something must be terribly amiss if one so dauntless as that huge African could show such fear on his visage.

Celeste tried to calm her wildly beating heart and concentrate on acting her part well. She'd do the task the Captain required, keeping her eyes lowered and her shoulders hunched so he'd not suspect a thing. Then, as soon as she was able, she'd race for the entrance to the hold and disappear into the darkness and the safety of her storeroom prison. Suddenly the excitement of her adventure seemed much abated. She was frightened, more frightened than she could remember being in many years.

A terrible sense of foreboding had descended upon her the moment she'd turned and discovered Damian Castillo staring at her. Something in his face, something in his eyes, had filled her with dread. Outwardly he'd done nothing amiss, only called for the apprentice she was pretending to be.

Damian now stepped aside and let her pass into his quarters first. He looked backwards, to see if others lounged anywhere near the entrance, then closed the door. To Celeste's dismay, he locked it. He turned to face her, standing very straight. He did not move. Her imagination fled in thousands of errant directions.

He knew. He must know. What other reason could there be for his strange behaviour? Yet she would not let him see the worry on her face. She would act out the charade to the bitter end.

"Well, Cap'n," she said in English, mimicking the accent of a London street urchin. "I don' see nothin' here what needs doin'."

Damian smiled. Slowly, wickedly. "Nay, I don't suppose you would."

Celeste shrugged. "Well, if you tell me what you're needin' done I'll get to it and out your way. I know a cap'n has got business to 'tend to, and I don' want t'be a bother to ya."

Damian canted his head. "You're English, aren't you, lad? How, then, did you come to be sailing aboard my ship?"

"Pirates." Celeste wiped her mouth with her sleeve. "Captured my ship, they did, and me with it. Killed my family but left me alive, seein's how I could work."

Damian nodded. "What's your name?"

"Evan Couch, m'lord. Now, about that job you was needin'—"

"You know, Evan…a ship's lord such as myself is a very powerful man. Whatever I say is the law aboard my own vessel."

Celeste nodded. "Aye, Cap'n. I know that. 'Tis why I came here so quick to do service."

"And you also realize, Evan Couch, that there are many rewards for those who please the lord of the vessel."

"Aye, Cap'n. Like I said—"

Damian stepped forward, so near Celeste could barely suppress a shudder. He reached up with a firm hand and grasped her chin, raising her face. Her eyes met his for one brief, frightened second before she quickly averted her gaze.

"You're a handsome lad," Damian said. "So attractive you could almost pass for a woman."

Celeste's stomach lurched.

"So attractive I'm convinced you *are* a woman."

Celeste could not speak.

Damian studied her closely. "Take off your clothes. We'll see if you tell the truth. Either way—male or female, pirate's slave or stowaway—an unexpected boon for me. Remove your clothing."

Celeste stared at him aghast.

His eyes were hot with intensity. They never left her as he reached down to unfasten the points which connected the upper stocks of his hose. "Watching you move about the decks in man's garb has had quite an effect on me." He hitched his thumbs into his breeches and drew them down. "Quite an effect. Look for yourself and see."

Celeste felt her insides churn. The man's nakedness was appalling and he wanted to... She gasped for air and wheeled away. "Nay, m'lord," she stuttered. "You mustn't... Such things aren't decent!"

He chuckled, moving closer. "Come now. There's reward in this for you, should you please me well." Suddenly Celeste found herself grasped firmly from behind.

"Nay, m'lord!" she gasped, trying to wrench away. "Release me or I'll yell and alert the other sailors."

He shrugged. "Yell all you want. They know me well enough. I dare say none will venture anywhere near this room."

His laughter came again, malevolent, tinged with excitement.

At that moment a knock sounded on the door, accompanied by a strident voice. "Captain! Captain!"

"Go away!" Damian growled. "I don't wish to be disturbed!"

"I'm sorry, sir," came the reply, "but the steward says your presence is needed on deck immediately. Two of the seamen have engaged in a knife fight. There's been a bad scene, sir, and you must come attend to the matter immediately."

"Damn the bloody bastards!" Damian released her and wheeled about, jerking his hose up over his hips. He turned and pointed at her. "You...stay right where you are! If you think to flee my presence, remember I am lord of this ship. There's no place for you to hide, and should you try I'll be neither gentle nor forgiving when I find you."

With that, he turned and left, the key clicking in the lock before his footsteps hurried away. Celeste shivered, her hand flying involuntarily to her throat in an effort to keep down rising gorge.

A moment later she heard the key twist again. She looked about frantically for something which could be turned into a weapon, determined not to let Damian Castillo touch her. If she must, she'd geld the man.

The door swung open. Barto stood in it. "Celeste, come!" He motioned frantically. "Hurry!"

She raced towards him. "Oh, thank God! You'll not believe what Damian thought to do."

"Oh, aye," Barto whispered as they hurried towards the deck. "I know. Now, come. No more words until we have you safely ensconced in your storeroom."

For once Celeste made no complaint. That cramped storeroom with its cockroaches and hard pallet on splintering planks had never been more appealing.

Chapter Thirteen

They entered the port of Sanlúcar in mid-afternoon of the following day. Diego Castillo, standing at the ship's rail, knew relief like he'd never known it before. They'd almost made it. So far Celeste was safe. His brother hadn't discovered her presence.

Diego's hands worked at their tasks but his mind was far away, making plans. He'd wait for the crew to become busy with their preparations for docking, then he'd ease below to talk to Barto. He needed to get Celeste off this ship immediately, even though it would mean sending Ricardo ahead to procure rooms in a decent inn. Every hour she remained aboard was another hour of possible danger, for Damian had acted more bizarrely than normal during the last twenty-four hours, practically tearing the ship apart looking for an apprentice who, apparently, did not exist. The entire crew had been engaged in the search, but luckily the steward in charge of the storeroom had wisely held his tongue, thanks to the generous coin Diego had slipped into his palm. Celeste's hiding place had not been ransacked, as had the rest of the vessel.

But Diego could not rest. His brother seemed more mad with each passing day. Twice Damian had called for him, and while Diego might generously call that which had passed between them conversation, it had in reality been little more than two strange displays of his brother's aberrant emotions.

Damian remained convinced that their father was trying to murder him and that his younger twin was the heir of choice. He would rant and growl by turns, proposing all manner of remedies for remaining alive and in control of his father's wealth. Only by sheer dint of will had Diego withstood the extraordinary demonstrations, especially when Damian had repeatedly proposed striking his father dead before Alejandro could kill him first.

Diego had realized in those moments that the eerie light in his brother's eyes was madness, sheer madness, and that nothing he could say would return reason to his brother's tormented mind. Instead, he'd held his tongue and listened, gleaning more information about his brother than he had ever wished to know.

Oddly enough, the only thing which seemed to bring comfort to Damian was the sight of Diego's priestly robe, so Diego wore it constantly now. At times he'd feel as if he were being watched, and he'd turn to find his brother's bright stare upon him. Once he'd passed near enough that his brother had reached out and seized the silver crucifix in an iron fist, jerking Diego towards him by the heavy chain. Fearing violence, Diego had been surprised instead when his brother had gazed upon the image of Christ with a strange reverence. Damian had kissed the cold silver and let it drop, pivoting away on one booted heel to bark out commands at the crew as if nothing odd had occurred at all.

Yet the same robe which brought comfort to Damian did not bring comfort to Diego, even though he feared what the uneasiness might mean. On the exterior, he seemed much as when Celeste and Barto and Padre Francisco had found him. He'd abandoned his brother's appearance and gone back to his own. He was cleanshaven once again, and his hair had grown longer.

On the inside, however, he was different. Before he'd been

at peace—or imagined that he had been. Now he experienced emotions that left him scarcely able to rest and made him feel raw and vulnerable.

More than once he'd considered simply fleeing this responsibility he'd undertaken. More than once he'd wished to simply walk away from Celeste and his family and return to his quiet cell with its warm-smelling leather books, and to his peaceful chapel with its candles that threw fragrant, flickering shadows upon the altar and cross of gold.

But each time he thought of leaving something cold and ferocious gripped his heart and he knew he could not leave. At first he'd convinced himself that Celeste needed him. He was not the sort of man to leave her defenceless.

Now he knew better.

His feelings had little to do with honour and everything to do with love. He'd never been more fearful of anything in his whole life.

He'd asked God to take away his desire for her. It had only deepened. He'd prayed to somehow find strength to withstand what he felt. Instead, he'd come ever closer to consummating his carnal lust. There had been no solace for him, not anywhere. And soon, very soon, he'd have to let her go.

He thought about the future. Either Celeste would be married to Damian or she would not. If she decided to go through with it, he'd attend the ceremony with his heart slowly fragmenting into quivering flesh, hearing those beautiful, sacred vows as she promised them to his brother. To love. To honour. To cherish. Even knowing that Damian would never love or honour or cherish her.

And, worse, there would come that moment when Padre Francisco joined their hands and pronounced them man and wife. Diego would want to gasp at the rending of his heart, knowing the finality of that moment, like death itself.

Beyond that he could not even consider. The thought of his brother tasting her sweet flesh was more than Diego could bear. The thought of Damian burying himself within her, giving her the seed from which would come the Castillo heir... Diego closed his eyes. He just couldn't think on it.

And yet Celeste had said she'd not marry Damian. At first that knowledge had been a comfort, knowing she'd not be abused by Damian's cruelties and lusts.

But then Diego had realized that he'd lose her, too.

At least if Celeste married his brother she'd be part of the family and he might see her occasionally, as painful as that would be, as bittersweet the torment. He'd ache to hold her, though he could never let her know it. But he'd see her. He could enjoy her smiles, see her grow large with child, hear her coo over the cradle of her baby—and almost, *almost,* he would be able to pretend it was he who'd made her smile, he who'd given her the child she carried, he who'd grow old at her side.

But if she did not marry Damian he'd lose her. She'd go back to England and soon, much too soon, they'd receive word through a cousin or a friend of a friend that Lady Celeste Rochester had married some titled nobleman and begun another whole life.

And that thought hurt more than he had ever imagined it would.

Diego had never dreamed he'd be thankful for sin, but there it was—and he smiled at the irony. With the sailors gone to visit the taverns and whorehouses, the ship was almost completely deserted. He could slip Celeste, Barto and Hettie down the gangplank without anyone knowing.

Celeste seemed remarkably subdued, as she had been for the last day or two. He wasn't sure what had brought about the change, and he wasn't sure he liked it. She seemed miserable. Her face was pale and wan, her thoughts distracted in a way that disturbed him. He'd questioned Barto about it, but the big man had shrugged it off. "She's tired of being confined," Barto had said. "Tired, and unsure about many things. The nearer we come to Seville, the nearer she comes to making her decision about Damian."

Now, as Diego led Barto, Celeste and Hettie through the darkness, each cloaked against the cooler air of night and carrying small bundles of clothing, he pondered Barto's words and debated what course of action would be best. The agony was that he'd spent years bearing the problems of others, listening with a tender heart and counselling with as much wisdom as he could find.

But Celeste he was unable to help. His emotions were too entwined. The most logical choice was that she return to England and marry well, but Diego couldn't bring himself to wish that for her.

Still, he wanted to give her comfort somehow, and so, after he'd ensconced them safely in their rooms at the Strutting Peacock Inn, he wandered the streets and pondered and prayed. The wares in a merchant's display caught his eye and he stepped closer to look.

A few minutes later he stepped away again, smiling, tucking a small leather-wrapped purchase underneath his arm.

Celeste opened the door at his knock, her face curious and expectant. "Diego?" She sounded breathless. "You've returned?"

"It occurred to me that perhaps you haven't yet supped," he said.

She looked perplexed. "Of course I have. You yourself brought me my meal of ship's biscuit and salted meat."

"Ship's biscuit and salted meat! What kind of decent food is that? I wonder if you'd accompany me down to the common room below for something more palatable?"

The excitement which lit her eyes and the speed with which she accepted his proffered arm caused a strange buoyancy to come to his heart. With a nod to Hettie, he pulled Celeste into the hallway.

"Hold one minute!" Hettie called from behind them. "'Tis not meet for a young lady to accompany a gentleman without a proper chaperon. I'll get my shawl and—"

Diego fixed her with a stern look. "Nay, madam. Your desire

to maintain propriety is admirable, but I think society bears no ill will towards any man who wears this garment." He waved his hand down the length of his robe. "Certainly a young lady should be safe from slanderous assault while with a priest, wouldn't you imagine?"

Hettie frowned and stammered, unable to come up with a suitable reply. Before she could find her tongue, Diego had turned his most sincere smile upon her and stepped quickly out, closing the door with finality behind him.

Celeste squeezed his arm as they walked away down the dimly lit corridor. "Oh, Diego! You did it! I've never seen Hettie at such a loss for words." She giggled, and then muffled the sound with a delicate hand against her lips.

Diego stopped and looked down at her. Her eyes grew dark and wide in the soft glow of the single candle which lit the confined space. And then, as if he had no care at all for his reputation or for hers, he gathered her into his arms and savoured the sultry taste of the woman he loved.

Celeste had not expected Diego to kiss her. Indeed, she hadn't expected him to return to the inn and knock at her door. But when she saw the mischief in his blue eyes, and the jaunty demeanour with which he greeted her, she could no more deny him her presence than she could fly to the moon. Her very being yearned for him, as it had every single minute she'd spent locked away in the cramped storeroom. His daily visits there had been hurried and brief, and the worry which had tinged his brow had affected her as well.

But tonight Diego seemed different. His eyes gleamed with something that made Celeste respond to him immediately. She was only too glad to accompany him wherever he wished to go, although she knew it was not food for which she truly hungered.

And now he'd kissed her, pulling her so tightly against him that her breasts scrubbed against the coarse robe he wore, the silver crucifix pressing painfully into the warm cleft of her bosom. His mouth was warm and hungry, with a fervency that made her heart beat wildly. When at last he loosened his grasp and let her pull back he was breathing hard, his nostrils flaring. His eyes were deepest sapphire.

She could only stare up into his face, wanting to pull him to her again but knowing such an action would be foolhardy and dangerous. Madness, it was, the way she felt about him. Such madness, to want him so badly she hardly cared what anyone thought, or what might be said if they were discovered here in this dark corridor, wrapped in an embrace the likes of which no priest should ever know.

"I should say I'm sorry for that," Diego said, his voice husky with desire. "But I'm not. I've missed your company. I've missed you."

"Don't be sorry for anything. I would that we might fill up our store with memories enough to last for ever! I would that you might kiss me again and again, and do more besides. I love you, Diego. I cannot but wish to share that love with you, in whatever form it might take."

She saw Diego's eyes begin to burn and knew he understood what she asked. He hesitated for the briefest of seconds, then drew in a deep breath and stepped backwards. "Come, my love. We need to be in the company of others, lest I forget all but this moment and do something we'll both regret for ever."

"I'll not regret. I'll never regret one moment I've spent with you."

Diego smiled, but the humour did not reach his eyes. He reached out one finger to trace the delicate tilt of her nose. "Aye, you would regret. When you grew big-bellied with my child and bore the shame of his bastardy, you would regret."

"Nay, I would not. I want to bear your seed, Diego."

She heard the sharp inhalation of his breath. When he spoke, his voice sounded oddly strangled. "Sweet mercy. You know not what you say."

"I do know what I say." Her hand came up to caress the firm

line of his jaw. "I want to know you, Diego. Every inch of you. I want you to place your seed within me. I want to bear your child."

"I cannot let you endure the shame."

"It would be no shame to me. Whatever the world might say of me, I'd know in my heart that I'd chosen the right thing."

"I cannot marry you, Celeste. Even without my vow…the Church's rules of affinity forbid it."

Celeste silenced him with a kiss. "It matters not. I don't care if I never marry, as long as you and I consummate our love. Making love with you would be binding enough. Tonight, Diego. We can become lovers tonight. And then, no matter what happens in my future, I would be content."

Diego struggled. His face was hard. "What then? Would you marry Damian and for ever wonder if the heir which springs forth is my issue or his?"

"I'll not marry Damian."

"Some other man, then. Some English nobleman with a fine name and a fancy title. One who'll never question why his young wife did not stain the sheets with her virginal blood, and who'll never wonder why his firstborn son looks nothing like him? Dear God, Celeste!" He pulled away and stared at her. "I cannot deny that every fibre of my being strains towards the offer you're making me. Believe me, I'd love nothing better than to have your sweet flesh beneath me. I've been long tortured with the want of you. But think on it. Think what our decision would mean to others."

"I don't care about others right now. I don't care about the future. I only know that I'm about to lose you, Diego, and I don't want to leave you without…without knowing. Without memories. Without your child growing within me." She pivoted away, hugging herself tightly. "I know I seem wanton, but I don't care. I know I'm being selfish. I don't care."

Her voice cracked. "I know all your reasons for putting me aside, Diego. I know about Leonora, but, curse it all— I want you the same as she. I envy her, Diego. She made love with you. She knew what it felt like to look into your face as you sheathed yourself within her. She stroked your skin in that moment when you lost control and shuddered and gave her your seed. She carried your child… Dear God, how I envy that woman!"

Diego pulled Celeste backwards into his embrace and held her gently. "Nay, Celeste. Don't be grieved this way." He turned her to face him and reached up a gentle finger to wipe away the tears that had begun to trace down her cheeks. "Don't envy Leonora. I didn't know then what love was meant to be, and I never loved her well enough. My love for her was a selfish thing. An immature thing. A lustful and careless thing, with far too little understanding and far too little wisdom. The love I bear you is nothing like it."

Celeste began to cry.

"Don't cry, my sweet Celeste. For truly…" He took her hand and placed it on his chest. "You alone have my heart. I pledge it to you this day and for eternity. This vow I make to you now is as binding to my soul as any words of matrimony I might speak. I pledge my life to you. I pledge my heart to you. I will never love any other but you, and I shall love you to my dying day. This is my solemn vow to you, Celeste." He withdrew a small, leather-wrapped bundle. "Sealed between us this day with this." He withdrew a ring and placed it on her finger, a ring of three pearls entwined in a ribbon of gold.

Celeste stared at it, and then raised questioning eyes to his face.

"Three pearls," he whispered. "One to represent the love I bear you. One for the love you bear me. The third for the love of the Almighty, who has now witnessed this, my troth to you. Gold, because love is worth much. And pearls, because they signify purity and integrity—which, in spite of all, we still must maintain." He drew her again into his embrace. "So no, my love, I cannot give you my child. I ask you to be content with my heart in its stead, and to wear this ring as a reminder that wherever you go in this world, whatever your future brings, you shall always, *always,* have the love of Diego Castillo."

He kissed her gently and turned, leading her down the corridor to the staircase.

Later, the serving girl who brought them food must have wondered how it could be that a pale young woman and a kind-eyed priest could smile at one another with such tender fondness, even as tears ran, unheeded, down their cheeks.

Chapter Fourteen

⁓⁓⁓⁓⁓

Barto's knock came early. Celeste and Hettie struggled to shake off sleep and greet the muted light streaming in through shuttered windows. Hettie donned her wrapper and went to the door, opening it just enough that Celeste could see the tiniest sliver of her protector and friend through it. His voice was quiet but its deep tone travelled. They were to dress and eat quickly and be on their way. Diego had purchased horses. They'd ride to Seville, rather than return to Damian's pirate vessel, now disguised as nothing more than a merchant ship flying the flag of the King of Spain.

Celeste didn't mind not going back. Her body craved activity. The thought of returning to the dark storeroom, even for the short trip up the Guadalquivir, made her feel anxious.

Then there was the possibility that she might be discovered by her betrothed. The mere thought made her skin crawl. She'd not yet forgotten the utter panic she'd felt, or the horror. She still hadn't completely come to terms with the man's depravity. Each time she thought of it utter revulsion made her nauseous.

As Hettie combed her curls into order she looked down at the ring on her finger, determined to think on happier things. And right now the happiest thing she could think of was Diego. Oh, his kisses! How they had warmed her, that she would have chanced discovery in his arms in a public corridor! His kiss had inflamed her past reason, past caring for aught save more of his sweet passion. She was too much in love.

She had wanted more than his kisses, but here in the light of a new day her face flamed at the memory of the things she'd said. Surely she'd been mad to say them, mad to wish for the infamy of a bastard child, fathered by a *priest!* She must have taken momentary leave of her senses.

Thankfully, Diego had not taken leave of his. He'd understood the consequences more clearly than she, and now she was thankful his sanity had prevailed.

Yet, in a strangely logical way, the things she'd uttered were *right.* She wanted badly to lie with Diego and to get with child by him, to bear him a son with golden hair and blue-green eyes. To be his woman.

She ran a fingertip across the ring and tried not to cry. Diego would say that she already *was* his, and that nothing short of death could take that away from her. But how odd that it didn't seem so, not until their flesh was made one.

She sighed. Hettie stopped combing, her face suddenly wary in the silvered mirror. "What are ye thinking now, that you sigh like the world rests on your tiny shoulders?"

Celeste shrugged. "'Tis nothing. Nothing that can be changed, at any rate."

"Ah, lamb. You're pining for the love of the Padre. I guess he's pining for your love, too, since he gave you that pretty bauble you're wearing on your finger now."

Celeste glanced up. "You noticed it?" Celeste traced the ring with one finger. "Aye, he gave it to me. A token, I suppose, of our time together. I just wish…"

Hettie shook her head. "Nay, love, don't even put it into words. A priest can do nothing about such feelings. He has to bury them."

Celeste's eyes filled with tears. "I want him, Hettie. I know it's wanton of me, but I cannot help what I feel."

"Ah, lass, don't be thinking such thoughts. He can't wed you."

"I know," Celeste said, looking down at her hands folded in her lap. "Sometimes I wonder if that would even matter. Can two people not share a true bond even without words spoken to make it public? Could they not feel as committed to one another regardless of ceremony and vows?"

Hettie straightened painfully. "You cannot mean these things. You cannot mean you'd lie with him, and him a priest."

Celeste didn't answer.

Hettie stepped back. "You must not do that. You know it would be wrong!"

"My heart says differently. I love him."

"He's sworn to the Lord!"

"Aye, I know it. And for that reason we've restrained our feelings until now."

Hettie let out a breath. "Thank God above for small mercies. It would not do for you to conceive his child."

Celeste raised her head. "I'd not be ashamed to conceive his child. I love Diego Castillo. I want no other."

"What of your betrothal? Your marriage? What about Jacob?"

Celeste drew in a sharp breath. "There will be no marriage to Damian. Indeed, there may be no marriage to anyone."

Hettie's brows drew together ominously. "And what about your brother?"

"I'll manage."

"A woman alone?"

"I have wealth. I can leave England and take Jacob with me. I can go…other places."

Hettie's eyes narrowed. "Places like where? The Spanish Indies? And what would you do there? Dally with your priest until you grow big-bellied with his child? What would be the result then? The world would know what you'd become—the kept mistress of a priest! My Lord, child! Your love has led you to folly! You'll destroy yourself and you'll destroy him."

Celeste burst into tears. "I know!" she cried. "God help me, I don't know what to do. I love Diego so much I hurt all the time. I want him, but each day carries me closer to leaving him!" She dissolved into sobs.

"There, there," Hettie soothed, drawing Celeste into her arms. "We'll devote ourselves to prayer, and in time all will be made plain to you, you'll see." But in her heart, Hettie knew there was a bit more to be done than pray, and that she'd be the very one to do it.

Barto was not the frivolous sort, and Celeste could only marvel at his present demeanour. He fairly danced as he led her, blindfolded, along the uneven pathway towards the stables.

"Slowly, Barto!" Celeste complained. "It's bad enough that you insisted on tying this scarf over my eyes, but to lead me so quickly over so rough a path! You must wish me to fall headlong so you'll be rid of my worrisome presence!"

Barto laughed. "Nay, *señorita*. No such devious plan." He grasped her shoulders. "Here. Stop here. Now take off that scarf and know that when a Spaniard buys a horse, he buys a *horse!*"

Celeste tore at the scarf, not even wincing when the knot came loose with several strands of her hair.

Before her stood the most magnificent horse she'd ever seen, a white stallion with flowing mane and tail and the lovely, delicate head of an Arabian. On its back, a beautifully tooled sidesaddle. "Oh, my goodness!" she breathed. She moved forward, her hand extended.

The horse pricked curious ears in her direction, whuffling slightly and nodding his head as she drew apace. Celeste touched his nose and looked into the warmest, most intelligent brown eyes she'd ever seen on an animal. Her heart did a crazy dance within her breast.

Barto chuckled. "His name is Farolillo," he said. "It means 'fairy light' in your English tongue, I believe."

Celeste was rubbing the stallion's neck and ears, but she stopped and looked at Barto. "You say Diego purchased him for me?"

"He did. Early this morn. Ricardo came ashore yesterday with orders to purchase our mounts. And, while Diego was most specific in his instructions to purchase you a mount of excellent quality, even Ricardo was reluctant to pay the amount of coin that this one—"

"Diego wanted me to have him? But why? Any horse would have been sufficient for the ride to Seville, and I don't wish to spend more of the Castillos's wealth than is necessary."

Barto smiled. "Ah, my lady, you're not at all like other women if you're loath to spend a rich man's coin. The Castillo family has more than can be enjoyed in a lifetime, thanks to Alejandro's skill with investment. But, see here, Diego purchased this gift for you with his *own* money. He wanted you to have something rare and special. Something, he said, as precious as the time you've spent on your adventure."

And something to say goodbye, Celeste thought. She resumed stroking the horse. "Farolillo. There's a name I must practise. My tongue stumbles over it. Farolillo."

Barto grinned. "Call him Faro, if that's easier. Diego was quite taken with the name, you know. He said something about how apt it was. A fairy light for a fairy princess."

Celeste looked up. "Oh, Barto! He didn't!"

"Aye, he did." Barto leaned closer and whispered. "Diego's in love with both of you, fairy light and fairy princess."

Celeste tried to ignore the sudden flip of her heart. "What an honour. To share his affections with a horse!"

The next moment the stable boys who laboured nearby stopped in their tasks and looked in their direction, perhaps wondering what had caused the huge black man in the yard to guffaw so loudly and with such obvious enjoyment. That was, until they noticed the vibrant beauty of the delicate lady beside him, who struggled, against great odds, to keep from laughing, too.

Diego was inspecting the great ropes of hemp that would be used, along with the capstan, to raise the heavy anchors

when it was time to move out of the bay and up the Guadalquivir. He was running his hands along their rough surfaces,
looking for frayed or weak places, when Ricardo's shadow fell
across the deck beside him.

"Diego, I'll take over that task," he said. "There's someone
here who needs to talk with you."

Diego frowned. "Right now?"

Ricardo grinned. "You're ready to make haste to Seville, I
see. But, aye, I think you'll want to talk to this visitor. 'Tis
Hettie, Diego."

Diego straightened abruptly. "Hettie? But she's supposed
to be leaving for Seville this morning!" He wiped the grime
off his hands and hurried to follow Ricardo down the gangplank.

Hettie stood among the bustle on the quay, her dark cloak
pulled up over her head to shield her fair skin from the strong
sunlight. "Padre Diego!" she said, extending her hands.

Diego took them and leaned down to kiss the old lady on
the brow. "Lady Celeste is well, I hope?"

"Aye, she's well, and mighty pleased with the lovely horse
you bought her."

Ricardo groaned. "Now, isn't that always the way? I find
the animal and Diego gets all the credit."

Diego grinned at him. "When you put down your half of
the purchase price, perhaps I'll share the lady's gratitude with
you."

Ricardo held up his hands in a helpless gesture. "Ah, but
there's the problem. I'm a poor *encomendero* whose priest has
led me to such generous acts of penance that I can scarce afford
to buy a lady a meal, much less a beast as fine as that you
bought for Celeste. And truly, Diego, had I known you to be
so wealthy—"

Diego waved him off. "Nay, Ricardo, no more. Had you not
spent so much of your earnings on your sinful ways, you'd be
a wealthy man today, far wealthier than I. Off with you now,
and let me speak with my visitor in peace."

Ricardo laughed, and moved away with a shake of his head.

"Please forgive us, *señorita*." Diego smiled. "We are like schoolboys released from our lessons now that your mistress has reached safety."

"Aye, and she's doing well, Padre. She bade me give you this." Hettie pulled a letter from the folds of her cloak. "Told me to put it into your own hand, she did."

Diego looked down at the letter, at the lovely flowing script that adorned it. "Thank you, Hettie. You've done well. But tell me. Were you not supposed to have left by now?"

"Aye," Hettie said. "But Barto took my mistress to eat after letting her see the pretty horse—and he is a lovely beast, m'lord, such a lovely beast—!"

"Celeste liked Farolillo?"

"Oh, she did. I've never seen her quite so delighted over any gift ever in her whole life, unless it be the ring you gave her last night—"

Diego frowned. "You know about the ring?"

"It's the reason I hurried to see you 'ere we left. To give this letter into your own hand and to have a talk with you, Padre Diego. A private talk about my little miss and the terrible things you're doing to her heart."

"Now, Hettie—"

"Nay, *señor*. You will listen to what this old woman has to say, if only because that Scripture you teach from says you're to show respect for your elders."

Diego raised an eyebrow. "I'm listening."

"The lass loves you past all distraction. You must feel something for her, too, else you'd not be presenting her with these fine gifts."

"Aye, I love her. I suppose there's no shame in admitting that, even though I be a priest."

Hettie studied his face. "And 'tis true that you've not…ah…deflowered…my little lamb?"

Diego stifled a groan. "Nay, Hettie. She's still most virtuous and untried."

"That's good, for I swear before all that's holy if you ever so much as lay your finger where it is not supposed to be—"

Diego held up a hand. "Hettie, please. I intend to stay true to my vow to God."

"And if you don't, you'll answer to more than God, *señor*, because—"

"Truly, Hettie, my brother will never have to—"

"Nay, I do not mean your brother. You doubtless know as well as I that my lady has no wish to marry him. And if she doesn't wish for something she'll ne'er do it, she's that stubborn."

"You're disappointed she's changed her mind?"

"Nay, I'm not. I never cared for the gentleman, though he is your brother and a wealthy man of title. I'm upset because she loves you to the point of leaving behind everything she was ever taught to be and everything she ever planned to do— leave it all, and for what? To hie herself off to your tropical island and get bastard whelps off you despite the fact that you are a *priest*."

Diego choked. "What are you talking about?"

"That's what she said this morning. All kinds of foolishness about running away and she didn't care if she bore your child and that there could be commitment between two people even without the vows of matrimony—"

"Dear Lord!" Diego felt as if someone had just kicked him in the groin. "Hettie, I love the girl, but I've never proposed that she do anything so foolish. Are you quite sure she was serious? Perhaps that was just her frustration speaking."

"I cannot be sure," Hettie admitted. "But it frightens me that she's not even considering how difficult life would be for her as a woman alone. And she thinks to raise Jacob on her own, too, as if it would be of little import whether he grew up without a proper education or—"

"Jacob? Who is Jacob?"

Hettie stopped in confusion. "You don't know? She's never told you?"

"Nay. Told me what?"

"About her brother. Her wee brother, only six years of age. Nay, seven, he must be now, since he had a birthday two weeks ago."

"I thought Celeste had no close kin."

"She doesn't, save for Jacob. Her parents are dead, and the little lad…oh, he's suffered from the loss. Hasn't spoken one word since his parents died. It's why my lamb's been so set to marry. She wanted to take Jacob out of that monastery and give him a home where he can laugh and smile and talk again."

Diego drew in a deep breath. "And now that she loves me she'll not marry Damian, and there'll be no marriage and no help for Jacob. Am I following you?"

"No matter that she'll not marry Don Damian, for he'll not be good to either of them. But I'd hoped she'd return to England and marry a fine lord who'd give the lad a proper education and help him make his way in the world."

"Only now she won't."

"Aye, that be what she's saying, Padre, and she's always been an impetuous girl who goes after her wishes, even if they be contrary to common sense."

Diego could well believe that. "What do you want me to do?"

"If you weren't a priest sworn to God, I'd tell you to marry the lass posthaste," she said. "But, since that can't be done, you'll do her the greatest kindness by setting her away from you."

"She'll be leaving soon enough, anyway."

"Aye, but as long as she thinks you love her she'll follow you to the ends of the earth, not settle down and put herself into a sensible marriage."

"So what are you saying? That I must pretend I don't love her? That I must act as if she means nothing to me?"

"Aye, Padre, that's exactly what I'm saying."

"That would be a lie, Hettie. I long for her with every waking breath."

"I know. But 'tis oft said the sharpest cut is the kindest. In this case it might keep the lass from destroying herself."

Diego nodded. He understood the truth that stared him in the face. The problem was, he didn't know if he could do it. It might possibly keep Celeste from destroying her life, but he knew without any doubt that it would definitely destroy his.

Chapter Fifteen

❧❧❧❧❧❧

Five days later, as Padre Francisco stood on the street outside the high wall that enclosed the Castillo estate, he could not remember any time he'd felt more uneasy about a task of pastoral care. He dreaded what lay before him.

Barto looked down at him and sighed. "It's an awful wait, I know. Yet a few more minutes and all will be accomplished."

"This waiting gnaws at me. Where are they? Why haven't they arrived yet?"

Barto shrugged. "You know Damian. He should have been a player on the stage, where he could for ever put his dramatic bent to practical use. I'm glad Celeste is safe at the inn and won't see the way he'll likely shock his poor parents."

"Break their hearts, you mean," Francisco muttered. "They know nothing except that the twins are both now in Seville, safe and sound. I sent them that message last night, only that and nothing more. Damian threatened to cut out my tongue if I breathed aught else."

"They'll be disappointed that Diego is now a priest."

Padre Francisco nodded. "More disappointed yet to realize that Damian is their only heir. Each day he grows more bizarre."

Barto placed one heavy hand on the priest's thin shoulder.

"I also dread seeing the pain that will come to Alejandro's face at the realization. But he'll be strong. He and Anne will weather this blow as they've weathered all others. And don't forget they still have us."

Francisco shook his head. "A poor, poor substitute we be for the dream that will die today."

Barto frowned. "Perhaps the dream won't die yet. Do you not remember the prayers we've prayed?"

Francisco grunted. "I'm not sure 'twas the right thing to pray for Diego and Celeste to marry. It seemed right at the time, but now?" He grimaced. "I'll try once more to convince Diego to leave the priesthood, for Alejandro and Anne's sake. Yet I doubt the result."

"Oh, ye of little faith. But no matter. I *believe.* Diego and Celeste are meant for one another. All will work round to that end."

Padre Francisco rubbed a weary hand across the tight muscles at the base of his neck. "I hope you're right, Barto. It would be a comfort if it comes to pass." He peered down the street and nodded his head in the direction that led to the harbour. "I'll try to keep that comfort in my heart during the next several minutes, for look, here the twins come yonder. It's time for the reckoning, whatever the end of it."

"Remember, my friend, that there's something in your scriptures that says knowing truth will set you free."

Francisco nodded. "Let's hope such good happens from this enterprise today."

Barto could tell, however, from the way the priest's steps lagged, that he was having a hard time convincing himself of that.

Oh, well. If it was true that faith moved mountains, then one big, heathen African would just have to muster enough faith for both of them.

It was too much, Diego thought. Simply too much. For ten years he'd been away. For six of them he'd known the quiet idyll of the tropics. He missed it now, in the noise and hustle of this city which had grown and changed while he'd been gone. There seemed too much of everything—too much noise, too many people. It set his nerves on edge.

For two nights now he'd slept only fitfully, his mind in confusion over what to do.

He knew he should put all Celeste's hopes to a sudden and calamitous death. He should walk away. But some things were easier said than done.

Sometimes loving someone was a cross to be borne, not a precious feeling to be enjoyed.

He and Damian rode together through the winding lanes of the older part of town, where the Castillo family home stood like a sentinel overlooking narrow tree-lined streets. Diego tried to put thoughts of Celeste aside. He'd soon be with his parents again, a reunion that should be joyful for him.

It should. Ten years had passed in near solitude. He'd missed them during every single day of it. Yet the joy he felt now as he neared his family home, as he passed the church where he'd studied, the market where he'd played while his mother bought shellfish and rice for paella... All the anticipated joy was swallowed up in worry that Damian would do something rash.

His brother had been quiet. Much too quiet.

Diego studied Damian from beneath lowered lashes. His twin had dressed simply. He carried on a pleasant enough conversation. That worried him. Damian seemed almost *sane*.

Diego was relieved to see Padre Francisco and Barto awaiting them. Barto wore a pistol tucked in his belt. That was reassuring.

Barto's presence told Diego that Celeste had made it to Seville. He hoped Barto hadn't brought her *here*. Diego dismounted and shook hands with the huge man. "The package I asked you to guard is now safe?"

Barto's lips twitched. "Aye," he answered, aware that Damian listened carefully to their exchange. "I left it back at the inn. I didn't think you'd wish for it today, but I can retrieve it if you wish."

Diego shook his head. "Nay, no need. Perhaps I can return with you there after I've met with my parents."

Padre Francisco gestured towards the heavy wooden portal, elaborately carved with an intricate floral motif. "Well, gentlemen. Your parents await you in the master's chambers, eager to embrace you both again. Indeed, this is a day for celebration. A captured son has been ransomed and an estranged son has been returned. They are nearly beside themselves with joy."

Diego chanced a glance at Damian. His twin's face was a mask, an impenetrable mask.

They entered the hall. Diego was assaulted by a multitude of familiar sensations. The smell of the citrus oil with which his mother polished the dark woods of the furniture, the dull clicking of his booted heels against the floor tiles, the aroma of Mediterranean food which wafted from the kitchen, where even now servants prepared the midday meal. There was the rug upon which he'd played with his toys as a boy. There was the collection of books that he and Damian had used in school, in the case of English walnut his mother had ordered shipped to her all the way from her homeland. And there, beside those books in a place of prominence, was the little clay bull he'd made for her when he'd been ten and enamoured with *la corrida*.

Feeling swept over him. He was *home*. He wished he were alone, so he could ease through the rooms slowly, sensation fully savoured, fingertips grazing each beloved piece of furniture, every remembered texture and treasure. He hadn't been prepared for the sudden inundation of warmth when he walked into this place. He was being herded past all of it much too quickly, into the courtyard, where the fountain bubbled and flowers blossomed in a riot of colour, and then pushed past even that towards the large, comfortable suite of rooms his parents claimed as their most private quarters.

They paused at the doorway while Francisco announced

their presence. Diego unconsciously ran his hands down the front of his robe, down his thighs in a nervous gesture.

Seeing it, Barto smiled. "It's been a long, long time. *Bienvenidos a casa,* Diego."

Diego merely nodded, unsure of his ability to speak.

The door opened and there they were, his mother in the forefront, his father following in his wheeled chair.

Diego felt breathless, looking again into those beloved green eyes. His mother's beauty had faded but slightly, though her blonde hair now glinted with touches of silver. Maybe she was even more beautiful than he remembered, with her eyes wide, her lips parted, her face full of joy. She held out her arms. Diego fell into them like the lost boy he suddenly felt he'd been for ten years.

"Mamá!" he breathed. "How beautiful you are!"

She seemed unable to speak. When their embrace ended, he knew she'd felt the same rush of emotion as he from the glinting of tears in her eyes. She turned and embraced Damian, too.

Diego stepped forward and clasped his father's hand. "Papá."

His father nodded, also suspiciously close to tears. An awkward moment of silence passed. Alejandro gestured towards Diego's robe. "You…you're a priest, Diego? *Dios mío,* how you must have changed."

"Aye, Papi," Diego said, reverting back to his childhood name for his father. "I'm not the same. I hope 'tis not an unwelcome shock."

His father shook his head. "Nay, my son. You're here, alive, and finally, *finally* among us again. I grieve nothing at this moment. It's a surprise, merely that. I didn't know."

Damian came forward and bowed low before their father. Alejandro held out a hand to him and Damian took it.

Alejandro smiled. Diego knew from the expression on his father's face that Damian was wrong in thinking his father capable of murder. The relief and gratitude on his father's face was genuine.

"And Damian has also returned to me, alive and unharmed," Alejandro said, nodding. "This is a day for thanksgiving to our Merciful Saviour, and a day for feasting and joy. Both my sons are home again."

Anne came to stand at his side, one delicate hand resting on his shoulder. He reached up and covered her hand with his in a loving gesture. "Ah, I am a happy man this morn," Alejandro said, his voice quavering.

He turned to where Barto and Padre Francisco stood quietly.

"My friends," Alejandro began, wheeling himself forward slightly before extending his hand. "I know not how to convey my gratitude."

The two muttered embarrassed comments, not sure how to acknowledge the tears shining in their friend's eyes.

"But tell me." Alejandro looked around. "Where is my dear *palomita?* Where is Celeste? No harm has come to the child, I pray."

Barto and Francisco looked at one another quickly, perhaps noting the stiffening of Damian's body and the way he turned accusing eyes in their direction. "Nay, Alejandro," Barto began. "The *señorita's* in fine health, and none the worse for her adventure. She'll likely join us on the morrow."

"*Bien.*" Alejandro smiled, looking back to his sons. "There's too much we've missed, but we can eat and talk at the same time. Gloria and the kitchen staff have a huge meal prepared. It will be a joy to gather once more at the same table, as when you were boys."

Diego nodded. His father, too, seemed much changed. He appeared gentler, softened by grief or years or both, as if life's small pleasures no longer went unappreciated.

Such knowledge was both honey and vinegar. Diego realized how much he loved his father, and how much he'd missed him.

A prayer formed in his heart, not spoken in words but whispered deep in his soul, that he might find peace with his family at last, and that he might be home to stay.

Anne took Diego's arm and pulled him towards the door. "Come along, everyone. The meal awaits." She laughed happily. Diego was pleased at the joy which shone in her eyes.

It was good, so good, to be part of the family again.

Alejandro let darkness creep into the room without bothering to light the lantern that sat easily within his reach. His mind was distant; he hardly noticed the waning light, or the way the last peach-coloured rays of sunlight filtered through the one tall, narrow window of his study.

A priest, he thought with a kind of helpless desperation. *Dear God, why did he have to become a priest?* His stomach tightened, then his chest, and Alejandro knew he could no longer avoid the tears he'd fought most of the afternoon. He bowed his head into a hand that seemed suddenly old and gnarled with pain.

He did not cry selfishly. He did not protest that Diego would never bear children, even though that hurt almost past belief.

Yet ever since Alejandro had discussed the journey with Barto and Francisco, he'd realized how badly his younger son still hurt, and how strong a stranglehold the guilt yet had over him. The wound had never healed.

Of all men, Diego would have suffered. Diego was the sensitive one, the loving one. He'd ever thought about the needs of others more than his own. That was why nobody had seen the tragedy coming. No one could have imagined Diego would take Leonora for himself.

In retrospect, Alejandro supposed he should have considered the possibility. Damian had never appreciated the girl, and she would have been disappointed in that. Her tender heart would have sought out someone to ease the pain, and who better than Diego, who listened with such compassion?

There had been signs. Alejandro should have seen them. The surreptitious glances between them. The shy smiles when they thought no one watched. The way Diego had sometimes appeared startled and uneasy when Leonora walked into the room on Damian's arm.

There had been those clues, but Alejandro hadn't seen them in time.

And what now of Celeste? Alejandro grunted, thinking how Barto had asked him outright if he'd wanted her to make love with Diego.

Well, what if he had?

Maybe it would have been better had she given herself to the younger twin. Alejandro couldn't say he'd sought that end deliberately, but had he done so subconsciously? Perhaps there had been a beautiful logic to his choices, even if intentional they had not been.

He rubbed his chin thoughtfully. Barto had said there was a strong attraction. Only Diego's vow and sense of honour kept them apart. Both he and Padre Francisco doubted they'd been intimate lovers, despite appearances. Both agreed that probably Celeste remained untouched, except for her heart, which was now firmly pledged to Diego.

She would refuse to marry Damian, especially now that she knew the whole truth about him.

So Alejandro would lose her, too. There'd be no lovely grandchildren with Celeste's fiery locks and dark eyes, none with her spirit and gaiety. His little dove would soon fly from him.

There was a knock at the door. Alejandro called admittance, straightening in his chair and wiping the visible signs of his grief away with a firm hand.

Diego entered, frowning at the gloom. "Papi," he said hesitantly. "I was about to take my leave, and didn't want to go without wishing you goodbye first." He gestured towards the lamp. "Should I light that for you?"

"If you would." Alejandro wished his voice didn't sound so gruff.

"Are you all right?" Diego asked. "We've not tired you overmuch, have we?"

"Nay, *hijo.* I'm not tired, only reflective. So many emotions have been aroused today, seeing you again. I need time alone to think them all through."

Diego made a short sound of agreement and lit the lantern. In the soft glow, Alejandro studied his son. Diego was a man now, tall and muscular, as fit as if he laboured in fields rather than over books. His hands were slender, but not soft, the nails short and neat. Alejandro wondered about Diego's life as a priest on an *encomienda* in the Indies. Had he been happy there? Had his choices brought him peace?

He looked up abruptly into his son's eyes, eyes so like his own except for the hint of green that he'd inherited from his mother. "Are you content, Diego?" he heard himself ask.

Diego didn't answer immediately. Alejandro saw his jaw tighten and knew the question touched a raw place.

"Why do you ask?"

"Because I need to know," Alejandro said, the gruffness returning to his voice again. Damn it all, but he would not let his son see him cry. "I can bear all things if only you've found peace."

Diego considered that for a moment. "I thought I had," he said softly. "I've enjoyed serving God, and serving the people."

There was silence. Alejandro sighed. "I wouldn't have sent her, had I understood what chaos it would bring to your life."

Diego glanced towards him. "You've spoken with Francisco."

"Aye. He told me all."

"Even that I have feelings for Celeste?"

"Even that."

Diego drew in a long, unsteady breath. "I've not touched her, Papi. I couldn't help falling in love with her. I did try. But I've remained true to my vow. I honoured the troth she made with Damian."

Alejandro smiled, but it was coloured with sadness. "For once, I almost wish you'd not learned so much from your mistakes."

Diego frowned. "What do you mean?"

"Only that I'd not be sorry if you'd failed in your restraint. I love the girl, Diego, and would that she might bear my grandchildren, however that should come about." Alejandro looked away, his eyes filling with tears. "Now I'll lose her, too."

"I'm sorry," Diego said quietly. "But I...I just *couldn't*. She was not mine."

"Francisco says she is, and that you love her, too."

"Aye, I've already admitted it. But I pledged my life to God's service. How can I turn my back on that?" Diego stood. "I'm sorry, Papi. I can't think of these things just now. I need to go. As with you, this day has savaged my emotions. I need some time..." He ran his fingers through his hair. "I'll return in the morning. Perhaps by then you'll understand that I've done the only thing I knew to do. I made the only choice I knew to make."

He turned and left. Alejandro Castillo felt his heart break when the door slammed shut behind his son's tall, broad-shouldered form.

Moment by moment.

He'd get through this day moment by moment.

Diego stood in the courtyard, breathing deeply, trying to straighten out his tangled thoughts.

Everything was happening too quickly. He needed to slow down, to focus, to ground himself somehow against the buffeting winds of change.

But it was hard when all his mind could think about was Celeste. He hadn't seen her for six days, and he hungered for her presence. It was all he could do not to rush to the inn and take her into his arms. But if he did there'd be no containing the emotion.

Barto joined him, the big man equally reflective as they stood gazing at the bubbling of the fountain, inhaling the heady floral scents that seemed more intense with gathering darkness.

"What's on your mind, Diego?" Barto asked.

"I dare not confess it," Diego replied. "And yet you must already know. You always appear just when I'm most in need of a confidant."

Barto smiled. "Uhm. Then you're thinking of Celeste." He scratched his head. "She's well, Diego. But I deemed it best that she not be present when your family was reunited. I didn't know how things would go."

"A wise decision."

"But you're hungry to see her, is that it?"

Diego gave a noncommittal grunt.

Barto laughed softly into the darkness. "When are you going to give up the fight?"

"I don't think I can. It would be against all I know, all I've believed. I don't want to live with regret as my constant companion."

"Then what have you been doing for the last ten years?"

"That cannot be undone. You do see, however, why I'm not willing to go through it again." Diego turned away, wanting to end Barto's probing questions. There were things he'd rather not discuss at the moment. "At what inn is Celeste staying? I want to check on Farolillo."

"Celeste is at the Gallina de Oro. No doubt she'll be overjoyed to see you. She plagues me with questions about you each time I visit her there. But Farolillo's in your father's stable."

"Farolillo is here?"

"He is. Celeste bade me bring him here and see him into the care of your father's groom. That horse proved quite a handful on the road, chasing Hettie's little mare about until the poor girl was vexed with worry."

Diego smiled. "Which poor girl? The mare or Hettie?"

"Both, I think." Barto grinned. "Celeste managed to control that rutting stallion, but she was relieved when she could leave the saddle behind."

"I should've found her a gentler mount."

"He's spirited, but then so is she. Already they're quite enamoured of one another."

"I'm pleased she likes the gift."

"Aye, she does. Though I warrant you 'tis not the gift she treasures so much as the giver of it."

Diego didn't respond to that. He turned away. "I'll be at the stable," he said, tossing the words back over his shoulder as he strode away.

The stable was deserted. The grooms and stable boys had gone home. The premises were dark, and quiet, save for the creak of the stable door, the swish of sand beneath his feet, the soft nickering of horses. Diego felt his way into the blackness, his fingertips trailing over the rough textures of wood and stucco until he found a lantern and lit it, suffusing the area with light.

Farolillo was in a stall at the far end, gazing out of the half-door with a curious expression. He seemed to welcome the company as Diego let himself into the box and held out a hand. Farolillo nuzzled him. Diego chuckled.

"*Sí, muchacho,*" he said, stroking the horse's velvety muzzle. "You recognize me? Nay, but you recognize what I am. A lovesick fool, just like you are, both of us constrained by walls when all we long for is a good romp with our pretty fillies."

Farolillo whuffled agreement. Diego began to brush the animal, letting the rhythmic sound calm his thoughts.

He should be content, he knew that. A great deal had been accomplished this day. He'd been reunited with his family. Damian had let the past lie buried. It was more than Diego could comprehend that he might take up his place within the family again.

He should be content, and in most respects he was. If only he didn't have to go to Celeste and end any dreams she might have about their future together.

Perhaps in time the hurt would ease and Diego would think of her without this awful tightening in his gut. He'd like to imagine her happily married, laughing with her children in a garden filled with sunshine and flowers.

He'd like to know he'd done the right thing by letting her go. She must go on with her life, but…perhaps sometimes she'd ride out on Farolillo to windswept fields and lie alone in the tall grass. Maybe she'd think of him.

Nay, he couldn't ask even that much of her.

It had to be ended, for both their sakes. He'd go to her tonight and they'd talk. It would soon be over. All but the pain.

He stepped to the half-door and then out of it, jerking with surprise at the dark shadow that appeared from nowhere.

"What's the matter, brother?" Damian asked. "Did I startle you?" His laughter was not pleasant, hissing harshly through the taut line of his lips.

"I thought you'd gone."

"I waited to speak with you. There are a few things we need to clear up. Some old business."

Diego was instantly wary. "What business?"

"Oh, this and that. You know, crimes of passion, sins of the flesh...that kind of thing. You do know a little about those, don't you, Padre?"

Diego didn't answer. Damian moved closer until he stood near his brother's tense form. "I want you to know...you don't fool me for a minute, Diego," he said. "'Twas ever the way with you. You could make everyone believe you were so virtuous, the good twin, the one who was upright and trustworthy. And then, when they were off their guard, completely trusting in you, you'd stab the knife into their back without so much as a flinch."

"That's not true," Diego said quietly. "I never meant to do you harm. I didn't mean to fall in love with Leonora. I didn't mean for her to die. Aye, I did an evil thing and, aye, I acknowledge you've every right to be angry. But you wrong me if you think I did any of it with vicious intent."

Damian tapped the top of his boot with his riding crop. "I hated you for it, you know. I hated you for the whispers that followed me wherever I went, for the stares, the smirks of those who thought it amusing that I'd been cuckolded by my own brother."

Diego looked down. "I'm sorry."

"I swore then that I'd kill you some day. Perhaps I still shall."

"I hoped time had healed your wounds," Diego said quietly. "Perhaps it will help you to know that time has not healed mine."

Damian snorted. "A small measure of justice, to be sure, that you truly loved the selfish little bitch."

Diego's jaw tightened.

Damian smiled. "I'm glad you suffered. I'm glad you've spent ten years feeling the bite of the serpent. Ah, that does make me feel better."

"You're a cold man, Damian."

Damian quirked an eyebrow. "You don't know the half of it."

"What do you want from me?"

Damian raised the quirt and touched it to his brother's chest. "I want answers."

"Answers? About what?"

"Come now. You're no fool. Tell me why you've come home."

"To effect the proxy wedding between you and Celeste."

The quirt moved before Diego could sense it coming, swiping a vicious blow across his face. Stunned, he reached up with one hand, feeling the sticky wetness of blood. He looked at his twin in disbelief.

Damian stared at him, his face hard and unyielding. "I want the truth."

"What I said was the truth," Diego answered coldly.

"But not the whole truth." Damian's eyes narrowed. "I'm no fool. I've seen you and Barto with your heads together, your voices low. I've seen the looks which pass between you."

"You've seen whatever you wish to see."

"If there's nothing astir, then tell me why Celeste went to the Indies to find you."

Diego drew in a sharp breath.

Damian smirked. "Aye, I know that. You see, Maria the

scullery maid fancies herself in love with me. It's a small matter for me to gain from her all the information I want about my parents and their business. And last night, after a mighty fine toss in her bed, I discovered that Celeste Rochester left here some time in May. She hasn't yet returned. Or has she?"

"You'd been abducted. She wanted a wedding. She did what had to be done."

"Hmm. I wonder. I'm more convinced than ever that you're part of the plot. You wish to succeed me as heir, don't you?"

"I've no wish to usurp your place. All I want is to go about my life in peace, ministering to others in the name of the Lord—"

The quirt struck again, harder this time, and across his mouth. Diego tasted the sickeningly sweet taste of his own blood. He raised his head until his eyes met his brother's.

"That is enough," he said tersely, his nostrils flaring. "You've struck me twice without cause. You'll not strike me again."

"And what will you do? Fight me? Aye, come on. I think I'd like that."

Diego stood, struggling to maintain his composure. Anger coursed through his veins, but something in his brother's steely gaze made him wary. "Nay, I'll not fight you, Damian. You're due your pound of flesh, if you must take it to ease the anger between us."

Damian sneered. "You were never a coward before."

"I'm not a coward now. But neither is there wisdom in fighting a madman who believes his own lies."

"They're not lies. Father brought you here to take my place. You were to wed Lady Celeste. Indeed, you've probably already claimed her as your own."

"I never touched her. I honoured the betrothal she made with you."

"I'll see soon enough. Celeste will lie with me. With *me*, do you hear?"

"That is for the lady to decide."

"Nay, 'tis for *me* to decide, even if I have to force her. Tonight. The lady will spread herself for me tonight."

Diego forced himself to stay calm. "To what end? To prove your superiority over me? What good will that do?"

"You'll never have her. I shall have foiled that part of the plan, too. I'll have the money, the title, and the woman you want."

In a flash of illumination, Diego suddenly knew what Damian intended. It made sense now, why his brother had played along so calmly today, why he'd been so undisturbed by his twin's return to the fold. Diego understood the rest of it now, the thing Damian did not say.

"You're going to kill me, aren't you?" he asked quietly.

"I am." Damian smiled. "I might say how sorry I am, dear brother, but the truth is I've wanted to kill you for years. Perhaps some day I'll thank Celeste for bringing you straight to me, so I can skewer your guts out and string your bloody entrails across the rigging of my flagship. I've long dreamed of that beautiful sight. Sometimes I'd lie in bed thinking of it. By tomorrow it will be more than a dream. I'll have your kidneys on my breakfast plate."

"You are mad."

"Mad?" Damian snorted. "What is *madness*, really? Is it the need to avenge a wrong done you by the brother you trusted? Is it the rage which coils around your heart when you're shamed by a *woman*? Is that madness? Then, aye, I am mad."

"My death will not ease the torment you feel."

"Perhaps not." Damian shrugged. "Perhaps the urge to kill will come again and again. Perhaps I'll have to avenge my father's duplicity, and my mother's sinfulness. Perhaps Celeste will have to pay for her part in the scheme, too. I know not where it will end." He shook his head in mock sorrow. "I do know, however, where it begins. 'Tis time for you, Diego. Time for that sweet sacrifice."

Damian grasped the silver crucifix around Diego's neck and jerked it over his brother's head, pulling it over his own with frantic motion. "Time to take up your cross, Diego. Time to pay, time to pay." He drew his sword.

Diego retreated, quickly surveying his surroundings. "Don't do this," he said. "It won't ease your pain."

Damian laughed. He tossed the sword to Diego's feet.

Diego looked up, bewildered.

"Take it," Damian gestured. "It shall not be said that I murdered you without honour. You will fight me fairly."

Diego shook his head. "I refuse to fight you at all. Would you murder an unarmed man?"

"You'll fight me, damn you. You'll fight me. You want her. You want the title. You want the money. You'll fight me."

"Nay. I don't want the money. I've no desire for the title. I'll not fight."

"But you want *her*. You want Celeste. You'll fight."

Diego could not speak. He could only stare at his brother while his brother stared at him, each trying to discern the thoughts of his adversary, each trying to decide upon the next move. Long moments passed, long moments where time was a hideous thing.

Diego turned, striding towards the door. He heard his brother's snarl of rage, heard the jingle of a horse's harness, and turned just as his twin leaped against his back. Damian's arm pinned his own in a crushing vice before something tightened about Diego's throat. A strip of leather, the reins of a bridle snatched from the wall.

Diego pulled at the leather with his one free hand to keep it from tightening any more. He twisted hard, trying to break away from Damian's grasp.

"Nay!" Damian panted near his ear. "You'll not escape, you deceitful bastard! Fight me or die!"

Diego struggled, his breath stilled, every muscle straining. Ordinarily he could claim superior strength and use his large frame to garner the advantage, but his brother had always been his even match in both size and strength. Now Damian's strength was empowered by madness, and Diego realized with a sickening certainty that he would not be able to break the power of the grip which coiled around him. In a minute more, perhaps two, he'd lose consciousness and it would be over.

He let go of the leather which twisted round his neck, feeling it bite even more deeply, and reached upward. Damian grunted in pain when Diego snatched his hair, tearing at it, tearing a great shock of it loose. Still Damian's hold did not loosen. Diego gouged at his brother's eyes, anything that might get Damian to weaken the stranglehold around his neck. Nothing helped. He bent, trying to throw his brother forward over his back, over his head, but Damian planted his feet and resisted with equal strength. Time was running out.

Sensing blackness hovering over him, Diego grew desperate. His brother's breath in his ear, ragged and hissing, tortured Diego with his own burning need for air. His hand reached out to the wall, feeling along its rough planks for anything he could use. His fingertips grazed something. *There.* A stick of some sort. He grasped it and brought the end up over his shoulder in a quick thrust, a jab towards his brother's eyes. Damian cried out and immediately the stranglehold lessened. His brother stumbled backwards.

Diego could not straighten right away, only breathe in huge gulps, his throat raw and stinging. His brother shook off the daze of his pain and staggered towards him again, a large bruise already appearing on his cheekbone.

Diego wanted to cry out to him, wanted to yell…*what?* A plea? A warning? He knew not. The gleam in his twin's eyes was not of this world. It was feral, made of hellfire itself. Nothing Diego might say could lessen the burning of it.

He wanted to speak but could not, could only gulp in air with heavy, rasping breaths while his brother straightened and turned and staggered towards him in a frightening, surrealistic nightmare. Diego felt he waded in deep water, his limbs unresponsive. He meant to flee, turned to flee, could not move quickly enough. Out of the corner of his eye he saw Damian stoop and snatch up the sword. Its blade glinted wicked silver as Damian rushed towards him in a blur of time and motion, coming straight for him.

Diego hardly had time to breathe, and no time to think. His brother who'd been across the room was now upon him, thrusting a blade towards his heart with swift, practised strokes. Diego parried them with the long, heavy stick he held. The blade whittled away the wood of the handle, sending splinters flying with every blow. Diego crouched low, circling with cautious steps. The door was behind him, only a few paces away now. Soon he'd be able to flee.

Damian sensed his intent. He roared his frustration and came at Diego in a rush, sword raised, his face contorted with a snarl. Diego shifted the tool in his hands so that the heavy, weighted end of it might push his attacker away, then stumbled backwards in surprise when his brother plunged into it and impaled himself on the sharp tines of the pitchfork Diego hadn't realized he'd held.

A shrill, keening cry broke past Damian's lips. He stiffened, looking down at his chest and the spreading crimson of his blood. "You!" His intense eyes met Diego's shocked gaze. "You've murdered me."

Damian's face blanched. He crumpled to the ground, the long handle of the pitchfork clattering against the rough planks of the wall as he fell.

The large door behind Diego opened and Barto rushed in. He stopped short, seeing the scene before him—Diego, sick with horror, and Damian, lying motionless in a pool of blood.

"My God," Barto said, pressing forward. He knelt beside Damian, feeling for a pulse, a heartbeat. He looked up at Diego. "What happened here? What have you done?"

Diego choked on the words. "I think I just killed my brother."

Chapter Sixteen

Something was wrong; Celeste knew it. Everything within her whispered the worry. She smelled it in the air, felt it in the wind, heard it in the pulsing of her own blood. She knew there was trouble.

She had thought it odd that she didn't see Barto for three full days. He'd finally come with news. She couldn't return to the Castillo home; there had been a disagreement between Diego and Damian. Don Alejandro, worried for her safety, wished her to remain at the inn.

More than that Barto wouldn't tell her. He left her with more anxiety than answers, and a burning need to know the truth.

Something was wrong, and she was afraid. What if Diego was...?

Nay, she refused to consider that. Diego couldn't be dead. Wouldn't her heart somehow know that?

But he might have had to flee.

She imagined Diego all alone, his hopeful dreams fragmented, mocking him like the torn, wind-tossed banners of a vanquished army. Perhaps he was wounded, perhaps in pain. He might need her. She imagined his heart cried out for her.

She had to know.

She would not stay here in this dreary inn, day after loathsome day, not when she could find Diego and give him ease and comfort. Any who thought she'd be content with waiting did not know the resolve of her English blood. Nay, she would find Diego. She would know the truth.

But she wouldn't go to Barto or Francisco or any of the Castillos. She would go to Fernando. That was the way. Fernando had always liked her. He'd always appreciated her kindness towards the servants, always praised the way she'd treated the horses well.

Fernando would tell her all she wanted to know. And he would lead her to Diego.

Her gold did not bring her the explanation she asked for. Fernando looked worried and shrugged, refusing to speak. But he'd given her something much better. He'd taken her by the hand and led her straight to Diego.

He was in the chapel, kneeling at the altar rail, praying.

Praying out loud, praying earnestly in deep, well-modulated Latin. For once, Celeste wished she'd paid more attention to her lessons at the convent—to Latin, with its words as sturdy and long as a well-built Roman road, with its verb declensions and histories of Gaul.

Maybe if she had, she'd know what Diego was praying in such dark and anguished tones.

Maybe she'd understand.

She spoke his name. Diego jumped up as if startled and whirled to face her, his face betraying a conflict of emotions. She frowned, thinking how little he seemed to want her there. He was immediately uneasy, his stance like one prepared to flee, nervously poised on the balls of his feet with hands half clenched. He would barely meet her gaze.

"What are you doing here?"

"I've come to be with you."

"You shouldn't have."

She moved closer, her heart thumping with fear at what she saw in his eyes. There was no warmth there, no happiness at her presence, no encouragement. He looked away quickly, avoiding her gaze.

"Diego, what happened? Barto said—"

"I don't want to talk about it. Not to anyone."

"Not even to me, Diego?"

"Most especially not with you."

Celeste could hardly believe the words. Something speared her chest and held her pinned, unable to breathe, unable to think. "I love you," she said. "Don't do this. Don't be like this. Think of what we've shared and all we mean to one another."

Diego turned away and ran a hand through rumpled hair. He drew in a deep breath and looked up at the cross. "There is nothing for us now. It's over."

Celeste gasped. Diego's jaw hardened at the sound.

"How can you say that? How can you deny what we've been together? Do you not remember—?"

"'Tis *over*, Celeste," he said harshly. "Forget all that's passed between us."

Celeste shook her head and moved to him, her hand reaching out to touch the firmly muscled arm beneath the coarse wool of his robe. "Nay, I cannot forget. You promised me...with *this!*" She held up the ring he'd given her. "You made a vow and called it as sacred as any betrothal we might swear."

Diego did not speak, but she saw his eyes fill with tears.

"Diego," she said, more gently. "Tell me what's happened. I can bear it, whatever it is. I can strengthen you, love you through it all, no matter how grim it is. No ill news can make me leave your side, nor will it change my love for you. Share it with me."

He did not speak for long moments. Finally he looked at her and Celeste trembled, awaiting the truth.

"I was happy in the Indies," he said. "At peace with God and with myself. I had worthy, productive tasks to fill my days, and prayer and scripture and a peaceful cell to fill my nights. That's gone now, all gone. There is no more."

"No more what? I don't understand.".

"No more peace. I wish to God I'd never come home."

"Why?" she asked, afraid of the anger in his face. "What happened?"

"It was wrong to come back. I should have remained where I was. I should never have listened to you."

"Then...you're blaming me?"

He looked away. "I'm blaming *us*. It was wrong to leave my place, to forsake my people, my vow, my God. It was wrong to fall in love with you."

Celeste shook her head, denying the sting of words that bit into her heart. "You don't mean that. Tell me you don't mean that."

He looked at her. "The past cannot be undone."

"Do you wish it undone, Diego? Do you wish you'd never met me? Do you regret kissing me and lying with me and loving me?"

Diego's jaw tightened. His words were quiet. Deliberate. "I do. My weakness has brought me great pain."

The words ripped into her heart, but pride bade her stand still, her back straight, her chin raised.

"Go home, Celeste," he said. "Go back to England. Marry a good man, have children and be content."

Celeste wanted to scream at him, to slap the coldness off his face, to break through to the core of something, anything, that was warm and passionate and loving. She wanted Diego back, not this shadow who looked like him but wasn't.

Instead, she looked away, blinking back tears. "Is that what you truly want?"

It took him a long moment to answer. Celeste waited. Like one who'd survived the single great wall of a hurricane, she stood in the quiet eye, awaiting the rest with dread too deep to be articulated. "Aye," he said. "That's what I want."

At that moment, the chapel doors opened with an echoing crack. Padre Francisco stood in the bright sunlight streaming in from the outside. "Diego!" he called. "You must come! Come quickly—right now!"

Diego raced down the narrow aisle and out through the door without even a glance back towards Celeste.

At first there was no feeling. Only a deep wounding, a burn so profound there was no pain. Celeste sat on the carved pew, staring into the candle flame burning on the altar. She heard the words he'd said again and again, perceiving with the un-comprehending, blunted reasoning of a beast.

Then anger came. It was cataclysmic and volatile; she wanted to lash out and hurt him, to wound him as cruelly as he'd wounded her, to flay him with rage.

Celeste made it out of the chapel doors and down the garden path before her fury became anguished tears. She wiped at them and ran, heedless of her surroundings, until she rounded a stucco wall and ran headlong into someone.

"Celeste!" Padre Francisco steadied her with a hand on her shoulder. "My Lord, child! What is it? Why do you weep so?"

"It's Diego! He...he sent me away! He's ended everything between us. He told me... Oh, Padre, how can I bear it? He told me there was nothing for us, that he wished he'd never loved me, that I must return to England and forget all that ever passed between us!"

Celeste lost control then, and began to shake.

Padre Francisco drew her into his arms, his own eyes filling with tears. He let her cry until her tears soaked his robe. He whispered soft words of caring until, much later, her sobs subsided.

"*Why*, Padre?" she asked, pulling away to look up into his face. "Why would Diego say those terrible things to me?"

Padre Francisco drew a deep breath. "Because he loves you, Celeste. He loves you. And he does not wish you to bear the shame of that."

Celeste frowned, thinking the Padre must be wrong. He hadn't seen the coldness in Diego's eyes.

"I don't understand," she said. "What shame?"

Francisco turned sorrowful eyes in her direction. "The shame of loving a murderer."

* * *

Diego met his mother outside the door to the room where his brother lay, sick and feverish, smelling of unguents and death.

"He's worse?" Diego asked, breathless from the speed with which he'd come.

"Nay, he's no worse," she said, her expression weary. "Mayhap he's a bit better. He's awake now, and calling for you."

Diego nodded, swallowing down uncertainty. He pushed open the door.

"Don't tire him," his mother said in a low voice.

Diego approached the bed cautiously, wondering if his brother had fallen asleep again. His eyes were closed. They fluttered open when he spoke Damian's name.

"You came," Damian said.

"Of course."

"I…feared…you would not."

Diego looked down. "We are brothers. Regardless of all that's passed between us, we are brothers."

Damian nodded. Diego was struck by how pale his brother looked. His face was nearly as white as the pillow on which he lay.

"I'm dying," Damian said quietly.

"Nay, don't think it," Diego answered. "The doctors—"

"An angel came. I will die."

"An angel?"

"Aye. I must…" He drew in a deep, laboured breath. "…make peace."

Diego looked away. "I'm sorry. I didn't know I held a pitchfork. I never meant to harm you."

Damian's eyes met his, piercing blue. "I would have killed you."

Diego couldn't answer. There was a long, awkward silence. His brother seemed to be weakening, as if every word came at the cost of his strength.

"My time…short," Damian whispered. "Please…"

"It's all forgiven," Diego said. "I hope you will also forgive me."

Damian relaxed visibly against the pillows. His eyelids fluttered down. Diego waited, but Damian did not speak more. After long moments, Diego turned to leave.

"I'm sorry," Damian whispered.

Diego turned his head. "Aye," he said. "I'm sorry, too."

His footsteps were muted on the soft carpet as he left the room.

Some nightmares never seem to end, Celeste thought as she let herself be led through the crowd towards the waiting ship on Barto's arm. The worst nightmares lasted for ever, and this week seemed made of them—terrible, insubstantial horrors that shaded the hours of passing night and grew even darker when daylight came. She wished she could awaken, stretch, yawn, and find the worry gone like an ephemeral dream. But it was no dream. This nightmare was reality.

Damian had died four nights past. Barto had come for her the following day, and she'd been with the Castillo family ever since, their grief touching her even though she was not, and now never would be, part of their family.

It had grieved her to see Alejandro and Anne accept sorrow with stoicism and quiet strength.

It had grieved her to be near Diego, to see his shoulders weighted with heaviness.

It had stirred her to see the servants looking downcast, and to hear their whispered comments that one son had murdered the other.

It had angered her that the authorities had come to question Diego. She'd wanted to proclaim that Diego would never have intentionally murdered his brother, that he wasn't that sort of man.

But Celeste had said nothing, for the truth was…she wasn't sure who Diego was, not any more.

He'd barely looked at her. When their eyes had met, the man who'd stared out of them had not been the one she'd known. His gaze was blank, withdrawn, as if life had ceased to burn in his heart.

He'd left Seville without even saying goodbye. Anne had met her at breakfast with the news, reluctant to tell her that Diego had departed for the Indies at daybreak. It had surprised everyone, Anne said. She begged Celeste to forgive all her two sons had done to bring grief. Celeste had somehow weathered that scene, hugging the older woman and replying with gracious words that she barely remembered, though her heart had been cracking into tiny splinters.

It was over. Diego was gone.

Celeste sat in the chapel for what seemed like hours, remembering all that had passed between them. She remembered the moment she'd first looked into eyes reflecting sky and forest, filled with compassion as deep as the river he'd pulled her from. She remembered his voice, the richly accented timbre that made her insides quiver.

She remembered his body, the way his hands had felt upon her, the night of love they'd shared and being held while she slept.

She glanced down at the ring on her finger and remembered the vow he'd made. What of that? In the end, she supposed it had meant nothing. Because she remembered, last of all, the coldness in his expression when he'd blamed her for his grief.

Tears blurred her vision. She rose and walked down the aisle until she stood before the altar, beneath the cross. She twisted the ring from her finger and laid it gently, reverently, on the altar rail. Then she turned and left the place, and the memories, behind.

Now, as she stood with Barto and they gazed towards the ship which would be taking her home to England, she wished she could feel something. Anything. Her heart must have died and been interred in the warm, sun-baked soil of Spain. She felt numb, and weary, and she longed to be away from this place which reminded her of the love she'd lost without even knowing why.

"I wish you'd consider staying," Barto said quietly. "I meant what I said about going to Diego. I'll convince him of his foolishness. At least, I will try."

Celeste tried to smile, but it probably looked as weak as it felt. "Thank you, Barto. You've ever been a friend to me, and I'll never forget you. But I doubt anything will bring him home again."

"He owes you an explanation."

Celeste looked down. "Some things are best left alone."

Barto looked away. "I'm going to find him. I'll try to convince him to leave the priesthood. I owe that much to Alejandro and Anne. Diego is their only son now. He is the heir." He drew in a deep breath. "As it is, the Church will get all they've worked for. Seems a shame to me." Barto's tone turned bitter. "Alejandro told me it was a fitting penance for his sins. Can you believe that? As if the man hasn't suffered enough. Now he must live with the knowledge that his work, his dreams—indeed, his whole life—it was all for naught. How he and Anne will bear that burden, I truly do not know."

Celeste nodded, unable to speak.

"And what of you, my lady? What will you do now?"

Celeste drew in a deep sigh. "I shall marry another."

"But you love Diego."

"He no longer loves me." She shrugged. "It's a small thing, now, to wed whomever the King shall choose for me. Just a matter of going through all the motions, really. My heart is numb. Surprisingly, that helps. I can do now what I must do. Perhaps I cannot feel joy, but neither will I feel pain." She squeezed Barto's hand. "I will survive."

Barto seemed unable to speak. He looked away, towards the ship where mariners sweated in the sun to make final preparations for departure. "I don't know what happened," he said finally. "I had enough faith for both of us."

Celeste looked puzzled.

"The prayer," he said. "Francisco and I...we prayed for you, for Diego, that you might find happiness together." He frowned. "I suppose God didn't hear us."

Celeste squeezed his hand. "He heard you, Barto. There were moments of great happiness." She looked towards the ship. "They just didn't last."

Barto grunted a reply, letting her take his arm and pull him towards the ship that would take her far, far from the Castillo family, and the man he had prayed would be her destiny.

Chapter Seventeen

Ricardo Alvarez rarely ventured to the island's port area at dusk. There was too much danger, and too much temptation for a man who'd once been prone to excesses involving wine and women.

But this evening was different. He had important business to conduct, and no time for sinful dallying. Besides that, he'd be with a priest, and had no wish to be chastised for the state of his immortal soul.

The tavern into which he walked was noisy and boisterous. Two ships had docked that day, and their crews were making the most of their time on land. As Ricardo sidestepped two seamen who took turns embracing a lusty wench, he scanned the churning muddle of colour and sound, finally seeing the man he sought sitting alone at a corner table, sipping slowly from a tankard of ale.

Francisco held out a hand when he neared. "Ricardo," he said, sounding relieved. "You got the message. I was half afraid you would not. Our ship had only just docked when I sent it this afternoon."

Ricardo smiled. "I got it, Padre," he said. "I've been expecting you every day for the last month. I'm pleased you were not delayed in this season of storms. October is sometimes a bad month for them."

"The Lord protected me. He knows I'm on an urgent mission."

Ricardo nodded, his smile disappearing. "*Sí.* Diego needs you."

The priest's warm gaze flew to Ricardo's face. "Does he?"

"He does, though he'd be nailed to a cross before he'd admit it."

Francisco caught the sleeve of a serving girl who passed nearby, and ordered a drink for Ricardo before settling back against the high back of his chair. "Tell me," he said. "He's not improved since you wrote to Alejandro?"

Ricardo shook his head. "Nay, he's no better. He is Diego, but he is *not* Diego. He still serves the people, still preaches the message of Christ, still goes through all the motions. But Padre, there's no light in his eyes any more. There's no *ganas*. No heart, no desire. He's a mere shadow of the man he was."

Francisco's expression darkened. "Does he ever speak of home? Of his parents?"

"No."

"Of Celeste?"

"No."

"Then he's condemned himself to a grievous penance." Francisco sighed and took a long draught of his ale. "What do you suggest?"

Ricardo shrugged. "If I knew what to do, I wouldn't have sent for you. I thought you might have more success reaching him, where obviously I have failed."

"I've spent long hours in prayer concerning this, and only one possible action comes to mind. You are familiar with the scriptures, Ricardo?"

"Well...some of them. I'm no scholar, Padre, and I don't pretend to be."

"But you do remember the famous story of David and the woman Bathsheba?"

"You mean the same David who killed the giant Goliath? Aye, I remember him. My mother taught me as a child. I loved that story, especially when the lad cut off the giant's head."

Francisco smiled patiently. "The same David, but at a later time in his life. This story occurs long after David became a man and King of Israel, and it relates to his most heinous *sin*, rather than his most rewarding victory."

Ricardo grunted acknowledgement. "Seems I recall that story, too. Did he not seduce somebody's wife and have the woman's husband killed to cover up what he'd done?"

"He did."

"So you're telling me Diego seduced Celeste?"

"No. No, nothing like that. What I'm getting at is what came later, when God sent Nathan the prophet to confront David about what he'd done."

"I don't remember."

"Nathan realized that David would be resistant to the truth if it were set out before him too abruptly. So the wise prophet chose a more circuitous route. He told a story, a simple story, a story of two men. One was wealthy, with a multitude of sheep. One was poor, with only one little lamb. The rich man was greedy and stole the lamb of the poor man, slaughtering it for himself. Naturally, King David was outraged when he heard of it and demanded the villain be brought to justice."

"Of course he would. It was wrong."

"Nathan then looked the King directly in the eye and told him, 'You, King David. *You* are that man.'"

Ricardo sucked in his breath. "A powerful kick in the behind."

Francisco smiled. "Yes. Much the same sort of kick as our beloved Padre Diego needs, don't you agree?"

Ricardo grinned wickedly. "Oh, yes. I agree completely. So…when and how do you plan to put the imprint of your sandal on Diego Castillo's backside?"

"Soon, Ricardo, but first I'll need your help."

Ricardo leaned forward, his eyes gleaming. "You've got it, Padre. Let's talk."

Guillermo Nuñez was twenty years old, the youngest son of Spanish parents who'd come to the island in the earliest days of its settlement. Diego had always liked him, for the youth was bright and artistic, with a disposition towards goodness that warmed Diego's heart.

But this time goodness had gone too far.

"What do you say, Padre?" Guillermo asked with an earnest expression. "I can be on the next ship to Spain if you'll give me those letters of recommendation."

Diego tried not to scowl. "Guillermo," he began. "I know you mean well in this. I know you love your mother and want her dream fulfilled, but…"

Guillermo smiled. "She's very pleased, Padre. She thought when my brother died that her dream of having a priest among her sons had died with him."

Diego nodded. "He was a good man. He would have made a fine priest. But just because the Lord took him does not mean another must step in to fulfil—"

"But I *want* to do this," Guillermo said with an almost tragic eagerness. "My other brothers have no aptitude for it. They prefer an active life and don't care for books or study. It must fall to me."

Diego drew in a deep breath. "I think you should think this through more carefully. The sacrifices of the priesthood are many and hard to be borne."

Guillermo met his gaze without flinching. "I am resigned to those sacrifices. I've given them much thought already."

Diego looked up towards the cross on the wall. "You'll never know great wealth. You'll toil for souls amid suffering and perhaps even danger. You'll never know a woman, never sire children."

"I am prepared to surrender those desires."

There was a long silence. Diego didn't understand why Guillermo's decision hurt so badly. He'd known the lad since Guillermo was twelve, had seen him grow into fine manhood. Many things about the younger man reminded Diego of himself in younger days. Why, then, should he not rejoice that such a one would seek to follow in his footsteps and train for the priesthood?

"Will you give me the letters, Padre? The ship is bound for Spain within the week, and I can be on her if you'll—"

"I don't want to give you those letters." Diego met Guillermo's green-eyed gaze. "I don't feel right about it. If you wanted the priesthood for yourself, then...maybe. But you only seek to please your mother."

Guillermo's face registered disbelief, then distress. "No, you don't understand! It's not just for my mother. It's for myself, too. It's for my brother! God knows how I miss my brother!"

Diego had buried Guillermo's brother and remembered now the whispers of the villagers that the older brother had died to prevent the death of the younger ones, including Guillermo, during a robbery of the family home.

He dealt gently with Guillermo's guilt.

"He loved you, too," he said softly. "And he would want you to find God's will for your life. Your *own* dream, Guillermo, not the one he left behind. You seek to honour him, I know, but your brother's dream does not fit you. You'll never be happy within it, no matter your best intentions."

Trust me, I know, he wanted to say.

Guillermo's face reddened. Diego had never seen him angry before. "I've chosen it, Padre. I *will* see it accomplished, with or without your help."

Diego shook his head. "Your determination is admirable, *hijo*. But you're overlooking something of grave import. One cannot simply *choose* the priesthood. One has to be *called* into it. Called by God himself."

Guillermo drew in a long breath. Diego sensed the struggle within him.

Then suddenly, unexpectedly, the young man looked full into Diego's face. "Called by God? Perhaps He *has* called me. Tell me, Padre Diego, how did it feel when God called you?"

The single question slammed into Diego.

It seemed to pull him out of reality and place him into some airless void where time ceased and truth flowed with painful clarity all around him.

It speared his heart, bled his soul, made him want to cry out with utter anguish.

Guillermo studied him intently, his eyes almost wicked in their intensity.

The answer would not come. Diego was many things, but a liar he was not.

Those eyes would not lose him.

He sat, unable to move, stupidly dumb as he grappled with the pain in his chest.

"Padre, are you all right?" Guillermo said in a low voice. "Is aught amiss?"

What could he say? That, aye, he was all right?

Or that, aye, something—*everything*—was terribly amiss.

He stood, unable to remain seated beneath the hard scrutiny. "I feel unwell," he said in a low voice. He moved towards the door that led from his private cell to the chapel's sanctuary, then suddenly halted.

Padre Francisco sat on the first pew, nearest the open door. He met Diego's startled expression with a knowing one.

"Excellent advice, Diego," he said quietly. "Your wisdom is more advanced than your years."

Diego overcame his surprise and crossed the stone floor to stand beside him. Behind Diego, Guillermo eased out of the small room and stood hesitantly.

Francisco smiled at the youth and withdrew a small bag of coins. "An excellent performance, *hijo*," he said.

Diego's eyes narrowed. *"Performance?"* He looked back at Guillermo, who came to take the proffered payment with a small shrug.

Francisco waited in silence as the young man departed the chapel.

"Explain," Diego said tersely.

"You know the scriptures, Diego. King David had Nathan the prophet to point him to the truth." Francisco looked up into Diego's face. "You have me."

Diego could not answer.

Francisco patted the seat beside him. "Sit, Diego Castillo. We must talk."

Diego sat, knowing he could no longer avoid the truth. And for the first time, no longer wishing to.

Chapter Eighteen

Lady Evelyn chuckled as she handed the skein of yarn across to Celeste. "You did it again, my dear," she said. "That makes at least three times in this one day alone."

Celeste lowered the tapestry on which she'd been working and looked up at her friend, one eyebrow lifted. "Did what?"

"Said *'gracias'* instead of 'thank you.' You've been back home in England for—what is it? Nearly five months now? And still you slip and do that. Regularly. Your time in Spain affected you a great deal."

Celeste made a small, non-committal reply. Lady Evelyn had no idea. No idea at all.

If the older woman noticed Celeste's sudden reticence, she pretended she didn't. Instead, she kept up a steady stream of chatter, all the while busily plying her needle.

"'Tis almost time to sup," she finally said with a sigh, "But we must wait, in case Harold should arrive and be hungry. He's always hungry. You'd think he'd be wide of girth, as much as he eats, but..." She trailed off, rising to glance past the curtains at the steady rain that made this day in early December a miserable one. "Nay, I don't see their mounts. Truly, I had expected Harold's return long before now."

She sat down again, smoothing her grey hair. Gentle eyes of blue met Celeste's. "I don't know how you can sit there sewing so calmly when Harold and the King are meeting with the foreign emissary to discuss final details of your betrothal. Are you not even the least bit anxious?"

"I trust both men to do what is best for me."

"Oh, they will," Lady Evelyn nodded. "You know Harold Ashton would do anything to ensure your happiness, dear. He did so love your parents. Like family we all were, though not blood kin. And he's certain the man the King has chosen will be perfect for you. I marvel that you want to hear nothing at all about him. Not even his name. You'd think that since you'll be sharing it for your whole lifetime—"

Celeste held up a hand. "It's enough to know that my father's dearest friend is making the preparations and that he's in agreement with the King's decision. There will be time to learn of my betrothed later."

"But Harold says—"

"Nay!" Celeste interrupted, somewhat harshly. Hearing her sharp tone, she drew in a deep breath and looked down at her lap. "Please, Aunt. I…I'm not nearly so brave as I'm trying to appear. I fear if we discuss the matter, I might…"

Lady Evelyn was instantly regretful. "Oh, love. I am so sorry. I should have believed Hettie when she told me you'd… I mean…"

"Hettie? What did she tell you?"

Evelyn had the good grace to look chagrined. "That there'd been someone—someone in Spain. And that he'd broken your heart."

Just hearing the words caused the sob to break through. One tiny, ragged sob, quickly smothered by a trembling hand.

At least Lady Evelyn did not try to stop her when she rose and fled the room, her tears making little splashes onto the marble floor of the foyer as she fled towards the stairs and the quiet haven of her room.

* * *

Two days later, Celeste entered the cool, dim interior of the monastery behind the ascetic figure of the monk who'd answered her summons at the door. He pointed out a bench in a room so large that the fireplace at the far end, as huge as it was, and as amply stacked with the burning skeletons of crackling logs, could not hope to adequately heat it all.

She lowered herself to the seat, pulling on the sleeve of the monk's habit just as he would have hurried away. He turned to her with an expectant look.

"How is he?" she asked. "I mean, is he…any better?"

"Nay, m'lady. Not since you were here last week. Even the carved horse you brought him hasn't forced words from his tongue, though we can all tell the gift means much to him. His eyes are most expressive. Those of us who care for Jacob know well how to read his thoughts within them. But speak? Nay, he has not."

At the tears that filled her eyes, the monk's hand covered hers and gently squeezed. "Don't lose heart; Jacob's a bright lad. He'll recover in his own time, and when he does he'll never cease to amuse you with his wit."

Celeste watched him depart. The news had been what she'd expected, but not what she'd hoped to hear.

Minutes later she heard footsteps and turned as her brother raced into the room, one hand clutching a carved horse on wheels. He was followed by the monk at a more leisurely pace.

The animation on Jacob's face brought some measure of cheer into Celeste's day. He jumped into her outspread arms. She hugged him fiercely.

The monk laughed as he joined them. "It's plain he's glad to see you," he said, before whispering that he'd be in the next room should she need anything. He looked back with a kind smile as he departed.

Jacob *did* have expressive eyes, and he used them to tell Celeste a myriad of important things. Aye, and to ask her questions, too. *Why have you come? Why are you here?* He studied her face for the answers, his plump fingers stroking her hair, curling around her chin, touching the delicate velvet braid that trimmed her cuffed sleeves.

"Oh, Jacob," she finally sighed, dropping the cheerful one-sided conversation she'd been attempting. "I know you're wondering why I'm here when it's not my usual day to come. But, please, just let me hold you. Sometimes I miss you so much. I miss our family. I miss *home*."

Sensing her distress, he climbed up onto her skirts and laid his head against her bosom. Celeste, inhaling the warm, soft fragrance of his hair, felt the hot prickle of tears. A sob caught in her throat. Jacob felt it more than heard it, and pulled back to look into her face. A wayward tear decided at that moment to slide down the slope of her cheekbone.

Jacob's eyes immediately darkened with shared pain. He reached up with both arms, pulled her face down to his, and, in a gesture that broke Celeste's heart, kissed the tear away.

It was then that she knew why she would sign those papers which awaited her. Those papers which would bind her to a stranger for the rest of her life.

Celeste had prayed the dream would not come again, but it did. She was with Diego, her heart pounding at the sight of the thick mane of tawny hair skimming those broad shoulders, of brown hands resting on trim hips, and that easy smile that made the dimple deepen in his lean cheek.

"Diego," she whispered. "Where have you been?"

His eyes met hers. "Searching for you, my love."

"Why did you leave me?"

"To seek truth. I had to know it. I had to find it."

"And what is the truth? Do you know it now?"

He pulled her near, so close she smelled his warm, masculine scent, the scent of sunshine and salt spray. His shirt was coarse against her breasts. "I do. I know I love you, Celeste. I'm coming for you."

Pain speared her soul. "It's too late, Diego. I am promised to another, one whose name and face I do not know because I'm afraid of what I've done."

Diego raised her hand to his lips and kissed her fingers, each one gently in its turn. When he lowered it, there was the ring of three pearls which he'd given her. "Do you remember this ring?"

"Aye," she whispered. "Three pearls. One for the love I bear you. One for the love you bear me. The third for the love of the Father, who cares for us both. White pearls for the virtue to which we must, even now, keep ourselves true."

Diego smiled. "You haven't forgotten."

"Nay, Diego. I cannot forget."

His lips drew closer. "Then, my love, *believe.*"

The great hall of King Henry VIII into which Celeste and Lady Evelyn were ushered was more long than it was wide. Celeste had time to study it as she walked, trying to keep her composure.

The men were gathered at the far end of the room, seated around a table of carved walnut with papers spread across its marble top, watching them approach. She recognized King Henry and his Lord Chamberlain. Her father's lifelong friend Harold, Lord Kentford, and his lawyer. And another, the one who drew her gaze. He, likewise, looked up from his paperwork and stood watching her enter, his expression transfixed somewhere between admiration and awe.

Celeste leaned closer to Lady Evelyn. "At least he's not ancient. I don't mind the grey at his temples. He's neat and clean and his eyes are kind. And he's tall. I like men who are tall."

Lady Evelyn nearly broke her stride. Her face held a mixture of disbelief and surprise. "Whatever are you talking about, my dear? That man there is not your future husband. He's merely an emissary sent to conduct the formalities."

Celeste did not know whether to be relieved, pleased, or disappointed. The old saying about a known foe being better than an untried friend came to mind. Perhaps her future spouse was so doddering with age that he couldn't make the journey. Or so ugly he didn't wish to shock her with his countenance. At any rate, her curiosity would not be appeased. Not this day.

Within moments she was presented to King Henry, sweeping into the deep curtsy that was required. He smiled and extended a hand. "Lady Celeste, dear kinswoman, if 'tis possible, you've grown even more lovely than on the fortunate occasion of your last visit here."

"Thank you, Sire," she said. "It is an honour to be here with you and to serve my country in this capacity."

King Henry chuckled. "Aye, lovely, intelligent, *and* diplomatic." He turned to the other men. "You see? We've chosen well the woman who shall represent our fair land in the court of King Carlos I. If any can foster the friendships which will encourage peaceful cooperation between our two nations, this worthy young lady shall do so." The other gentlemen smiled and nodded their agreement, and the King turned his attention back to Celeste. "'Tis little wonder, then, that your future husband has forsaken all to seek you out. You're certainly worth all his trouble and more."

The words puzzled Celeste.

"Both King Carlos and I wish you great felicity in this marriage. Although its original purpose was to ally our nations, we pray God that there shall be the added benefits of marital bliss and mutual joy."

Celeste curtsied again. "I thank you, Sire. May it be as you have said."

At a gesture from the King's Lord Chamberlain, the tall emissary stepped forward. "Lady Celeste, I apologize that your betrothed is not present today. He did wish it, and embarked from Palos some days ago with that purpose in mind. However, his ship was blown off course by a storm in the Channel."

Celeste inclined her head in a gesture so poised it was almost regal. "I quite understand, good sir. The winds of the Channel are oft contrary and at times thwart even the most worthy intent."

The man's eyes softened with respectful admiration, before his lids lowered and he moved around the table, addressing the men as he went. "He did, however, send a fast courier with the necessary documentation, all properly signed and in order. I have checked it myself."

He reached for the papers spread upon the table. "These first two are the required Papal dispensations. The documents are rather thick and wordy, but you can easily see on the final page of each the signature and seal of Pope Leo himself." He handed them to the nearest man, who happened to be her own dear Uncle Harold. After a brief perusal, he handed them on to the King's Lord Chamberlain. He caught Celeste's eye and gave her a wink, grinning when she raised a questioning eyebrow.

"This sheaf of papers documents in quite notable detail the lineage of the family into which Lady Celeste will be marrying, as well as their current financial status and the provisions made for her, for any future heir and for all other offspring which shall proceed from this union." He stroked his beard absently as he peered at Lord Harold and the King. "You may certainly take as much time as you like to study them. They are detailed and lengthy."

The King cleared his throat and leaned forward in his chair, his fingertips grasping the carved arm. "What think you, Mr Oliver? You've read them. Tell me in brief—will Lady Celeste profit from this union?"

The lawyer nodded. "Aye, Sire. She shall indeed. The family's bloodline is impeccable. Their claim to noble rank cannot be questioned. In addition, their financial status is secure. Their holdings are most impressive, and their generosity towards the lady herself... Well, I may say, Sire, that I've never seen such generosity in all my twenty years of service."

"Good enough," the King said, settling back into his cushioned chair. He nodded to Lord Harold. "Shall we sign the papers to make the match official, then? I believe the gentleman has sent his signed document of betrothal already?"

"Indeed, Sire. It lies here on the table, beside that which Lady Celeste must now sign."

The King nodded. "Then, my dear cousin, nothing remains except your agreement."

Lady Evelyn pulled her forward. As Celeste stood, looking down at the soft vellum parchment which awaited her, she saw Diego Castillo in her mind, all golden and glorious, his eyes sea-green in his tanned face. Her stomach did an awful roll. The air seemed oppressive around her. She heard his voice. *Believe.*

Her eyes travelled to the matching parchment beside hers. There, on the bottom of the page, was the bold signature of the man she would soon wed. Curiosity compelled her to read the name, but alas, the scrawl was wild, careening across the page as if he had been frantic with haste. She could make out only a few letters of it. His name would remain a mystery. Her fear had bade her ask both Harold and Evelyn not to speak of him. Now pride would not let her rescind the request.

She raised her eyes. Uncle Harold watched her, his expression filled with compassion. Their gazes locked and he nodded almost imperceptibly. She closed her eyes and saw Jacob's dark eyes. She reached for the plume and dipped it quickly into the bottle of ink. Then, with her heart pounding, she signed her name.

The rest of the ceremony passed in a blur. There were betrothal gifts, sent by the same fast courier. "Your betrothed was disappointed in not being able to present them himself," Mr Oliver said, adjusting his spectacles. His kind eyes met hers. "As the wedding will take place in three days, you'll soon be able to thank him personally."

Celeste's heart dropped to her feet. Three days? Three days was all the time she had to prepare herself? Sweet Lord above!

Her betrothed was certainly not going to give her any opportunity to change her mind. She suddenly wanted to cry. Her legs felt weak. She had to force herself not to grasp the table for support. Only the thought that she was a Rochester kept her from buckling.

The gifts were presented one at a time. First there was a spectacularly beautiful set of brush, comb, and mirror, superbly crafted in gold and inlaid with a rainbow of precious jewels. She heard Aunt Evelyn's sharp intake of breath. "Gracious! Have you ever seen anything so fine? It must have cost the man a fortune!"

Mr Oliver smiled. "The note which accompanies it explains that it was created by Italian craftsmen, my lady, and purchased especially for you in Rome. Your betrothed writes that, while you surely need nothing to enhance your beauty, he does hope the gift will please you."

"Thank you. He is most kind."

Mr Oliver reached again into the leather satchel and pulled out another gift, a soft, sheer veil that seemed spun of air. As she took it, Celeste marvelled at the fabric. It was unlike anything she'd ever seen, woven of threads so silken that every breath of wind stirred the cloth and gave it a magical life of its own.

"Again, your betrothed hopes you'll like this small token, woven in the Orient. Although he adds that it is a shame to cover burnished curls as glorious as a sunrise."

Next he handed her a cloak of soft wool. It was indigo blue, finely woven, and embroidered with an intricate floral pattern of red and yellow flowers in leaves of green that trailed down its hemmed edges. "This gift comes from his homeland of Castile, although, as with the veil, he writes that it is with sadness he would cover a womanly form so comely and so well made."

Celeste squelched a spark of irritation. Her betrothed had never seen her hair or her form and was far too glib with his words.

A command softly spoken to an attendant brought the next

gift—a puppy. Celeste raised her eyebrows incredulously at the small, wriggly bundle of curls. "This gift is not for you, my lady," Mr Oliver said with a smile. "It's for your brother—Jacob, I think his name is? And the message to accompany this gift is that the love of this little pup will have to do until the love of a family can supplant it."

Celeste drew in a sharp breath, feeling tears spring to her eyes. Through the blur, she raised her gaze to her Uncle Harold's and found his gentle eyes upon her. He must have told the man her situation. But, oh, what a great relief it was to know her brother would be welcome, and that her future husband's intent was to provide him with a home. Celeste swiped at a tear which threatened to fall.

Mr Oliver reached into his bag once again. "This final gift," he said, "is of particular worth to your betrothed. He instructed me to hand it over with great care. Indeed, that I was to place it on your hand my own self, as in his stead."

"And was there a message to accompany this gift?" Celeste asked.

Mr Oliver shook his head. "Nay, my lady, there was not. He writes merely that you will already know what it means."

He drew open the small box and came to her, placing a ring upon the third finger of her left hand. Celeste held it up and her breath caught. A ring of three pearls. Three. So similar to that which Diego had given her. Yet so different, too, for this one had the deep red of a single magnificent ruby woven into the design. Three white pearls and a red ruby. Her betrothal ring, and, aye, she did know what it meant.

It meant a lifetime without the man she loved.

Chapter Nineteen

Cruel, it was, the dream that came to her that night. She and Diego lay together on a riverbank, clothed only in moonlight. His hand reached up to stroke her hair, then slid down to cup the fullness of her breast, its warm weight resting against his palm.

"I've come for you," he said.

"Nay, Diego. It cannot be. I have bound myself to another."

His eyes glittered with hurt. Her throat tightened.

"Why, Celeste?"

"Because of what I learned from you. Love does what is best for others. It is not selfish."

"I taught you this?"

"Aye, you did, when you wisely chose to set aside your manly desire for my good. Do you not remember, my love? You would not give me your seed. You would not let me bear your child, though I greatly wished it."

His fingertip circled around the softness of her nipple. She felt the tender bud begin to harden. A burn started in her body.

"Would you bear my son, my love?"

She closed her eyes. "Would that I might, Diego, but I am bound by sacred oath to another."

"Would you bear my son?"

She drew in her breath at the heat that melted within her body. "I cannot."

"Would you take my seed?"

"Oh, Diego. It is my heart's fondest wish."

He kissed her lips. *"Believe."*

It was the eve of Celeste's wedding. She went to bed early, subdued, and hoping that sleep might bring solace for her anxious mind. But she found herself fitful and unable to relax. It was those dreams. They made her almost afraid to close her eyes. Even long after she awoke her body burned with desire for the man she could never have. Her body ached with unappeased need, her breasts tender and craving Diego's touch, her woman's flesh moist and ready for a man made only of shadow and memory.

And yet she lived for those dreams. In the five months since she'd come home, her conscious memory of Diego had dimmed enough to get her through the days of loneliness. She'd forgotten how he smelled, how he tasted. She'd forgotten the lithe grace with which he moved, and how his eyes sparked fire when angry. She'd forgotten the feel of his flesh against hers.

At first she'd welcomed the small mitigation of pain that such forgetfulness brought her, but as time went on it frightened her. The man of flesh was becoming a ghost.

But then the dreams had begun. And while she knew the pain of that sharp, bittersweet moment of waking, when each time she'd realize anew that Diego and his love were lost to her, she also had those tender, hungry dream moments to relive. Oh, they seemed so real. Diego seemed so real.

Her worry now was that soon both hunger and dreams would cease, driven away in the moment when another man would take her into his arms and claim her body. She didn't know if he'd be young or old, hasty or gentle. But if, perchance, he should appease the desires of her young body, then the dreams of Diego might depart and leave her heart forlorn. The thought made her want to cry.

An unexpected knock on the door of her bedroom interrupted her thoughts. Hettie's voice called; Celeste jumped from the bed to let her in, noting as the elderly maid entered that the wrinkled cheeks were red with exertion and her eyes bright with excitement.

"He's here!" Hettie panted. "Oh, m'lady. Who would've believed it?"

"Who? My bridegroom?"

"Nay, not he! There'd be no surprise in that." Hettie sat upon the bed and pulled Celeste down to sit beside her. "Diego. He's here in London."

Celeste's hand flew unbidden to her chest. "Oh, Hettie. He's not."

"Aye, he is. I went to early Mass this eventide, thinking to pray for your happiness on this eve of your nuptials. So intent was I on my prayers that I hardly noticed when someone slipped into the pew beside me. Only when there was a touch on my arm did I realize—"

Celeste could not breathe. "He's here. He's come for me."

"Aye, that's what he told me. Used those very words, in fact. He's forsaken the priesthood—not the Church, mind you, just the priesthood. He's come for you."

"Did you say aught of my betrothal?"

"I did. I thought the lad ought to know what he stood up against."

"Oh, sweet mercy! Now he thinks I care naught for him, that I made haste in finding myself another match."

"Nay! He understands your reasons."

"How could he? He knows nothing about Jacob."

"Aye, but he does. He's known of him for months."

Celeste's head jerked around. "How could Diego have known about Jacob months ago? You…you told him, didn't you?"

Hettie looked at the floor, shrugging one shoulder. "And what if I did? 'Twas what was needful to be said at the time. You were the cause of it yourself, you were, talking all sorts of foolish talk about a man and a woman not needing the bond of matrimony to be committed to one another, and wanting to hie yourself and your brother down to Diego's isle, heedless of the laws of God. And what would ye have got there but a babe in your belly and a foul name for yourself? Ah, lass. Your dear mother would've rolled in her grave."

Celeste stood abruptly and paced the floor beside the bed.

"You'd have corrupted a man of God," Hettie muttered, studying her young charge's face.

Celeste didn't answer.

"You'd have struggled, m'lady. A woman all alone—"

Celeste spun round. "Enough, Hettie!" Then, hearing the sharp tone with which she spoke, she drew in a deep breath and quieted her voice. "I know all those things. I know you did what you thought best. But, Hettie, don't you see? Diego Castillo is the most noble man alive. Knowing about Jacob, he would never have allowed me to accept less than an honourable marriage, and since he couldn't offer me that…"

"Aye, love. He set you aside. I was glad for it at the time, but seeing you grieve these many months has made me wonder if I wasn't an old fool."

"Where is he?"

"He's taken a room at the Merry Whistler. He and Don Ricardo."

Celeste spun around, throwing open the armoire that held her gowns. "Hurry, Hettie! Help me dress!"

"What are you going to do? You can't get out of your betrothal. Not now, with the King himself a witness to it."

"We shall see."

"What are you going to do?"

Celeste was already pulling her nightshift over her head. "I don't know for sure. Only that I cannot in good conscience place my hand into that of another man on the morrow without at least talking with Diego first. I love him, Hettie. If nothing else, I want him to know that much."

"I'll go with you. Only give me a bit to catch my breath."

"Nay, not this time. I'm going alone." Celeste held up a hand to stop the wave of protest. "I care not for propriety, not tonight. Say no more. Your meddling has cost me enough already."

Hettie harrumphed, settling Celeste's gown into place, then tying on her sleeves. "He's got his friend there with him, but 'tis unseemly to go by dark of night to a gentleman's bedroom. You'd best be certain that talking is *all* you'll be doing."

"Now that," Celeste said, meeting the old woman's stare, "is something I may not be able to promise you."

Ricardo scratched his head and drew on his wool cape. "How long did you say I was to dawdle about in the tavern? Not that I mind, since you're buying the drinks. But just so I'll not interrupt anything…ah…*important*."

"I don't know exactly," Diego answered.

"Are you sure she's coming?"

Diego breathed in deeply. "She's coming. Or at least I hope to God she is."

Ricardo turned round and raised an eyebrow. "And are you going to tell her?"

"I don't know. That depends on whether she loves me. I fear she does not. I said some terrible things to her when last we spoke."

"You weren't yourself. You'd just come back to a home filled with memories, seen parents you hadn't seen in ten years…"

"And killed my brother."

"Aye, let's not forget that. Though the bastard deserved it."

Diego frowned. "Don't speak ill of the dead."

Ricardo clucked his tongue. "Only for your sake will I refrain, *amigo*. Otherwise I'd say the bastard deserved it."

"Ricardo!"

"*Está bien, está bien.* But you must at least acknowledge that Celeste would never have been happy married to him. She'll be much happier married to you."

"That is if we get married. Tonight should be the moment

of truth. I will not expect her to marry me if she does not love me. She deserves better than that."

"She loves you, Diego. I know she still must. She surely must have understood that you'd gone over the edge, that darkness swallowed you up for just a while."

"I left for Hispaniola without even saying goodbye."

Ricardo grunted. Diego stood and paced, his hands nervous. Ricardo poured a drink and handed it to him. "Drink this. Then you'll at least be calm, whatever happens tonight."

Diego gulped at the drink, knowing the fine Madeira would help but little. He set down the empty glass and resumed his pacing. "I love her," he said. "But what will I do if she no longer loves me?"

"It really shouldn't matter."

Diego snorted. "Not matter? Of course it matters!"

"Nay, it really doesn't. All the arrangements are in place."

"That's where you're wrong." Diego ran lean fingers through his hair and faced his friend. "If I discover that she loves me not, there will be no wedding tomorrow. I'll release her to find another she might love better than me."

"You would defy the wishes of the King of Spain, Diego? After all he did to help you procure those dispensations from the Pope?"

"If I must. I'll not marry Celeste unless she wants me as I want her."

"Hell and damnation. Every day men marry women who don't love them. Oftimes they don't even *know* them."

"That's not what God intended. There should be love, Ricardo. On *both* sides."

Ricardo sighed. "You're a hopeless romantic, Diego, for one who spent nearly ten years as a priest."

"Perhaps I'm a hopeless romantic *because* I spent ten years as a priest."

Ricardo laughed. "Aye, perhaps there's truth in that. You've waited years for this. But look here, *amigo*. What a beautiful night of love will your wedding night be, eh?" He turned and walked to the door. "Let's hope it is all you ever dreamed it would be."

Diego lifted an eyebrow. "Assuming there's a wedding first, of course."

Ricardo laughed. "Of course, my virtuous ex-priest. Of course." He shut the door. Diego could hear him, laughing still, make his way down the hall towards the stairs.

Celeste had almost convinced herself she could control her excitement by the time she stood in front of Diego's door. She'd spent well-nigh the entire ride reminding herself that she was betrothed to another, and that she owed that nameless man a virtuous bride on his wedding night. By the time she mounted the stairs to Diego's room she felt sure she could handle those strong feelings.

Then Diego opened the door.

Not even in her dreams had he appeared so appealing. He towered above her in the close quarters of the dimly lit hallway, his shoulders broad and magnificent in a shirt of crisp white linen beneath a doublet of forest-green brocade.

He drew her quickly into the room, closed the door, then knelt before her and kissed her hand in a gesture so tender her heart melted.

She started and pulled her hand away. "Nay, Diego."

His eyes darkened with hurt, quickly masked. "You came," he said quietly.

"Aye, I am here."

He stood, his eyes roving over her hungrily. He lightly fingered the veil which covered her hair, the one her betrothed had given her. Something softened in his face. He tugged at the laces of her new cloak and pulled it from her shoulders, his eyes never leaving her face.

"You are even more lovely than I remembered," he said in a voice husky with emotion.

She swallowed hard at the sweet tension which filled the space between them.

"Ah, Celeste," he said, his voice a warm growl. "You came." His hand raised as if he would touch her, draw her near, then clenched and dropped. He turned away and gestured towards where two chairs were pulled near the fire. "Please, come sit with me."

"Why are you here, Diego?"

He halted, his body stiffening. "Hettie did not tell you?"

"Aye, she told me something."

Diego turned to face her. The hunger in his eyes tore her breath away. "I came for you, Celeste. I love you."

Her breath stilled. It was the desire of her heart to fling aside all hindrances and rush to his embrace, to tell him how much she loved him, too. But her conscience pulled at her.

She walked to the chair nearest the fire and set herself on the edge of it, ignoring the pained look that crossed his face at her lack of response. "You are no longer a priest? How could that be?"

He breathed in deeply and moved to sit beside her, his long form so near that their knees brushed. Even that brief, accidental contact made Celeste's stomach tighten.

"'Tis a lengthy story. I'll save the details for another time," he said. "Only that I realized I had never experienced a true call from God. I entered the priesthood for the wrong reasons, to absolve myself of the guilt I felt over Leonora's death."

He leaned forward. "I didn't leave the priesthood because I'd fallen in love with you. You must never feel you came between me and my vow to God. You were only His instrument, sent to show me that I was on a path He never intended."

Celeste lowered her eyes, afraid he might read the conflict of emotions there. Diego was free, no longer a man of God. Now simply a man. There was no more vow of celibacy. He was free to court her, free to marry her, free to make love with her.

Except that she was not free.

"What are you asking of me, Diego?"

He studied her for so long that she grew anxious. "I want

you to forgive me," he said finally. "I know I hurt you with the cruel words I said, with the callous way I left you. All I can say is that Damian's death made me fearful and wild for a time."

"I knew that. Somehow I knew that. Of course I've forgiven you."

Relief was evident in his expression.

"You came all this way to ask forgiveness of me?"

"Nay. I could have done that much in a letter." His eyes met hers. "I came all this way to make you my wife."

Celeste closed her eyes, unable to breathe.

"I want to marry you," Diego said. "I want to lie with you, love you, protect you, give you my seed. I want to spend my days hearing your laughter drift through my world, letting your sweet song cajole me to sleep. I want to finish my days with you by my side. Would you have me?"

She couldn't answer, couldn't look at him.

He finally spoke, acknowledging that which stood between them. "You are betrothed to another."

"I didn't know you would return."

She opened her eyes and looked at him. His face was gentle, his eyes filled with compassion.

"Do you love me, Celeste?"

A sob caught in her throat. "Aye, Diego. I love you. But tomorrow I shall be joined to another. By this time tomorrow night I shall have become his wife in truth. But, oh, how can I bear it?"

Diego pulled her into his arms, smoothing her hair. "Shhh. Don't cry, my love."

Celeste swiped at her tears. "I cannot bear the thought of his touch, not when it's you I desire. I cannot bear the thought that he'll kiss me and touch me. Oh, Diego, what have I done?"

"You did what you had to do. You did not know I would return."

"Aye, but know this, Diego Castillo. I will never love my husband. I will never love any other but you. Each time he makes love to me it will be your face I shall see. And when I bear his child I will wish that it were yours. Oh, how I will wish it could have been yours!" She dissolved into sobs.

Diego rocked her, his breath soft against her hair. For long, long minutes they held one another, letting love wash over them in gentle, undulating waves that had nothing to do with desire and had everything to do with tenderness. He traced her lips with a fingertip, but he did not kiss her. She caressed his hair and stroked the firm lines of his jaw. She touched her lips to the pulse at his throat. He whispered "I love you" and kissed her cheek.

Inevitably, the feeling deepened. Their breathing quickened. It happened all at once, like quicksilver racing through their veins. Celeste pulled Diego down to her and kissed him, her tongue parting his lips and tasting of the silken depths of his mouth. He groaned, his embrace tightening.

When they finally pulled apart, she trembled, her loins hot and throbbing. "I must go," she said. "If I stay…"

"Celeste…"

"'Twould be wrong, Diego. Even though our love feels so right."

He looked away, the muscle in his jaw working with some strong emotion. "Celeste, there's something…I really must tell you…I'm—"

She laid a finger across his lips. "Shhh. Say no more. I'm afraid if I hear it I'll lack the strength to leave you."

"But this is of great import, and you—"

She stilled the words with a kiss, putting all her love into the gesture. He seemed to forget all else, as she'd hoped he would. He groaned and pulled her near, deepening the kiss until she had to pull away, trembling.

"I must leave you now. Please, Diego. Be content to know that I will always love you." She stepped away, noting that his eyes had become darkest blue and stormy with passion.

His gaze followed her to the door. She drew her cloak around her shoulders and laced it, trying to ignore the longing in his eyes.

Only by sheer will did she keep herself from forsaking all her good intentions. She ached to return to him, catch his hands, and lead him to the bed.

As she turned to go, he called her name.

"Believe," he said simply.

And Celeste—looking into those eyes so blue, so green, so warm—could not. Even though she so desperately wanted to.

Chapter Twenty

Celeste would be married, King Henry had decided, in the same chapel in which he'd wed Catherine, his own beloved Spaniard. It was not large, but the atmosphere was restful, as if the prayers of many lingered there and now gave off an aura of tranquillity.

Candles burned, their fragrance filling the air. Large bouquets of English flowers added their own incense, plucked that very morn from the King's hothouses.

Celeste stood in the vestibule, peering towards the altar while Hettie fussed with the folds of her new gown. Aunt Evelyn had gifted her with it. Truly, if there were ever a gown fit for a royal wedding, this one was. It was of costly ivory silk from Cipangu, cut and sewn by the best seamstresses in all of London. The neck of the bodice was seeded with tiny pearls, virtuously demure and yet alluring. Of her bosom it showed little but promised much, and, as Aunt Ev had said, would doubtless please the man who stood beside her to pronounce eternal vows this day. Except that Celeste cared not a whit if he were pleased. Far better for her if he were not.

"Where is he?" Aunt Ev whispered harshly, handing Celeste a gilt-edged prayer book. "I see Harold, the King and Queen and their attendants, and the cleric who is to perform the rite. But of your bridegroom not so much as one hair of his head."

"He's probably so decrepit with age that he cannot make it up the steps," Celeste murmured bitterly. "Or perhaps he waits until I am already at the altar and dare not run from his unsightly visage."

Aunt Ev smiled. "I've not seen him myself. But Harold met him early this morn and swears he's a right pretty man to behold, and not at all decrepit. Perhaps your…ah…*duty* this eventide will not be overly burdensome."

Celeste felt her face grow warm, thinking of the talk she'd had with Aunt Ev earlier. The older woman had been painfully forthright and thorough, describing in intimate detail the way in which a man coupled with his wife, and giving her instruction on how a dutiful wife might please her husband. She'd finished up by saying, with her indomitable honesty, that even though Celeste might not love the man in the beginning, if he were gentle and gave her pleasure, surely she'd eventually learn to care for him deeply.

Well, Celeste knew better than that. She'd endure his touch, at least long enough to give him an heir. But that was all she would ever give him. Her heart was Diego's. His alone.

Diego. She wondered where he was at this moment, thankful that he didn't know the day or hour of her nuptials, thankful that he'd not have to endure the pain of seeing her place her hand into that of another to swear the vows he'd wanted to hear for himself. Tears prickled behind her eyelids. She knew that one day soon she'd hear he'd boarded a ship and sailed back to Seville. It would be over.

The music began, the swell of the organ making the hackles rise at the base of her neck. Her stomach rolled. "It's time, dear," Aunt Ev said, handing her a bouquet of flowers.

Celeste turned and moved down the aisle, having never felt more alone in her life. And where was he, this mysterious bridegroom? He still had not taken his place at the altar.

She was nearly there herself before the heavy door behind the priest opened and two men stepped out. The man in front was tall and resplendent in a black velvet doublet and black silk hose. He wore a heavy gold chain and pendant bearing his family crest. She raised her eyes to his face.

Her heart stopped beating. Indeed, she stopped walking, unable to move, the music flowing on past her as she tried to find her breath in the sudden void of air.

Diego!

The priest gestured and Diego moved forward. Ricardo stepped into place beside him. Diego's dark eyes never left her, his expression filled with concern. He raised an imploring hand.

Diego?

Celeste's mind was a jumble of confusion. None of this made sense. She could only stare, trying to understand, afraid to believe. The priest held up one hand and the organist stopped the music. Celeste still had not moved one step closer to the altar.

"Come, my child," the priest urged. "Take your place at your bridegroom's side."

She stood, transfixed. "Diego?" she murmured. "You? You are my bridegroom?"

"Aye."

"But how? You did know of this yester eve?"

"Aye."

"And you let me weep? You let me believe I must betray my love for you to wed someone else?"

"I had to know if you yet loved me. If you had not, I would have given you freedom to choose another."

She hesitated, considering his reply. "I understand that," she said finally. "But why did you not tell me after I'd confessed my love to you?"

"I tried, if you remember. But then you kissed me, love, and told me to content myself—"

The priest cleared his throat. He turned to Diego, his voice quiet and solemn. "Sirrah, 'tis not meet that these intimate matters be debated here before these assembled guests. Perhaps we should adjourn to a more private chamber?"

Diego looked forlorn and uncomfortable. He turned anguished eyes towards her.

She raised one hand to him, in an unconscious gesture of supplication that he might help her understand. In the winking flames of the candles the ruby in her betrothal ring sparked into flame. She looked at it. Three pearls and a ruby, the rich, deep colour of passion. She looked up at Diego, at his frightened eyes, and she understood now what he'd been trying to tell her.

Celeste moved forward to the altar. "Nay, Father," she said, her voice clear and strong. "There's no need. I am ready to pledge my vows to this man." She placed her hand into Diego's warm palm and smiled up into his face. "Quite ready, indeed."

Diego groaned as someone pressed another cup of wine into his hand. He did not need more wine, not when upstairs there awaited him something—someone—altogether more intoxicating than anything in this great banqueting hall. But one could hardly say nay to the King of England.

The feasting, dancing, drinking, and merriment had gone on for hours now, for King Henry was a youthful, exuberant man who liked such joviality. Throughout most of the festivities Diego had been separated from Celeste, always able to see her glittering eyes and flushed cheeks from across the expansive room, but unable to touch her or speak with her. It was a curious custom, this English game, making a man wait to bed his own wife while everyone in the room twittered behind their hands and speculated about how long the bridegroom would bear with such restraint.

Thankfully, a man who'd been a priest knew a great deal about restraint. Diego had good-spiritedly conversed with the men, smiled at their ribald humour, endured their teasing suggestions about how best to tame a fiery Englishwoman, and swallowed more wine than even a Spaniard should have consumed.

His patience would soon pay off, he hoped, for only a short while before Celeste had been led in a triumphal procession of giggling females up the broad stairs to a suite of rooms above. While he would have preferred to take his bride to some place of his own choosing, the King had insisted on playing host for this one special night, chuckling at what must have been a stricken look of discomfort on Diego's face.

"Don't worry, sirrah," the King had said. "We shall give orders. There will not be attendants outside your rooms tonight. You and your lovely bride can carouse to your heart's content without fear of being disturbed." He'd slapped Diego on the back. "Never shall it be said that the King of England is less than a worthy host, eh?"

An eternity passed before a young woman came to whisper words in the King's ear. He turned to Diego with a wink. "Your lady awaits you, sir. You are dismissed, to consummate what we all hope shall be a long and prosperous union. Please know that the King of Spain thanks you, and I thank you. And perhaps when this night is ended your satisfied bride will thank you, too."

The King guffawed at his own joke as a reddened Diego bowed before him and turned to bound with a grin up the stairs, amused that England's monarch had obviously had a bit too much to drink.

Celeste did not hear Diego enter the room. She had meant to be waiting for him, a vision of feminine loveliness in his bed, her soft pink gown contrasting softly with the crisp white linens. As it was, he caught her by surprise.

She was bent over the fire, wrestling with a large and heavy kettle of water for his bath. When she turned with it, awkwardly, clumsily, he was suddenly there, his hands taking the iron vessel from her. The accidental brush of their fingertips brought a gasp to her lips. He smiled down into her eyes, as if he knew how urgently her stomach had fluttered at his nearness.

"A small woman like you shouldn't be trying to lift this all by yourself," he said quietly, his gaze touching her everywhere, making her feel strange. "Where do you want it?"

"There," she said, gesturing to the nearby tub. "I thought you might like a bath. I've already had mine." That Diego was her husband now, that he was here in the room and would bathe in her presence, was almost unbearably stimulating. She felt her face grow warm and turned away.

She heard him pour the water into the tub and place the kettle once again near the fire. She busied herself with straightening the room and fluffing pillows, trying to ignore Diego as he undressed. It didn't work. Even the smooth glide of his garments as he lowered them to the floor made her insides somersault.

She was nervous. Excited and nervous. It seemed a dream come true at last. Diego was her *husband*. He had taken her hand and spoken vows to her and soon, very soon now, he'd lead her to that bed and make her his woman in all truth.

It was everything she'd ever wished for, and she was so anxious she could barely breathe. Even without looking at him she was aware of everything about him. Sweet tension hummed between them, electrifying the air all around them, making even her skin tingle.

She sought a distraction, and seated herself at a small writing desk. Her eyes averted, she nevertheless heard the gentle splash of water as Diego lowered himself into the tub. Only then did she chance a glance in his direction. He eyed her thoughtfully, brow furrowed slightly as if perplexed. Her nervousness must be apparent to him. Either that, or he was as nervous as she.

That thought brought a smile to her lips. It eased her own discomfort to think that tonight her new husband would have done with ten years of chastity, and that he would do so within her arms. He would reclaim his full rights as a man, and he would make of her a woman.

She opened her journal and began to write. So much had happened since she'd closed this little book...

She'd become engrossed in the words by the time Diego's voice startled her. "What are you doing?" he asked.

She looked up. "I'm writing in my journal." She smiled at his raised eyebrow. "I began one the day I left for Spain. At first it was simply a way of keeping a record of my journey to share later with Jacob. But I've become rather enamoured of the practice, and now I write something each evening before I retire. It helps me sort out my thoughts, understand my feelings."

He reached for the bar of soap. And, oh, his arms were wonderfully lean and muscular. Soon they'd encircle her and hold her close against his body. Celeste swallowed hard, trying to concentrate on breathing.

"What are you writing now?" he asked. "What feelings are you trying to understand tonight?"

Only Diego would have asked such a question. Only Diego would have cared. Celeste's heart warmed at the love between them, at his tenderness and desire to know her as a woman.

"I'm writing of how pleased I am that you were my bridegroom. Last evening I wrote of all my anxieties. Of my great sadness at losing you, and of my worry that I'd done the wrong thing, even though I made the only choice I could have made for Jacob's sake."

She brushed the feather of her quill against her lips and smiled at Diego. "He liked his puppy, Diego. Never have I seen him so happy, not since our parents died. And he said a word! Just one, but it was a start. The puppy was jumping up, licking him all over his face. Jacob laughed and, without giving conscious thought, he told the puppy 'No!' I heard it, but could scarcely believe it. Oh, Diego, it brought tears to my eyes."

Diego smiled, silent for some time. "And what of your betrothal gifts?" he asked finally. "Did you like them?"

"Oh, aye," she said, remembering their richness and the words which had accompanied each one. "Strange now to think you were the one who chose them. It gives me pleasure, knowing that."

The muscle tightened in his cheek. "Lady, you do not yet know pleasure."

The words shot through her, snatching her breath with their blatant sexuality. This was not Diego the restrained priest. This was Diego the man. Her husband.

He met her gaze. His burned with a new intensity. "Tonight, Celeste, you will learn of pleasure."

The words thrummed through her, making her breasts tighten. How could it be that Diego's mere *words* could make her so breathless?

She lowered her gaze. "I tremble at the thought of learning of it with you, my husband."

He studied her. "Do you tremble with delight, Celeste? Or with fear?"

Their gazes locked. His burned with the same dark fires she felt. "Both," she answered truthfully.

He nodded. "Then turn aside for now, my sweet, and let me rise from this water. It grows colder and I would don my robe."

She looked towards the fire. "There is more water."

He chuckled. "Nay, good wife. We'll save it for later."

The words brought to her mind an immediate vision of their two bodies entwined in the one tub together. Heat suffused her face. Though she didn't lift her eyes to Diego's nakedness as he stepped from the water and towelled himself dry, she sensed his amusement and wondered if he somehow knew her wanton thoughts.

There was a slide of silk as he donned his garment, soft footsteps as he came to her. She lifted her eyes to his face when he halted beside her.

He took the quill from her fingers and laid it aside, then drew her up into his embrace. "Come to me, *preciosa*." His voice was a marvel of warmth. "Come, my dearest love."

He folded her into his embrace, then took her hand and placed it on his chest, delicate fingertips against his bare skin, covering it with the firm pressure of his own. "Feel my heart," he said in his rich Spanish accent. "How steadily it beats. And while it does I will ever love you, ever protect you. My sweet Celeste, set aside your fear. I will not hurt you."

"I know," she whispered. "I'm not afraid. It's only that I want so badly for this night to be beautiful. We've waited so long." She looked away. "I know little of how to make love to a man, Diego. I fear I'll not be pleasing to you."

A low growl escaped his throat. He pulled her more firmly against him, until her breasts scrubbed softly against his chest and her soft belly pressed against the hard ridge of his arousal. "Have no worry, sweet wife. You are already well on your way to pleasing me," he murmured.

For long minutes he held her, unhurried, enjoying the pleasure of touch alone, letting his warmth become her warmth, rocking her gently against his pelvis, the small motions tingling through her core.

He lifted her chin to look into her eyes, seeming surprised that tears glistened on her lashes, so overwhelmed was she by the emotion between them.

"You are so beautiful tonight," he said in a reverent whisper. "Can I believe that you are my own wife? A substantial being, and not some ethereal forest nymph who shall disappear with my heart when the gilded rays of morn cast their light into yonder window?"

She smiled, her fingers slipping around his neck to twine into the softness of his long hair. "Kiss me, Diego, and you shall see."

Their lips came together, gently at first, just a breath of softness, dew upon dew. Celeste's hand slipped beneath his hair to the corded sinew of his neck, pulling him down to her. She felt herself tremble—or was it he?

Her tongue licked at his lips, tasting the sweetness of wine on his breath. This kiss had qualities possessed by none before it, free of guilt and shame as it was, and freely Celeste savoured it, sipping at Diego, tasting him, teasing him with shameless provocation.

He responded beautifully, equally ready to sample delight. He answered the darting of her tongue with his own, leaving her breathless and giddy when he finally left her lips to trail fire across her eyes, her brow, the sensitive places near her ear.

"I love your hair," he whispered. "I oft dreamed of it wrapped around me as I loved you." She shivered at the thought, her eyes closing. Diego reached up and gently tugged it down, untwining the elegant coil until her coppery curls fell in loose disarray around her shoulders to her waist.

He skimmed his fingertips down its length, causing her swift intake of breath at his lightest stroke against her breast. "Those dreams were in my mind when I bought the jewelled hairbrush. That night I dreamed I brushed your hair. It was like finest silk beneath my palms."

He leaned near, his words a sighing of breath against her ear. "Always, *always,* those dreams ended with you in my arms."

Celeste's eyes opened, searched for and found his. She caught her breath at the hunger she saw within them. "And now, Diego?"

"This is no dream, Celeste. But, aye, it shall end the same way."

His lips found hers again. With scarcely any effort at all, he caught her up into his arms and carried her across to the bed. Her arms held him, pulled him down with her onto the soft feather mattress. "Nay, love," he said, rolling so that he lay beside her and not upon her. "I'm heavy. Too heavy for you to bear."

She laughed, surprising herself with the soft and provocative sound. "Oh, Diego. If only you could know how I've longed to bear you. Your body. Your sorrows. Your sons."

He closed his eyes. "Ah, love," he murmured. "You know not what you do to me."

"Whatever I'm doing now, it is not the half of what I long to do."

He kissed the beating pulse in her neck. "And what do you long to do?"

She smiled and trailed her fingertip down his chest. "I want to see you. All of you."

His eyes glittered fire. He loosened the belt of his robe and drew it off.

Celeste's eyes took in his form, exulting in his lean, angular beauty.

"I want to touch you."

Diego captured her hand and placed it over his heart.

"Not there," she whispered, her fingertips curling against the honey-coloured hair of his chest.

Diego struggled to breathe at the very thought that his wife wanted to explore his body. He shuddered as her hands slid downward, so slowly downward, skimming past his ribs, his belly...downward. His breath completely stilled when one delicate fingertip touched his smoothest skin. A groan escaped his lips when her hand boldly closed around him.

Such exquisite pleasure, her hand on his shaft, her eyes watching, darkening, when his muscles began to jerk beneath the maddening sensation of her touch. She grew bolder, tormenting him until he could no longer keep himself from that primitive rhythm a man instinctively knew. He taught it to her now, pulsing himself firmly against her hand.

When he would halt her, she boldly sought out other places, caressing his body, stroking his thighs, growing bolder as she discovered how to please him. It *all* pleased him.

"Do you like me to touch you, Diego?" she whispered.

He could not speak, only answer her caresses with a wild, primitive sound. She responded with a soft sound of triumph, and Diego knew then how it felt to be a beast tamed to hand. Celeste had him now—tied, tethered, trussed—and he could only quake beneath her touch, revelling in the wild beauty of her utter possession.

She lowered her head, the touch of her tongue supplanting that of her fingertips as she licked his most sensitive skin. That nearly sent him over the edge. His every sense reeled. He could have screamed with the excruciating pleasure of her warm, wet mouth.

Instead, he grasped her head, fingers lacing through her hair. "No, Celeste. No, I cannot bear it."

Her expression was one of hurt. "You don't like that?"

"Aye, I like it. Far too much. So much that I'm about to lose control, and I don't want our pleasure to end, not just yet. Not when I want so badly to make sweet love to you."

She sat back, letting his breathing slow, letting the shaking in his limbs gradually subside.

He gathered her into his arms, stroking the hair cascading down her back. "You, my sweet virtuous wife, are a wondrous surprise. Who'd ever have thought you'd know to do that?"

She made a womanly sound of pleasure, a proud she-cat rejoicing in her power over him.

Diego smiled at it. It was time he reminded her that possession could be a mutual thing. Her eyes followed him, half veiled and languorous, as he carefully unlaced her bodice and spread it open so that the lovely curves lay exposed to his view.

Celeste gasped when his hands cupped her fullness.

Diego strummed his thumbs across the rosy peaks. Celeste moaned. The sound pleased him, and he teased them, pulling at them gently, watching as Celeste's dark eyes grew more and more distant beneath his touch.

His lips found her. Celeste gave a strangled cry. "Aye, oh, Diego!" Her hands came up to tangle in his hair.

The tension in her body increased, and Diego also knew triumph. Celeste was his love, and he wanted her to burn, to burn brightly, to burn for him.

His tongue, his hands, his body ignited her.

He knew by the way her features became taut and etched with strain, by the way her hips lifted and rotated. She longed to answer that age-old call.

"Celeste," he whispered, slipping down her gown so that she lay naked against him. "Your name reminds me of heaven, and your body is that of an angel."

By now Celeste was past comprehension. She could only moan and pant, her head tossing from side to side, her chest heaving.

Yet her body sought its pleasure, hips rising to the rhythm of his touch.

He stopped stroking her to change position; she gave an anguished cry. "Nay, Diego, don't leave me!"

He embraced her tightly, murmuring against the fragrance of her hair. "I know, little one. I know how those fires burn."

He used one knee to separate her thighs and then moved between them, stretching out over her, his shaft hard against soft, moist woman. He ached to enter her, but made no move to do so.

Celeste was not as patient. Her body responded to the pressure of his. Her hips ground against him. Diego shuddered at the wave of pleasure which rolled over him, through him, reverberating like thunder to his core.

It was time. He had waited so long he was beginning to hurt. "Celeste," he whispered. "I cannot hold off much longer. I must have you, my love, if you are ready."

"Please, Diego. Oh, please."

He parted her with his fingertips and eased himself just inside her, waiting there, letting her tight sheath stretch slowly to accommodate him. Her arms wound tightly around him, her nipples teasing his chest.

His legs quaked, every instinct urging him to hurry, to thrust himself into her softness. Still he moved carefully, so carefully, using short forward thrusts to let her adjust to having him within her. But her warmth was agony, the sweetest of torture chambers.

Celeste gripped his shoulders as he entered her, holding her breath. He looked into her eyes, seeing in them excitement and just a hint of fear. He kissed her. "I'm trying not to hurt you," he said.

"It doesn't hurt, not yet."

But it was about to. Diego had just come to the barrier he'd been expecting. He paused, wanting to prepare her somehow, wanting to tell her he was sorry for what he was about to do, wanting to thank her for the precious gift of her virtue.

"Celeste, look at me," he commanded. She looked at him. "Wrap your arms around me." She did. He drew his hips back and drove forward, feeling the tearing in her body that felt almost like a tearing of his own.

Celeste gave a cry, her fingernails digging into his back.

"I'm sorry. I'm so sorry," he whispered.

She didn't answer right away. He bent his head and kissed her, wanting to hurt for her, needing to share her pain. He waited for what seemed an eternity, letting the burning in her body subside. "I didn't want to hurt you," he said. "I'm sorry."

She drew a deep breath. "It isn't bad. Already the pain eases. It is worth it to me to become your wife. Oh, Diego, how I've longed for it!"

"I promise you, love. There's no more pain, only pleasure."

"I tremble at the thought of learning of it with you, Diego."

Diego looked into her eyes. "Do you tremble with delight, Celeste? Or with fear?"

Celeste smiled softly. "With delight, Diego. Only with delight."

He closed his eyes, knowing a great relief. She was so brave, so generous, so giving. He would spend a lifetime seeking to make her happy and still not be worthy of her. In the thunder of his heartbeat he heard a prayer. *Let it be good, let it be good for her.*

His hips moved more quickly now. He stretched forward into her, wanting to fill her, to know her hidden places, to touch her womb. His hips caressed her, pouring into sweet motion all the love, all the longing he'd ever felt for her. He moved in the timeless dance of lovers, calling her to join him.

She understood. Her eyes found his. Their gazes locked. Her breathing grew ragged; her body grew taut with a tension he understood.

"Oh, Diego," she moaned. "Oh, Diego, oh!" Her hips began to rise steadily against his. Her nipples tightened, her breasts expanded and quivered with need. Her body arched wildly against his. Her chest heaved with her gasps and then stilled as she held her breath. A fine, fine sheen made her skin glow in the firelight. Oh, she was near the summit now, if only she dared take that spectacular flying leap over the edge.

Aye, she dared. She screamed his name as her muscles convulsed around him. He slowed just a bit, holding her close against his heart while she soared past the firmament and drifted down to the realm of mortals again.

Her sigh was the signal for his hips to take on a quickening rhythm. Celeste opened her eyes and watched his face, her expression so filled with love he wanted to sob at the beauty of it. He would paint her. Yes, he would paint her.

But not just now. Now he would love her.

Upwards he climbed—towards the cliffs, towards the summit, hurtling ever faster towards the summit's raw edge. As he neared the moment of his own satisfaction he heard Celeste's voice as from a great distance. "I love you, Diego. I love you and I want your child." She closed her eyes, her lips still moving. *"Almighty God, please give my husband an heir this night. I love him so. Please do not deny me this!"*

But the sun burst into brilliance all around him, exploding with astonishing intensity. It seemed a long, long time before he was lucid enough to remember exactly what Celeste's prayer had been.

When he did, he closed his eyes, his heart hammering at the thought. For Diego Castillo was a man who firmly believed in answered prayers.

Epilogue

September 12, 1518

Diego believed he was alone and so hadn't prayed in silence. He usually preferred to pray aloud, and in the Spanish that was his native tongue rather than the Latin he'd used as a priest. Spanish was the language of his heart. He felt sure that if God ever spoke directly to him, the Almighty would do it in Spanish. It was always the language Diego used when he needed to pour out his most ardent prayers.

Today was one of those times. For that reason he was kneeling at the altar rail in his family's small chapel, praying aloud and earnestly in a language that anyone in the whole Castillo family could comprehend. So he was a bit embarrassed when a shadow fell across his face and he looked up to see that he was *not* alone.

"I knew I'd find you here," Barto said.

"It's a good place to be, given the circumstances, wouldn't you think?"

Barto nodded. "Oh, aye. You'll get no argument with me on that. I've learned much about this business of prayer of late."

Diego eyed him dubiously. "You, Barto?"

Barto chuckled. "Aye, I have. Indeed, were it not for me and my fine prayers, you'd not be kneeling here today. There'd be no need of it."

"You speak in riddles, my huge African friend. What have you to do with the situation in which my lady and I now find ourselves?"

Barto laughed and clapped his hand on Diego's back. "You thought it was all your idea. It wasn't, you know. Padre Francisco and I prayed for this day as far back as your brother's pirate ship."

"Sweet merciful Jesus."

"Aye, he is sweet. Merciful, too. And that's why I believe he's going to answer that prayer you were praying as I walked in. Everything will work out, Diego. God didn't give you that sweet little woman to let you lose her now. Set aside your fears and be at peace."

Diego rose, shaking his head. "A lot you'd know about it."

He heard Barto's laughter even as he pushed open the heavy brass-trimmed door and blinked against the brilliance of the sunshine.

Diego heard his name called and turned. Jacob came flying at him, a blur of knees and elbows and boyish smiles, followed by Sam the dog. The rather *large* dog. Jacob jumped into Diego's arms, babbling excitedly. Diego could barely follow the boy's words.

"Nay, Jacob," he answered. "Your sister cannot play with you in the courtyard today. Aye, I'm glad you understand. Shall I get Alicia to play with you instead?"

Jacob pulled a wry face. "Not Alicia. She's afraid of Sam."

"Well, Sam *is* a bit unruly sometimes. Maybe you could talk Fernando into riding with you. Sam could romp along behind. Would you like that?"

"I suppose it will have to do," Jacob said, looking a bit crestfallen. "You know, Diego, if I'd known I'd not have Celeste to play with, I don't think I would've prayed so hard for this."

Diego's lips twisted. "So you're to blame for the rough

spot we're in?" He tickled Jacob's belly. "I'll remember that."

"Don't blame me," Jacob said. "I just prayed. God did what he wanted."

Diego smiled. "You're so right."

Diego entered the house. It was cool after the heat outside, and much too quiet. Normally the servants would be busy with preparations for the evening meal. But at the moment everyone seemed too preoccupied to go about their usual activities. He hoped there would be at least a little bread and cheese in the kitchen. Maybe some chilled wine. He'd gone hours without eating.

He was in the kitchen, cutting slices from a cold slab of meat, when he heard a noise behind him. "There you are, my son," his father said.

"Aye, Papi. Would you care for any of this meat while I'm cutting?"

"Nay, I had some fruit a while ago. And you'd best eat quickly."

Diego's head jerked round. His father smiled. "Your mother sent me to find you. She says it's almost time."

Diego spun, heading for the door. His father caught at his sleeve. "Nay, don't be in too big a rush, *hijo*. Eat first. You don't need to be at Celeste's side this very moment. First babies take their own sweet time."

"But it's been all day."

His father smiled. "Aye, it has. Seems like there ought to be some way to speed up the process, but the truth is, babies come when they will come."

Alejandro watched in silence while Diego finished his food, then wheeled his chair across the tiled floor. Diego moved to open the door and they made their way along the arched portico towards the courtyard. Alejandro chuckled. "You'd think a former priest would know a bit more about patience."

Diego snorted. "The good padres never had to endure *becoming* one," he said dryly.

"Well, look at my example, then. Your mother and I have prayed for this moment for years."

Diego's eyes rolled upwards. "Not you, too."

"What is that supposed to mean?"

"Only that while Celeste and I thought *we* were making this child, it seems that Barto and Francisco and Jacob and both my parents had all been busy petitioning well in advance. Under those circumstances, Celeste's pregnancy was unavoidable."

Alejandro laughed. "Then it was a mighty good thing that you...ah...*refrained* until vows were spoken."

Diego's lips twisted. "Without a doubt."

Alejandro looked past the fountain towards the room in which Celeste was giving birth. "Ah, Diego, my son. On this day I'll look for the first time upon my grandchild. It will be the second happiest day of my life."

Diego raised a questioning brow. "The second happiest? Which was the happiest?"

Alejandro looked up at his son, his eyes filling with tears. "It was the day I looked for the first time upon Damian and upon you."

Diego would have replied but for the knot in his throat.

A few moments later, the door opened and his mother looked out. She motioned for Diego. "Come, my son. Your child is on the way. It's just a matter of a few minutes now."

Diego hurriedly entered the room, his eyes adjusting to the dimness after the bright sun of the courtyard. Celeste was on the bed, her face red, her hair wet with perspiration. There was blood. An awful lot of it, it seemed to Diego. And Celeste was moaning, squeezing Hettie's hand as a new contraction came.

"Is she all right, Mamá?" he asked, hearing the odd note of panic in his voice.

His mother patted his arm. "Aye, Diego. She's fine. Everything is progressing just as it should. She's calling for you, though. She wants you to be at her side to welcome your child into the world. She's convinced it will be a son."

Diego moved towards her, feeling sick with guilt over the pain and the blood. If more men were present at births, perhaps they'd not be so quick to— Ah, who was he fooling? As soon as Celeste felt herself ready, he'd be back in her arms again. He craved her touch as he craved air to breathe. He truly couldn't leave his beautiful wife alone. Even if childbirth were awful.

"Celeste?" he ventured. "I'm here."

Her eyes opened. "Oh, Diego!" She grasped his hand. "I'm glad you came quickly. Margarita says he's coming and— *aarrgh!*" She grimaced, and squeezed Diego's hand so tightly he feared the bones would snap.

Margarita spoke in a firm tone. "'Tis time to push now, my lady. When I tell you, bear down with all your might." Celeste took a deep breath and looked at her husband. "Soon, Diego."

Margarita nodded. "Now, dear. Push and push hard."

Diego watched as Celeste groaned and pushed until her legs shook. She was so brave to have wished for this moment. And so strong to bear it with such dignity.

"Rest now," Margarita commanded.

Celeste breathed, quick panting breaths.

Margarita looked at Diego. "I see the head. Once more and perhaps the babe will be here."

The resting was soon over. Celeste pushed again, rested, pushed again. Within moments the child slipped out into the midwife's arms, giving a lusty yell as soon as those little lungs could fill with air.

Diego squeezed Celeste's hand. "A son, my love. A fine, healthy boy."

She breathed in, deeply. "Count his fingers and toes."

Diego grinned. "All there. Everything's there. He's perfect."

In a short while Diego's mother brought the baby to him, wrapped in a cloth of soft linen. Diego knelt down on one

knee so Celeste could see the miracle they'd made together—
with some help from Barto and Francisco and Jacob and his
parents. And God.

The baby blinked and looked at them with the wizened
features of an old man. His eyes were blue and he was, at least
in Diego's mind, the most beautiful child in all of Spain. His
heart twisted in joy so sharp it felt like pain.

His son.

"What shall we name him?" Celeste asked, her voice
sounding weary now.

"'Tis a custom in my country to name a child after a person
for whom one has great respect and admiration." He smiled
into her eyes. "I'd like to name him Tomás Alejandro Castillo.
If you agree, of course?"

Celeste's eyes softened. "Thomas? After my father?"

"Aye. I never knew him, but I know he reared a wonderful
woman. So, aye, Tomás for your father, and Alejandro for
mine. What say you?"

She stroked the baby's head with a slender fingertip. "I say
you should take Thomas Alejandro to meet his family. He is,
after all, the new Castillo family heir."

Diego almost ran with his new son to the door, then remembered something he'd forgotten. He hurried back to
his wife, who smiled at his excitement. He kissed her
soundly on the lips. "Thank you, my sweet. As long as we
live I'll never forget this moment. You've made me a happy
man today."

Celeste smiled. "Happiness is such a fleeting thing, Diego.
I'll have to keep you busy, making the next child and the next,
so you can have such days of happiness fairly often."

Diego shook his head, his eyes misting soft. "Ah, Celeste.
How I treasure you. Our children will never, ever doubt that
their parents love one another, and them, beyond all measure."
He leaned forward and placed a kiss upon her brow. "Rest now.
May your dreams be beautiful, my sweet love."

"They will be, Diego. They will be."

* * *

Celeste watched her husband carry their new son towards the door and through it, towards the waiting arms of his family. She raised grateful eyes to heaven, eyes that now filled with tears. A year ago it had seemed that happiness was an elusive thing, and that her search for it often brought more pain than pleasure.

Now she knew differently. Happiness was all around her, in the loving arms of family like Alejandro and Anne and Jacob. In the loving hearts of friends like Ricardo, Barto and Francisco. And though there was sometimes pain, more often there were moments of greater pleasure.

Celeste closed her eyes, a smile upon her weary face, and drifted towards sleep, her last conscious thought a memory of beautiful eyes of blue—those of her husband and those of her son.

* * * * *

THE ROYAL HOUSE OF NIROLI
Always passionate, always proud

The richest royal family in the world—united by blood
and passion, torn apart by deceit and desire

Nestled in the azure blue of the Mediterranean Sea, the
majestic island of Niroli has prospered for centuries. The
Fierezza men have worn the crown with passion and pride
since ancient times. But now, as the king's health declines, and
his two sons have been tragically killed, the crown is in
jeopardy.

The clock is ticking—a new heir must be found before the
king is forced to abdicate. By royal decree the internationally
scattered members of the Fierezza family are summoned to
claim their destiny. But any person who takes the throne must
do so according to The Rules of the Royal House of Niroli.
Soon secrets and rivalries emerge as the descendants of this
ancient royal line vie for position and power. Only a true
Fierezza can become ruler—a person dedicated to their
country, their people…and their eternal love!

Each month starting in July 2007,
Harlequin Presents is delighted to bring you
an exciting installment from
THE ROYAL HOUSE OF NIROLI,
in which you can follow the epic search
for the true Nirolian king.
Eight heirs, eight romances, eight fantastic stories!

Here's your chance to enjoy a sneak preview of the
first book delivered to you by royal decree…

FIVE minutes later she was standing immobile in front of the study's window, her original purpose of coming in forgotten, as she stared in shocked horror at the envelope she was holding. Waves of heat followed by icy chill surged through her body. She could hardly see the address now through her blurred vision, but the crest on its left-hand front corner stood out, its *royal* crest, followed by the address: *HRH Prince Marco of Niroli*...

She didn't hear Marco's key in the apartment door, she didn't even hear him calling out her name. Her shock was so great that nothing could penetrate it. It encased her in a kind of bubble, which only concentrated the torment of what she was suffering and branded it on her brain so that it could never be forgotten. It was only finally pierced by the sudden opening of the study door as Marco walked in.

"Welcome home, *Your Highness*. I suppose I ought to curtsy." She waited, praying that he would laugh and tell her that she had got it all wrong, that the envelope she was holding, addressing him as Prince Marco of Niroli, was some silly mistake. But like a tiny candle flame shivering vulnerably in the dark, her hope trembled fearfully. And then the look in Marco's eyes extinguished it as cruelly as a hand placed callously over a dying person's face to stem their last breath.

"Give that to me," he demanded, taking the envelope from her.

"It's too late, Marco," Emily told him brokenly. "I know the truth now…." She dug her teeth in her lower lip to try to force back her own pain.

"You had no right to go through my desk," Marco shot back at her furiously, full of loathing at being caught off-guard and forced into a position in which he was in the wrong, making him determined to find something he could accuse Emily of. "I trusted you…."

Emily could hardly believe what she was hearing. "No, you didn't trust me, Marco, and you didn't trust me because you knew that I couldn't trust you. And you knew that because you're a liar, and liars don't trust people because they know that they themselves cannot be trusted." She not only felt sick, she also felt as though she could hardly breathe. "You are Prince Marco of Niroli…. How could you not tell me who you are and still live with me as intimately as we have lived together?" she demanded brokenly.

"Stop being so ridiculously dramatic," Marco demanded fiercely. "You are making too much of the situation."

"*Too much?*" Emily almost screamed the words at him. "When were you going to tell me, Marco? Perhaps you just planned to walk away without telling me anything? After all, what do my feelings matter to you?"

"Of course they matter." Marco stopped her sharply. "And it was in part to protect them, and you, that I decided not to inform you when my grandfather first announced that he intended to step down from the throne and hand it on to me."

"To protect me?" Emily nearly choked on her fury. "Hand on the throne? No wonder you told me when you first took me to bed that all you wanted was sex. You *knew* that was the only kind of relationship there could ever be between us! You *knew* that one day you would be Niroli's king. No doubt you are expected to marry a princess. Is she picked out for you already, your *royal* bride?"

* * * * *

Look for THE FUTURE KING'S PREGNANT MISTRESS
by Penny Jordan in July 2007,
from Harlequin Presents,
available wherever books are sold.

THE GARRISONS

A brand-new family saga begins with

THE CEO'S SCANDALOUS AFFAIR
BY ROXANNE ST. CLAIRE

Eldest son Parker Garrison is preoccupied running
his Miami hotel empire and dealing with his recently
deceased father's secret second family. Since he has
little time to date, taking his superefficient assistant
to a charity event should have been a simple plan.
Until passion takes them beyond business.

Don't miss any of the six exciting titles in
THE GARRISONS continuity, beginning in July.
Only from Silhouette Desire.

THE CEO'S
SCANDALOUS AFFAIR
#1807

Available July 2007.

THE ROYAL HOUSE OF NIROLI

Always passionate, always proud.

**The richest royal family in the world—
a family united by blood and passion,
torn apart by deceit and desire.**

Step into the glamorous, enticing world of the
Nirolian Royal Family. As the king ails he must find an
heir…each month an exciting new installment follows
the epic search for the true Nirolian king. Eight heirs,
eight romances, eight fantastic stories!

It's time for playboy prince Marco Fierezza to
claim his rightful place…on the throne of Niroli!
Emily loves Marco, but she has no idea he's a royal
prince! What will this king-in-waiting do when he
discovers his mistress is pregnant?

THE FUTURE KING'S PREGNANT MISTRESS

by Penny Jordan

(#2643)

On sale July 2007.

www.eHarlequin.com

HPI2643

REQUEST YOUR FREE BOOKS!

Harlequin® Historical
Historical Romantic Adventure!

2 FREE NOVELS PLUS 2 FREE GIFTS!

YES! Please send me 2 FREE Harlequin® Historical novels and my 2 FREE gifts. After receiving them, if I don't wish to receive any more books, I can return the shipping statement marked "cancel." If I don't cancel, I will receive 6 brand-new novels every month and be billed just $4.69 per book in the U.S., or $5.24 per book in Canada, plus 25¢ shipping and handling per book and applicable taxes, if any*. That's a savings of close to 15% off the cover price! I understand that accepting the 2 free books and gifts places me under no obligation to buy anything. I can always return a shipment and cancel at any time. Even if I never buy another book from Harlequin, the two free books and gifts are mine to keep forever.

246 HDN EEWW   349 HDN EEW9

Name _____ (PLEASE PRINT) _____

Address _____ Apt. # _____

City _____ State/Prov. _____ Zip/Postal Code _____

Signature (if under 18, a parent or guardian must sign) _____

Mail to the **Harlequin Reader Service®**:
IN U.S.A.: P.O. Box 1867, Buffalo, NY 14240-1867
IN CANADA: P.O. Box 609, Fort Erie, Ontario L2A 5X3

Not valid to current Harlequin Historical subscribers.

Want to try two free books from another line?
Call 1-800-873-8635 or visit www.morefreebooks.com.

* Terms and prices subject to change without notice. NY residents add applicable sales tax. Canadian residents will be charged applicable provincial taxes and GST. This offer is limited to one order per household. All orders subject to approval. Credit or debit balances in a customer's account(s) may be offset by any other outstanding balance owed by or to the customer. Please allow 4 to 6 weeks for delivery.

Your Privacy: Harlequin is committed to protecting your privacy. Our Privacy Policy is available online at www.eHarlequin.com or upon request from the Reader Service. From time to time we make our lists of customers available to reputable firms who may have a product or service of interest to you. If you would prefer we not share your name and address, please check here. ☐

HH07

◆ HARLEQUIN®

Mediterranean
N I G H T S ™

---

*Experience the glamour and elegance of cruising the
high seas with a new 12-book series....*

MEDITERRANEAN NIGHTS

Coming in July 2007...

SCENT OF A WOMAN

by

Joanne Rock

When Danielle Chevalier is invited to an exclusive
conference aboard *Alexandra's Dream,* she knows it
will mean good things for her struggling fragrance
company. But her dreams get a setback when she
meets Adam Burns, a representative from a large
American conglomerate.

Danielle is charmed by the brusque American—
until she finds out he means to compete with her bid
for the opportunity that will save her family business!

Romantic
SUSPENSE

**Sparked by Danger,
Fueled by Passion.**

Mission: Impassioned

A brand-new miniseries begins with

My Spy

By *USA TODAY* bestselling author

Marie Ferrarella

She had to trust him with her life....
It was the most daring mission of Joshua Lazlo's
career: rescuing the prime minister of England's
daughter from a gang of cold-blooded kidnappers.
But nothing prepared the shadowy secret agent
for a fiery woman whose touch ignited something
far more dangerous.

My Spy

#1472

Available July 2007 wherever you buy books!

COMING NEXT MONTH FROM

HARLEQUIN®
HISTORICAL

- **SEDUCTION OF AN ENGLISH BEAUTY**
  by **Miranda Jarrett**
  (Regency)
  No self-respecting Italian rakehell could ignore the lush beauty he spots on a hotel balcony, but no sweet English rose would succumb to passionate seduction...right?

- **THE STRANGER**
  by **Elizabeth Lane**
  (Western)
  Haunted by his past, he has never stopped wondering what happened to Laura. Will Caleb's secrets deny them a future together?

- **UNTAMED COWBOY**
  by **Pam Crooks**
  (Western)
  Riding the trail, Penn McClure only wants to satisfy his wild need for revenge—yet his heart may not escape unscathed!

- **THE ROMAN'S VIRGIN MISTRESS**
  by **Michelle Styles**
  (Roman)
  Beautiful Silvana Junia has a reputation for scandalous, outrageous behavior. Still, when she agrees to become Fortis's mistress, she has no idea of the consequences....